YOU POOR MONSTER

a novel by Michael Kun

YOU POOR MONSTER[1]

— or —

THIS SHOULD ANSWER
YOUR QUESTIONS, MY SON[2]

a novel by Michael Kun[3]

MacAdam/Cage

MacAdam/Cage
155 Sansome Street, Suite 550
San Francisco, CA 94104
www.macadamcage.com

Library of Congress Cataloging-in-Publication Data

Kun, Michael.
  You poor monster : a novel / by Michael Kun.
    p. cm.
  Includes bibliographical references and index.
  ISBN 1-59692-119-6 (hardcover : alk. paper)
1. Identity (Psychology)—Fiction. 2. Attorney and client—Fiction.
3. Baltimore (Md.)—Fiction. 4. Divorce—Fiction. I. Title.
  PS3561.U446Y68 2005
  813'.54--dc22

                                                        2005003688
Manufactured in the United States of America.
10 9 8 7 6 5 4 3 2 1

Book and jacket design by Dorothy Carico Smith.

Portions of this novel have previously appeared, in different forms, in *Fiction*, *Other Voices*, and *Cottonwood*. An earlier, different version entitled *Our Poor Sweet Napoleon* was serialized in *The City Paper* in Baltimore, Maryland.

For my wife

Editor's Note

Shortly before this book was to go to press, the author revised it dramatically (for reasons that will become apparent), removing an entire subplot involving the narrator's marriage, excising several chapters, and rewriting a great many sections (some to my delight, some to my dismay—my favorite scene is now in the waste basket). As you will see, the author also added endnotes. Out of respect for the author, and because my own boss is standing over my shoulder demanding that I hand over the final version of the book before we miss our deadline, I have left the endnotes intact, unexpurgated, except for those where I was unable to read the author's handwriting. It is left to the reader whether, when and how to read the endnotes. They may be read as you proceed through the main text, or they may be read after you have completed the main text. In fact, you may ignore them altogether if you would like. As the author would say, "Do what you want. It's your book. You paid for it."

This statement applies to everyone but Alexander, who should read and reread the endnotes at every opportunity. To you, Alexander, I offer my sympathy and love. You will always know how to reach me, though I will understand if you choose not to.

Is a lie a lie if you know it's untrue,

or is it just a story?[4]

—*Hamilton Ashe*

Chapter One: Eyes and Lips and Hips and Waists

First, a story:

Sam Shoogey killed seven men, sent them to their graves, turned their bodies to fertilizer and their thoughts to pure blue air. It was no accident. He killed them intentionally, all seven of them, and he did so in a manner grotesque and violent, a manner often referred to as cold-blooded by newspapermen and television reporters and people who like to read paperback detective novels beside pools or oceans or while traveling by airplane.[5]

He shot the men with a gun, sent pieces of metal the size of a baby's thumb through the air, and those babies' thumbs sailed and darted and dove, ceasing to be babies' thumbs at all and becoming instead metal bees, bees that bit through flesh and then the tissue and white bone beneath.

But all this happened during the war, so it was all right and Shoogey could still go to Heaven.[6]

He could still go to work, where he made a living selling insurance policies (life, fire, automobile, etcetera, etcetera). He could still go to the movies with Jane, who was mad about movies and, he suspected, occasionally believed herself to be starring in one. He could still go the bar for a drink (scotch and soda) if a drink was what would satisfy him. He could go to the dry cleaner's and the supermarket, to the country club and the hardware store, where men, often much older than he, still patted him between the shoulder blades and said, "Hey, Shoo," in the most fawning of tones.

"How's it going, Shoo?" they said.

Or, "There's good ol' Shoo."

Or, "There he is, Number 84," a reference to the number embroidered on both front and back of the jersey he wore when he played football at the University of Maryland, before all the madness with the babies' thumbs and bees, before he started turning men into fertilizer and pure blue air.

But Shoogey would not be thinking of the number he wore on his football jersey. He would be thinking of an entirely different number. He would be thinking of the number of men he'd killed.

Seven.

The same number as Deadly Sins, he often thought.

The same number as the Seas.

As Wonders of the World.[7]

As Dwarfs.[8]

As Brides for Seven Brothers.[9]

When he returned to the States, Shoogey told Jane about what he'd done, or, at least, he tried to. When he'd started to tell her about the first man he'd killed, her face became the reflection of a face in a foggy mirror. Her skin turned the color of flour. She covered her mouth and ran to the bathroom of their motel room outside the base when he told her of the sound his gun had made: *pop pop*. Shoogey was left to stand outside the closed door, able to do nothing more than say, "Jane? Jane, honey, are you okay? Honey?" He'd not even told her the details of how he killed the man, just the fact that he'd done it in a clearing on a cool June night, just the fact that he'd pulled the incurved trigger: *pop pop*. Just enough to send her fleeing to the bathroom.

After several minutes with his cheek and ear against the bathroom door, Shoogey returned to his seat on the edge of the bed. The flowered bedspread was slick to the touch, as if someone had spilled a drink on it recently (not Shoogey or Jane). The mattress was soft and concave. When he closed his eyes, the image he saw was not Jane, but a soldier sleeping in a muddy foxhole. He opened his eyes. A breeze came through the window and made the horrible tan curtains billow and dance and produce a soft, scolding noise: *sheesh-sheesh-sheesh*. A sliver of moonlight slipped through a crack between the curtains and the curtain rod. Finally—finally—Shoogey heard Jane turn on the faucet, heard her brush her teeth vigorously. The toilet flushed. For several minutes, he heard nothing at all and wondered whether she'd fallen asleep in the tub or, worse, crawled out the window to seek another man with whom to share herself.

Then, happily, the water ran from the faucet again. She was not sleeping, had not left.

"Please," Jane said, finally emerging from the bathroom. She wiped her lips with a discolored beige washcloth. Her lipstick had left pink clouds on it. "Please, Sam, sweetheart, darling. Please, let's talk about something else, something more pleasant and bearable. I can't allow myself to think about this matter."

Jane was dressed in a thin blue nightgown, the type Shoogey had dreamed of during those months sleeping in the mud of the woods, and she was trembling slightly, as if the light breeze were pushing her hands, her chin, the soft flesh on her neck. She curled a finger against her nose. She brought the washcloth to her mouth. She chewed on it the way she'd seen women do in the movies with their handkerchiefs when they were disturbed by a stolen necklace or a troubling letter.

"Please, Sam," she pleaded, "promise you won't ever talk about this untoward matter again. Promise me that."

"I promise," he assured her. He raised one hand and extended three fingers, folding his thumb and little finger into his palm. "Scout's honor."[10]

Neither moved. Shoogey remained seated on the bed. Jane stood in front of him, her bare legs still browned from her trips to the beach with her parents. He imagined her playing volleyball in the sand, leaping, smashing the ball with her little browned fist. He imagined her lying on a blanket, wearing her red-and-white one-piece bathing suit, reading a paperback book or a movie magazine.

They both seemed to stare at a spot on the thin brown carpet near Shoogey's feet. The spot was black and the size of a bug, but it was not a bug.

"Maybe he didn't die," Jane said brightly. "Maybe he was only hurt, and the doctors fixed him up. Maybe he had a small Bible in his pocket, and the bullet hit the Bible like what happened in the movie *The Return of a Hero*, so he didn't die.[11] The Bible saved him. A Bible, or a silver cigarette case.[12] Maybe he's home with his family at this very moment, just like you are. He's showing them the Bible or the cigarette case, and telling them how it saved his life, and they're all having a laugh."

"That's an interesting theory," Shoogey said, listening to the longing that came not from his heart, but from other, less savory organs. He'd never seen a girl as lovely as Jane, and was certain he never would again.

But the man *had* died. There was no doubt about it. Shoogey had shot him through the *nose*.

Jane sat beside him on the bed. She placed a hand on his knee, squeezing it. She looked into his eyes. Hers were blue, the color of cornflowers. He did not forget that color during those nights in the woods. The blue nightgown, the blue eyes. The mad-spaghetti mess of red hair. The long, browned legs.

"Maybe you didn't even hit him," she said. "Maybe you're not as good a shot as you think you are." She laughed, and there was more than a little nervousness in her laugh. She stared into his eyes as if she were pleading with him. Was she asking him for the truth, or was she asking him to lie to her?

Shoogey had only a moment to decide which course he would take, and, his eyes on her legs, he chose the latter. "It's possible," Shoogey said. "It's possible I missed him entirely."

It was, to the best of his recollection, the first time he'd ever lied to Jane, and for that he knew he would go to Hell.

"You probably hit a tree," Jane continued.

"It's possible." The cloth of Jane's nightgown was so thin it seemed she had created it of her own breath. It allowed him to see the outline of her breasts, the curve of her thighs, the elastic at the waist of her underpants.

"Or maybe you hit a shrub."

There had been no shrubs.

"Yes," he said, "it may very well have been a shrub."

"There, you had me all worried for nothing," she said. "My Sammy couldn't hurt a fly."

Jane pushed her fingers through his hair, then smiled a contented and mysterious smile. She kissed him on his cheek, then his lips; he'd forgotten what a kiss was like. He breathed deeply, as if going underwater; she had a faint breakfast cereal-y smell.[13]

Next, his lips found her ears and her eyelids. He undressed her and pulled back the bed sheets—they smelled strongly of bleach—pushing her (slowly, slowly) onto the mattress before removing his clothes (quickly, quickly).

They spent much of the week that followed in that bed by the base, with the slick bedspread and the bleached sheets and the bug-shaped stain on the floor, pushing against each other like wrestlers, pushing until they were tired and aching, then resting and starting again after a bite to eat or a drink of tap water or a long, leisurely nap. Later that year, they had a baby boy (Rudolph; eight pounds, eight ounces; red, wrinkled). How strange it was to think that, after all those months of killing, he would have a child to hold. And it had all happened because of his lie. Shoogey knew that if he told Jane about the other six men he'd killed, she could never have looked at him again that night and for many more nights. She certainly would not have permitted him such intimate access to her body that first week after his return to the States.

Their son was the result of a lie, and, though he tried, Shoogey would never forget that. The boy grew and changed (white, smooth-skinned), and Shoogey held him infrequently, did not gurgle and talk nonsense to him. He came to understand that he would never love his son the way he knew he was supposed to, never show him those endearments that fathers often bestow upon their first-born boys. Shoogey would be cruel to the boy when kindness was in order. He would ignore the boy or, on occasion, ridicule him in the guise of teasing. When the boy achieved something or other, as he was wont to do—he was a clever and athletic boy who would frequently win contests in mathematics or place first in a race—Shoogey still could not love him. Shoogey was not a stupid man. He knew his feelings were unreasonable, but he also knew a man cannot control his feelings. The heart does not reason; the heart does as it wishes.

As the years passed and their children grew—they'd had a second child, a daughter (Susannah), who received all of Shoogey's fatherly attention—the only one of the seven men he'd killed whom Shoogey could recall in any detail was the first one, the one he'd killed in a clearing on a cool June night, the one who did not have a Bible or a silver cigarette case in his breast pocket, but instead was shot in the nose. Over the years, the other six men had become faceless, then forgotten, like the women who follow a first love: just eyes and lips and hips and waists. Then, nothing.

* * *

As often happens in both the best and worst of stories, there would be a telephone call, and that call would change Shoogey's life as dramatically as a wedding or a birth or a disease might.

In this case, the telephone call came while Shoogey was working in his office, doing the things insurance salesmen do. He was making telephone calls. He was writing letters, reading brochures and reviewing application forms. His door was shut to the world when his secretary's voice appeared through the static of the intercom.

"Yes?" Shoogey said, somewhat diffidently. He was reviewing a life insurance policy, measuring methods to increase the premiums which, not coincidentally, would result in a greater commission for one Sam Shoogey.

"There's a phone call for you," Anne said. She was not much of a secretary—her typing was slower than most and she was prone to errors when hurried—but she had been his secretary for six years. Sometimes Shoogey thought that the only reason he retained her was to hear her voice, her vowels dripping like honey from the spoon, the way homegrown Marylanders speak, an occasional reminder that he was home and safe.

"I asked you to hold all my calls," he said, momentarily losing his place in the policy he was reviewing.

"The gentleman said it's important."

Shoogey sniffed. "They all say it's important. Who is it?"

"A Mr. Lombardi. Robert Lombardi."[14]

That was all it took to remember everything: the babies' thumbs turning into bees, the bodies into fertilizer, the thoughts into pure blue air. All he'd needed was to hear Bobby Lombardi's name, a name he'd not thought of for ten years and not heard for many more.

Shoogey picked up his telephone and greeted Lombardi calmly and reasonably.

"Hello," he said in a voice more quiet than usual.

The reply was not so quiet: "Shoogey! Good ol' Shoo! Number 84! It's me, Bobby Lombardi! How are you? How the hell are you?"

Shoogey resisted Lombardi's efforts to joke and kid like the war buddies Lombardi likely imagined they had once been. Shoogey's mind was not so prone to tricks of time.

"Fine, thank you," he said. "And you?"

"Well, I'm doing great, Shoo! I'm doing fantastic!"

"Good."

There was a brief pause before Lombardi said, "Is everything okay? Am I calling at a bad time?"

Any time would be a bad time for Lombardi to call, but Shoogey didn't say that. "Everything's fine," he said.

Lombardi explained that, as luck would have it, he happened to be in Baltimore for a convention and thought he'd look up his old pal Sam Shoogey. He'd obtained Shoogey's phone number from another of the men in their platoon, Jimmy Birnberg. Shoogey did not remember Birnberg, but upon mention of the name he nodded and said, "Mm hmm," as if he did.

"Good ol' Birnberg," Lombardi said.

"Yes," Shoogey said. "Yes."

"Listen. I'm going to be in your neck of the woods tomorrow."

"Is that right?

"Yes, it is. In fact, I'll probably be driving right by your office building. I could stop by and we could go out for a drink."

"I'm afraid tomorrow's a very busy day," Shoogey said. "I'd be lucky if I had ten free minutes." It was true, more or less. He had too much work to finish before Anne packed up her belongings and went home, and he had promised a client that they would go to a baseball game that night. A few minutes really was all Shoogey could allow.

"Well, ten minutes ought to be more than enough time," Lombardi said. "Ten minutes for a couple war buddies to catch up."

So, against his better judgment—and his judgment was normally quite good—Shoogey agreed to meet with Lombardi the next day.

"Terrific," Lombardi said. "I can't wait to see you."

"Yes," Shoogey said. He already knew what Lombardi wanted. "Yes."

As he hung up the phone, Shoogey found himself perspiring and flexing his fingers the way people do when they are plagued by arthritis.

Lombardi had not been Shoogey's favorite in the platoon, but then Shoogey had not had a favorite. They were all crude and, unlike Shoogey, uneducated. On the transport plane that carried Shoogey from the States, he'd imagined that he would be assigned to a platoon, and that among them he'd find one man with a similar background. He'd imagined that he and this unnamed man would spot each other like lovers in a dimly lit hall, their eyes meeting and knowing every-thing. He'd imagined that he and this unnamed friend would swap jokes and talk about books and music, and that when the war was over, they'd settle in the same town and have barbeques with their wives and their children; Jane and his unnamed friend's unnamed wife would become fast friends. Shoogey had imagined all this and more, creating a wonderful, lifelong friendship that would never happen. Instead, among his platoon, Shoogey was the odd man out among the belching and farting and cursing. They were the type of men his mother had never approved of, the type of men Jane did not approve of, the type of men Shoogey struggled not to become. Say what you will about his football teammates—and there was much not to recommend about them—they were gentlemen, more or less.

Lombardi was a large, portly, thick-necked Italian. He was nearly as tall as Shoogey, six-foot-two, with black hair that curled in all directions like a schoolgirl's. He spat, he swore, he blew his nose into his open hand. He fancied himself as a comedian, though his jokes were childish and often ended prematurely when he realized he no longer remembered the punchline. Worse, he made Shoogey the butt of a great many of his jokes.

"Did you hear about the football player on the submarine?" Lombardi once said. "He got warm, so he had a screen door installed."

Or, "How many college boys does it take to screw in a light bulb? None. College boys don't know anything about screwing."

Two days later, Lombardi told this joke: "How many Jews does it take to screw in a light bulb?" (Shoogey was Jewish, Lombardi was not). "None. Jews don't know anything about screwing."

"It's the *same* joke," Shoogey protested.

"But it's still funny," Lombardi said, and the laughter of the others seemed to confirm that opinion.

Shoogey grew distant from the others in the platoon. He read when he could, he wrote letters to Jane when he was too tired to read. They were the type of letters written by a prisoner on death row, which was how Shoogey felt. He'd felt as if he were in the woods alone, never feeling the trust and loyalty in his colleagues that he'd been told over and over that he must have. Instead, all he felt was indifference. Worse, Shoogey knew in his heart that he would die, and he knew that the heart knows such things. It was, after all, the same heart that had told him he loved Jane. He had no choice but to trust it. He was going to die in those woods.

It was June fourth when Shoogey was paired with Lombardi on

night patrol. The air was thick and smelled of summer, but there was a chill in the night air that was at once unseasonable and reassuring. It quickened Shoogey's step as he patrolled the woods. It emboldened him like a stiff drink or a firm kiss upon the lips. In the years that came, he often wondered whether it was the chill air that made him do what he did.

The ground was dry and firm beneath Shoogey's boots as he pushed his way through the woods, hunched like a grandmother just as he'd been taught in boot camp. ("Keep your heads down! Down!") The reports on the radio were that there were no enemy soldiers within ten miles, but Shoogey kept hunched nonetheless, trying to ignore the ache developing in his shoulders and the small of his back. He kept hunched because he knew in his heart that if he walked upright, it would become a habit, and he knew that habit would cost him his life.

Thirty yards to the right, Lombardi made his way through the woods. The radio reports had liberated him. Normally, he was a good soldier, but now, knowing there was no one for miles, he ducked his head as he walked rather than hunch, and he let his rifle hang from its strap like a handbag. From time to time, Shoogey heard Lombardi fart, then laugh. Fart, laugh. Fart, laugh. An imbecile's symphony.

In the quiet, starry night, Shoogey began to relax, too, imagining that Jane was fast asleep under the same sky. He imagined her wearing a thin blue nightgown, her legs browned. He imagined the smell of her hair, fresh with shampoo. When he tried to straighten up, he found that his shoulders had stiffened and locked into place like a statue of a perfect soldier. The ache in his back grew worse. His ankle, which he'd broken in the Cotton Bowl, screamed. To his right, he heard the farts and the laughs and the crackle of twigs beneath Lombardi's heavy feet.

When they reached a clearing, Shoogey paused to look at the perfect moon, but only did so for a moment, allowing himself to think of Jane before turning and heading back. He walked twenty quick yards. Only then did he realize that there were no noises from Lombardi's direction. No farts, no laughs, no crackle of twigs. Shoogey turned back. He began perspiring, and the tips of his fingers and toes felt cold. He made his way back to the clearing, careful not to make too much noise. There was Lombardi, standing in the clearing, looking as big as a snowman beneath the light of the moon. He stretched his arms. His rifle and helmet were at his feet, as if he were setting up for a picnic.

Then Lombardi, the comedian, the fat Italian comedian, began to sing. He tipped his head back and began to sing some lunatic song he'd made up about detergent:

Comet,
It tastes like gasoline,
Comet,
It makes your pee turn green,
Comet,
It makes you vomit,
So buy some Comet and vomit today.[15]

Shoogey began to whisper Lombardi's name, but the words clung to his lips like breadcrumbs and remained there. Across the clearing, he saw the glint of moonlight against metal and he was able to discern the dark outline of another snowman standing upright, as big and as stupid as Lombardi. If there were time, Shoogey would have raced across the clearing and tackled Lombardi, but there wasn't that kind of time. Instead, Shoogey dropped to one knee, and before he knew what he'd done, he'd pulled the trigger.

The baby's thumbs darted out.

The baby's thumbs became metal bees.

The metal bees crossed the field and passed through a man's nose; skin and tissue and white bone parted.

Lombardi dropped to his belly, covered his head, screamed.

"Jesus Christ!" he shouted. "Jesus H. Christ!"

"Shut up, you moron!" Shoogey yelled, then he fell to the ground and, propelling himself with his elbows and the swivel of his hips, crawled to Lombardi's side. Lombardi wrapped his arms and legs around Shoogey more tightly than Jane ever had. Across the clearing, Shoogey could hear moaning and growling, soft but audible nonetheless.

"We've got to make sure he's dead," Shoogey said.

"What?"

"If he's not dead, he'll yell for help, and then we're all goners."

Shoogey freed himself from Lombardi's embrace and began to crawl through the clearing, careful not to raise his head lest he lose it. Lombardi followed close behind. The groaning grew louder, and when Shoogey reached the man, he was surprised at what he saw. He was not surprised by the blood or the hole in the man's face; he'd prepared himself for that while crawling. No, what surprised him was the man's face. He'd expected the man's face to be twisted into a grimace, but, instead, in the light of the same moon under which Jane slept, he could see that the man was smiling. The man had large, wet eyes and sharp cheekbones like a fashion model, and the moonlight bounced off his teeth and made the blood gleam. Still, he made noises like those made by a dog Shoogey's father had once struck while driving on a dark highway. The dog had suffered for nearly an hour before dying.

Shoogey turned toward Lombardi and bunched his lips as if to say, *Look at what you've done. You've ruined everything.* He thought about shooting the man again, then realized that the sound of another gunshot would make them easier to locate. There was only one way to proceed. Shoogey rubbed his hands together as if trying to warm them over a campfire, then spread his fingers across the man's throat and did what he had to do, not knowing that it would rearrange all of his own molecules and create some new and different being. With his hands, he made fertilizer, he created pure blue air. When the task was complete, Shoogey took the man's rifle and ammunition, then rummaged through the man's pockets. There was no Bible, no silver cigarette case. Instead, he found a small, color photograph of a plain-looking woman. She was smiling awkwardly and holding a baby on her knee; on the back, there was handwriting that Shoogey could not read. Three weeks later Shoogey found someone to translate the words: "Baby and I are waiting with much hope and know that God is with you." Only God hadn't been with him. He'd been with Shoogey and the farting, belching moron, and only God knew why He'd made such a choice.

* * *

Anne's voice came through the intercom again.

"Yes?" Shoogey said. He held a policy on his lap; he'd been holding it there for several hours.

"It's Mr. Lombardi," she said, and she escorted him into the office. Lombardi had grown heavier. Much of his thick black hair had fallen out, leaving gray wisps over his ears and a semi-circle of taut pink flesh atop his head. His stomach hung over his belt like a rain-soaked canopy. He wore a poorly stitched navy suit with brown shoes. Even with the shine of fresh polish, the shoes could not hide their age.

Lombardi grinned, showing all his teeth, and he stepped toward Shoogey, opening his arms wide to hug Shoogey to him. Shoogey escaped by retreating behind his desk.

"Shoogey, it's great to see you," Lombardi said, and his pleasure seemed sincere.

"How much do you want?" Shoogey said matter-of-factly.

"What?"

"Money. How much do you want?"

"What?" Lombardi's eyebrows curved together, meeting briefly.

"That's what you're here for, isn't it? You're here for money?"

Lombardi's skin grew pink, then red. "Well, I thought—"

"—You thought you'd stop by and hit me up for some money since you heard I was doing well. You thought you'd come by and make some small talk and then bring up your financial difficulties as if in passing so I'd be the one to suggest throwing some money your way. It's okay, it's not a problem. Just tell me how much you want and I'll write you a check."

Shoogey opened the center drawer of his desk and produced a black leather checkbook. He opened it and held his pen over a blank check.

Lombardi's mouth fell open slightly.

"Go ahead," Shoogey said, "tell me your figure. I won't haggle with you, just tell me your figure. But understand, once I write you this check, that'll be it. I don't ever want to see you again. I don't ever want to hear from you again."

"But, Sam…."

"Ever. Do you understand? This is your one shot, so you better make your number high."

Lombardi rubbed his forehead where his curls used to be, then inspected his palm. Saying nothing, he turned and walked toward the door, but he didn't seem capable of opening it. His fingers touched the knob, but couldn't turn it.

"Five thousand dollars?" Lombardi said. His back was still turned to Shoogey. "Is five thousand dollars too high?"

"No," Shoogey said, "five thousand dollars is fine. Now that wasn't hard, was it?" and he began writing.

"Will you do me a favor?" Lombardi said.

Shoogey stopped writing for a moment. "What?"

Lombardi turned, his chin buried in his chest like a mourner, and returned to the desk. "Please don't make the check out to me," he said.

"Who would you like me to make it out to?"

"Make it out to Birnberg," Lombardi said. "Jimmy Birnberg."

Shoogey did so. But when he finished signing his name to the bottom of the check, Shoogey did not set his pen down. He passed the check across the desk and nodded to instruct Lombardi to leave, then, when Lombardi had left his life forever, he picked up a notepad and began to write about the men he'd killed, seven in all. Those angry, troubled words would be the end of his career in insurance and the beginning of his career as a novelist. He would dedicate his first book to his son, now fully grown and bearded and as muscular as a bear. Over red wine and a steak dinner, Shoogey explained everything to his son. "This should answer your questions, my son," he would start. "I killed seven men, sent them to their graves, turned their bodies to fertilizer and their thoughts to pure blue air." When he was done, he would ask his son for forgiveness. "Rudolph," he would say, "I'm not a beast, just a man, and a weak one at that. I would bring back those seven men if I could, each and every one of them, and I would relive every moment with you, only differently this time." And the son, not being equal parts of his mother and his father, but being more of his mother, would forgive Shoogey. Shoogey and his son would hug one another on the steps outside the restaurant, the rain falling upon their drunken faces and their hunched shoulders (neither one carried an umbrella). The rain and their tears would become indistinguishable.

* * *

That is Shoogey's story.

It is, by all reckoning, a compelling and disturbing and oddly sweet story, one that is more compelling and disturbing and sweet when told by Shoogey himself.

Over the years, I heard Shoogey tell that story no fewer than a dozen times. He told it at parties, over dinner, whenever the occasion permitted, with a diligence to detail that was so admirable as to be horrifying, so horrifying as to be pitiful. It pained him to tell the story, yet tell it he did, over and over, in the unabridged, King James version. Never once did he change even the smallest element of the story, never once did he rearrange even the thinnest blade of grass in the telling. Jane's nightgown is always blue and thin, and she always smells of breakfast cereal; Lombardi always farts at the same moment; Shoogey's bullets always end up in the man's nose (never his chest, never his stomach, always his *nose*); the size of the check he hands over to Lombardi never wavers; Lombardi always asks for the check to be made out to Jimmy Birnberg; it is always raining when Shoogey hugs his bearded son. Yet, the only elements of that story I can swear are true are these: his name was Sam Shoogey, he had a wife and two children, and he was a generous and guilty-minded man. That is all. The rest—the great majority—is either untrue or, as hard as I've tried, I am unable to confirm.[16]

But that is the way life often is for men like Shoogey, men possessed by fear and wonder. The cruelest flowers, the most elegant wrecks. For men like that, try as they might, cannot help but lead raucous, untidy lives. For men like that, it is often left for the rest of us to sort out their lives, to try to make sense of what may in fact be senseless, find meaning in details that may in fact be meaningless. And, for men like that, things are bound to end badly.

For Shoogey in particular, things would end badly, as badly as they could. The truth is that he would in fact kill two people, send them to their graves, turn their bodies to fertilizer and their thoughts to pure blue air.

I know this to be true. I know this because I was his lawyer, and, despite my occasional protestations, I was his friend.[17]

Sam Shoogey killed two people. You can trust me on this.[18]

Chapter Two: This Will All End Badly

This will all end badly.

Shoogey assured me of that the night he appeared at our door looking like a smashed vase that had been hastily pieced back together.[19]

It happened soon after Angie and I bought a house in Baltimore. It was the city where we were both born and reared, where I first met Angie, where I met her again years later (thank God), where we were married (white church, white steeple), where our daughters (first Katie, then Claire) were born and reared.

Baltimore was built on the harbor, and the damp ocean air has left much of the city the pearly color of flounder—the buildings, the streets, even the sky at noon. It is a color that suits an industrial city: factories and warehouses and freighters tied up to the docks on the harbor, where the water is still too brown to be green. But the city is not all gray. No, there are pockets of green land here and there, parks and ball fields, and neighborhoods so lovely that you would swear you were lost in some New England hamlet. Flowers. Trees. The smell of things growing. The smell of things being cut.

The house Angie and I bought was located in a comfortable, tree-lined section of the city known as Mount Washington. The trees were certainly what you noticed first about the neighborhood, lovely, thick-trunked oaks. In the summer, they held a plush, fragrant umbrella over the neighborhood; in the winter, their bare brown limbs reached toward the sky like the beseeching arms of a gospel choir. The streets in the neighborhood were quiet and infrequently trafficked, perfect for children's play, and though there were several apartment complexes in the area, all with fancy names meant to suggest some rich heritage— "The George Washington Estates," "The Gables" and other, similar nonsense—most of the homes were one-story affairs like ours, with front porches and short, asphalt driveways and, of course, the trees. They were homes that attracted all types: young families, like ours, who viewed them as "starters," and older couples who had seen their children grow and leave, or who had suffered economic reverses. And people like Shoogey, whose reasons for living there were matters of idle speculation.

It wasn't long after I began practicing law that we bought that house.[20]

I had taken night classes at the law school while teaching history classes during the days. I taught history at Magruder High School in Baltimore, the very same high school I'd attended as a boy and Angie as a girl. The Revolutionary War. The Civil War. The Spanish-American War. Two World Wars. I was a fair teacher, perhaps better than fair, and I would like to think that my students liked and respected me. They knew about my night classes and, perhaps because I was a student, too, they often confided in me about the indignities and heartaches they suffered. I tried to assure them that the indignities and heartaches would all end once they graduated, once they found jobs they liked, once they met perfect girls (or boys). That was, after all, what happened to me. Or so I thought.

After graduating from law school, I resigned my teaching job at Magruder to work for a law firm by the name of Morrisey & DeWitt in downtown Baltimore.[21] Compared with what I'd been paid as a teacher, Morrisey & DeWitt paid me well, and Angie and I were able to make a substantial down payment on our house as a result. It was a small cottage of a place, just big enough for Angie and me and our daughters. The house was painted the rusty color of tobacco spit, with shutters that peculiar shade of yellow one associates with a colicky baby. The house didn't remain those colors for long; we had it repainted blue and white at the earliest opportunity. Blue and white, the colors of the

Magruder High School athletic teams, as chance would have it. We kept the basketball hoop over the garage door.

We had only been living in the neighborhood for a week or so when Angie and I first noticed Shoogey. His house was on the same side of the street as ours, six doors down, and when we drove past one evening, we noticed him lurking in the half-darkness by the hedges in his front yard. His head was bowed, his arms locked to his sides, his body twisted into a question mark of sorts. It wasn't until a white rat scurried from between his feet, then slowed, then stopped and resolved itself into a golf ball that we realized what he was doing.

"Who practices his putting in the dark?" Angie asked.

"Our neighbors, apparently. It could be worse though."

"How?"

"He could be skeet shooting," I said.

"Yes, that would be worse. Promise me you won't ever do that."

"What, play golf at night or skeet shoot?"

"I was thinking about golf, but you might as well include the other one, too."

We didn't meet Shoogey that evening. In fact, we didn't even know his name and wouldn't for several weeks more until the night we heard a rap at our front door. There were several knocks, each louder and more urgent than the one that preceded. It was nearly midnight, and I had to search for my teeth on the nightstand. My own teeth had been knocked from my mouth during a basketball game in high school, and I've been forced ever since to wear a dental plate made by an orthodontist here in Baltimore, a Dr. Miles Mansfield.[22]

Even after all these years, they still rattle around my mouth some, making a noise only I can hear—*brack-a-brack-a-brack*—like dishes clanking, like some giant piece of machinery running without oil.

My teeth in place, I grabbed the first thing I could lay my hands on—a broom we'd left in the hallway after one of our continuing, desperate attempts to clean the mess the previous owners had left for us. Old newspapers and magazines. Boxes of crackers and rotten apple cores and orange hulls under the sink.[23] Mildew and stained carpeting.

Barefoot, I carried the broom down the hall. My teeth rattled, or I imagined that they did. I groped in the darkness for the light switch in the living room, then flicked the porch light on as well, and I peered through the windowpane: gnats floated drunkenly around the yellow bulb of the porch light, and our neighbor shielded his eyes, a hand at his brow like a serviceman saluting, his head bowed almost precisely as it had been when he'd been practicing his golf game in his yard, which may have been how I recognized him.

I opened the door and our neighbor squinted, battling the lights to look at me. He was a tall man and on the thin side of things. Slumping, he gave the impression of having plenty of muscles and tissues and blood, but very few bones. He wore a lopsided gray suit and a limp, stained shirt, and he'd just shaved: there were flecks of drying blood on his cheekbone and jaw. As for his hairstyle, it was no style at all; his thick, black hair stood up in all directions like the weedy lawn before a haunted house.

"Hello. How are you?" he said. Before I answered, he volunteered, "I'm fine."

"Good," I said.

"Are you Ashe?" he asked. "Are you the one and only Hamilton Ashe?"[24]

"I am," I lied. There's actually another man named Hamilton Ashe, a tailor in Atlanta to whom I once spoke to on the phone to discuss our shared name, but I'm sure the man at the door wasn't looking for him. The man extended an enormous hand to me. I took it cautiously in my own. All but his thumbnail were bitten to the cuticles.

"I'm Sam Shoogey," he announced, "the novelist. I live down the street." He tipped his head in the direction of his home.

"I know."

Suddenly, a tremendous smile crept over his face as if there were some smaller man living within him, pulling at tiny wires connected to his lips and the corners of his eyes. He raked his fingers through his hair in an attempt to give it some semblance of order.

"Oh, you've read my books?"

I shook my head to confirm that I hadn't, which I later regretted: it wouldn't have been too much for me to fib. "What I meant was that I know you live down the street," I said. "We've seen you. In your yard. You were playing golf. We saw you."

"Oh." The small man released the wires, and Shoogey rubbed the tip of his nose to conceal his disappointment. "I thought you meant that you'd read my books. Well, I suppose most writers' work isn't fully appreciated until they're dead. I'd like to think my death is eagerly awaited." He forced a smile. "In any event, my friend, I need your help," he said, then he stepped gingerly into the house like a man easing himself into a rowboat. Once inside, he described a small circle, surveying the living room which was in a state of disarray. The furniture was clustered in the center of the room and draped with old, thin bed sheets. If the paint on the outside of the house had been bad, the inside was unbearable. The dining room had been left the dark, brilliant red of a matador's cape, and the paint on the windowsills and the wainscoting was chipped, revealing the yellow wood beneath. Angie and I had been spending our evenings and weekends scraping and sanding and painting like madmen.[25]

Masking tape framed the windowpanes, and the sweet, intoxicating smell of paint permeated the house like the faint whiff of a turkey dinner cooking.

When he'd completed his circle, Shoogey gave me a puzzled look.

"What were you going to do with *that*?" he asked. He gestured toward the broom, which I'd forgotten was in my hands.

"Nothing. I thought you might be a burglar."

"Were you planning on cleaning up after I stole everything?"

"No" I said, embarrassed. "I guess I was going to smack you over the head with it."

"Before or after I shot you?"

"Hopefully before."

I leaned the broom against the wall.

"Well, I don't have a gun, so I suppose it's a good thing for me that you didn't take a swing at me.[26] Now, I understand that I probably took you by surprise, my friend. I was just in the need of some assistance, and I believe you're the man I'm looking for."

When I asked him what he needed help with, he said, "Well, you're a lawyer, aren't you? Braverman says you're a lawyer. You know, Braverman down the street."

Shoogey tipped his head again, in the same direction as when he'd indicated his own address.

"Braverman? I don't know anyone by that name. We're new here."

Shoogey parted his lips to speak again, but just then Angie called from the hallway. "*Ham?*" she said. "Ham, who are you talking to?"

"It's Mr. Shoogey from down the road."

"Sam," he called to her pleasantly. Then, to me, he said, "Everyone calls me Sam," which was the first lie he ever told me: no one—*no one*—ever called him Sam. Shoogey was Shoogey, like Dillinger was Dillinger, Picasso Picasso, Gandhi Gandhi.[27]

But mostly Dillinger Dillinger.

"Who?" she said.

"The golfer," I answered.

"*Who?*"

"The skeet shooter."

Angie took several small steps down the hall, then bent slightly and peered at us, pinching her bathrobe closed at the neck with one hand, at the waist with the other. She and Shoogey exchanged squints. Then she pitched her head to one side, sending her black hair flying in a manner that a boy might find charming and beguiling and that might very well send the heart racing, that might make him want to caress the nape of her neck.

"Is everything okay?" she said.

"Everything's fine," Shoogey said, swatting at the air with one hand. "Just a little matter I need to discuss with your husband. I'll just be a second, then I'll be on my way and—" he paused, searching for my first name, which I provided him only after making him wait an uncomfortable moment. "I'll be on my way, and Ham will come back to bed, and you won't even know he was gone. His absence will be like a dream."

Angie took two more steps down the hall. She bit down on her lip.[28]

"Can I fix you both some coffee or something?"

"A scotch-and-soda would be nice," Shoogey said matter-of-factly, "if you don't mind." If he was joking, nothing in his expression revealed it.

Before Angie could answer, I said, "I'm sorry, Mr. Shoogey, but we don't have any scotch," which was true. I turned to Angie and gave her a look to assure her that everything was fine, but she remained fixed in her spot in the hall. "Really, sweetheart," I said. "Everything's okay. I'll be back in a minute. Go ahead. Go back to sleep."

Angie turned and disappeared down the hall, and Shoogey waited for the murmur of her slippered footsteps to dissolve before turning toward me again.

"No scotch, huh? You must have some hidden somewhere. A house without scotch is like a church without a collection plate." He began to stroll around the living room, then removed his suit jacket, revealing the entirety of his unlaundered shirt. Shapeless brown and gray stains had formed on the chest and armpits, and black dots the size of pinheads colored his frayed collar.

Shoogey removed a drop cloth and took a seat on the couch, then extended his arms like wings across its back. He crossed his legs at the knee in a manner that struck me as somewhat effeminate, then folded his suit jacket across his thigh. I sat across from him in a love seat that was also covered by a drop cloth.

"Your problem?" I reminded him.

"Yes, as I was saying, Braverman says that you're a lawyer. He says that you're a damn good one, that you work for a law firm downtown, Morrisey & DeWitt."[29]

At that time, I'd only been out of law school for ten months or so and, contrary to whatever Braverman may have told him, I'd done nothing to distinguish myself in the field, and probably never would. Momentarily, though, I was flattered by Braverman's description. "I don't know how Braverman—"

"—That's a fine firm, Morrisey & DeWitt. You know, I'm awful friendly with Tom DeWitt. He and I go back a long, long ways. Do you know Tom?"

I said that I didn't, and Shoogey sniffed. "Tom was my roommate when I attended the University of Maryland. A real down-to-earth guy. We played football together. Even played in the Cotton Bowl together. A real experience that was. His brother's Carl DeWitt. You must know Carl."

"Not really."

Shoogey's eyes widened dramatically and he raised his voice slightly, scolding me: "You work for the man's law firm and you don't *know* him? Well, I'm just shocked, just shocked as can be."

"It's a big law firm," I said in my defense, "and I'm in a different department than Mr. DeWitt. I'm in the corporate department, he's in litigation. They're two completely different worlds." I held my hands far apart to demonstrate.

"Well, you really should get to know Carl DeWitt. He's a prince of a man, just a prince. He'd give you the shirt off his back, that's the kind of guy he is. That's the kind of guy *I* am, too. I'd give you the shirt right off my back in a second. Not this one, of course"—he gestured to indicate the shirt he was wearing—"this one I wouldn't give to a dog. But my point's the same. I'd give you anything you needed, no questions asked, be it a shirt, money, food, a scotch-and-soda, you name it. It's that kind of thinking that gets me in trouble, though. You're generous and people just take and take and take, and then one day you have to say no, and—boom—they stab you in the back. You got any kids?"

"Two." I held up two fingers on my right hand.

"Girls or boys?"

"Both girls."

Shoogey swatted at the air and grinned. "See, that's something we've got in common already. I got a girl, too. Probably quite a bit older than your girls, but the same chromosomes. I've got a girl and a boy. Anyway, I've got some troubles, and I need a lawyer. I need a good lawyer, and Braverman says you're tops."

"Well, if it's strictly a legal matter, we could talk about it tomorrow at my office since it's so late now. We could set up an appointment for the morning."

I started to rise from the love seat, but Shoogey merely pursed his lips and shook his head slowly side to side. "Oh, I wish we could, my friend, I really do, but I need to talk with you immediately. You see, my wife's filed for divorce. Years and years gone by, and they mean as much to her as the wind. She's trying to take everything from me, right down to my toenails, but I can tell you more about that later. She packed up her things and went to her mother's and—well, I can tell you more about that later, too. My problem, my *immediate* problem, you see, is that I fired my lawyer this afternoon. Stanley McGee—know him?"[30]

I shook my head, no.

"Well, you don't want to know him. The man's got no balls. No *cojones*, as they say in Spain. It got to the point where I finally said to the guy—this is a true story—I said to him, 'Stand up and drop your pants.' And he said, '*What?*' And I said, 'You heard me, McGee. Stand up and drop your pants so I can tell once and for all if you've got any balls.' I know it's crude of me to talk that way in your home, seeing as you've got girls and all, but, you see, my wife and her lawyer are robbing me blind, and he was practically helping them. Like he's an accomplice. Serves me right, though, for hiring a goy. We have to stick together," he said, and he crossed his middle finger tightly over his index finger and gave me a sly, wicked smile. "Me, you, Braverman, Lebowitz, Rubin—"

"—Mr. Shoogey?"

"Sam."

"Sam, I'm not Jewish," I said, which technically is true: though my father is Jewish, my mother is Roman Catholic and that was how I was reared. In Sunday school, I recited the Apostles' Creed, the Lord's

Prayer, the Hail Mary. I don't know a word of Hebrew or Yiddish.[31]

"No? God, with a name like Ashe, I thought for sure you were a good Jewish boy. Braverman said you were Jewish."

"Well, I'm not, and I don't know Braverman."

"I guess that makes sense if you think about it: a Jewish boy named 'Ham'? Something of a contradiction, isn't it? Sort of like a Muslim named 'Flank Steak.'[32] Or a diabetic named 'Hershey.'[33] Oh, we could make a splendid game of this, couldn't we?" He spoke a little too loudly now, hammering home his little joke as if he were trying to ring the bell at the state fair.

"How about an alcoholic named Bob Budweiser?"[34]

Shoogey coughed once, then twice, like a sheep bleating. "Go ahead, you give it a try."

I stopped Shoogey by raising my hand beside my face, the same gesture I'd used countless times to hush my daughters. "Mr. Shoogey, whether or not I'm Jewish is neither here nor there. The important thing is that I'm not a divorce lawyer. Like I told you before, I'm a corporate lawyer. I work on things like reviewing contracts, helping out with sales or mergers. I don't do anything with divorces. That's not my specialty. But what I can do is I can find the names of some good divorce lawyers in town, and then I can pass them on to you tomorrow morning. We may even have some lawyers in the firm who handle divorces."

Again, he shook his head slowly side to side. "No, no. We can't do that."

"Why is that?"

"Well, my friend, it seems as if I have a hearing tomorrow morning at nine o'clock. It's called a pen-something hearing."

"*Pendente lite*," I said before I could stop myself: pen-den-tay lie-tay. "It's Latin."

"That's it—pen-den-tay lie-tay. They're going to determine how much temporary alimony I have to give my wife until the divorce is final, things like that. But, see, you knew what it was called. You know what you're talking about. You'll be fine. You're hired. Congratulations, you've got yourself a client. Now, let's have a drink to celebrate."

"Knowing that term is nothing special, Mr. Shoogey. Like I said, it's just a Latin term. They teach you a lot of Latin terms in law school. It doesn't mean I know anything about divorce law. You really need someone who specializes in handling divorces."

Shoogey walled his eyes up into his head and chewed his lower lip. "I can't very well go in there alone, my friend, and you're the only lawyer I know. Other than Carl DeWitt, of course, and I can't very well call him at this late hour." He rotated his wrist as if to look at his watch, but he didn't look at it. "I can't very well call up a man of his stature, the name partner in one of the best law firms in town, to talk to him about my little problem. Unless, of course, you recommend it," he crooned softly.

Shoogey had me in a bind, and you could tell he knew it. He knew that I couldn't refuse a friend of Carl DeWitt's without considerable risk to my job. Striving to shape an answer that would get me out of this predicament, I came up empty.

"Fine," I finally said. "Fine. I'm going to have to do some research first before I even figure out what kind of questions to ask you at the hearing."

A smile oiled Shoogey's face. Relief or satisfaction, it was hard to tell. "Good. You do that. You figure out what to ask me, and I'll tell you everything you want to know. You ask me who shot Liberty Valance, and I'll tell you.[35] I'll cooperate fully."

I told Shoogey to meet me at my office at seven o'clock the next morning so we would have time to prepare for his hearing.

"Seven o'clock it is," he said. "Seven, that'll be easy to remember. It's the number of Deadly Sins. The number of Seas. The number of Wonders of the World. The number of Dwarfs. The number of Brides for Seven Brothers. The number of Commandments, if you don't count the last three." He rose and headed toward the front door, then stopped in his tracks. Suddenly, his expression was sober. "There's one thing you should know." He wagged his index finger in the air. "My friend," he said, "this will all end badly."

When I didn't respond, he continued: "I know that for a fact. I know it will all end badly. You see, I went to see my wife the other night to try to patch things up, but we couldn't even talk in a civilized manner, in a manner that people who live in a civilization should speak. Eventually, I lost my temper and I said some horrible things to her. Horrible, terrible, evil things. You see, she was slapping me and beating her fists against me like she was pounding bread dough—*boom! boom! boom! boom! boom!*—and it just went on and on. Before I knew it, I'd lost my temper. Oh, the things that came out of my mouth. I'm ashamed. I just said them to get her away from me, mind you, but I said them nevertheless. That's when I realized that this will all end badly. There's nothing you personally can do about that. I guess I just need you to control the damage. I need you to make sure I walk out of this with something other than the shirt on my back. Particularly, this shirt."

"We can talk about all that in the morning," I answered with a cock of my head and a too-big smile meant to usher him toward the door. He followed my suggestion, carrying his suit jacket by his fingertips. His shirt, stained as it was, had every right to be foul, but it wasn't at all; instead, as I stood beside him now, it seemed that if the shirt gave off any odor at all it was—was it possible?—the faint, sweet smell of peaches.

Shoogey pulled his jacket on, then extended his hand to me, and we shook. He pushed the door open and stepped onto the porch, where the gnats greeted him like a long-absent friend, diving for his lips.

"I'll be there at seven o'clock on the nose," he said. Then, as if he'd forgotten something, he turned and added, "My friend."

Chapter Three: A Cake On Her Birthday

The thought of Shoogey dancing in my head, a peach-fragrant specter demanding a drink, made for a restless sleep that night. Over and over, the words he'd spoken nagged at me like a song: *This will all end badly. This will all end badly.* Angie didn't sleep well either, her head lolling back and forth in the midst of some dream. She'd already fallen back asleep by the time I'd shown Shoogey out, and though I'd wanted to wake her to tell her all about our neighbor, I'd thought better of it and let her sleep.

It was still dark when I climbed out of bed. The alarm clock ticked beside my head, and the sawing noise of the insects outside leaked into the bedroom, as they did during the deep summer, which it was now; it was July. The wind moved the leaves in the oaks that drooped over the roof. The moony darkness of the hour—too black to be day, too light to be night—reminded me of nothing so much as rising to feed our daughters when they were no larger than sacks of sugar, of staggering around the kitchen and warming bottles on the stove. The girls were asleep, though. You could hear their little girl breathing if you passed their room.

I trod quietly through the bedroom and stripped off my pajama top, careful not to wake Angie, her eyes still shut tight like winter windows, the bed sheets covering three-quarters of her body, revealing her delicate, white upper arms. A small, curving scar on her neck, the result of a bicycle accident, was hidden by the twisted fabric of her nightgown.[36]

Drunkenly, I made my way down the hall to the bathroom, wearing just my pajama bottoms, and I locked the door behind me. My fingers still on the knob, I unlocked the door and returned to the bedroom, pulling a clean pair of boxer shorts from the pancake stack of shorts in the bureau, then retraced my sleepy steps to the bathroom.

I inspected myself briefly in the bathroom mirror, then shaved too quickly, missing spots here and there (I later noticed), brushed my teeth and showered before returning to the bedroom. In the half-darkness, I was able to pick out a charcoal gray suit and a white cotton shirt from the closet. I'd purchased them both at Jos. A. Bank Clothiers—"Joe Bank's" is how most people refer to it—which is where most of Baltimore's legal community seemed to buy their clothing, like schoolboys buying uniforms for the new semester.[37]

At lunch, no matter where I dined, invariably I'd see dozens of young men in their charcoal gray Joe Bank's suits and know, instantly, that they were lawyers, as if they'd all been cut from the same bolt of cloth. Myself included, of course.

Angie and the girls were still asleep when I left the house. Outside, everything looked like Sunday morning. The streets were deserted at that early hour, save for a pink-and-blue truck with NU-DY-PER BABY SERVICE painted on the side, a giant safety pin piercing the U. There were no cars, no pedestrians cramming the sidewalks, and I must admit that it made me uncomfortable seeing the city like that, like stumbling across an old relative stripped to the skin, flesh sagging. I parked my car in the lot two blocks from the office and arrived at work shortly after five o'clock. The guard in the lobby, a thin black man with a narrow face and big cow eyes named Harry Addler was watching a black-and-white television monitor. He had skin the color of raisins, and when he spoke his voice was damp and swollen like a raincloud.

I said, "Good morning, Harry," and his head snapped up as if I'd not merely greeted him, but poked him with a pin, too. He arranged a smile on his face and waved, then said, "Good morning, sir." He did not know my name yet. There were hundreds of people who worked in that building, coming and going, then coming again; he could not know all of us. As I waited in the elevator bank we exchanged the glances of recognition shared by people who are familiar but have never taken the time to learn anything about each other. We shared the same initials (H.A.), and, as far as I knew, no more.[38]

Reaching my office, I hung my suit jacket on the plastic hook that jutted out of the back of the door like a curled finger, then headed toward the firm's library, stopping at Carl DeWitt's office on the way to leave a short note on his black leather blotter—

Mr. DeWitt:

Please see me as soon as possible about your friend Sam Shoogey. I'm afraid this is urgent!

Signed,

Hamilton Ashe, Corporate Dept.

Though I'm sure DeWitt hadn't been in his office for many hours, the air there was still brown with pipe smoke.

As I walked toward the library, I flicked on row after row of fluorescent lights. They were the same type of lights they'd installed at Magruder High School during my teaching days, and the hard light they gave off made the skin on my hands seem a ghostly white, like onion peelings. The library had the odor that I will always associate with the practice of law: that stale smell of the interior of an antique desk drawer.

Floor-to-ceiling bookcases lined the walls. I made my way along them, plucking volumes that suggested they might be helpful, then I settled in to read case after case of bitter marital disputes, of husbands stealing their wives' savings, of spouses struggling for possession of houses and cars and jewelry. Some were almost funny in that sorrowful way of a Russian story. The names of the cases, printed in solemn black letters atop of each page, shared an unmistakable, ironic symmetry: *Smith versus Smith. Haplish versus Haplish. Rigoli versus Rigoli.*[39] There were many, many more.

By the time the morning sun had snuck in and softened the glare

of the fluorescent lights, I'd compiled a list of nearly a hundred questions to ask Shoogey, all neatly printed on a yellow legal pad. I left the
library, and, suddenly, standing in the foyer beside the dull-hued portraits of men who'd been dead longer than they'd been alive, there was
Shoogey—or someone who bore some faint resemblance to him, like
cousins or half-brothers. In any event, it was not the same man who
had lumbered into our home just hours before. This Shoogey was
clutching a long, white flower box under one arm and, under the other,
another smaller box wrapped in shiny, mint-green wrapping paper. A
plastic bag dangled from the fingers of his right hand. In the light of
day, he had a ruggedly agreeable face, with deep crags carved into it, not
unlike the cowboys in the cigarette advertisements. The night before, it
had been impossible to assign an age to him. Now, he appeared to be
no more than thirty-five, but as he moved closer, approaching with the
pleasing, rolling gait of a sailor, that estimate seemed very, very low. It
was clear that there was some weather on the bark: perhaps he was fifty
or even sixty, it was impossible to say. His black hair was slicked back
with some lotion to keep it looking shiny and healthy, and he wore a
double-breasted, pinstriped suit, a starched shirt that was so white that
it nearly became another color, and one of the most beautiful ties I've
ever seen, a paisley tie the color of pea soup; the tie was like nothing
sold at Joe Bank's. Then, I smelled it again: the clear, distinct fragrance
of summer peaches.

"My friend, I can't apologize enough for my behavior last night," he
said when he reached me. "It was inexcusable, absolutely inexcusable.
It's just that I've been going through some very rough times of late,
much of which is my own doing, which only makes matters worse. You
can't control some things in life, but you can control your own
behavior. Your demeanor, your conduct, etcetera, etcetera, etcetera.
Normally, I live by a simple motto: *sic biscuitis disintegrat*. Roughly, that
means, 'That's the way the cookie crumbles.'[40] But this time, well,
because of the gravity of the circumstance, I'm afraid that motto fell by
the wayside. In any event, it was rude of me to call on you at such a late

hour, and even ruder to behave the way I did."

He held the flower box out to me.

"Roses," he announced, "for your lovely wife. She must think I'm horrible, the way I barged in so late. And then asking for a drink, too! What a nightmare. Anyway, please give her these as my way of apologizing." Next, he handed me a plastic bag. Inside were two dolls, each dressed like a beauty pageant contestant. "For your girls," he said. "At least I hope I remembered correctly. You did say you had girls, didn't you?"

"Yes."

He pretended to wipe his brow. "Thank God. If you had boys, giving them these dolls might be the first step toward careers in modern dance. Or interior design."

"Now this," he said, handing me the other box, "this is for you, my friend. Go ahead, open it."

He folded his arms across his chest and a look of pure, childlike glee came over his face as he watched me peel off the wrapping paper and pull out a bottle containing an amber liquid. As I wasn't much of a drinker, I had to read the label to see what it was: scotch.

"That's for the next time someone barges into your place and asks for a drink." He smiled broadly, then clamped his hand on my shoulder and jostled me. "I'm just kidding you," he explained. "It'll never happen again." Then he held up three fingers on his right hand, folding his thumb and pinky inward into his palm and said, "Scout's honor."

"Where did you get flowers so early in the morning?" I asked. "And dolls? And alcohol?"

"You need to know people," he said. "You need to know people who know people. And those people need to know people." He squeezed my elbow.

With that, I ushered Shoogey into my office, for the first time feeling somewhat embarrassed by it. They were hardly the accommodations I'd expected upon arriving for my first day of work some months earlier. The office was nothing like the offices of lawyers I'd read about in novels or seen in the movies. No mahogany desk, no antique bookcase or leather armchairs. Instead, the office was just a cubbyhole only slightly larger than a pool table, with a veneer desk meant to simulate some unknown wood, a matching credenza, and two metal chairs with frayed wicker seats that would catch your pockets or your belt loops if you weren't careful. I placed Shoogey's gifts atop the credenza, then took a seat at my desk, and he sat across from me, crossing his legs in precisely the same manner as the evening before, only now his movements seemed infused with no small degree of elegance. His sober eyes shone like June blackberries, and when he spoke, it was in a musical voice that poured forth like great, thumping waves. *Aren't we having a lovely time*, he seemed to say, *despite the circumstances.*

"You really must believe me when I tell you that last night was out of character for me," he said. "I'm normally a very decorous person. As straight as an arrow. In fact, in all of the books I've written—five, if you're counting—I've only cursed once. Once. It was in a book called *The Screaming Wall*, the fourth of the Napoleon Game novels—all of my novels are mysteries involving a private investigator named Napoleon Game. He'd been a war hero, then became a private investigator when he returned to the States. In the book, a woman murdered her husband, then hid his carcass in a cavity in the basement wall. Napoleon Game knew the woman was a murderer, he knew it the way you know water's about to boil, but he just couldn't find the body. Until he pounded his fist against the basement wall, that is. Then her husband's transistor radio clicked on and sound leaked through the bricking. The idea for that book came to me when Jane and I heard banging and clanging at Braverman's house. We thought Braverman had killed his wife. Can you imagine that? I mean, Braverman?" Shoogey paused for a moment, shut one eye and wagged a finger at me. "Did you say you hadn't met Braverman yet?"

I nodded.

"Well, we'll have to correct that. You'd like Braverman. Surely you've seen him around the neighborhood. Big ears." Shoogey brought both hands to the sides of his face and flapped them back and forth as if imitating the breathing of fish, hands for gills. "He has *huge* ears. You sure you haven't seen him?"

When I shook my head no, Shoogey returned his hands to his lap: "Anyway, as I was saying, Jane and I heard all this banging and clanging at Braverman's house. We thought he was burying his wife, or vice versa. Fortunately, they were only installing a new bathroom. I didn't think that would be such an interesting subject to write about, though. I wrote about a murder instead."[41]

He looked at me, waiting for a smile, which I dutifully gave him.

"In any event, as I was saying, *The Screaming Wall* is the only one of my books in which anyone curses. It only happened once. A character by the name of Gregory Hafets used a word that begins with the letter F and rhymes with 'fuck.' Actually, it *was* 'fuck.'"[42]

I couldn't help but let out a laugh.

"There," Shoogey said with a small amount of pride, "I knew I could get you to laugh. I knew you had a sense of humor. Anyway, this character, Gregory Hafets, said, 'Fuck you' to Napoleon Game. I didn't think anything of that until the book was published and the good people of Casper, Maryland—do you know Casper?"

I said that I didn't.

"Oh, it's just a little fishing town about eighty or ninety miles from here, no bigger than a box of Cracker Jacks.[43] It was where I grew up. In any event, the good people of Casper gathered to discuss the offensive word contained in my novel. Basically, they had a 'fuck' meeting. Some people argued that the book was dirty. Heck, the dictionary's dirty if you look closely enough. Anyway, they said the book should be banned from the town library. Others argued—rightly, in my biased opinion— that the First Amendment to the United States Constitution—the Constitution—guarantees all writers the right to say whatever they want. At one point, my mother rose and said, 'I just want all of you to know that we have never used that word in our home. Never. Not once,' which was true. But she said the book should be allowed in the library nonetheless. Bless her heart. Well, the debate went on and on, and in the end they voted not to ban the book from the library. Instead, on page two eighty-four, they crossed out the word 'fuck' with a black felt-tipped pen and wrote 'cook' above it. C-O-O-K. That's how it reads in that one copy: 'Cook you.' Because of the great anguish it caused her, I promised my mother that there would be no more cursing in any of my books so long as she's alive to read them. Once she passes on, though, I'm free to curse to my heart's desire."

I found myself smiling the genuine, approving smile I usually reserved for my daughters. I took out my notepad and pulled the cap off my pen and reminded him that we needed to get to work.

"Well, if you're going to be taking notes, there's one thing I should tell you up front," he said, "and that's that a lot of people think I'm a genius. It's not true, though. I'm no genius. Far from it. I'm miserable with state capitals, and I couldn't even name a dozen U.S. Presidents if I tried. Just watch. Washington. Lincoln. Truman. Both the Roosevelts. Babe Ruth. Was Milton Berle ever President?[44] I'm kidding, of course; I know he wasn't President. In any event, the first time I ever heard someone say it—'Sam Shoogey is a genius'—back when I was in grammar school, I thought they said, 'Sam Shoogey is Jesus.' Which is quite a compliment for a young man, you must admit."

"Yes. Yes, it is," I said, preparing to ask him the first question on my pad. "But back to the matter of your divorce—"

"—I really can't believe that this is happening, that she's divorcing me," Shoogey said before I could start my question. "You know, my friend, I've known Jane most of my life. I've known her since college, back when I was still considered a genius. Or Jesus, depending on your hearing. She was the sweetest little girl in the world then: cut her open and you'd find chocolate. And she had a voice—it was as pretty as the sun going down. I used to write her poems, you know. Not that that took much effort: everything rhymes with Jane. 'Train.' 'Drain.' 'Cellophane.' 'Chicken lo mein.' 'The rain in Spain falls mainly on the plain.'" He leaned forward, toward me, and in a tone that was conspiratorial he admitted, "I didn't write that last one. That's from *My Fair Lady*.[45] I wouldn't want you to think I was a plagiarist."

I smiled again—when had I smiled so much or so willingly?—and Shoogey shifted his weight in his chair as if settling in to tell a long, long tale. "Anyway, I've known Jane Plain Chicken Lo Mein since freshman year of college. You know, I met Jane—"

"—Mr. Shoogey," I said. I tapped my pencil against my legal pad. "I hate to interrupt you, but we really don't have a lot of time before the hearing. I've prepared some questions for you like I told you I would. Basically, they're the questions that I'll ask you at the hearing, but I'd like to go over them now for a couple reasons. First, it'll give me some of the information I'll need. And second, it'll be good practice for both of us."

"Sounds like a good idea," Shoogey said. "Braverman said you were good. Shoot."

One by one, we proceeded through the questions I'd prepared.

His full name was Samuel J. Shoogey III.

He lived at 626 Hampton Lane, Baltimore, Maryland.[46]

His wife's name was Jane Deborah Shoogey. Her maiden name was Peel.[47]

He'd grown up in Casper, Maryland.

He'd played football at the University of Maryland.

He'd served in the armed forces.

He'd worked as an insurance salesman before becoming a novelist.

He'd written five novels, all involving the private detective Napoleon Game. ("Several of them have sold nicely," Shoogey was quick to explain. "They've been especially popular in Europe. I don't know why that is. Maybe they gain something in the translation.")

He loved his parents.

He loved his children (Rudolph, Susannah).

He loved America.

It went on and on, and I found Shoogey to be an unusually engaging man, though, on at least three occasions, I caught him looking not at me, but over my right shoulder and out the smoky gray window behind me. Each time, I swiveled in my chair to see what was happening outside—an automobile accident perhaps, or a rainstorm coming—but there was nothing of interest there, only the black building across the street and the beginning of the rush-hour traffic below. It wasn't until he excused himself to use the men's room that I realized that he'd been inspecting his own generous reflection.

When he returned from the men's room, Shoogey had a puzzled look on his face. He adjusted the knot in his beautiful tie.

"You're a smart man, aren't you, my friend," he said. "Well, I was just thinking. Are you familiar with a little book by the name of The Bible?"

I confirmed that I was.

"Well, bear with me a minute, okay. After God created the heavens and earth, he created Adam, right?"

"Right."

"Then Adam and Eve had two children, correct?"

"Right."

"Then there was all that family business between Cain and Abel where Cain ended up killing Abel, correct?"

"Correct."

"A horrible thing for a brother to kill a brother." He paused for a moment to inspect the ceiling. "In any event, Cain ended up having children, and they had children, and so on and so on, right? You know how they say it in The Bible: 'And Cain begat So-and-So, who begat So-and-So,' right?"

"Right."

"Now, my friend, here is my question: who was the mother of Cain's children?"

"What?"

"You heard me. Who was the mother of Cain's children?"

I thought for a moment before saying, "Maybe I don't know The Bible that well."

"Ham, my friend, there was only one woman on earth, wasn't there? The only woman on earth was Eve, right?"

"Right."

"So," he said, "using the powers of logic, the only person who *could* have been the mother of Cain's children was Eve—his mother!"

I shook my head. "That can't be right, can it? Maybe Cain had a sister."

"So, you're saying he slept with his sister."

Now I looked at the ceiling. "Are you sure about this?"

"I don't know. But if it's true, that's one really troubled family, isn't it? Maybe that's why we're all so troubled, because the very first family was incredibly troubled. Murder. Incest. Snakes. Apples. It'd make a pretty good book, don't you think?"

I nodded.

"Sure makes me feel a bit better about *my* family situation," Shoogey said.

He returned to his chair, then flicked a casual finger toward my legal pad. "Now, are you finished with your questions?"

"Not at all. I've still got to ask you some sensitive questions. I've got to know what kind of terrible things your wife might say about you. There's an old expression lawyers use," I said, and trying to feign some amount of experience I repeated an expression I'd heard for the first time no more than a week prior: "I can't help you through the snake pit unless you tell me where the snakes are."

Shoogey gave me a weak, compulsory smile. "Feel free to ask whatever you want. Pick through the bones of my life like it was a filleted fish. You're my lawyer. You're entitled to know whatever you want. I will volunteer that I sometimes leave the toilet seat up. I hope that's not a major offense."

I looked down at my pad. "First, I need to know if you've ever used any illegal drugs."

"Never."

"Good. How about alcohol?"

"I know what you're thinking, my friend. I know, I know, I know. But last night was an exception. An aberration. I drink from time to time, *socially*, but I'm strictly an amateur. I'm still eligible for the Olympics."

"Okay. Have you ever struck your wife?"

"Never."

"Good. How about your children? Have you ever hit them?"

"Never. I never even spanked them, for godssakes."

"That's good." I looked down at the next question on my pad and paused. I suspect I may even have blushed.

"What is it, my friend?"

"Well, I'm sorry I have to ask you this, Mr. Shoogey, but I need to know if you've ever had an affair."

"Never," he said, slicing the air with his palm.

"Never?"

"Never." He held up his right hand, his thumb and pinky folded across his palm. "Scout's honor."

I wrote the word *NEVER* on my pad and circled it, then moved on to another question. Then, when I glanced at my wristwatch and saw that it was nearly twenty minutes to nine, I escorted Shoogey out of my office. We took the elevator down to the lobby, where Harry Addler was still standing guard. He grinned slightly—I don't recall having seen so many of his teeth before—and he waved.

"Good luck," he called out.

I started to respond, then realized he was speaking not to me, but to Shoogey.

"I don't need any luck, Harry," Shoogey said. "I've got my good friend Ham working for me."

* * *

Once we were inside the courthouse, Shoogey hiked his shoulders a little, holding his arms out to his side. He casually craned his neck as he inspected the vast, colorful murals that lined the corridors. One after another, a stream of men of all ages passed us, most in their gray, Joe Bank's uniforms, carrying tan briefcases which caught the morning sun as it darted through the architecture, turning their briefcases gold.

I'd never been to the courthouse before. I had never appeared before a judge. It was only as we approached that my hands grew moist and my mouth dry, causing my dental plate to slip. *Brack-a-brack-a-brack.* To remedy my nerves, I repeated to myself the first words I planned to speak: "Good morning, Your Honor, my name is Hamilton Ashe. Good morning, Your Honor, my name is Hamilton Ashe. Good morning, Your Honor, my name is Hamilton Ashe."

A series of painted arrows on the walls pointed the way to the courtrooms, and I followed them, guiding Shoogey up a creamy marble stairwell that curved and flowed like descending water, the steps waves out of waves out of waves. We found the courtroom with little trouble. It was warm and small and had the smell of a solemn classroom. We made our way to a walnut table across from the judge's bench. Once there, Shoogey sat quietly beside me, looking only once at the other table when his wife arrived with her attorney.

Jane Shoogey was small and pale, like a smart child, with a friendly, open face that was attractive, though not extraordinarily so, and hair the color and viscosity of drying blood. An intricate network of freckles graced her face like stars, beneath her eyes, on the bridge of her nose. And, like her husband, her age was utterly indiscernible. Was she forty? Fifty? Sixty?

Jane Shoogey smoothed her skirt and settled into her seat, then ran a hand through her tresses. She turned her head slightly, and she and Shoogey looked at each other with tense, unhappy eyes. Then, as if responding to some sudden, sharp noise, they looked away at precisely the same moment.

"Good morning, Your Honor," I practiced. "Good morning, Your Honor." Shoogey touched my wrist with his fingertips and nodded.

It wasn't long before the judge entered the room, and while he seemed to be that sort of man who might normally carry a wind of silence with him, a man of substance and might, there was no need to quiet us; we were already silent, and the few spectators in the gallery sat attentively, as if waiting to have their photograph snapped.

The judge was a sixty-year-old man by the name of Wallace Doughty, a thick, squat man with a heavy face and little hair, with the black eyes of a cat framed in thick tortoise-shell eyeglasses.[48]

He welcomed us, then essayed something in the nature of a grin when I said, "Good morning, Your Honor, my name is Hamilton Ashe" a bit more stiffly than I'd intended.

"First time in court, counselor?" the judge asked.

"Yes, Your Honor."

"Well, I'll try to make it as painless as possible then, although I warn you that my dentist makes the same promise."[49]

"Thank you."

"I believe you mean to say, 'Thank you, Your Honor.'"

"Yes."

"Yes, what?"

"Yes, Your Honor."

"There," he said, "not too painful yet, is it?"

"No," I said, then fortunately remembered to add, "Your Honor."

The hearing moved along smoothly, and when it came time for Shoogey to testify, he was wonderful, simply wonderful. I had grown more and more comfortable myself, strolling about the room as if I were in my socks in my living room, and I worked through the questions I'd asked Shoogey that morning. He answered each one thoughtfully, tipping his head to one side slightly as he listened, his legs crossed at the knee throughout. There was only one occasion when I became uncomfortable again.

"Mr. Shoogey," I said, "would you please tell the court what you do for a living?"

"Well, my friend," he answered, "I happen to be the world's greatest writer."

Judge Doughty leaned forward and gave Shoogey a stern look, his head bobbing. "That's not very modest of you, Mr. Shoogey," he said, and Shoogey replied, "I'm sorry, Your Honor, but I am under oath, aren't I?"[50]

Judge Doughty released a bomb of a laugh—if he didn't actually rattle the bench, it was only because the wood was solid—and Shoogey's eyes flicked about the room as if he were trying to satisfy himself that he'd left everyone suitably charmed. Even his wife seemed to fall momentarily under his spell, watching him with some fascination, the corners of her mouth curling slightly, almost imperceptibly; she looked not at his face, though, but at his pea-green paisley tie. I was struggling to suppress a giddy smile myself. When I was through with my questions half an hour later, I'd completely forgotten that, just hours before, I had despised Shoogey.

Mrs. Shoogey's attorney was a man by the name of McClellan, Henry McClellan, whom I had met for the first time that morning.[51]

He was a thin, balding man, and he wore a poorly stitched navy suit that is not available at Joe Bank's. When I finished examining Shoogey and returned to our table, McClellan approached the witness stand deliberately, shuffling his feet like a pallbearer. He folded his arms across his chest and asked question after question in a dull voice that did not have the power to hold my attention, like the voice of a man narrating a filmstrip on cloud formations: cirrus, stratus, cumulus. But Shoogey listened and responded to each question confidently: "Yes, sir." "No, sir." "I don't recall, sir." Finally, when it looked as if he were ready to complete his examination, McClellan cleared his throat.

"One more thing," he said. "Mr. Shoogey, have you ever had any extramarital affairs?"

Shoogey stared hard at me and answered, "Never."

And that should have been that, as they say. Only it wasn't.

McClellan started toward his seat, stopped, scratched his temple, then turned back toward Shoogey. "Let me put it this way," he said. "Have you had physical intercourse with any woman other than your wife during the course of your marriage?"

When Shoogey said, "What do you mean?" I was overcome with a sensation so strange that I can't describe it, though I doubt I need to; it might best be compared to seasickness.

"I mean sexual intercourse," McClellan said. It appeared that he was about to make a gesture with his hands, but he stopped himself. He cleared his throat again instead. "Have you engaged in sexual intercourse with any other women since you were married?"

"Oh, sure," Shoogey answered.

"How many times?"

"Geez, I don't know. A hundred? A hundred fifty?"

There was silence in the courtroom, the kind of absolute silence that is normally only found underwater. The silence seemed to shock Shoogey, and he gazed about the room at all the faces gazing upon his. Then he looked past McClellan at me, his expression precisely the same expression I've seen couples exchange at auctions when trying to determine whether they should bid higher.[52]

Fortunately, Shoogey stopped at a hundred, a hundred fifty.

It seemed that no one was breathing.

"A hundred, a hundred fifty?" McClellan repeated. He wore an astonished look on his face. Though attorneys are often rightly accused of being overly theatrical, I sensed that McClellan's expression was genuine. In fact, his body was tipping dangerously backward as if reeling from a blow. I thought he might fall over and hit his head on something. "A hundred, a hundred *fifty*?"

"Oh, heck, sure," Shoogey answered. I don't know if Shoogey made any gestures or facial expressions himself as I was no longer watching him. In my mind, I pictured him undoing the button on his slacks, leaning back in his seat, and rubbing his belly like a man who'd just downed a tremendous Thanksgiving dinner. Turkey, potatoes, vegetables, cornbread and butter, a slice of pie for dessert. I looked at his wife: her mouth had gone sour, her face sagged.

McClellan began his next question, halted, then adjusted his suit jacket with a tug of his lapels. He asked Shoogey to name all of the women, and Shoogey made a sporting attempt to do so, calling out name after name like the graduation list of an all-girls' high school. Tammy This. Sally That. The names rolled off his tongue musically, finally running together like raindrops. Sharon. Nancy. Jeanne. Trudy. Lynn. Karen. Meredith. Amy. Laura. Ann. Carla. Debbie. Maria. Anna. Susan. Patricia. Beatrice. Barbara. Marilyn. Tierney. ("Tierney, like Gene Tierney?" "Yes.") Stephanie. Christina. Lee. Rebecca. Gretchen. Mary Beth. Mary Ellen. Mary Jane.[53]

In all, it took nearly two hours, slowed some as Shoogey searched his memory for names. I stopped jotting down the names after thirty or forty. I remember this much, though: there were two named Serena. I also remember thinking, *Who knows two girls named Serena? Who?*[54]

Later, when the judge shuffled off to his chambers to consider the testimony, I pulled Shoogey aside in the hallway, giving his elbow a sharp squeeze. I was barely in control of my temper. My shirt felt damp at the collar and armpits with the warm sweat of a breaking fever.

"A hundred, a hundred fifty," I said in a loud whisper. "A hundred, a hundred fifty. Dammit, Shoogey, I asked you this morning whether or not you'd ever fooled around with another woman, and you said no. You looked me right in the eye and said no. How can I represent you if you won't tell me the truth?" And then I did something I rarely did: I cussed. "How the *fuck* am I supposed to represent you if you won't tell me the truth," I said.

Shoogey was unruffled. His fingertips were dipped in his pants pockets. "Now, now," he said, "there's no need to use foul language. You never asked me if I'd fooled around."

"Yes, I did."

"No, my friend, I'm afraid you're mistaken. You asked me if I'd had any affairs."

"It's the same damn thing."

"No, it's not. An affair means dinner. An affair means movies and dinners and sneaking around. An affair means telling another woman that you love her and buying her a cake on her birthday. No, no. I would never do anything like that. I wouldn't even think of it, telling another woman that I loved her. Jane's the only woman I've ever loved. She's the only woman I've ever written poems for. Now, a one-night stand is a completely different thing, on a business trip or something of that nature. It has nothing to do with your heart," and he actually pulled his hand from his pocket and patted his chest when he said that, in a way that was almost endearing. Almost, I say, because it's difficult to forget the numbers a hundred, a hundred fifty. They are, in this particular context, unusually large numbers, numbers that stick in your mind.

Shoogey ran his fingertips over his gorgeous, pea-green paisley tie and grinned as if expecting a pleasant surprise. No such surprise was forthcoming, though: Judge Doughty returned to the courtroom after the briefest of recesses and, in a booming, insistent voice sounding like something more than the voice of a man, but of the entire universe, he awarded Shoogey's wife a substantial amount of alimony—the number I no longer recall—until the final divorce hearing.

"You will pay this amount every month, Mr. Shoogey," he said, "or you will face the wrath of this court." As he made this pronouncement, he glared not at Shoogey, but at me, as if I'd committed Shoogey's deeds. Then, exiting, Judge Doughty picked up a sheet of paper and crushed it as if he were crunching my bones.

"That isn't right," Shoogey said minutes later when we were alone in the courtroom. He fingered a knot in the table. "What he just did just isn't right. Can I talk with the judge and tell him that he's made a terrible mistake? He just got the wrong impression of me. If I could just talk with him man to man and smooth things over."

Pushing my notepads into my briefcase, I explained that he couldn't do that, then put a hand on Shoogey's elbow to compel him out of his seat. He slumped as he walked, and he rubbed at his forehead, causing a few strands of hair to stand up at odd angles. We didn't talk as we walked through the corridors, inspecting the murals instead, paintings of the peoples of ancient civilizations huddled over some documents that presumably contained their laws, their lifeless eyes seeking solace in Shoogey's.

I wished Shoogey good luck, reluctantly shook his meaty hand, and left him standing on the steps in front of the courthouse, a statue of something I could not name. As I crossed the street, I heard him call out to me, "You did a fine job, my friend. Braverman was right about you," but I walked on, pretending not to hear him over the hustle and bustle, the car engines and the music seeping through their open windows. "A superb job, my friend!"

The sky had changed since morning. A promise of rain had darkened the day, a sky of new clouds shaded the sun as if seen through the blur of teary eyes. Here and there, black spots of rain appeared on the sidewalk. The rain began to fall more heavily, the way it is always meant to do in Baltimore where, the saying goes, "If it isn't raining now, just give her a minute."

As I walked past the shops on the way to my office, I discovered that I was shaking my head side-to-side in an exaggerated way, as if I'd imagined this Shoogey, as if I could expel him from my memory by force. By the time I reached the office, the rain was falling in a swift screen and my suit jacket, which I'd pulled over my head like a shroud, was soaked through and through. I rode the elevator to our offices, but I didn't walk directly to my own. Instead, I stopped at Carl DeWitt's first, hoping to have a word with him about his friend Shoogey, but I found his office dark, the lights off and the blinds drawn against the sunlight. I returned to my office, where I found a slip of paper floating on the seat of my wicker chair. The message on the slip, written in sweeping script that might be mistaken for the hand of a high school girl, read: "Your wife called. Call back ASAP."

When I telephoned, Angie's first words were, "Who on *earth* was that terrible man last night?"

I explained to her what had happened the night before, beginning, "This will all end badly." I described the hearing as well, doing my best to imitate McClellan and Shoogey both:

"Have you had intercourse with any women other than your wife?" I asked.

"Oh, sure," I answered.

"How many times?" I said.

"I don't know, a hundred, a hundred fifty?" I answered.

"A hundred, a hundred fifty?" Angie shrieked, and I pictured her placing her hand over her open, wan mouth. "Ham, you're pulling my leg. Tell me you're pulling my leg."

I told her I wasn't, that that was precisely what Shoogey had said. I even folded my thumb and pinky into my palm and said, "Scout's honor."

"Jesus, Ham, who even knows a hundred, a hundred-fifty people?"

"Sam Shoogey," I said, "and apparently he knows them in the biblical sense." Then I said, "Hey, speaking of The Bible, do you know who the mother of Cain's children was?"

"What?"

"Cain, from The Bible. Who was the mother of his children?"

"Why?"

"No reason," I said. "You know, forget I asked."

Finally, I told Angie I'd be home by seven o'clock for dinner. "Seven," I said, "the number of brides for seven brothers."

"Okay, we'll see you then. Bye, honey."

Not a minute passed after we hung up, not even enough time to hang up my coat, before my phone rang.

"Ham, have *you* ever had intercourse with a woman other than your wife?" Angie wanted to know.

"That depends. Does the time you dressed up like Ann-Margret count?"[55]

"*Ham.*" I pictured her biting her lip.[56]

"Of course not, sweetheart," I said, and I said goodbye again and returned to my work.

The rest of the day passed slowly and without event. The rain washed against my window, then abruptly stopped, and I reviewed documents in silence at my desk. I ate lunch, I wrote several letters and returned a few telephone calls, though my mind wandered to thoughts of Shoogey now and again, thoughts that made me feel strangely happy about my own state of affairs. At the end of the day, I pushed some documents into my briefcase and pulled Shoogey's gifts from the credenza and drove home. As I did, I was filled with a certain amount of joy as I thought about my family, about going to the beach with Angie, about the hole to China that the girls and I had started digging in the back yard, about sitting at the dinner table and eating dinner with them, eating meals that tasted of happiness and had nothing to do with eating.

Around the last bend, I could see the light of the television set glowing gas-blue through the curtains of our living room. I eased the car into the driveway at seven o'clock, more or less, just as I'd promised. The evening collected in the gray shadows among the trees. The air smelled of new grass. I walked up the curving path to the porch. There, I found a thin white box. Its raised blue lettering read, "Braverman's Menswear. Quality Menswear For Over A Quarter Century." Inside, the pea-green paisley tie.

Chapter Four: The Allergic Boy

When was it exactly that I first heard Shoogey's story about the men he killed, the story that begins this book? When did I first hear about all the fertilizer and the pure blue air?

Was it a week after I met him? Was it two weeks? Three? More? It's impossible to say exactly because after his court hearing ("A hundred, a hundred fifty"), Shoogey disappeared. Every indication was that he'd left for good. Though I could see the roof of his house through the trees, I didn't see him; he didn't practice his golf game in his yard in the days following the hearing, and his house remained dark at all hours like a movie theater that had been shut down and boarded up. A rainbow of oil marked the spot in the driveway where his car had rested, and his lawn grew high, then higher, then yellowed, then died. God only knew where he'd gone, though I can't say I gave it much thought, returning as I did to my normal routine. Already I'd forgotten what he looked like, the color of his eyes, the shape of his head. He'd already disappeared, like a stranger you'd talk with in the line at the grocery store who becomes a blip on the screen of your history, so that someday, when you see someone who resembles him, you would pause, and crinkle your nose, and fold your arms across your chest, and concentrate and concentrate and concentrate and concentrate until, finally, you give up, shake your head once or twice, and say, "Hmm." All that remained of Shoogey for me was the smile; it hung in the air like the Cheshire Cat's.[57]

It was no small amount of time, a month perhaps, before Carl DeWitt appeared at my office door, catching me by surprise. I'd never seen the man this close before: I'd only observed him from a distance in the hallways or on the sidewalk in front of the building, leaning on a wooden cane, waving it here and there before him as if to rouse creatures in hiding.

He rapped the curl of the cane against my door, a pipe drooping at a dangerous angle from his lips. DeWitt had a peninsula of iron-gray hair on the top of his head surrounded by red, mottled skin. He did not have a handsome face. Instead, somehow, it was all mouth—all gums, all lips, all fat, brown tongue. The immediate impression he gave upon such close inspection was that of an infant who'd been stuffed and stretched by some new and uncanny medical procedure—stuffed and stretched and a pipe stuffed in its mouth as a gag, the way bar patrons will shove a cigar in the mouth of a moosehead protruding from the wall, or set a baseball cap atop its head. He held up a slip of paper, then in a tone of mild impatience he said, "Are you Ashe?"

I admitted as much with a nod and said, "Yes, sir," then wished I hadn't added the "sir."

"What's this all about, Ashe?" He waved the slip of paper, and a long moment passed, the slip of paper rustling in fingertips browned from packing tobacco into the bowl of his pipe. Finally, I recognized it as the note I'd left on his blotter the morning of Shoogey's hearing. Whatever the time that had passed, it had been sufficient to make me forget about the note's existence.

"Oh, that's about Sam Shoogey," I said at last, then I started to explain: "He showed up at my home a while back ranting and raving about—"

"—Who?"

"Sam Shoogey," I said, more loudly this time. When DeWitt didn't show any sign of recognition, my stomach twitched. "He said he knew you. He said he was a friend of your brother Tom. I think he said they were roommates in college." I went on and on, but nothing I said seemed to stir any memory in DeWitt.

"Hum." DeWitt's fat brown tongue flicked out to wet his bloated lips. He arched an eyebrow and stared at my note. He stroked the back of his neck as if it were sore there.

"Well, he said he knew you when he showed up at my house ranting and raving about how he needed a lawyer for a divorce hearing the next morning, so I helped him out. He gave me a tie." I looked down at my chest and touched the tie I was wearing. "Not this particular tie, but a tie."

"Hum. Let me check into this," DeWitt said, then departed, still clutching the note. His reaction left me with the cold, unmistakable feeling that, on top of everything else, Shoogey was a fraud. He didn't know DeWitt. He'd never even met DeWitt, and I should have known that from Shoogey's smile alone: it was too friendly, the smile of a man trying too hard to please; it was too familiar, as if he'd known you longer than your own parents had. It was a smile that was fraught with deception. In the next hours, I grew crazy with questions I wanted answered, and, though I tried, it was impossible to concentrate on my work. The phone rang, but I could only stare at it absently. The papers on my desk moved, but were not attended to. As the morning progressed, I found myself growing angrier and angrier, until DeWitt reappeared at my door, the mild, sweet odor of tobacco preceding him like the whistle before a train.

"Mr. DeWitt, I can't even begin to tell you how—"

"—Calm down, calm down. I just got off the phone with my brother and with Shoogey," he said. He poked the cane at me, missing my nose by no more than an inch. "Shoogey said you did a hell of a job the other day. Top drawer. You've got yourself a big fan."

"So you do know him?"

"Sure I know him—Shoogey, the writer. Sure, sure. If you'd have said he was the writer—which you didn't—if you'd have said that, I would've remembered. I couldn't place his name at first, probably losing some of my memory, so I called Tom, and Tom reminded me who he was. I haven't seen Shoogey more than once or twice in the past ten or fifteen years." A grin came over DeWitt's thick, stained lips, but it came slowly and in pieces, as if he'd learned to smile from a series of still pictures. "I think we all went fishing the last time I saw him. Now, there's going to be a lot of work that needs to be done in his divorce before the final hearing, and I'd like you to make it one of your top priorities, as a personal favor."

"You want me to stay on the case?"

"Of course. Shoogey doesn't want someone else. He specifically asked for you."

I tried to reason with DeWitt, explaining that I was already too busy, that I didn't know a thing about divorce law—the same arguments I'd tried with Shoogey. My voice took on an unpleasant, whining quality, which did nothing to persuade him.

"Don't worry," he said. "You'll acquire the expertise. Besides, like I said, Shoogey doesn't want anyone else. So, you do whatever you need to do to become an expert on divorce law."

"But that's not something I'd like to be an expert in. I'd rather concentrate on my regular work." I passed my hand over the landscape of documents covering my desktop.

DeWitt poked his tongue into his cheek.

"Mr. Ashe, you seem to think we're having a discussion when what I'm doing is giving you a direct order. Now, you're an M & D"—I'd heard people at Morrisey & DeWitt refer to themselves as M & D's before—"and I just happen to *own* M & D." He spoke calmly despite his strong words. "You have no choice in this matter, so accept your fate and do a good job." An unspoken "or else" hung in the air like crepe paper, precisely where he'd intended it to hang.

DeWitt made a clicking noise with his tongue, then left. His pipe smoke left a damp and lingering odor in my office like the smell of fresh grass that follows the mower, only much less pleasing. He was gone for a moment, then returned.

"Oh," he said, "Shoogey is coming by to have lunch with you at noon. I assume you'll change your schedule if you need to do so."

"Yes, sir."

"Good."

* * *

Shoogey arrived with a newspaper folded carefully into thirds like a love letter. He was dressed in a blue-and-white seersucker suit, the very type that is popular among Southern gentlemen—and worn by no one in Baltimore.[58]

With it, he wore a starched blue shirt and a brilliant red tie that was even more spectacular than the tie he'd left on my porch. The tie had thin blue diagonal stripes and tiny gray spots that shone like iron filings in the light.

Shoogey greeted me enthusiastically, smiling a sweet smile that had in it perhaps a trace of an apology, though I may have been mistaken.

"Ham," he barked. "Ham, my friend, it's good to see you. Awful good to see you. You did a great job the other day. Did I mention that, a great job? You looked very comfortable, very poised. A real lawyer."

I thanked him half-heartedly.

"In fact, it wasn't until halfway through the hearing that it struck me that you reminded me of someone I used to know. It's amazing, the resemblance, really. I should have spotted it right off, but there I was, all wrapped up in my problems, just thinking, 'Me, me, me, me, me.' But the resemblance is remarkable. It's not like when someone says, 'You know, my cousin looks just like Marilyn Monroe,' and then you meet the cousin and she has black hair and is missing teeth and weighs as much as a refrigerator loaded down with bricks.[59] No, the resemblance truly is remarkable, like you're his doppelgänger."

Shoogey could use a word like "doppelgänger" and not sound as if he'd meant to impress.

I asked whom I reminded him of, and he said, "I mean this as a compliment, my friend, so please take it that way. You remind me of a boy I knew growing up in Casper. The same features, the same hair, the same smile. He was very sweet and guileless. His name was, well, I don't recall his *given* name—it may have been Walter, it may have been something else.[60] In any event, he was shall we say 'height impaired.' He was always the smallest boy in the class, so we all called him Napoleon after Napoleon Bonaparte, who was very short."

I assured him that I knew who Napoleon Bonaparte was; I'd taught history, where his name has a way of popping up. Napoleon, Hitler, George Washington, Abraham Lincoln, etcetera, etcetera, etcetera.

"You taught history, is that right? See, I didn't know that about you. That's something that I didn't know about you, something interesting. Anyway, would you mind if I called you Napoleon from now on?"

A thought struck me at that moment.

"Isn't that the name of your detective? In your books?"

Shoogey gave me a smile very different from the overly friendly one he'd given me before. This one was sincere, there could be no mistake.

"You have a very good memory, my friend. You're right, you're quite right. The name of the detective is Napoleon Game. I named him after the boy I used to know. In any event, Napoleon,"—he drew out the first "o" of Napoleon, then held the newspaper out toward me—"in any event, there's something I want you to see. I searched and searched for this, and I was finally able to track it down in one of my file cabinets. I've got file cabinets in the cellar with everything in them. I save every-thing. I mean, every little *thing*. Just like an old lady. Letters, newspaper articles, tickets from ballgames, you name it. Anyway, you see, one morning many months back, as I was eating breakfast—nothing fancy, just an English muffin and coffee—I came across an article in *The Sun* about infidelity.[61] Infidelity, I believe, is good breakfast reading. As good as anything else, I suppose. Certainly it beats reading the obituaries. It beats the obituaries hands down."

Shoogey turned the newspaper over to me, and we both settled into our chairs. I unfolded the paper and gave it a slight snap with my wrists.

"It's that one there," he said, directing me to an article entitled, "Sex, In and Out of Wedlock." There was a cartoon of a man and woman walking toward a motel with their shoulders hunched and raincoats hiding the tops of their heads as if to shelter them from a storm. The man and woman weren't walking on solid ground, though. They were walking on a tightrope. The artist had drawn squiggly lines beside the rope to indicate that it was trembling.

"In the article, among a variety of statistics, it says that university researchers have found that seventy-five percent of all married men are unfaithful to their wives. Seventy-*five* percent. Imagine that, Napoleon. My first thought upon reading that number was that it must have been a typographical error. I called a friend at the newspaper, though—Jack Bowman, do you know him?—and he assured me it was accurate: seventy-five percent.[62] Imagine that. The article reminded me of something I once heard, though I don't recall who said it. He said that infidelity becomes a temptation for all men, so much so that it becomes the answer to every question great or small. Someone will ask you, 'How are you today?' and you'll think, 'I wonder if I should cheat on my wife.' 'What time is it?' 'I wonder if I should cheat on my wife.' 'Who was the sixteenth President of the United States?'[63] 'I wonder if I should cheat on my wife *a lot.*'"[64]

I laughed against my will, which seemed to urge Shoogey on.

"The article also reminded me of something my father once said at the dinner table. He said, 'Why go out to buy milk when you've got a cow at home?' I don't think he chose his words as carefully as he could have. I remember the look my mother gave him. It wasn't a pleasant one. She's no longer with us, my mother. She passed away. Anyway, you should read that article."

I asked why.

"Well, my good friend Napoleon, I got the impression that you were somewhat disgusted by some of my admissions the other morning, about my bodily contact with certain women who do not have my wife's name, and I thought that reading that might help you understand. I think you'd be surprised how many people are unfaithful. Very surprised."

"You might be right, but thus far I don't think I've ever met anyone who's cheated on his wife."

"Sure you have. How about Braverman?"

"I don't know Braverman."

"Are you sure?"

"Yes, I'm sure."

Shoogey squinted critically.

"Well, I suppose you'd remember if you'd met him. I mean, he's got those godforsaken ears. You should meet him. He's a good man, despite the ears. Always in a good mood, always friendly. A regular Pollyanna. If he were in a prison, Braverman would be running around saying, 'We've got the best darn cell block in the whole penitentiary!' You know, he owns and operates his own company, distributing menswear throughout the state."

"Is that right?"

"Braverman's Menswear," Shoogey explained, "is one of the largest distributors of suits, shirts, ties and shoes in Maryland, perhaps the largest. As for Braverman himself, he's a very sharp dresser, which only makes sense. He has access to fine clothing. Many poor dressers, I believe, are poor dressers simply because they don't have the access to fine clothing. Don't you agree?"

Having no opinion on the subject, I agreed. Then I pointed to the jacket of his seersucker suit and said, "You seem to be doing all right."

"Why, thank you." He held his arms out in front of him as if he were carrying a tray of hors d'oeuvres. "As a matter of fact, I purchased this at Braverman's store. I had him order it specially for me. It's the same suit Gregory Peck wore in *To Kill a Mockingbird*.[65] They're British, you know. Seersucker suits, I mean. The British wore them in India to keep cool. The name comes from the Persian *shir o shakkar*, which means 'milk and sugar.'[66] I believe that refers to the different textures of the cloth, the blue stripes having a different feel to them than the white. You should consider getting one."

I let my head tip to one side to suggest that I was considering it.

"Braverman would give you a discount."

"I don't *know* Braverman."

"That's right, isn't it? Well, back to the charming little subject of infidelity. As I was saying, one night I met Braverman for dinner and he confided in me that for years he'd been involved with his secretary, Denise, a thin-waisted, busty woman." Shoogey held his hands in front of his own chest, curving his fingers into his palm as if in the throes of an arthritic seizure. "At first, it was something of a shock for me to hear that. I mean, those ears—how could she? It was one of those"—returning his arthritic hands to his lap, Shoogey caught a glance of his wristwatch, then said, "Hey, it's about lunch time. Do you have lunch plans?"

I said I didn't.

"Come on, I'm buying," he said, and he took my jacket off the hook and dropped it to my lap before I could refuse. "I know a great place, a fantastic place that you'll just love. In fact, Braverman's the one who showed me. What a coincidence—there we were talking about Braverman, now we're going to one of his favorite restaurants. What are the odds of that—three-to-one? Four-to-one?"

We took the elevator to the lobby. As always, Harry Addler stood at the guard station, his black-and-white television monitor blinking. He waved to Shoogey.

"We're getting some lunch," Shoogey said to him. "Can we bring you back something?"

"No, thank you," Harry said. He lifted a small brown paper bag. "Celia made me a meatloaf sandwich."

We continued out the front doors.

"Do you know Harry?" I asked Shoogey.

"This is Baltimore," he answered. "Doesn't everyone know everyone here?"

When we reached the street, Shoogey unbuttoned his coat, letting it flap in the soft winds, then he spread his arms out to his side, his palms up as if checking for rain—there would be none—and tipped his head back as if he were drinking in the sunshine that splashed on his face.

"This blessed plot...this earth...this realm...this Baltimore," he announced. Then he tilted his head to look at me with one eye open and the other closed. "I'm quoting Shakespeare, my friend. Except for the part about Baltimore, of course. I added that myself."[67]

Shoogey led me to the corner, then hailed a cab with some small, undetectable gesture. The raising of his chin perhaps, the wag of a hidden finger. He refused to tell me where we were headed, instead telling me about Braverman's infidelities in some detail—though some of those details seemed to defy the immutable laws of physics—only stopping now and again to tap the cabbie on the shoulder and point him off in a new direction. When the cab finally pulled to the curb, it was in front of a restaurant with a simple red sign that read "Cuban-Chinese Food." The same words had been painted on the window, by someone with a very shaky hand.

"Have you ever had Cuban-Chinese before, Napoleon? I hope not. Have you?"

I said that I hadn't even heard of such food before. In fact, had I not seen the sign, I would've thought he was pulling my leg; even with the sign right in front of me, it seemed as if he was giving my ankle a subtle twist.

"Are you sure you haven't heard of it?"

I assured him I hadn't.

"Then you'll learn a little something today, my friend. You see, there's a fairly large Chinese population in Cuba," he said in the thoughtful, measured tone of a museum guide. "The Chinese sailed there sometime in the mid-nineteenth century, and they worked the fields, peeling sugar cane or doing whatever it is you do to sugar cane. I believe you peel it, though I really should look that up.[68] This was about the same time that the railroads were being built in this country, not coincidentally by cheap Chinese labor."[69]

Shoogey stopped outside the restaurant door.

"So," he continued, "over the years there's been this group of Chinese people in Cuba, just multiplying each generation. First there were, say, a thousand of them. Then, the next generation, there were three thousand. Then ten thousand, and so on and so on and so on, *ad infinitum*, all working the fields. I wish I knew more on the subject, but unfortunately I don't. Of course, the reason we don't know much about it is Castro. He's cut the outside world off. We can only imagine how terrible it must be down there, with the economy the way it is, the poverty, the overcrowding. But you're going to love the food."

Only then did Shoogey allow us to enter the restaurant. Expecting it to be empty, I was surprised to find a small gathering of people milling about the entrance, waiting to be seated. A young black woman wearing a tight pink dress that clung to her thighs leaned against the wall. Her fingers were braided in her boyfriend's, a thin white man who stared at the laces of his tennis shoes with great interest. Two elderly women, in their seventies perhaps, swayed slightly to very different songs playing in their heads; they held their purses close to their chests as if they contained not only enormous sums of money, but the secrets to the universe, too. Five or six young men sat in straight-back chairs along the wall, reading newspapers—*The Sun, The Afro-American*— and a Hispanic couple paced back and forth, their eyes fixed on the red-brown carpet, which was worn in spots and stained in others. Shoogey left me for a moment and spoke to the manager, whispering. The manager nodded, and Shoogey returned to my side.

"Cough," Shoogey said to me.

"What?"

"Just do me a favor and cough, okay? It's a signal for the manager over there."

"Fine," I said, and coughed once, then twice, into my fist.

I caught Shoogey and the manager as they exchanged glances that could only be described as conspiratorial. Their eyes met for an instant, as if they were bank robbers soundlessly saying, *The coast is clear.* Then Shoogey looked away, casually bringing two fingers to his cheek as if to scratch an itch. The manager looked down at a spiral notepad, then announced, "Shoogey, party of two."

The manager led us into the dining area, which wasn't much larger than a living room. Still, there must have been at least forty people crowded in there, eating. The room wasn't decorated in any distinguishing way, just plain yellow tablecloths weak from washings. The only view was of the street, and the street revealed nothing.

Shoogey ordered for the both of us, and the meal was soon delivered to our table by a thin Chinese man with very white teeth. Like all of the waiters, he wore a white jacket like a hunting coat. His features suggested that he was often smiling.

Shoogey scooped rice onto my plate, then covered it with our entrees, the names of which I don't recall. One dish began with an "s." It was orange and heavy-looking. Another began with a "ch." That dish was red, the color of a fire engine.[70]

I was more than mildly surprised by the food, which I confessed to Shoogey. It was spicy, but pleasurably so, with a fruity taste that remained.

"I have to tell you that I was surprised by it at first, too," he said. "I'm mostly a meat-and-potatoes kind of person myself, and I'm not ashamed of that. Meat and potatoes, a slice of key lime pie for dessert. But Braverman got me to stop that, always dragging me off to some new place."

Throughout the meal, Shoogey regaled me with stories of the famous men and women he'd rubbed elbows with, with his thoughts about love and hate, and life and death, and heaven and hell, and other light subjects. He uttered one lovely phrase after another. He quoted Christopher Marlowe and Teddy Roosevelt and Walt Whitman and Thomas Hobbes and Abraham Lincoln.[71] He was cheerful, and he was grave, and he moved from one to the other with amphibious ease, his face hanging before me, taking over the room.

When we were finished with our meal, Shoogey paid the check, leaving the waiter a sizable tip, and we stepped out onto the sidewalk. I said goodbye and extended my hand, but Shoogey refused to take it.

"Where are you going?" he said. "The day's still young."

I explained that I had to return to the office, and he shook his head.

"Oh, don't be silly, Napoleon. Don't be ridiculous. On a day like this, you shouldn't be inside. It's Baltimore, and for once it's not raining or threatening to. How could you possibly go back inside? Now, let's enjoy the afternoon." His face was bright with recklessness, all pink and excited.

I said that I couldn't, in a tone that sounded suspiciously like the whine I'd used earlier with DeWitt, but soon we were in another cab and headed toward the waterfront, toward an area of town known as Fells Point. The area is known for its shipyards, as many as sixteen or so at one point. It's where many immigrants first touched ground and where boats once deposited loads of rum and Indian meal, coffee and salmon from New England. Now, it's better known for its taverns, which is where we were headed.

Shoogey pointed the way to an Irish bar by the name of the Cat's Eye Pub, where we listened to Irish music and had several glasses of ice-cold beer that, perhaps because of my truancy, tasted finer than any I'd ever drunk in years and years and then some.[72]

Afterward, we stopped at another bar, then another—there may have been one more—then took another cab several miles north to the Senator Theater, a lovely old movie theater with an enormous screen framed by a red velvet curtain.[73] We took in a matinee, a western called *Aim High*.[74] The theater was nearly empty. Everywhere, cowboys and Indians turned each other into fertilizer and pure blue air.

When the movie was finished, we walked to a nearby schoolyard and watched a Little League baseball game. The boys were no more than ten or twelve years old, but they played with great skill, the balls snapping in their mitts, their bats cracking. Shoogey and I sat in the stands with all the pretty mothers, and we made a point of cheering equally for both teams. When the game ended and the teams shook hands and diverged, Shoogey and I stopped at another bar, this one by the name of Jerry's Belvedere where we ordered a pitcher of beer.[75]

"I have something to show you," he said. "I might as well tell you seeing as you remind me of Napoleon."

With that, Shoogey reached into the inside pocket of his suit jacket and produced a small notepad with the words *Poor Napoleon* written in solemn black letters on the cover.[76]

"This is the book I'm working on," he said. "Or, at least, part of it. The other notebooks are at home. I can't tell you how excited I am about it. Really, I guess I've been working on if for about ten years, maybe more. I can feel that this is going to be it, this is going to be my big break. The great American novel. Romance. Comedy. Tragedy. Fatty foods. Everything American."

"What's it about?"

"Oh, *never* ask a writer what his book's about because he might actually tell you. There's nothing a writer likes more than to talk about his writing."

Perhaps it was the alcohol, or perhaps it was the simple fact that he was charming me again, but I told him I'd love to hear about his next book, which made him smile even more broadly.

Then he began his story: "There was a boy I knew when I was a youngster growing up in Casper. His name was Walter Something-or-other.[77] He lived on Nayatt Road, which ran perpendicular to our street, Briarwood Road. We lived at 11 Briarwood Road in a brick house with black shutters. It's funny what the mind chooses to retain. I can't recall what shirt I wore yesterday or what I had for dinner on Saturday night, but I can still recall our telephone number in those days. Want to know what it was?"

I said, "Sure."

"It was 486-1175. Don't try calling it now. If you call it now, you'll be connected with a construction company called SMP Construction. I know: I've tried. A hundred times I've called expecting to hear a younger version of myself answer, but each time it's the same thing: 'Hullo, SMP Construction. Hullo? Hullo?'[78] Anyway," he continued, "as I was saying, there was a boy I grew up with. We were in the same class from kindergarten through high school. If you look at any picture of our class from any of those years, for all the changes—people moving to other towns, people moving to our town, clothing styles changing, etcetera—there were always two constants: me in the back row with the taller boys, and Walter Something-or-other standing in the front row with the shorter boys. Now, in those days, people weren't as sensitive about every little thing as they are today. If someone was fat, you called them fat, and it was no big deal. There was even a comedian at one time called Fatty Arbuckle. Today, they'd call him Stocky. Stocky Arbuckle. Today, everyone tries to ignore the most obvious of things. Back then, if someone was short like Walter Something-or-other, you acknowledged it, and it was no sin. He was short, so everyone called him Napoleon."

"Like Napoleon Game in your novels," I said.

Shoogey touched the tip of his nose, smiled a little and said, "Bingo. I won't pretend it was an inspired nickname. He was short, and Napoleon was short, so, voilà: Napoleon."

Shoogey tipped his head back the way people do when enjoying a cigarette, the smoke filling their lungs. He wasn't smoking. "By the way," he said, "did you know that Napoleon was the person who came up with the idea of putting buttons on coatsleeves? Of course, I'm referring to Napoleon Bonaparte, not *our* Napoleon. It seems he did it so his army would stop wiping their runny little noses on their coatsleeves.[79] Anyway, there's a funny little story about Napoleon. *Our* Napoleon. In the sixth grade, he was absent from school every Monday, or nearly every Monday. He'd be at home perspiring and gurgling and twisting in his bed. He'd be red, and his face would be bloated like a cream puff. Every Monday, or nearly every Monday, the same symptoms. Perspiring, gurgling, twisting, red-faced, bloated like a cream puff. It took doctors months to find out what was wrong with him."

"What was it?" I asked.

"He was an excellent speller."

"What?"

"He was sick because he was an excellent speller."

"I don't understand."

"Well," Shoogey said, "every week our teacher, Mrs. Krall, would give us a list of spelling words to learn.[80] 'Together.' 'Particle.' 'Judicial.'

Then, on Fridays, she would give us a quiz. Napoleon always won. Always. He was, as I've said, an excellent speller."

Shoogey took a sip of his beer and looked at me as if he'd explained everything.

"Yes?" I said.

"Oh, I almost forgot the most important part. Each week, Mrs. Krall would present the best speller with a giant Nestlé's chocolate bar. And Napoleon would take it home and eat it. By Monday morning, he'd be as sick and as puffy as a woman pregnant with triplets."

"The teacher gave him spoiled candy?"

"No, no, for godssakes, no. What a horrible thought. What kind of teacher would give spoiled candy to her own students? No, no. It ended up that Napoleon was allergic to chocolate. Just couldn't eat the stuff at all."

I nodded. "So did he stop trying to win the spelling bees?"

"No, he kept winning them, but Mrs. Krall would give him peanut brittle instead. It's funny, but I just remembered that for a while we started calling him 'Nestlé' instead of Napoleon, but it didn't stick. We went back to calling him Napoleon. So, the book I'm working on is about him, more or less."

Shoogey patted his pocket where the pad was.

That was when I said, "But you've written about him before, haven't you?"

"I've used the name, yes. But this book's actually about him. It was all very sad. He died during the war."

"I'm sorry to hear that."

"Yes. Well, it was very sad. But that's what war's all about. If people didn't die, it'd just be a big dance. A big cotillion."

"You were in the Army, weren't you?" I asked, remembering something he'd told me when we'd been preparing for the *pendente lite* hearing.

"Yes."

I asked Shoogey whether he'd been in battle. He confirmed that he had, then inhaled deeply as he prepared to tell me his story, the story that begins the book that you hold in your hands.

"My friend," he began, "you should know that I killed seven men, sent them to their graves, turned their bodies to fertilizer and their thoughts to pure blue air. Seven. The same number as Deadly Sins, as the Seas, as Wonders of the World, as Dwarfs, as Brides for Seven Brothers."

It was a sad and compelling story, and I sat quietly and listened. My mouth may even have fallen open on several occasions: he was a magnificent storyteller, and he knew his story well, knowing when to allow his words to race at you, knowing when to pause, and take a sip of beer, and give you the notion that the story was finished, when in fact it was not.

I heard about Jane in her thin blue nightgown at the hotel near the base. (I could imagine her young and beautiful, could see how she could send a young man's heart racing.)

I heard about Jane becoming ill when Shoogey told her about the first man he'd killed. (I could picture that too, as if it were in a movie: Jane, in the bathroom, crying; Shoogey outside his cheek pressed against the bathroom door, praying that she would still love him.)

Lombardi farting in a clearing. (Childish, bullying, insecure. I knew boys like that when I was at Magruder, and more when I taught there years later.)

Shoogey sending two bullets through the air, the bullets passing through a man's nose. (I may have worried.)

Shoogey doing what he had to to silence the man. (This is where my mouth may have fallen open.)

Shoogey mistreating his son. (I thought of my daughters and wished to hug them.)

Lombardi visiting Shoogey at his office and leaving with a check for five thousand dollars. (It was over.)

The check made out to someone named Jimmy Birnberg. (It wasn't over. There was still a question remaining.)

We sat in silence for several moments. Was he finished? Was he pretending to be finished? I waited for him to take a large mouthful of beer, which seemed to confirm that his story was complete.

"But who was Jimmy Birnberg?" I asked him.

"What?"

"Jimmy Birnberg. Who was he?"

"Heck if I know," Shoogey said. "All I know is he's got five thousand dollars of my money. Not an unreasonable price for a little peace of mind, don't you agree?"

It was dark when our cab driver dropped me off at the parking lot so I could retrieve my car. I shook Shoogey's hand and said goodnight. Before closing the door, though, I said, "By the way, I'm curious about something."

"What?"

I suspect he anticipated another question about his story. Instead, I asked, "What did you say at the Cuban-Chinese restaurant to get us seated before everyone else?"

Shoogey smiled. "I told him you had tuberculosis and needed to eat immediately," he said. "It always works. No one even knows what tuberculosis is anymore."

Then he closed the cab door. The cab drove off.

Chapter Five: Meet Syd Braverman

One of the next times I saw Shoogey, I mentioned Jimmy Birnberg again.[81] Why would Lombardi ask that the check be made out to Jimmy Birnberg? Why?

"Maybe Jimmy Birnberg was someone you'd gotten into an argument with during boot camp," I said. "Maybe he was someone who had a vendetta against you."

Shoogey ignored me.

"Or maybe," I said, "he was someone you borrowed money from and he never forgot about it. He calculated the interest, and it finally reached a total of five thousand dollars."

"So, have you heard from Jane's lawyer lately?" he said, and the message in his voice told me he wished he'd never talked to me about the war, about how he'd killed seven men, how he'd shot one in the nose. But he had, and the story he'd told stuck with me, the way the cold can seep into your bones and make you feel as if you'll never be warm again. Perhaps that's why I have a memory of spending much of the following months with Shoogey, of meetings and dinners, of trips to bars and movies, of listening to his stories and his rambling ruminations, his rantings and his malarkey. It's a memory that is for the most part inaccurate, a trick of time. I was busy at work in those days—far too busy, looking back on it. There were a great many clients to meet with, countless letters and contracts to read and write and reread and rewrite, and a telephone ringing all day like the bell at a prizefight announcing the rounds, only the rounds came too quickly and there were far too many of them. There were other humdrum duties as well, duties that in retrospect never seem nearly enough to fill a day, but they did and then some. The darkness would seep into the sky, and I would sit in my little box of an office and watch the offices across the street as everyone turned off their lights and left—to go home, to go to the movies, to eat dinner, to bathe, to watch television, to look for someone to love and to stroke their hair at night. Still, in those late hours and those paltry, thoughtless chores I found the small gift of quiet and solitude.

Angie and I continued painting the house in the warm, windless evenings of that summer; because of my late hours, she shouldered the redhead's share of the work. We finished painting the living room, and at long last we removed the bed sheets from the furniture and carried them into the kitchen to start work there. The kitchen bore no relation to the needs of our small family. It was a large room, much larger than we needed; it could have been used to feed a family twice the size of ours, and it needed no small amount of work: the cabinets were dented and smudged, the walls were moist with grease, and the floor tiles curved like toenails too long between clippings. Worse, the faint smell of roasting chicken loitered in the air. If you closed your eyes, you could smell the chicken fat burning, you could hear it popping in the pan. *Pop-pop-pop-pop-pop.*

Angie finished painting the kitchen and the bathroom one after the other, then we carried the supplies to our bedroom and took down the curtains, and started painting there, beginning with the window frames. We painted until we ran out of paint one night, and we looked to the next work-free nights like holidays. With the curtains down, our bedtime activities were limited—limited, unless we were willing to share our marital secrets with our new neighbors, which we weren't— but those were pleasant nights nonetheless.

"Do me a favor," Angie said one night, her legs braided in mine, her breath on my neck.[82] She had been painting the dowels of the banister that day. She smelled lovely of turpentine.[83]

"Anything," I said.

"Say something sweet to me."

"Okay," I said. "Cookies, cake, chocolate candy."

Angie breathed against my chin. "Tell me a story," she said. "Tell me the story of how we met." It was a story she liked me to repeat from time to time, though occasionally I wondered why. To remind her why we were there, together, with a house of children and bills to pay off? To remind her what she was like when she was younger? I must admit that I enjoyed telling the story, too, and the reasons for my enjoying it are a bit of a mystery as well. I must also admit that the details of the story changed once in a while, as we would add some piece of new information we'd suddenly remembered or thought perhaps we'd remembered.

"If I remember correctly," I said, "you were there."

"I know, I know, but I just like to hear it. It's like watching a movie. It's like reading a book. Was I nice?"

"You were beautiful and sweet," I said, "as sweet as cake batter."

"Oh, I like that," she said, and she kissed my neck. "Go on, go on."

"But I didn't always know you, and I wish that I did. I wish I'd known you when you were a little girl, growing up in North Carolina."

"What was the name of the town I lived in?"

"Is this a quiz?"

"Mm hmm."

"You lived in a small town in North Carolina called Burlap— burlap, like the sacks—before moving to Baltimore and moving into our neighborhood."[84]

"How small was Burlap?"

"Burlap was so small that the high school didn't even have a basketball team."

"You're doing good so far." I could tell her eyes were closed. She was approaching sleep. I looked over. She was biting her lip.[85]

"As a girl, you had hair the color of peanut shells, though it would grow to be as black as black can be, and round cornflower blue eyes. I've seen photographs: what a gumdrop you were then. Your father had plain brown hair, the color of a paper bag, though later it turned as gray as a field mouse, and your mother's was that white-blond that you associate with Californians, though she wasn't from that state; you were all from North Carolina.[86] Or, as you would say, Carolina, just Carolina, as if there were no such place as South Carolina."

"Well, South Carolina's just plain disgusting."

"Then your parents moved you up to Baltimore, and you were my neighbor. You wrote songs and played the guitar, and you'd read books beneath the trees that grew behind your house."

"How did you know that?"

"I could hear you singing, and I could see you from my window."[87]

"You could?"

"You know I could. Then I went off to college."

"This sounds sad. Did we ever see each other again?"

"Not for a long time."

"Oh, no, this is a sad story."

"Not at all. It has a happy ending to it. You see, I bumped into you several years after we'd graduated. I bumped into you in the grand-stands of a football game at the school on a pale, brisk November after-noon. You were with one of your dear friends in those days."

"What was her name?"

"I don't remember."

"At least tell me her first initial."

"I don't remember that either, sweetheart."

Angie pushed her head into the crook of my arm. "Me neither."

"Let's say her name was Nancy."

"Okay, I was with Nancy."

"So, there you were with your very close friend Nancy, and in that sweet voice of yours, you called out my name when you spotted me: 'Hay-yum.'" With that beautiful Carolina accent of hers, that was the way she pronounced my name, as if it were two syllables. Hay-yum.

"Did I look pretty that day?"

"Pretty as a picture."

"You don't remember, do you?"

"I remember it more than anything else in my life," I said, which is true. "That day at the football game, you were wearing a heavy sweater, the color of cream of tomato, and two stray locks of your hair fell across your forehead, sort of like parentheses. You had a carefree expression that suggested you were mildly intoxicated."

"I was *not.*"

"You were *so.* Remember, you'd had a few sips of bourbon from a bottle that Nancy had hidden in her sock."

"Oh, you're right. Sorry. That Nancy was such a bad influence, wasn't she?"

"So there you were, pretty and drunk—a young man's dream if ever there was one. Faint puffs of breath, like cigarette smoke, rose from your lips. As for me, soon I was smiling the smile of a rogue altar boy all day, walking around with the prettiest girl in the world on my arm."

"Is that when you realized you loved me?"

"Yes. I realized that I loved you, that I always had, that I always would. I realized that I wanted to spend every moment with you, that every moment without you would be a wasted moment, and that I could only bear those moments with the thought I'd see you again."

"Tell me more."

"You're falling asleep."

"No, I'm not. Please tell me more."

"That evening, we ended up in the woods behind the high school, and we undressed and kissed and started to push against each other. Only, just then, the alcohol we'd consumed that evening worked its way up my body like salmon swimming upstream, and I found myself gagging and, finally, asleep in the woods with leaves attached to my sweaty skin."

"Can we leave out the vomiting part?"

"Sure. I found myself suddenly very ill and I fell asleep in the woods with leaves attached to my sweaty skin. Better?"

"Much."

"When I awoke, you were long gone—"

"—I had to go home. I couldn't wake you up, and I had to go home or I'd be in trouble."

"But you'd covered me with your coat. I was embarrassed by the whole event and expected that you would never see me again. Still, there was the small matter of your coat, a blue pea coat. I returned it to you the next morning, along with a bouquet of flowers and a note that read:

Angie —

It was a perfectly wonderful day until I made a fool of myself. I hope you'll forgive me. Please let me take you out next Saturday for a drink.

Only I'd crossed out 'drink' and written 'ice cream cone' above it."

"That was a funny note."[88]

"Thanks. Anyway, the angels who watch over eager young men made sure that you forgave me. That following Saturday, we ate chocolate ice cream cones and eventually returned to the woods behind the school, not far from where I'd left my mark, and we undressed and kissed and pushed against each other with that energy and aimlessness that only young lovers can summon. You kept repeating my name over and over like the chorus of some pop song: 'Hay-yum, Ham-yum, Hay-yum.' When we were through, we rested on the cold, fallen leaves."

"That's a lovely story. Did we end up getting married?"

"Yes. It was the most beautiful wedding in the history of mankind."

"More beautiful than when Prince Charles and Princess Di got married?"

"Much more beautiful."

"How did the bride look?"

"Like an angel. It is now illegal to show pictures of her to future brides for fear of making them feel inadequate."[89]

"How did the groom look?"

"Like someone whose dreams had all come true. Like someone who had been touched by the warm hand of God."

"Did we have any children?"

"Two beautiful girls."

"Did we live happily ever after?"

"Of course we did."

I listened to Angie breathe.

"Can I ask a favor?" she said.

"Of course you can."

"From now on, can we change the story so I wasn't drunk when you saw me at the football game. It makes it a nicer story."

"Of course we can do that."

"And can we take out the sex and just say we were kissing."

"Of course."

Then we fell asleep. We slept well and woke up with the sun in our eyes.

Early that Saturday morning, we made plans to run a number of errands, including purchasing a can of paint so we could complete the bedroom. First, though, Angie and I had to take the girls to their ballet class. They'd just enrolled at the dance school, a small barn that had been converted into a studio, and as we pushed the girls into the car they looked adorable in their pink outfits, like pieces of candy. I dropped them off with Angie at the front door of the dance school, then ran some errands, filling the tank at the gas station and running the car through the car wash, then I stopped to get my hair cut at a barber shop called, simply, Larry's Barber Shop. The sign over the door was red-white-and-blue. *Larry's* in red. *Barber* in white, outlined in black. *Shop* in blue.

There was a wooden bench outside the barber shop, and there was an old Jewish man sitting there, his yarmulke covering the crown of his head as yarmulkes are meant to do. He was reading a thin paperback book, not looking up from it as I passed and entered the shop. I tried to see if it was one of Shoogey's books, since I had yet to find them in any bookstore, but I couldn't see the cover; the man had folded it back. A bell chimed when I opened the door, and it chimed again when the door shut closed behind me. There were two barbers, and two barber's chairs, and two long rows of mirrors lining the walls and facing each other so that, when you looked at your reflection, you saw a thousand

yous all standing in a perfect line, like a science experiment out of control. Other than the men already being attended to, their hair covering
the floor like fallen leaves, there were five or six others waiting their
turns. They sat in chairs in a row beneath the long, polished mirror,
with weathered magazines and *The Sun* in front of them, their heads
bowed like mourners. They didn't speak, and when one was called into
the red barber's chair, invariably someone walked through the door—
chime, chime—and took his place and his magazine. I sat among them
until I, too, was summoned into one of the chairs, which was as warm
as a lounge chair left in the summer sun. I gave the barber some brief
instructions about how I like to wear my hair—full on the top, short in
the back—then watched as pieces of my hair fell onto the cloth that
covered my chest and lap. They landed with the lightness of fireflies
upon me. When he was finished, my hair had been cut to nubs. It was
very nearly a crewcut, with nothing in the way of sideburns, and the
look on all one thousand of my faces was one of disappointment. The
haircut made me look young and lumpy and very, very vulnerable.

Outside, the old man was still sitting on the bench. He wasn't
reading his paperback anymore. It was folded open in a V across his
knee; it was not one of Shoogey's books. He was an old and handsome
man. He was neither heavy nor thin, but solid, and his hair was curly
and gray. He had a gold front tooth, not on the top row like you usually see, but on the bottom, and large, fleshy hands.

"Not bad," he said. "That's not a bad haircut at all. It really isn't. If
you wanna see a bad haircut, take a look at this," and he leaned forward,
doubling over and lifting his yarmulke like he was lifting the lid of a
cookie jar to reveal the bald spot on the crown of his head, round and
the size of a piece of fruit. He made me smile, which I suspect is exactly
what he'd intended.

"You ought to get your money back," I said.

"Believe me, I've tried," he said. Then he picked the book off his
knee and resumed reading.

I returned to the dance school and found the girls and Angie more or less in the same spot where I'd left them. Katie and Claire loitered, shoulder to shoulder, with several other girls who were talking with a pack of boys. The boys were seated on bicycles and giving the impression that at any moment they would shoot off. Angie stood off to the side, reading a *Redbook* magazine to give the girls ample room. When I pulled into the parking lot, Angie walked to the car first. She climbed in and ran her hand over my hair and said, "Should I kiss you or salute you?"

"Very funny."

"I knew joining M & D was like joining the military, but this is a bit extreme, don't you think?"

I frowned, and Angie kissed my cheek, and we waited for the girls. They walked to the car after a safe amount of time had passed, climbing into the back seat, and we drove downtown toward the library.

In Baltimore, if you drive downtown, you can't help but notice a clocktower that stands several blocks from the harbor, tall and gray with stones like those in a medieval castle in England or Ireland or Scotland or France or Italy; in fact, I've only recently learned that it was modeled after the tower of the Palazzo Vecchio in Florence. The clock faces—one each pointing due north, south, east and west—don't bear numbers, though. Instead, there are letters where the numbers rightly should be. A *B* at ten o'clock, an *R* at eleven, and so on and so on, spelling out the words *BROMO SELTZER*. A canny advertisement for a city whose inhabitants seem to be aggrieved with chronic indigestion. At one time the tower was topped by an enormous reproduction of a blue Bromo Seltzer bottle, the kind you may have seen in the drug store or in your own medicine cabinet. It was crowned with lights, and it revolved, spinning round and round.

If you use the Bromo Seltzer tower as your beacon—which you can do, even without the beaming blue bottle—several blocks beforehand you'll find a shoebox of a building with rows of display windows like those in a department store; though there were libraries closer to our home, this is the Enoch Pratt Library, the same library my father took me to when I was a boy.

That morning, the windows were decorated with model trains, which chugged and wound through a city constructed of entirely of books, stacked to form skyscrapers and bridges. Inside, we let the girls loose in the children's section to pick out some books for the weekend. Angie went off browsing through the rows of magazines, and I settled into one of the straight-back chairs to read the morning newspaper, which I hadn't had time to finish in the barbershop. I'd only skimmed over the headlines on the sports page when I was struck by a sudden thought. I returned the newspaper to the rack, then made my way to the card catalog by the door and pulled out the drawer marked *AUTHOR—S TO SM*. The cards were thick and tan and well-thumbed, and I made my way through them rapidly.

Sheldon, Henry
Shelton, Laura
Sherman, Margaret
Sherrard, Thomas
Sherwyn, Jackie
Shiller, Frances
Shilstein, Simon
Shilter, Scott
Shipp, Benjamin
Shipton, Catherine
Shipley, Frederick
Shires, James
Shirley, James
Shive, Susan
Shobe, Mark
Shofer, Jeanette
Sholer, Amanda
Shooman, Henry
Shoopster, Stephen
Shorrock, Paul[90]

There was no *Shoogey, Samuel.*

I thumbed my way through again, reversing my path this time. There was no card between *Sholer, Amanda* and *Shooman, Henry*, where there should have been several.

A thin teenage girl with limp brown hair was sitting behind the librarian's desk, reading a magazine and popping slivers of a chocolate bar into her mouth with fingers that were stained blue with ink. She was not a pretty girl, and her carriage, the slump of her tiny shoulders, the way she dug her chin into her chest, suggested she was well aware of that condition. For that reason, I decided to forgive her for the contemptuous look she gave me over the top of her magazine as I approached.

"Excuse me," I said to her in as friendly a voice as I could find, "but I was hoping you could help me."

The girl sniffed and looked at me again over the top of her magazine, but said nothing.

"I was looking for a book."

"Did you check the card catalog?" She spoke in a voice so tiny it sounded like it was coming from the bottom of a well. I felt enormous sympathy for her.

I said that I had.

"What's the title?"

I told her I didn't know. "I'm looking for any of the books by Sam Shoogey, or any books about a private investigator named Napoleon Game. Maybe you've heard of them."

She looked at me blankly. "I'm in high school. I only read what they make me read: *The Red Badge of Courage*, *The Scarlet Letter*, junk like that.[91]

The books you were looking for weren't in the card catalog?"

I told her no.

"That means we don't have them. If you want, I can check with some of the other libraries around here to see if they have them."

Her offer was extended in such a way as to make it clear that it would be a great imposition upon her time, and I had no desire to

make her life any more unbearable than it already was. There was
taunting, I knew. There were few friends and fewer boyfriends and
Friday evenings spent at home with her parents. Cheerfully, I told her
not to go to the trouble of calling those other libraries, then returned
to the newspaper and read. When Angie and the girls were finished
picking out their books some time later, we put them in the trunk of
the car and headed toward home. We were several blocks away when
Angie reminded me that we had forgotten to pick up a fresh can of
paint to finish the bedroom. I'd forgotten because I'd been thinking
about that poor girl in the library. Why Angie forgot, I can't say. We
made a detour to the hardware store, and I left Angie and the girls in
the car with the radio on while I ran inside. Passing through the aisles
filled with wires and bolts and thingamajigs hanging from racks, I
pulled a can of paint off a stack at the back of the store and paid for it,
and as I turned to leave, I found myself looking at the largest ears I'd
ever seen, enormous, fleshy mounds that jutted out like malignant
growths. They were pink and puffy with the conformation of scar
tissue, and they seemed to move on their own.

"You're Ashe, aren't you?" their owner said. "I thought you had
longer hair. But you're Hamilton Ashe, right?"

"That's right," I answered, mesmerized. "And you're Syd
Braverman, aren't you?"

Braverman beamed, smiling with thin, pale lips.[92]

"I see my reputation precedes me," he said. "Well, don't believe
everything you hear."

He was a short, broad man, built like a bagpipe, and he had a peculiar, prehistoric head, all lumpy like a clay figure a child would make
with a flurry of thumbs and a short attention span. If you could take
your eyes off his ears—no small trick, that—you would next notice his
nose, which was large and fleshy and somehow droopy, with a crook like
a thumb-joint at the bridge. Gravity seemed to affect him differently,
and not just the nose. It was as if all of his features were being pulled
downward toward the earth. His eyes, his eyebrows, his fatty chin.

But the ears. You were always drawn back to the ears.

Braverman put a gentle hand on my wrist, squeezing it slightly as if taking my pulse, then spoke in a creaky voice that seemed to confide things rather than speak them.

"You know, I wrote that jingle myself."

"What jingle?"

"The jingle that made my store so popular." Then, as if reciting a long-memorized verse, he closed his eyelids and said:

Guys who are wise
Know that smart dolls have eyes
For big handsome guys
Who buy suits, socks and ties
At Braverman's Menswear.[93]

He peeled his eyelids open, as if recovering from a sweet dream, and looked to me for approval.

"Yes," I said, "that's very nice." I'd never heard it before. I've heard it on the radio hundreds of times since.

"Thank you. As I said, it's just a little thing I wrote myself. I'm no writer. Not like Shoogey. That man writes like Hemingway, let me tell you that. Heck, you can tell just by the way he talks, can't you? If he was describing something that was tall and green, for instance, he'd say, 'It was tall and green like a pine tree.' Me, I'd just say, 'It was tall and green like a tall, green thing.' See? That's real writing what Shoogey does. Now, speaking of Shoogey, I understand that you've been doing a hell of a job handling his divorce. You know, I'm the one who told him he ought to go see you in the first place. I said to him, 'You know, Shoogey, I hear the new boy down the street is one heck of a lawyer. He works for M & D, Shoogey.' Thank God I had the good sense to tell him to go see you."

It was only then that he released my wrist, and out of a sense of obligation I thanked him for sending Shoogey to see me. Braverman bobbed his head, causing his ears to flap. Would he leave the ground and fly?

"Think nothing of it. It's my little way of saying, 'Welcome to the

neighborhood.' It was either that or a fruit basket." He patted the breast
pocket of his shirt, then looked at the ground around his feet as if he'd
just dropped something. "You don't have a cigarette, do you?"

I told him I didn't.

"Are you sure? I really could use a cigarette. Maybe in your
pockets?"

I told him I was sure: I didn't smoke.

"Well, I really could use a smoke. It's a vice, I know, but everyone
needs a vice. Do you have a vice?"

"I hadn't thought about it."

"Well, you should. Pick one. There are some very appealing vices
out there."

Braverman walked with me out to the sidewalk in front of the
hardware store. He moved slowly, as if he never got enough sleep. He
waved to Angie and the girls in the car. After a moment's hesitation,
they returned the greeting.

"You know," he said, "that Shoogey's a good egg. Don't listen to
what some people say about him. They don't know him. You've got to
really know someone before you can say the kind of things people say
about Shoogey, but they don't know him at all, so they should just keep
their pie-holes shut.[94] Me? I know Shoogey, and I say he's a good egg."

"That's good to hear," I said, suddenly curious to know the terrible
things people had to say about Shoogey.

"Well, it's true: Shoogey's a good egg. I would swear on The Bible
that that's true. In fact, that's not a bad idea. Now mind you, I'm no
lawyer—and I'm certainly not a lawyer at Morrisey & DeWitt, which is
one of the finest law firms in the entire country, and I mean that. I'm
no lawyer, but I imagine you'll probably need a character witness at
some point. You know, someone to get up on the stand who can say,
'Yes, sir, ladies and gentleman, I know Sam Shoogey and under oath—
under *oath*—I can tell you that he's a good egg.' What do you think—
is that a good idea? Yes? No?"

"I don't know if we'll be needing anyone, Mr. Braverman. But I'll keep this conversation in mind if we do."

Braverman bunched his lips.

"Good, good. Now, where are my manners. I really should let you get back to your lovely family. Maybe your wife has a cigarette? I could walk with you to your car."

"She doesn't smoke either."

"I don't suppose your daughters smoke."

"No, I don't suppose they do either."

"Well, I guess I could buy a fresh pack. That would be the logical thing to do. I'll go over to the pharmacy over there." He pointed to the pharmacy at the far end of the shopping center as if it were a historic landmark.

"It was a pleasure to meet you," I said.

"You, too. I'll see you at synagogue." He turned his back to walk off, dragging his ears with him.

"Mr. Braverman, I'm not—" I did not complete the sentence. Braverman walked on.

Climbing into the car, I handed Angie the paper bag containing the can of paint and said, "That was Syd Braverman. He's one of our neighbors."

She leaned toward me, to kiss me I thought, but instead she whispered, "Did you see them?"

"Did I see what?"

"His *ears*," Katie said. "They were as plain as *day*."

"God, Ham," Angie said, "you could catch a softball in them."

I started the engine, and Angie added, "You could hang Christmas ornaments from them."

Two blocks from home she said, "You could serve a Caesar salad in them. It wouldn't be sanitary, but you could do it."

Chapter Six: Napoleon Returns

For those who lived in Maryland, for those who knew how to crack open a crab and find the juiciest meat within its claws (twist, twist, careful now, pull, *gentle*, pull), for those who knew the squawk of a seagull watching you as you worked, Shoogey needed no more of an introduction than Elvis Presley, and Elvis Presley needed no introduction at all.[95]

If you lived in Maryland, you knew Shoogey. There was no way to avoid it.

Sundays belonged to the Lord. Monday through Friday, those days belonged to work or school. Saturdays belonged to Shoogey.

Saturdays belonged to Shoo.

"Shoo." It leapt from the lips like a wind of breath on a baby's cheek. It was what they'd taken to calling him when he played linebacker at the University of Maryland. Six-foot-four, with a neck like a thick lower branch of an oak tree and hands that would invariably find themselves squeezing whoever was silly enough to try to sneak the ball through his portion of the field. Hands that looked too large on Jane Peel's waist.

"Ladies and gentlemen," the public address announcer would say, "that tackle was made by Number 84, Samuel Shoogey."

"Shoo!" the crowd would yell, exhaling megaphones of cold breath into the Maryland air. "Shooooooooo!" Sometimes, they would even break into song, singing, "Shoo, Fly."[96]

Shoogey would dust himself off and pick himself up from the ground, always offering a hand to his opponent. He was, after all, a gentleman.[97]

That was how his mother had raised him. Coughing and cancerous, she'd died during his junior year at college; it was the only cruel thing she'd ever done to him.[98]

Returning to the huddle of teammates, Shoogey would look into the grandstands to see if he could find Jane Peel; he knew she'd always be there. He'd look for her face among the mural of 50,000 faces and somehow (the warm hand of God?) he would always locate her. The red hair. The blue eyes. The oval mouth calling his name: "Shoooooooo!"

How was it that he could find her week after week? How was it that he'd found her in the first place? How was it that he'd happened to sit at her table in the cafeteria? How was it that he'd convinced her to let him hold her hand and, later, convinced her of many other things?

There was only one answer he could come up with: the warm hand of God.

Shoogey would join his teammates in a rough circle and give them instructions about the next play.

"Shooooo!" he'd hear, and he'd have to flap his arms like a bird struggling to take off in order to quiet the crowd enough so his teammates could hear him.

"You go here," he'd say to one teammate. "You go there," he'd say to another. They'd nod, then clap hands in unison, then the crowd would raise their voices again.

"Shoooooo!"

Saturday afternoons, week after week, the radio announcers would dutifully explain that the fans were not booing Shoogey; no, they were worshipping him. Few needed the explanation. They worshipped him a dozen times a year—thirteen if there was a bowl game on New Year's Day—and they did it for four years running, until he graduated.

Shoogey graduated on a bright May day more than five months removed from his final football game. The morning of his graduation was more vivid than the morning of any of the games he'd starred in, more vivid even than the Cotton Bowl, where he injured his ankle; it would never be the same. There would be no career in professional football, which was fine with him; Jane hadn't wanted him to play professional football anyway. It was too dangerous, she thought. Of course, she did not know then that he'd wind up going to war, where men like Shoogey did not just end up in the hospital.

"Maybe you can get a job selling insurance in Baltimore?" Jane Peel had said when she visited him in the hospital after the Cotton Bowl. His leg was elevated and resting in a small hammock that hung from the ceiling.

"Only if you're going to be in Baltimore," he'd answered.

"It's always gray in Baltimore, isn't it?" she asked.

"Yes, but different shades of gray."

"Of course I'll be in Baltimore."

"Then we have a date."

The graduation day sky was clement and pure. It could not rain on this day. There were speakers who could not command anyone's attention. There were songs that were ignored. Then, finally, the students stood and formed a line leading to the stage. Shoogey stood in that line, much nearer the end than the beginning, awaiting his name and the applause that would follow. Jane was seated somewhere in the audience with his father, somewhere among the thousands of families and friends. He turned his head to find them. It could not have been more than ten seconds before he did so. Jane was wearing a blue dress.

The warm hand of God.

"Marie F. Sartron," the dean announced. The name crackled through the public address system, and a thin girl walked across the stage and accepted her diploma.

"Thomas P. Sellers."

"Francis M. Selmon."

Then "Julie Shines," and "Henry Shinniman," and "Wilson B. Shoob." [99]

Then, finally, "Samuel J. Shoogey, III."

It started quietly, just a few people here and there, and little by little others joined in the sound, swelling like a train approaching.

"Shooooooooo!" they yelled, like hundreds of gardeners swatting away bees. "Shoooooooo!"

Shoogey stepped onto the stage.

"Shooooooooo!"

The dean grinned awkwardly. He was a short and balding man whom Shoogey had met at more than a dozen banquets. The man had not been an athlete himself, but rather than holding them in contempt, he seemed to be in awe of young, athletic men like Shoogey. Shoogey approached the dean slowly. He convinced himself that it was his ankle that slowed his pace.

Shoogey took the diploma in his enormous hands.

"Shooooooooo!" the gardeners continued. "Shoooooooooooo! Shoooooooo!"

Then Shoogey suddenly lifted the dean from his feet, picking him up gently, the way you'd pick up a sack of groceries, and brought him slowly to the ground. It would be his last tackle.

"Shooooooooo!" the gardeners roared. "Shooooooooooooo!"

The dean was still holding his microphone, and, on his back with Shoogey still pressed against him, he announced, "That tackle was made by Number 84, Sam Shoogey."

The audience stood, cheering.

Shoogey picked himself up, helped the dean to his feet, then continued walking across the stage, limping slightly on his aching ankle. He looked into the audience at hundreds of gardeners, all of them with their gaping oval mouths like goldfish gasping for breath. He squinted as if the sun were in his eyes when, in fact, it was at his back, and he smiled for them.

"Shoooooooo!" the gardeners shouted.

"Shooooooooo!" Jane Peel shouted, curling her hands around the sides of her mouth.

Shoogey told me that story too many times to number. It was, he would tell me, the most thrilling day of his life. His eyes grew distant and wet whenever he told me about it, the way people's eyes often do when speaking of their wedding day or the birth of a child. The way they do when they realize that they have ceased to be who they once were: their molecules had changed, they were someone else now.

Jane Peel was right about Baltimore: it was gray.

Even the Baltimore sky was gray, gray as gunmetal and substantial, too—not blue and pebbled with clouds as are other skies, western skies—except when it opened up and moistened our steps, which was often, very often.

Sometimes, under the spell of another one of those gray Baltimore skies, under the weight of a thousand tedious tasks, it seemed as if every day were the same, as if my life had become nothing more than a series of mundane activities, one after another after another, and so on and so on like the reflections of infinity in barbershop mirrors. In large part, it was my job that was responsible for that feeling, day after day of reducing my thoughts to the percussive, sleepy language of the law: boom, boom, boom, boom, boom, *boom.*

But then there was Shoogey.

Somehow, he seemed to sense exactly when my mood was the worst, then picked that precise moment to pull me out of my mood. Sometimes it was a package that would surprise me at the office. One contained a beautiful pair of Italian loafers. They were the color of some rich and exotic wood. Another, a cassette tape of a jazz singer by the name of Helen Merrill that he had mentioned once in passing.[100] Sometimes it was just a postcard, written in the flawlessly oval Palmer method:

Dear Ham:

Hawaii is beautiful!

Unfortunately, I'm in New York City. But who can deny that Hawaii is beautiful!

   Eat Wheaties![101]

   Sam Shoogey

He needn't have signed it.

More often than not, though, he appeared in the flesh with plans for lunch or a quick get-away. A movie. A ballgame. Shopping. Drinks. You name it.[102]

Or he would just appear at my office and begin a story, like the story that began this chapter.

I would find him moving through M & D's hallways with the agree-ability of an old dog, or sitting in one of the thin, high-backed chairs outside my office with his legs crossed at the knee, smiling his gentle smile, tapping the tip of his nose to summon a thought and remem-bering everyone's name as if he'd just dined with them yesterday. He greeted them one and all, and only the most resolute did not seem taken with him:

"Good morning, Carole. Did you see the movie at the Charles The-ater yet? I think you'd absolutely love it. It's French. Yes, you'd love it." (She did.)

"Hello, Ted. That's a sharp suit." (It wasn't.)

"Hello, Cecily. And hello to you, too, Debra. I'm just waiting for my good friend Ham to get off the phone, but I'd be happy to postpone my meeting for a minute to share a cup of coffee with two such beautiful women."

At times like that, it was easy to see how he could charm women, even a hundred, a hundred fifty of them. Plain-faced women who wished to be treated as they'd seen prettier women treated. Romantic women who wished to calm the ferocious storms of his heart.

Angie was not charmed by Shoogey. She was plain about her senti-ments: "Ham, I don't want that disgusting man in our home. I don't want him near our children."

"He's my friend, sweetheart. He's not a bad guy."

"I don't care if he found the cure for polio.[103] I don't want him in our house. Do you hear me, Ham? I'm putting my foot down on this one. Heck, I'm putting my entire body down on this one. I don't want him in here."[104]

Shoogey in fact had not been to our home since that first evening when he'd materialized on our porch, so it was a surprise to see him there again one evening, in the porchlight, looking like a saint. Another summer had died late in Baltimore, and the bugs had left for autumn, going wherever they go. The unobstructed porchlight seemed as lemony-yellow and pure as a glimpse of the sun. It bounced off Shoogey's teeth like the lights in a toothpaste commercial. His teeth were perfect, the teeth of a man who brushed and flossed as meticulously as a mason laying tiles. The light bounced off his eyes, too, and off the lotion in his hair, and it seemed to leave a whitish ring above his scalp. Fortunately for both of us, Angie wasn't at home. She'd gone to dinner with her sister and had left me to take care of the girls. She'd left us spaghetti and meatballs for dinner, and a Tar Heel pie for dessert.[105]

"Ham, my friend, what are you doing?" he said with some excitement in his voice.

"Babysitting."

"Where's your better half? The old ball-and-chain? The old grapefruit?"

"The old grapefruit? That's not an expression."

"Well, it is now. So, where's the old grapefruit?"

I told him that she was having dinner with her sister.

"Where?"

"I have no idea."

"I wonder if they're going to D'Amico's.[106] I haven't been there yet, but I hear it's very good." Shoogey touched his nose. "Well, I suppose it doesn't matter. But if the old grapefruit's gone, let's go get a drink somewhere."

"I'd love to, Shoogey, but I can't. I told you, I'm babysitting the girls."

Shoogey peered past me into the living room. "Well, hello, ladies," he said to the girls, then he walked past me into the room. He crouched like a wrestler to talk to the girls, who were dressed in bright yellow pajamas that made them look like baby chicks. "Ladies," he said, "it's a certain pleasure to meet you both. My name is Samuel J. Shoogey. I hope this won't embarrass you, but let me say that you are without a doubt the most lovely creatures in the entire neighborhood. You two and your lovely mother, of course."

The summer was still in the girls' hair and in their faces, but still you could see them blush a little at Shoogey's compliment. They twisted and rocked side to side while they spoke with him. But they were restless, and soon they were running through the house like roughnecks.

"Come on, girls," I finally said, "it's time to go to bed."

"No," they both whined.[107]

"It's time," I said, pointing to my watch needlessly: neither one knew how to tell time yet. "Let me take you to bed so Mr. Shoogey and I can have a talk."

Shoogey smiled. "Would you mind if I told them a story to put them to sleep?" he said.

When I hesitated, he said, "Come on, humor me. My children are grown. I haven't had a chance to tell a bedtime story in years."

"You're not going to tell them about the war, are you?"

Shoogey looked at a spot on the ceiling. "Please. I know what stories are appropriate for children."

We walked the girls to their room, each of us taking one of the girls by the hand. I held Katie's hand, and I have no doubt that she felt short-changed. I tucked their tiny bodies under the covers, then balanced on the edge of one of the beds while Shoogey took center stage, the light from the hallway a spotlight that surrounded him as he stood just inside the doorway.

"When I was in elementary school in Casper, Maryland," he began, "there was a boy in our class by the name of Napoleon." He looked at me and winked. "Nobody knew Napoleon very well, but, all of a sudden, he became famous. You see, Napoleon could put his whole fist in his mouth."

"His fist?" Katie said, and she made one of her own.

"Yes, he discovered that he could do it when he had to stay home from school one Monday. You see, although he didn't know it at the time, he was allergic to chocolate." When Shoogey saw that the girls didn't know the meaning of the word "allergic," he said, "Whenever he ate chocolate, he would become very sick, like he had the flu. So he would have to stay home and listen to the radio in bed and eat from the trays that his mothers would bring up to his room. He would ask for books, too, and she would carry them up as well. It was in *Ripley's Believe It Or Not* that he got the idea about the fist. You see, there was a piece in *Ripley's*, just a drawing and a caption, about an Indian prince in the seventeenth century. He had fair skin and reddish hair, and the citizens doubted that he was in fact of royal blood. To convince them of his standing, he slipped his fist in and out of his mouth, not unlike King Arthur and Excalibur, Napoleon thought, only not as romantic. King Arthur, you see, removed a sword called Excalibur from a rock in order to prove that he was royalty."[108]

Katie and Claire looked at me. I nodded.

Shoogey continued, "So it was there, in his bed, that Napoleon made a fist with his right hand, squeezing his fingers tightly together, brought the fist to his lips, and pushed it in. It slid in easily and comfortably. He pulled it out, pushed it in, pulled it out, listening to the pop it made. It was the same pop that his cheek would make when he'd thump it with his finger."

The girls each tried to shove their fists in their mouths. Thankfully, they were unsuccessful and soon stopped.

"It's not easy, is it?" Shoogey said. "Anyway, Napoleon showed his parents, and, though they were amused at first, they told him not to do it again, that his face might stay that way, his eye's bulging like a bug's, his fist in his mouth, for the rest of his life. He continued nevertheless. He did it for his sister Charlotte while she watched television in the den, and she laughed so hard that she had to lie on her back on the rug, her shoulders flat against it. The dog barked and jumped onto the recliner.

"At school, during the pledge of allegiance, he did it for Rosemary

Scofield when no one else was looking. She laughed out loud, and the teacher made her repeat the pledge by herself in front of the class, by the chalkboard. Next, he did it for Roger Lever during gym class, and Roger laughed, too.[109] He stopped paying attention and was hit on the head with a basketball, right on the ear. Though it probably smarted, he kept laughing, and everyone thought Roger was acting strangely.

"Soon, everyone in school knew about Napoleon's trick. They talked about it in the lunchroom and in the hall between classes and whenever there was a substitute teacher. Everyone in the neighborhood knew about it, too. They all wanted to see Napoleon put his fist in his mouth, and they began to offer him things to see it done. Mrs. Kendall, who lived three doors down, promised to give him a piece of pecan pie if he'd do it, but she thought it was so funny that she let him eat the whole pie. She even poured him the last glassful of root beer though she'd been saving it for her husband for supper."

The girls were listening carefully, breathing when Shoogey did. They were smiling, as was I. There was something sweet and soothing to his voice, the tone that of a favorite uncle who brought sweets on his visits; the girls had no such uncle.

"A boy from the high school said that he would let Napoleon drive his father's new car into town if he'd put his fist in his mouth, but the boy laughed so hard that he let Napoleon keep it for a week and a half. Someone else gave him a toaster oven, and someone else gave him a baseball signed by Babe Ruth—he was a famous baseball player—and someone else gave him a clock in the shape of a mallard, and someone else gave him a dozen sirloin steaks.[110] Most people gave him money, though, and he bought a BB gun and a hi-fi system, and he went to all of the movies, sometimes seeing the same movie twice. That's how well he was doing.

"So, one day, Napoleon had a couple of his friends over to his house, and he stuck his fist in his mouth for them. His eyes were bulging like a bug's from their sockets. He was smiling, or at least trying to. It's hard to smile with your hand in your mouth.

"'Incredible!' one of his friends yelled. 'That's incredible!'

"His other friend said, 'Geez, Napoleon, I've never seen anyone do that before. You could make a bundle.'

"Napoleon nodded and pointed to his hi-fi system with his free hand. But then, Napoleon tried to take his hand out of his mouth, but it wouldn't budge. He kept pulling at it and pulling at it, but it was stuck in his mouth. His mother was at the bottom of the stairs, calling up to him. 'Napoleon,' she said 'Napoleon, what are you boys doing up there?'

"Napoleon was still trying to get his hand free.

"'Napoleon? Napoleon, I'm calling you,' his mother said, but all Napoleon could say was, 'Maggalumph. Maggalumph.'

"You see, in the two months since he first discovered he could put his fist in his mouth, Napoleon had experienced a growth spurt, as boys his age do. He was two inches taller, his pants legs fell to his ankles, his shirtsleeves were too short, he sometimes stumbled when he walked. His hands had grown, too, not noticeably, but enough to become caught in his mouth. So there he was, on the floor, on his back, tugging at his hand.

"'Maggalumph,' he said. 'Maggalumph.'

"His mother was still calling him. 'Napoleon, I'm not yelling for my health,' she said, just like your mother probably says sometimes.

"Well, Bill Bateman and Robbie Ellis didn't know what to do. They moved a couple steps toward Napoleon, but they got scared. Bill pulled his father's college ring from his jeans pocket and placed it on Napoleon's dresser. Robbie did the same with his baseball cards, then the two boys raced out of the room and down the stairwell as fast as they could, leaving Napoleon on the floor, rocking and mag-galumphing. His jaw was growing sore, and Napoleon tried to cry, but his eyelids wouldn't shut."

"Did they ever get his hand out of his mouth?" Claire asked.

"They had to hire a plumber to do it," Shoogey answered, "but they got it out."

"Good."

"Good," Shoogey said, "except do you know what plumbers charge? They charge a *fortune*. They're more expensive than lawyers, if you can believe that. It ended up costing Napoleon everything he'd acquired. He had to give the plumber the BB gun, the hi-fi system—everything."

"That stinks," Claire said.

Shoogey nodded in agreement. "So there's a moral to my story."

"What's that mean?" Katie said.

"A lesson. And the lesson is: don't ever try to put anything in your mouth you can't get out. Bowling balls, raccoons, automobiles—if you put them in your mouth, you won't be able to get them out. They're too big. Now, do you both promise you'll live by that lesson?"

They both nodded.

"You don't want things getting stuck," Claire added.

"Yes," Shoogey said. "Now go to sleep, little angels."

I kissed the girls goodnight, and Shoogey did the same, then we shut out the bedroom light and returned to the living room.

"You're very good at that," I said with more than a touch of admiration in my voice. I sat on the couch, and Shoogey took a seat across from me in the love seat. "You're very good with children."

"Don't act so damn surprised, my friend. I have two children of my own, you know."

I told him I wasn't surprised, but of course I was.

"Well, you can bet your bottom dollar that their mother wasn't the one who was telling them bedtime stories. Jane couldn't tell a story if you put a gun to her head. Not that I ever tried that approach, mind you."

"Well, it was a good story."

Shoogey's eyes scanned the room, taking in the details, the drapes, the tables, the lamps. "It's true, you know."

"About Napoleon? That's true?"

"Maybe it's not true exactly, but it could be. I once saw him put his foot in his mouth, which is close enough for me. Besides, my friend, there's an old storytellers' motto: if you tell a story five times, it becomes true."

"Is that so?"

"Damn straight it is, and that was the fifth time I told that one, so you can put it in the history books."

Then Shoogey paused and rearranged his features.

"You know," he said, "it's sad, but he died during the war."

"Yes," I said, "you've told me."

"That's right. Of course I did. Sad. Very sad."

"Speaking of Napoleon," I said, "how's your next book coming along?"

Shoogey said, "Fine," and patted his breast pocket where his notepad was usually housed. "It couldn't be going better," he said. "It'll be done any day now. Any day. Monday. Tuesday. Thursday."

"What about Wednesday?"

"Oh, no, my friend, it won't be finished on Wednesday." Shoogey spread his arms to his side as if to settle in for a long night.

"Can I ask you a question?" I said.

"Sure."

I'd wanted to ask for a while, but hadn't had the nerve. Finally, I said, "I can't seem to find a copy of any of your books. Not in the library, not in the bookstores."

He sniffed. "They're out of print for the time being. They've been out of print for a couple years now, though I'm sure they'll print them again once the new book is published. I keep telling my agent—"

"—Your agent?"

"Yes, my agent. All writers have agents, or at least the good ones do. I just didn't mention mine because I didn't want to sound pretentious. She's a wonderful woman. She's been my agent for years and years, going back to prehistoric times. Anyway, as I was saying before I was interrupted, I keep telling her we need to get the books back in print, there are people who want to read them, people like you, but she doesn't listen. She's more interested in movies these days. In fact I sent her the rough draft of my new book a short time ago, and she says that she thinks Hollywood would be interested in making a movie out of it. Of course, if they do make a movie out of it, I'd want you there on opening night—you and the old grapefruit." He said all of this matter-of-factly, as if he were accustomed to discussing Hollywood in our living room.

"A movie?"

"Yes, yes. She's thinking about Robert Redford or Sean Connery for the lead."[111]

"Robert Redford?"

"Yes."

"Sean Connery?"

"Yes. Who knows what could happen. If my book becomes a best-seller and they make a movie out of it, before you know it my name will be a household word. Like 'refrigerator' or 'egg timer.' Or, well, there must be other examples."

"Bath towel?"

"Yes, that's a good example."

Shoogey went on and on, much more calmly than I would have had I been in his shoes.

"Now, my friend," he said at last, "how about a nice drink for an old friend?"

"I'm sorry, but we don't have any"—then I remembered that we did have a bottle of scotch after all, the bottle he'd given me some months earlier. "You know, we *do* have some scotch in the house."

I left him alone when I went into the kitchen. I pulled the bottle of scotch out of the cupboard above the kitchen sink, the cupboard where we kept all of the household cleaners and sponges, and I peeled off the black band around the screwtop. I dropped several ice cubes into glasses, then filled each glass halfway with scotch. When we clinked our glasses together, Shoogey said, "To a truly great writer—me. Or, as the French would say, *moi.*"

For the next hour or so, we talked about the movie, tossing out the names of actors and actresses who should be in the movie, dismissing them almost as quickly. We each drank several glasses of scotch. Shoogey helped me wash out the glasses, then shook my hand and thanked me.

"It was an excellent evening," he said, "my friend. You are a man to be envied. You have a wonderful home, a wonderful family. And a wonderful neighbor."

He was gone before Angie returned. Though she didn't ask, I could tell she knew he'd been in our home that night. After she took off her jacket, she sniffed at the air. She walked toward the kitchen, then stopped abruptly and sniffed at the air again the way you might to determine if something were burning. She could smell it, too. Not the scotch. No, the smell of peaches.

Chapter Seven: Five Minutes With King Gilmore

The autumn passed, and in those long, lightless months I worked on matters of which I've chosen to have no memory. I wrote contracts for companies buying this or that. I reviewed contracts for companies moving here or there. I talked on the telephone. I wrote letters. Even working on Shoogey's divorce wasn't particularly interesting. Months passed, and in those months Shoogey and I pored through documents his wife's lawyer had turned over. At home, there were phone bills, clothing bills, a deed to the house, things of that nature. On the weekends, I often had to spend one or both days at the office, leaving it to Angie to take the girls to their ballet classes and to run errands. I cannot say I was happy. I cannot say Angie was, either. The girls were girls, meaning I can only assume they were happy.

Winter arrived, but you wouldn't have known it. It was not a harsh winter, not by any standard. The temperatures rarely dropped below freezing, and here and there you would see flowers that had remained to mock the season. Yellow flowers, pink flowers.

The first light snow did not fall until several nights after Christmas; the snow would melt quickly and pour down the sewers and leave no trace, like a burglar who wore gloves. The holiday had come and gone with little fanfare—a group of children bah-rum-pum-pum-pum-ming, a pageant at the girls' school that I nearly missed—but for the most part it had been a quiet and unspectacular one. I'd been at work so late most nights that I'd barely seen the holiday coming. Angie did most of the shopping. Most of the gifts were for the girls, just as it should be (dolls, dresses, board games), and Angie and I exchanged our gifts on Christmas Eve. We'd agreed that, because of the expenses we'd incurred in buying the house, we would only exchange one small gift each. She'd bought me a belt, and I'd given her a Henry James novel (I don't recall which.)[112]

"It's not exactly 'The Gift of the Magi,' is it?" she'd joked.[113]

I had to agree.

"Did they have one of your friend's books at the bookstore?" she asked, as she pressed the discarded wrapping paper into a ball..

"No," I said. I'd looked. There was nothing between "Sholer, John" and "Shoprey, Audrey" on the fiction shelves.

"Well," Angie said, "imagine that."

The snow fell the Saturday before New Year's Eve, the night that one of the families on our block (I don't recall which family) held a party. It was an annual event, we were to learn. It would be the only one we would ever attend.

Angie dressed the girls in the same holiday outfits they'd worn for their school pageant—Katie in a green velvet dress, Claire in red—and we made our way down the slick street hand-in-hand-in-hand-in-hand. With that thin cover of snow, as thin as the powdered sugar on a donut, the neighborhood looked lovely. The houses were all decorated with lights; many had electric candles in the windows, glowing orange and brilliant. One house had an electric Santa on the roof, complete with reindeer and sleigh.

At the front door, someone collected our coats and whisked them off to a closet or a bedroom. The girls ran off to join the smaller children in one of the bedrooms, Angie joined the women in the kitchen, and I found the men in the dining room standing over the food and talking gutturally about nothing in particular. Sports. Movies. Our jobs. Then, looking into the living room, I spotted Shoogey. Rather than speak with the men of the neighborhood, Shoogey stood at the fireplace with a group of teenaged boys forming a jagged semi-circle in front of him. He wore a green cardigan and tan, wide-wale corduroy slacks and chestnut-colored shoes the likes of which I hadn't seen since

I was a boy: they were called split-toed bluchers, and they were beautiful, as shoes go.[114]

As Shoogey spoke to the boys, he tipped his head back regally. His left hand pointed to his stomach as if he'd just consumed a plate of bad clams.

When he noticed me, he stopped in mid-sentence and waved me over with a windmill of one arm. I excused myself from the group in the dining room and headed toward Shoogey. He was surrounded by the pleasant aroma of burning wood, but the fireplace was empty and clean. The bricks were as red as if they'd just been laid.

"Come here, come here," he said. "Boys, this is the best damn lawyer in the town of Baltimore. I want you to know that. If you get yourself in trouble with the ladies, he's the man to talk to. Am I right?"

I forced a smile.

"Am I right?"

I said, "Yes," reluctantly. "As always, you're right, Shoogey."

"Do you have any business cards? You ought to give these boys your card."

I lied and told him I didn't: there were half a dozen business cards in my wallet.[115]

"Well, that's okay, my friend. You can give them all your cards later. Now, why don't you join us for a moment. We were just talking about a matter, but I don't recall what."

Shoogey tightened his jaw as if he were doing his thinking with it.

"Now, gentlemen, where were we? Oh, yes, I recall. You were telling me about Muhammad Ali.[116] Well, all I have to say is Muhammad Ali, Muhammad Schmali. Don't talk to me about Muhammad Ali. You want to know who a great boxer was, I'll tell you who a great boxer was—King Gilmore."

"King Who?" one of the boys asked, one of the younger ones.

"You've never heard of him, I know. But let me tell you why. Now, you boys don't know this, but when I was a young man I was a boxer. A professional. It was after I got back from the war. I couldn't play football anymore because of my ankle, so I took up boxing. The Sport of Kings, as they say."

I leaned forward with as much interest as the rest of his audience. Shoogey was a tall and athletic man, and I had no trouble seeing the boxer in him, especially when he stood as he did now, crouching slightly, his hands in balls.

"Really?" one of the boys said.

"Yes, sir." He held his fists in front of him, obscuring his face. "I had fifty fights, maybe more. Only lost but a dozen of them."

He pursed his lips and flicked his hands out at one of the boys, one after the other, rapidly.

"Wap! Wap! Wap!" he said. His hands buzzed past the boy's ears like mosquitoes in waiting, but made no contact. "See? I've got big, quick hands. Perfect hands for the sport. Perfect for protecting myself and perfect for fighting. They're a gift from God, these hands."

The boys stole looks at their own hands, bony and small for the most part.

"Were you Joe Louis?"[117]

"Lord, no." Shoogey coughed. "Lord, no. Joe Louis? Me? No."

"Who were you, then?"

"Sam Shoogey. Slammin' Sammy Shoogey, they used to call me." He held his hands in front of him again, and peeked over them. "Slammin' Sammy Shoogey, that was me. Everybody had a nickname in those days."

He gestured toward the boy he'd thrown the short punches at.

"What's your name, my friend?"

"Thomas Brody."[118]

"Bruiser Brody, that's what they would have called you."

He pointed toward another boy.

"How about you?"

"Frank Martin."[119]

"I hereby dub thee Marvelous Frankie Martin."

"Were you champion?"

"Nope, I have to admit that I never was, but I fought against a champion once. King Gilmore, the man I was telling you about. Well, King Gilmore was the champ before you were even born, and I used to be his sparring partner.[120]

"Do you know what that is, a sparring partner? A sparring partner means I used to get in the ring with him and practice with him. Practice fighting."

"How?"

"Well, it'd be just like a regular fight except it wouldn't count for anything. It didn't matter who won or lost. It was just so he could get himself in shape for one of his championship fights."

"Did you beat him?"

"No, sir. I never did really fight him, my friend, I just sparred with him, like I said. But I knocked him down once, that's true. That's how I lost my job, my job sparring with him. They don't want you around if you're going to knock the champ down because it makes him look bad. It makes him look like he's not much of a champ. Do you understand what I'm saying?"

"Unh-uh. How did you knock him down?"

"I'll tell you how I knocked him down. The King and I had already been fighting for three or four rounds—you fight for a couple minutes and that's called a round, then you get to sit down a while and rest up. We'd been fighting for three or four rounds, and I was still feeling pretty good. He hadn't hit me at all, and I was sitting there in my corner, just sweating like a dog, wiping myself off with a towel, and across from me, there was King with not one, not two, but *three* guys wiping him off and giving him water and talking to him. And I was just sitting there by myself. It was just me and nobody else. Nobody to help me. Nobody to give me any advice or tell me this or that. So I was just sitting there, thinking, 'Sam, enough is enough. One man's as good as any other man. There's no reason this man's better than you except that that's what they're saying.' So, when they rang the bell for us to get going again, all of a sudden I was as mad as can be, as mad as I've ever been. And I felt myself getting stronger, and I came out thinking, 'Nobody can beat me. King Gilmore can't beat me. I'm Slammin' Sammy Shoogey, for godssakes.' So I came straight at him and—*wap! wap! wap!*"

He flicked his hands out toward Bruiser Brody. The boy reeled back and laughed nervously. Shoogey looked at me. He didn't wink exactly, but he grinned that grin of his to the same effect.

"King, he kept standing there. So he threw a left—*whoosh!*—and I ducked under it and—*wap!*—I hit him in the stomach, then—*wap!*—I hit him in the chest with my right. So King, he backed up a couple steps, and I came in on him. *Wap!*—a left jab to his forehead. *Wap!*— another to his eye. Then—*wap! wap! wap!*—two left jabs to the side of his face and a right cross to his nose. Now, poor old King, he was staggering around, and I kept coming at him like a bull. Sam Shoogey, the bull. *Wap!*—a right uppercut to the stomach. *Wap!*—a left hook to his chin. *Wap!*—a straight right to his nose. Then, the big one—*wap!*—an overhand right smack up against his ear, and there goes King, just falling to the floor. Sounded like a building had fallen over."

Bruiser Brody was excited, though some of his friends looked about the room skeptically. "Did he get up?"

Shoogey shook his head fiercely, once. "Not for a while. They had to put vinegar under his nose to wake him up, and then when he woke up he said, 'I slipped.' I *slipped*. Did you ever hear of a man who has to be revived with *vinegar* because he slipped?"

"Nope."

"Me neither. Not in all my years as a human being on this earth have I ever heard of a man needing to be revived with vinegar because he slipped. That man had never been hit so hard in his life. Not before, and not since. But they ended up firing me anyway. There was a silver lining, though, as there are with many things in life. If I hadn't been fired, I never would've started my career as a writer. You know, Ernest Hemingway was a fighter, too.[121] That's something we have in common. See, a silver lining."

Shoogey's hair fell across his forehead, and he was talking to himself. To himself and to me. The boys had left as soon as they saw a cake unveiled in the adjoining room. In the dining room, several of the men shook their heads disapprovingly.

Braverman arrived late, so late that everyone turned their heads in surprise when the doorbell rang; earlier, the rings had made no sound. I was sitting at the dining room table, an arm's length away from the food, but I had no appetite. I was ready to leave, but Angie was still talking in the kitchen, and the girls were still playing in one of the bedrooms; their dolls were having a party, too. Braverman removed his coat and walked directly to the makeshift bar in the dining room—a bridge table covered with a green tablecloth. He joined me, carrying two glasses of scotch. He set one down in front of me, and I thanked him.

"So, how's the party?"

"Fine," I said. "Not too exciting."

"They've all been waiting for Syd Braverman to arrive, that's why," Braverman said. "Now that I'm here, just sit back and watch the fun."

"I didn't know you had that kind of power."

"Well, I do. If fun had a name, it'd be Syd Braverman."

Braverman and I sat back and scanned the room. He was having no effect; the party dragged on at the same speed.

"Maybe you should check your batteries, Mr. Fun."

Braverman smiled. "Give it a moment. I never said it was instantaneous."

He reached forward and fingered the material of my suit jacket, rubbing the lapel.

"There's polyester in that, you know," he said disapprovingly.

I told him I knew. It was one of my Joe Bank's suits.

"You know, what you really should try is a double-breasted suit. Have you ever had one?"

I told him no.

"You really should try one. It'd be perfect for your build. I was just thinking that when I saw you. We just got some super ones in all the way from Italy. You'd look sharp in one of them." He made an OK sign beside his ear with his thumb and index finger. The ears. Though it wasn't especially cold out, just cold enough for the precipitation to fall down as snow, his ears were bluish and wet.

"I have large ears, don't I?" he said suddenly. He looked at me sadly, and I leaned forward, pretending not to have heard what he'd said through all the noise, but there really was little noise, and he knew I'd heard him. He repeated himself nonetheless, then added, "You were looking at my ears, weren't you?"

I admitted that I had been.

"They're big, aren't they?"

"Mm hmm."

"You're not even going to do me the courtesy of lying to me?"

"Braverman, I don't know you well enough to lie to you."

He laughed. "You're right about that: you don't know me well enough to lie to me. Some people will do it at the drop of a hat. 'Oh, no, Syd, you don't have big ears. No, not at all. In fact, I didn't even notice you *had* ears until you mentioned it, that's how small they are. You'd need a microscope to see them. They're the size of *peas*.'"

"Well, they're most definitely not the size of peas."

"Thank you for your honesty," he said giddily.

"You're welcome. If it would make you feel better, I'd be happy to comment on your ears some more."

"Give it your best shot."

"Your ears are the size of bowling balls," I said, and he laughed again.

"They're the size of Volkswagens. They're as large as Portugal. They should have their own government. They should issue postage stamps."

Braverman was turning red as he laughed.

"I can criticize other things, too, if you want," I offered. "There's no reason to limit ourselves to your ears, is there?"

"Your breath stinks," I said, and Braverman laughed.

"No, really, Braverman, your breath smells like an outhouse after a Mexican dinner.[122] And your butt's fat and flabby. I've seen better looking butts on cattle."

His chest began to bob. He tried to take a sip of his scotch, but couldn't. Braverman began to snort. He put a hand on the arm of his chair to steady himself. His ears flapped, and he placed a hand over his heart.[123]

"Stop it! Stop it!"

"You've got the IQ of a shoe."

"Please!"

"A family of four could live in your nostrils—comfortably."

"Please stop!" Braverman seemed never to have been so thrilled as he was at that moment. Afterward, he never again looked so happy.

When I ran out of insults, Braverman put his hands on his thighs and breathed heavily, in and out, like someone who'd just finished a foot race. He noticed Shoogey's plight before I did. A group of the neighborhood men had surrounded Shoogey like a posse in a wild, wild west movie. One man, a man by the name of Cronin, Mick Cronin, poked an angry finger against Shoogey's chestbone, then wagged it under his nose.[124]

 Shoogey seemed as small as a young boy. He pawed at the floor with his beautiful shoes, his chin tucked into his chest.

"Come on," Braverman said, "we'd better save him."

I followed Braverman at first, but at some point I pushed past him and made a beeline toward Shoogey. I stepped in front of Cronin, like a referee separating two boxers, only why were there eight of them? Another man, a man by the name of Robert Plessy, pushed at Shoogey, and I slid my feet, using my hip to block him, too.[125]

"Stop it," I said. "Stop it, I'm his lawyer," as if that last pronouncement should have made them shiver. It did not.

Cronin spread his arms to his side, looking indignant and slightly bewildered.

"I don't care who you are, we don't want this guy here. He wasn't invited."

"I most certainly *was* invited," Shoogey answered. "In fact"—he slipped a hand into his back pants pocket and produced a card—"in fact, here's my invitation."

Cronin pulled the card from Shoogey's hand and studied it.

"It's addressed to Mr. and Mrs. Shoogey," Cronin said.

"And who exactly do you think I am, my friend?"

"It says Mr. *and* Mrs. Shoogey. You were invited because of her. She's welcome, and if she has to drag your sorry old carcass along, that's fine. Everyone has a cross to bear, and I guess you're hers. But nobody wants you here alone, Shoogey. I think I speak for everyone."

While the other men didn't confirm his opinion, they didn't say anything to contradict him, either.

"Well, my friend—"

"You're not my friend, you goddam Jew," Cronin said in an urgent whisper meant to be heard by the men in the room and not to travel any further. He said "Jew" with more than a bit of derision, as if *that* were the curse.

Shoogey did not seem offended. He looked at me blankly, and when he said nothing, I felt my jaw tighten.

"What did you just call him?" I demanded. "What the hell did you just call him?"

Cronin wouldn't repeat his remark, and his face and his bull neck turned red with embarrassment.

"My last name's Ashe. What do you think I am?" I said. "I'm Jewish, too, you know."

"Well, no offense. I didn't mean anything by it, it just slipped out. But this guy's going to get shown the door right now."

"We'll all leave," I said. "Nobody wants any trouble, and we certainly don't want to stay any longer. But you have no idea what this man's been through. You have no idea what it's like to sleep in the mud of the woods and to be forced to do unthinkable things merely because you're in a war. You have no idea what it's like to watch people being turned into fertilizer and pure blue air." Pleasantly, I called out to Angie and the girls to get their coats. The girls pleaded to stay with their friends, but I insisted. "It's late, and you have to get up early tomorrow."

"No, we don't," one of the girls said. Katie? Claire? "Tomorrow's Sunday. We don't have to get up early."

"Yes, you do," I said. "We have to get up early to go to a place we're going to."

"Ham, it's not even midnight," Angie said.

"Angie, New Year's Eve isn't for three days."

"I know, but we're pretending it's tonight."

I promised Angie I would explain everything to her later, and I helped her and the girls on with their coats. Angie eyed Shoogey suspiciously, as if she'd seen him stuffing silverware into his pockets. We found the hosts to thank them, then, with Braverman and Shoogey accompanying us, we headed down the street. A light wind flung what was left of the wet snow into our faces. The girls were on either side of Shoogey, holding his hands as they walked.

"Can Mr. Shoogey tell us a goodnight story?" Claire asked.

Now, Angie eyed me suspiciously. She dug a gloved finger into my palm. You could feel her fingernails.[126]

"I don't think so, Noodle," I said. "It's very late, even for Mr. Shoogey."

"I'd be happy to do it," Shoogey offered. "I know a story about a girl who danced in the ballet."

"Maybe another time," I said, "but thank you for offering."

The girls' shoulders dropped.

When we reached our house, Angie did not turn. Instead, she said good night to no one in particular, then led the girls inside. Braverman, Shoogey and I stood in the dim light of the streetlamp.

"Shoogey," I said, "I don't mean to pry, but do you mind if I ask you what that was all about?"

"What was all about?" he said, as if nothing had happened.

"Those men? Cronin?"

He waved a hand in the air, swatting an imaginary fly.

"Oh, that was nothing, my friend. That Mick Cronin isn't very fond of me. Oh, but is that an understatement! He hates me. He despises me. He detests me. He loathes me. He wants to pick the flesh from my bones tiny piece by tiny piece with a tiny, dull knife and wash my body down the sink little by little. He wants to toss me headlong before an automobile or perhaps a bus. He wants to kick me down a long flight of stairs, and put a blade between my ribs. He wants to lace me to a tree in the middle of a forest, bare, in the thick of winter. He wants to hit me with his fists until his fists are sore and bloody, and then he wants to hit me with something else. He wants to make me swallow poisoned pills, and he wants the pills to be bitter, too. I know all of this to be true. He told me. And, might I add, I don't particularly fancy him either."

"But why?" I asked.

"Who knows?" Shoogey shrugged. "Some people just never hit it off."

"That's true," Braverman interrupted. "That's very true, you know. You can't hit it off with everyone. It's impossible."

Shoogey held his fists in front of his face. "But I'll tell you this, my friend, if it'd come to blows, I'd have taken our friend Mr. Cronin apart."

Shoogey flicked his hands toward my head. *Wap! Wap!*

"Now, good night," he said. He shook my hand quickly. "And thank you for your assistance."

"Yes," Braverman said, shaking my hand, too. "Thanks for your assistance. You're a good egg, Ham." Then they walked off into the night, Shoogey hulking over his dear friend.

Our bedroom was already dark when I reached it, Angie already in bed. I stepped out of my shoes, removed my tie and began unbuttoning my shirt.

"I just don't get it," I said. "I don't understand the way they treated him tonight. It was too peculiar."

"Ham," Angie said, "he slept with Cronin's wife."

"What?"

"He slept with Cronin's wife," she repeated.

"Are you sure?"

"Well, I met his wife tonight."

"And she told you she'd slept with Shoogey?"

"She didn't have to," Angie said, matter-of-factly. "I knew it as soon as she introduced herself."

"How?"

"She stuck out her hand and said, 'Hi, I'm Serena. Serena Cronin.' Then she introduced me to another woman and said, 'This is the other Serena. Serena Moore.'"

"The two Serenas?" I said.

"The two Serenas," she answered.[127]

Chapter Eight: Frankenstein Mask

Shoogey's eyes were unfocused, his mouth slightly agape as if he were trying to solve a math problem in his head. He'd arrived at my office without warning, wearing blue jeans and a white T-shirt and leather work boots. But the jeans were too new, the shirt was pressed, and the work boots were brand-new clean, uppers and soles. I couldn't help but laugh at Shoogey's attempt to look rustic and casual.

He stood in the doorway with a puzzled look painting his face. "What is it, my friend?"

"Nothing, nothing." I may have rolled my eyes.

"I haven't had a chance to break these clothes in yet, that's all," Shoogey said. "But I'm going to get a chance today."

"And how's that?"

"I'm going to go out to see if I can catch something for dinner. Do you want to go?"

I ignored his question, trying not to laugh at him. He was going to *catch* dinner?

"You know," I said at last, "I never thought of you as an out-doorsman."

"Well, I am. I played college football, for godsakes, and back when I played, we played outdoors. None of that sissy stuff they do today, playing indoors on carpeting with the heat on. I grew up in Casper, on the water. I know a thing or two about the great outdoors."

"Are you going to tell me you're going hunting?"

"No. There's no challenge to hunting, standing a hundred yards away from a deer and then blowing its brains out. Where's the challenge in that, shooting a deer from that distance? No, if you want a challenge, try sneaking up close enough to smack one on the nose with a rolled-up newspaper. Now, *that's* a challenge, my friend."

"So that's how you're going to catch dinner—you're going to smack something on the nose with a rolled up newspaper?"

"No, I'm going to go fishing, and I'm taking you with me."

"Shoogey," I said, "it's January." I gestured toward the window as if to prove my point.

"What, there aren't any fish in January? Besides, it's warm out."

That was true. It still had not turned cold.

"Shoogey, I've got work to do," I said, which was also very true. There were contracts and letters piled on my desk, to be replaced by more contracts and letters once I was through reviewing these.

"Are we going to go through this every time?" He rolled his eyes casually. "Every time I want you to do something, you say, 'But *Shoogey*, I've got work to do,' in that whiny little voice of yours, and then we go back and forth, and then I twist your arm and we end up doing what I proposed we do in the first place. Now, let's just cut to the chase and pretend I've already suitably twisted your arm, and let's get the heck out of Dodge."

I brought both of my hands to my chest.

"I can't go catch fish dressed like this," I protested. I was wearing a gray suit with a white shirt and a blue-and-yellow tie. Blue with yellow stripes.

Shoogey stepped out of my office for a moment, then said, "Catch," and tossed me a burgundy shopping bag with the name of a department store written across one side. Inside was a package of white T-shirts, a pair of blue jeans, a pair of white athletic socks, and sneakers.

"I'd have bought you some jockey shorts, too, but I figured you probably had some on under your suit."

"I wear boxer shorts. And, besides, there's no way that these things are the right sizes."

"Bet me." He leaned against the doorway.

"I'm not going to bet you, Shoogey. I'm just saying that these things aren't going to be the right size."

"I'll bet they are. Now hurry up and get changed."

He left my office, closing the door behind him and immediately struck up a conversation with Carole, something about some movie he'd just seen. I twisted a wand to close the office blinds and undressed, then pulled on the jeans and one of the T-shirts. The jeans were snug, but they fit. The T-shirt and sneakers were perfect. I opened the door, and Shoogey stopped in mid-sentence. Carole was eyeing him adoringly, her hands fussing with her white hair.

"Good thing you didn't bet me," he said.

"Good thing. How did you know my size?"

"I traced you while you were sleeping. No, really, it's easy to figure out men's sizes—you just look at them. Now, let's get out of here. There are fish to catch." Then, to Carole he said, "My dear, dear woman, if anyone should ask where young Hamilton is, please inform them that he's in a very important conference with a client and cannot be disturbed."

"Certainly, Mr. Shoogey," she said, girlishly.

"It's Sam," he corrected her. He patted her hand.

We made our way down to the lobby, where Shoogey and Harry Addler exchanged waves, and we passed several M & D's, all of whom looked at me suspiciously. Shoogey had left his car parked in the fire lane in front of the building with its hazard lights blinking.

"Aren't you afraid you might get a parking ticket?" I said.

"There is nothing to fear but fear itself," he said. Then he cited the source of that quote: Franklin Delano Roosevelt.[128]

"Now get in the car. Dinner's waiting beneath the sea."

I expected we might drive to his hometown, Casper, to go fishing, but we didn't. Instead, we drove to Annapolis, where Shoogey rented a small tub of a motorboat and set off for blue water. There, I listened to Shoogey as he talked. His words flowed and flowed from some deep and mystifying source—bits of reflection, confession, philosophy and nonsense. Did he know what he was saying? Was he any more in control of his words than an epileptic in the throes of a fit?

"There was no such person as William Shakespeare. All his works were really written by Christopher Marlowe."[129]

"Women are usually eager to help someone."

"The best looking women are the redheads."

"Here's my favorite sandwich: turkey, a little provolone, lettuce, tomato, a healthy dab of Thousand Island dressing, and peppers."

"Women touch themselves in the places they like to be touched."

"Brooks Robinson was the greatest third baseman of all time."[130]

"I believe the cure for cancer can be found in splitting a hydrogen atom."

As for his efforts to catch our dinner, Shoogey was no man stupidly holding a string in the water, either, no dreamy fisherman who came home empty-handed with stories about the one thiiiiiiiiiiiiiiis big that wriggled off the hook; he knew what he was doing, twisting the bloodworms around the hook to keep them from slipping off, tying lures of red and green and yellow and pink to our lines. Later that day, we left a briny smell on the upholstery of Shoogey's car and carried half a dozen bluefish into his home.

* * *

Shoogey's house had precisely the same floor plan as ours, but its appearance was so drastically different that you might not notice that fact at first, or ever. When I realized it, I was overcome with a wave of embarrassment. Where our living room had soft, puffy couches and a recliner, Shoogey's had the stiff, sharp accommodations that one associates with the extremely wealthy, as if some rich relative had bequeathed him the whole lot: a yellow-gold couch with cushions as thin as the mattress of a hideaway cot, straight-back chairs with wooden arms twisted into roaring lions' heads at the ends, a marble coffee table that shone like the sea at noon (except in those spots where doilies and crystal bowls sailed), and tall silver floor lamps. The few objects in the room all had an incidental quality to them: an open book on the table, a pillow, a wooden box. All in all, the room had the airless quality of a museum, but a museum in miniature as these pieces were all packed into the small room, everything just a little too close, the couch too close to the chairs, the chairs too close to the endtables, like new lovers who cannot bear to be separated lest they discover their passions were not true.

If the living room was a museum, then the kitchen was a shrine to some god of cleanliness. It had an untouched quality to it. Everything shone too white, as if it were all brand, spanking new. The floor, the counters, the cupboards, the refrigerator, the dishwasher, the table and chairs—they were all white, a brilliant screaming white. Just stepping across the threshold gave me an uneasy feeling, but Shoogey didn't hesitate. He stepped into the room, leaving footprints on his way.

"I'd tell you to get a drink from the refrigerator," he said, "but the only things I have in the house are scotch and ice cream. I guess we could make floats."

He plopped the wet newspapers carrying our catch onto the counter.

"You're going to make a mess," I said.

"Well, I won't tell Mom if you don't."

"I mean, everything here is so neat and orderly."

"Oh, order schmorder. Jane always has to have everything spotless: for everything its place. It's a kitchen, for godssakes. It's supposed to be messy."

He pulled an enormous stainless steel frying pan from one of the cupboards.

"Regardless, you have a beautiful home, Shoogey."

"Thank you." He kept his eyes on his work, rubbing butter into the pan, then going to work on the fish with a jagged knife. "There's a good story behind this place, you know. I've got to go back a ways first and give you something of a prologue, if you don't mind. You see, many years ago I went to see my doctor because I'd grown quite heavy. How heavy, you ask. Well, I must have weighed a ton. In fact, when he put me on the scale it read 2,005 pounds. But I figure if you subtract five pounds for clothing...."

He looked up and waited for me to smile. I obliged him.

He sliced the head off one of the bluefish.

"So, the doctor said, 'Mr. Shoogey, we've got to do something about your weight. I recommend that you take up bike riding.' Well, I didn't even own a bike at the time, so on the drive home I stopped at a bike shop. And because I don't have a mind of my own, I let them talk me into buying one of the most expensive bikes in the place, a racing bike. And not just any racing bike, but a *Japanese* racing bike, the kind that weighs the same as a pen. In case you didn't know it, the Japanese make the most wonderful bicycles. They really do. That's what they do with all their technology instead of using it for the military. They have no military to speak of over there in Japan. That's why all the monsters invade it. Godzilla. Megalon. Mothra. The Smog Monster.[131] Those monsters aren't stupid. They do their research. They know the Japanese don't have a military."

He carved the fish open like splitting an apple.

"In any event, I bought a Japanese racing bike, as if I needed it. I rode it that afternoon when I got home, and again the next day, and that was it; I never rode it again. Never. It just sat in the garage collecting dust, a filthy monument to my stupidity. Everyone should have one, a monument to their stupidity; it keeps you from getting too stuck on yourself."

"Now," he continued, "several years passed. Pretend that you see calendar pages flying like they do in the movies. Jane and I bought a new house—*this* house, the one you're standing in this very moment, you lucky man, you. The moving men came"—he whacked the head off another fish—"now there's an interesting subject, moving men. Big, sweaty, burly, disgusting men. The last people you'd ever want in your home. And, yet, when you buy a new home, they're the *first* people you invite in. Pretty ironic, if you think about it. In any event, they came over and packed up all of our belongings and put them in a truck. Boxes, lamps, furniture, you name it. Only guess what—they forgot to close the back of the truck!"

"No!" I heard myself say.

"Scout's honor. They forgot to close the back of the truck. It was incredible. It's not as if their job is all that complicated. In fact, it seems to me there are three fundamental things movers have to do. Three and only three. You open up the back of the truck, you put the stuff inside, you close the back of the truck. It's like a heart transplant: you open the patient's chest, you put in the heart, you close the patient's chest. You never hear surgeons walking around town saying, 'Hmm, I wonder if I remembered to close that guy's chest.'"

"So, what happened to your things?"

"I'm getting there. Don't rush me." He scraped something gray and stinking out of the fish. "Jane and I waited and waited for the truck to arrive, and when it didn't show after three or four hours, we started making frantic telephone calls. We were positive they'd stolen everything. Finally, the owner of the company himself arrived and he said, 'Mr. Shoogey, Mrs. Shoogey, I think you should sit down. I have some very bad news to share with you.' So I sat down and he said, 'There's been a terrible mistake on our part. Somehow, our workers forget to close the back of the truck and some of your things fell out. We recovered everything except for one item. We couldn't find your bicycle.' Well, when he said the word 'bicycle,' a single thought went through my head: *don't laugh. Whatever you do, don't laugh. If you laugh, they'll never reimburse you for it.*"

"Did you laugh?"

"Are you kidding? You'd have thought someone died the way I behaved. They ended up reimbursing me in full for the bike, literally hundreds and hundreds of dollars. We ended up buying that refrigerator with it."

He gestured over my shoulder at the enormous white refrigerator, the size of a horse.

"In any event, I think there's a moral to that story. I'm just not sure what it is." I waited for him to rub his nose, then willed him to do it. *Come on, rub it, rub it,* I thought, and he complied. "Maybe it's, a fool and his money are soon parted. Or maybe it's, don't count your chickens before they're hatched. Or maybe there was no moral at all. Maybe it's just something that happened."

Shoogey laid the fish in the frying pan, shook some pepper into a spoon, then dumped it into his palm, then back into the spoon. "I always follow the old carpenter's rule: measure twice, cut once." He tipped the spoon over the pan. He followed the same rule with paprika and some greenish-brown spice I didn't recognize.

"Now," he said, resuming his story, "the truth of the matter is that we actually made a little money on the deal. I told a little fib about how much the bike cost. But I doubt I'll go to Hell for that one little fib. Besides, even if I did go to Hell for it, there are probably different level of Hells, don't you think? Take Hitler, for instance.[132] For someone like Hitler, he has to spend an eternity in a blazing inferno, fire everywhere, no relief. But for people who go to hell for some minor infraction, like cheating on their taxes or lying about the cost of a Japanese racing bike, I don't think they should have to spend an eternity in an inferno. No, that wouldn't be fair at all."

"What should they get then?"

"I don't know. How about extreme humidity?"

"Like Baltimore?"

"You mean we're already *in* Hell? That certainly explains why the television reception stinks."

I didn't remind Shoogey that, according to the story he'd told me time and again, the story that is the first chapter of this book, he was already going to Hell for lying to Jane about the men he'd killed.

Shoogey put the lid over the frying pan and wiped his hands clean on a dishrag that hung from the handle of the refrigerator door. He looked at his wristwatch.

"Listen, we've got some time to kill before we can eat. Do you know what we could do? We could watch some home movies while we're waiting. How does that sound? Does that sound okay?"

I said yes half-heartedly, which sent Shoogey rustling though the hall closet. He stepped out with a green steel projector and a metal tube, which opened into a small white screen. He set the screen up at one end of the room, the projector at the other, then turned off the lights.

The films were black-and-white and short, no more than three minutes each. The Shoogeys on the beach. The Shoogeys at Thanksgiving. His son (no beard yet) acting in a school play. His daughter opening birthday presents. Shoogey provided the narration for each, explaining who was who and what was what, and the smell of fish frying wafted into the room, the lovely aroma of the warming butter dancing beneath my nose.

There was a film of Shoogey fishing. There was one of him mowing the lawn. Then there was one of a man in a Frankenstein mask.[133] Bolts protruded from his neck. There was a scar across his forehead. He walked toward the camera, his arms extended before him as if he were pushing a heavy door. When only his head was still in the frame, he removed his mask, revealing Shoogey beneath. He was younger, maybe fifteen years or so, and thinner, but he had the same smile.

"I love you, Jane," he mouthed. "I love you."

* * *

I called Angie to let her know I would not be home for dinner.

"Are you working late?" she asked.

"Not exactly."

"You're with him, aren't you?" She had reached the point where she would not even call Shoogey Shoogey.

"Yes, Angie."

"Fine. Goodnight, Ham." She hung up.[134]

Shoogey continued adding spices to the frying pan.

"The old grapefruit hates me, doesn't she?"

"Please don't call her that, Shoogey."

"Okay, but she hates me. You can't deny that, can you?"

"I'm afraid I can't."

I expected him to make a joke, or to suggest a plan to win Angie over. Instead, he simply grew quiet and continued with his cooking. I set the table.

The fish was delicious, and the scotch complimented it well.[135] The ice cream had no place in the meal, but we ate it nevertheless as a side dish. Though Shoogey returned to his story about the moving men, I kept thinking about the film in which he wore the Frankenstein mask. He'd shown other home movies afterward, but it was the one with the Frankenstein mask that my mind kept returning to. There was no mistaking it: when he'd told his wife he loved her, he'd meant it. It was something that only another man who loved his own wife could recognize. The face grows slack; the eyes alight. He told Jane he loved her the same way I said those words to Angie.

Finally, I couldn't help myself. "Shoogey," I said, "can I ask you something?"

"Sure."

"I don't mean to pry, but if you loved Jane so much, why did you cheat on her?"

"Love schmove," he said. "It had nothing to do with love, my friend. You see, Jane and I couldn't have sexual intercourse. Technically, we could. Physically, we could. But it wasn't very appetizing. And though we'd all like to think we're driven by our hearts and minds, sometimes we're driven by less savory organs."

Prefacing my next question with another apology, I asked why he and his wife couldn't have intercourse.

"It's a very delicate matter, my friend." He leaned forward, his head over his plate, and curled two fingers into his palm to pull me toward him. He looked left, then right, as if someone might have snuck into the house to eavesdrop. "You see, Jane is a heretic."

A laugh burst out of my mouth before I could stop it. I put my hand over my mouth, then curled my fingers as if to wipe something from my lips.

Shoogey squinted at me.

"What's so damn funny?"

"Nothing, Shoogey, nothing. I'm sorry." I held up a hand in apology.

"Really, I want to know what's so funny."

I tipped my head a bit to one side.

"Well, nothing personal, but I don't quite see your wife as a heretic."

Shoogey exhaled loudly through his nostrils. "I didn't say she was a *here*tic. I said she was a her*pe*tic." I must have given him a blank look, which would make sense since I'd not heard that word before. He explained: "It means she has a communicable disease by the name of herpes. Someone who has herpes is 'herpetic.'"[136]

The last remnants of my smile disappeared.

"Shoogey, I've heard of herpes. Why didn't you tell me this before?"

He poked at his fish.

"It's not something I feel it's appropriate to discuss."

"Shoogey, I'm your attorney, remember? You can tell me anything."

"It didn't seem to be important."

"Well, it could be, depending upon how you answer this question—do *you* have herpes?"

Shoogey slumped back in his seat, taking great offense at my question.

"I most certainly do *not* have herpes. Here I have you in my home, for dinner, and you accuse me of something like that. I would never accuse *you* of something like that. I'm as clean as a whistle. You can have a doctor check me out if you want. Clean as a whistle."

Though Shoogey was upset with me, I continued in my lawyer's voice, which seemed to soothe him: "Did your wife have herpes when you were married?"

"No."

"Then how did she get it?"

"She got it at the hospital after our son was born. That's why when our daughter was born a couple years later, they had to do a Caesarian. You see, if the mother has herpes, they have to deliver the child by Caesarian or else the baby could end up blind."[137]

"Shoogey, how did your wife get herpes at the hospital?" I asked the question very deliberately so he would understand the importance of his response.

"She got it from the toilet seat. I wanted to sue the hospital, but she wouldn't let me."

There was a long silence while I considered whether I should tell him what should have been obvious. Anyone who ever took a health education class in high school knows you cannot contract herpes from a toilet seat. The disease simply cannot survive on a toilet seat; it requires what is known as a warm environment.[138]

I exhaled deeply, as if blowing out a hundred birthday candles.

"What is it, my friend?" he asked.

"I don't know how to tell you this, Shoogey, but your wife was cheating on you."

"What? How dare you say that about my wife?" He rose from his seat. "I know you're my lawyer, but how—"

"—Shoogey, I don't want to upset you, but please listen to me. Please sit down. You can only get herpes through sexual contact. You can't get it from a toilet seat. You just can't, plain and simple. Now, if you don't have herpes, then she got it from someone else."

Shoogey rubbed his knuckles.

"Oh, Lord," he said. "My wife was cheating on me? Jane?"

I confirmed that with a nod, then watched I something I'd never seen in my life and hope to never see again: I watched the soul drop out of a man's body.

Chapter Nine: Let's Build A Treehouse

The smell of peaches remained.

That was how I knew that Shoogey had already been in my office: the smell of peaches. It was only seven in the morning—seven, the same number as the Seas, as the Wonders of the World—and he'd already come and gone. There was no note on my desk, though, or on my chair, nothing to let me know he'd stopped by, just the smell of peaches. I hung up my coat, and just then, noiselessly, he appeared in the doorway.

"Ham, my friend," he said. "Good morning, good morning, good morning." He was in high spirits, or pretending to be: his voice a little too loud, his smile a little too large, showing too many teeth, his words coming too quickly. He paced as he spoke, tracing the outline of my office, but his movements were odd and disjointed, like the movements of a wind-up doll, each motion distinct from the one that preceded, from the one that followed. On closer inspection, his eyes were red-rimmed and his pupils dilated like a bottom-feeding fish: he hadn't slept, and whatever energy he had likely was generated by coffee, or something stronger.

"It's a gorgeous day out today, isn't it, Ham? Isn't it just a gorgeous day? Simply gorgeous. You know, on the drive downtown this morning I saw a robin, a beautiful, blue-breasted robin, and it put me in mind of a wonderful story. I hope you don't mind hearing a wonderful story on a gorgeous day like today. You see, when I was a boy, the local newspaper, *The Casper Chronicle*, used to print a story every year about the person who spotted the first robin of spring. They'd print a little story that would say, 'Lucky John Doe of Such-and-Such Street was cleaning his gutters when he happened upon the first robin of spring, blah blah blah.' And there'd be a photograph of John Doe of Such-and-Such Street, smiling like he'd just won the lottery. I don't remember if they'd give you ten dollars for spotting the first robin, but it makes a better story, so let's say they did, let's say they'd give you ten dollars. Well, my little friend Napoleon wanted to be in the paper, so every year he'd call up the paper in January or February and say, 'Oh, I just spotted a robin,' even though he really hadn't. There wasn't a robin within a thousand miles of Casper at that point, but he had to make sure he beat everyone to the punch and got his picture in the paper. And, of course, the ten dollars. Every year, for four or five years running, there was a picture of little Napoleon holding his check for ten dollars. Eventually, they figured it out and called Napoleon's parents, like he was some kind of criminal mastermind."

Shoogey was standing so close to the window that the tip of his nose bumped the glass. He stepped back far enough to allow him to inspect his reflection, to look at his wan and strangely eager expression. He stared into his own eyes for a moment, adjusted the knot of his tie, then squinted out the window at the Bromo Seltzer tower. One hand was nearly on the *B*. The other touched the *L*.

After a very long period of silence, I said, "That was a nice little story about the robin."

"Thank you," he said. "You're probably wondering what I'm doing here so early in the morning, aren't you?"

"As a matter of fact, yes."

"Well, I didn't come all the way down here just to tell you that little story about the robin. No, I came to talk to you about some matters relating to my little lawsuit. My little divorce lawsuit." He inhaled dramatically, as if he were about to reveal a well-kept secret. He clapped his hands together. "You see, I've been thinking a lot the past couple days, and I had an idea last night after you gave me that little piece of medical news about Jane. I had a terrific idea, and I had to see you straight away. I was going to come to your home and wake you, but I thought, hell, I should let the boy get his beauty sleep. But, now that you've had your beauty sleep—and now that I've had mine—I need a favor."

Something worried me.

I asked him what the favor was, and he said, "I need you to arrange a meeting. I need you to arrange a meeting as soon as possible—A-S-A-P, my friend—with Jane and her lawyer."

"I don't think that's a good idea. Considering the information you gave me, I think we ought to sit back a while. I think we ought to sit back and plan our next step carefully."

"Well, I've thought about it, my friend, and I think a meeting is exactly what we need. You see, like I was telling you, I have an idea. Actually, it's more of a plan than an idea. It doesn't quite rise to the level of a strategy; it's just a plan."

"Are you going to tell me what your plan is?"

"Do you want to know?"

"Yes."

"Are you curious?"

"Yes."

"Would you say that your curiosity is piqued?"

"Yes."

"Then say it."

"Say what?"

"Say, 'My curiosity is piqued.'"

"I'm not going to say that just because you want me to."

"If you don't say it, I won't tell you what my plan is."

"Fine," I said, then dutifully I added, "My curiosity is piqued."

"Say, 'Polly want a cracker.'"

I smirked.

"Just teasing, my friend. Do you want to know what my plan is?"

"Yes."

"Say it."

"I want to know what your plan is."

"Ha!" Shoogey arched an eyebrow. "I'll bet you want to know what my plan is, but I'm not going to tell you. It's a surprise, and the best way to ruin a surprise is to tell someone. I just want you to set up the meeting."

For the next several minutes, I tried to talk him out of having a meeting, but eventually, consented. Later that day I called McClellan to arrange a meeting for the end of the week. I tried to explain to him that I thought a meeting would be productive, and I dodged his questions about the purpose of the meeting, doing my best to conceal the fact that I was just as much in the dark as he.

"What's he going to do?" Angie asked me that night as we sat in bed.

"I haven't the faintest idea."

"I think he's going to try to kill her," Angie said. "I think he's going to shoot her right in front of you."

"No," I said, although the idea was not implausible.

"Please be careful," she said.

"I will."

"Really," she said. "I mean it. Your friend is a dangerous man."

* * *

Over the following days, I saw Shoogey shoot his wife a hundred times, a thousand times. It was like watching a movie over and over. Each time, he would produce a gun from somewhere—the breast pocket of his jacket, the waistband of his pants, a garter around his ankle. He'd make some dramatic pronouncement, often something vaguely Shakespearean. Then: *pop-pop.*

Sometimes he turned the gun on Henry McClellan.

Sometimes he turned it on me.

"Please don't go to the office," Angie said as she walked me to the car that morning. "Just call the meeting off."

"It'll be fine," I said, trying to be brave. When I arrived at work, I asked Harry Addler if he would stand in the reception area of our office. I did not tell him why.

Shoogey arrived half an hour early for the meeting. He was wearing an unseasonable blue linen suit, with a white shirt and a pale green tie with red spots the size of quarters. His shoes were brown-and-white wing-tip spectators, new or newly shined, the likes of which I hadn't seen since I was a boy.[139]

He carried a box of tea bags and a white bakery box.

Where was the gun? It did not appear to be in his suit jacket or at his waistband; there were no bulges there. It was not at his calf either, for the same reason. It was in the bakery box.

"What do you have?" I asked.

"This is Jane's favorite tea," he said, pointing to the label, "Earl Grey. She'll drink other kinds of tea, but this is her favorite. I'll need a tea pot, if you can arrange it."

"No," I said. "I meant what's in there?" I pointed to the bakery box.

"I'd rather not open it until later."

"I want to see it now."

"Fine," he said.

What would I do? Grab the gun? Push the box away? Run?

Shoogey lifted the lid to the bakery box and gestured for me to peer inside. He smiled that smile of his, that smile I'd come to recognize as half-invitation, half-prayer. I think it was at that moment, peering dumbly into the box, that I realized what Shoogey had in mind, why he'd asked me to set up the meeting, but I didn't have the nerve to try to confirm my suspicion or the heart to stop him. There was no gun inside. What was inside was something that was, at once, sweet and sad. He closed the box and sat, holding it on his knees.

"Please don't do this, Shoogey," I said. "Please, it's a mistake."

"I have to," he said. "Now, this is the way I'd like things to proceed, my friend. When they arrive, I'd like you to have your secretary escort them into the conference room, then let them sit there by themselves for a while. Got it? Then I'd like you to go in by yourself. Just say, 'Hello, how are you, blah blah blah.' Tell them that I've been delayed and that you'll have to wait for me before commencing. Then just look through your notes for a while, do something to keep yourself occupied until I arrive."

Shoogey looked to me for some sign that I understood his plan, simple as it was. I bunched my lips to show him I was thinking, then gave him a nod, dipping my head slowly.

"I go into the conference room," I said, "and I'll say, 'Hello, how are you, blah blah blah.'"

"That's right."

"Now, do you actually want me to say, 'Blah blah blah'? Won't they find that unusual?"

Shoogey's features tensed. "This is no time for joking, my friend. This is a serious matter. This is a matter of the utmost importance and seriousness."

I apologized, then repeated his plan to him. It wasn't long before Carole poked her head in my office to tell me the Shoogey's wife and her lawyer were in the lobby. I instructed her to show them to the conference room. Shoogey nodded firmly, the first step of his grand plan complete. I waited for him to give me a sign that it was time for me to join them. Several long minutes passed before he gave me the thumbs-up sign that pilots use. It was only as I rose that I noticed that his legs were trembling: the fabric of his slacks fluttered a bit.

The conference room was a large one with straight-back chairs to accommodate twenty people. Shoogey's wife and McClellan had taken seats beside each other at one end of the long oak table, the wood oiled so dark that it appeared black. Behind them was an enormous portrait of Carl DeWitt, a pipe drooping from his lips. The stillness of the room as I entered it was remarkable, as it often is in those places where sound and movement are given room.

Rising halfway from his seat, McClellan said hello quietly. Jane Shoogey said nothing. She looked up from her magazine when I entered, looked me square in the eye, then she returned to her reading when I greeted her with a brief and uncomfortable smile. She had the self-conscious mannerisms of a woman who had been stared at too often and too hard. She took one hand from her magazine to pat her hair. She ran a finger over one eyebrow, then the other, revealing a diamond the size of a filbert on her left hand: Shoogey had been a generous fiancé. I had no difficulty picturing a younger version of her in the stands at a football game, shouting "Shooooo!" or of her in a thin blue nightgown in a hotel room by an Army base.

"Is your client here?" McClellan asked.

"Yes, he's in the restroom," I improvised. I could hear his footsteps as he prowled outside the door, or imagined I could.

"Probably looking in the mirror," Jane said in a stage whisper. She had a silky voice, an elegant purr that barely made the acquaintance of consonants. Looking over the top of the magazine, she said, "You do have mirrors in the restrooms here, don't you, Mr. Ass?"[140]

"It's pronounced 'ash,'" I corrected her.

"Do you have mirrors in the restrooms or don't you, Mr. Ass?"

I told her that we did, and she said, "He could be in there for hours then, preening and primping. He could—"

The door swung open, and Shoogey stepped in carrying a teapot in one hand and the bakery box in the other. He looked around with the air of a small boy who'd just arrived at a birthday party.

"Good morning, Jane. Good morning, Mr. McClellan," he said.

He set the bakery box on the table. He carried the teapot toward his wife.

"Jane, I picked up some Earl Grey tea, your favorite. Can I pour you a cup?"

"I'm not thirsty." She turned the page of her magazine, though I knew she hadn't finished reading it: she'd only turned to that page a moment before.

"Okay, you're not thirsty. Maybe you'll have some later." He set the pot down on the table. "How about some pastry? I bought an apple, a cherry—"

"—I'm not hungry, either. Is this why you wanted to meet, to share a meal? To have *break*fast?"

"No, not at all. Why don't you just open the box and get a pastry."

He walked around the table again and set the box in front of her.

"I don't want a pastry. Why would I want pastry? Why? Tell me why?"

"Just open it and see the pastry I bought. They're wonderful."

"I don't *want* any pastry, for godssakes. Do I have to carve it into your forehead?"

"Okay, okay, maybe later," Shoogey said. I expected him to take a seat beside me, but he didn't. Instead, he returned to the head of the table. Somehow, he seemed smaller, dimmer, rougher in those next moments. Attempting to put his plan back on course, his movements were without grace. He moved as if he were wearing an itchy overcoat, and when he spoke, his words seemed rehearsed, but poorly so. Like a stage actor who had forgotten his lines, he spoke rapidly, hoping to touch upon something that would trigger a memory, breathing when he remembered a word.

"Now," he said, "I'm glad you're all here today because today is a very important day. Of course, all days are important in their own way, aren't they? Yesterday, for instance, nothing special happened, but it was important for other people. Maybe it was somebody's birthday, or their anniversary, or they're—well, I can't think of anything else important. Did I say birthday? I believe I did. In any event, today's an important day for all because I have an idea I'd like to share with all of you, a proposition that can resolve all of our problems. But first let me tell you something about myself. Jane already knows this, but Mr. McClellan and Mr. Ashe, you don't. You see, gentlemen, I'm not like other people. Of course, I am in some regards. I have two arms and two legs, I speak, I eat. But, you see, I'm different in the way I look at the world. Some people see a glass as half-empty. Some people see a glass as half-full. But me, I see the glass as being too damn large. And that's what we've got here today, we've got a glass that is too damn large. So what do you do when you've got a glass that's too damn large? You get a new glass, that's what you do."

The words seemed to fly straight through the open door and into Shoogey's gaping mouth. They didn't seem to rest on his lips long enough for them to be his own.

"A new glass is what we need. Now you're probably thinking, 'What does this guy mean, saying we need a new glass.' Well, that's exactly what I mean, that we need to start anew. We need to start fresh. Now, there's something I wrote that I'd like to read."

He opened the bakery box and reached into it. He pulled out not a gun, not even a pastry, but a sheet of white lined paper, like the kind a high school student keeps in his three-ring binder. He cleared his throat. "It's a poem I wrote for you, Jane. It's a little rough, but the message is what I wanted to say. It's called 'Let's Build A Treehouse In Our Souls.'"

Shoogey cleared his throat again, and this is what he read:

Funny how quickly everything changes
One day you're ten, and the next full grown
The things you thought permanent turn out to be stages
And life's what happens when you're not on the phone
We grow and we grow and we can't turn around
And each morning ten's further away
But as long as our bodies are here on God's ground
We'll always need a place to play

So let's swim across the Atlantic Ocean
Let's run like sheepdogs across the knolls
Let's go around the world by locomotion
Let's build a treehouse in our souls

Last week I saw a gray line in your hair
It shone like a single flashlight
I laughed and nearly kissed it, I swear
It looked like children playing at night
And I imagined them looking for frogs by the pond

I could hear one of them call around a tree
"When you need someone you can depend upon
Look for someone who looks like me"

Let's swim across the Atlantic Ocean
Let's run like sheepdogs across the knolls
Let's go around the world by locomotion
Let's build a treehouse in our souls

Sometimes I see someone I'm not sure I know
Look in a window, you might see what I mean
She's dressed in stockings and fancy clothes
When she looks more like herself in jeans
You already know how I feel about you
My little friend when I wasn't a child
You know I hope all your dreams come true
You know I hope you'll always find reason to smile

Smile as the years pass by your door
Smile at the things beyond your control
Smile when they say, "Mom, what are you smiling for?"
Smile, you'll have a treehouse in your soul

It was not a good poem, God knows, but Shoogey read it well, the tender quality of his voice giving a body to those words that could break the heart. His voice rose and fell, like the wind through some hilly geography, and I know that I never liked Shoogey more than I did at that moment.

When he completed the poem, he refolded it carefully, then slid it into the breast pocket of his suit jacket and looked at his wife with the earnest eyes of a schoolboy awaiting his reward.

No one spoke, each of us looking at each other in turn, then Jane rose from her seat.

"Sam?"

He looked at her eagerly and lovingly.

"Sam, you wrote a poem about the fact that I'm getting gray hair. Jesus H. Christ, that was the most pathetic thing I've ever heard in my whole lousy life. 'Build a treehouse in your soul'? You're a pathetic little man with a pathetic little poem and a pathetic little life. There, I think I've just broken the world's record for using the word 'pathetic' in a sentence." She turned to McClellan. "Do you see what I was stuck with? Now do you *understand*?"

The disappointment tugged gently at the corners of Shoogey's mouth.

"Jane," he protested, "I wrote that poem just for you. I meant every word of it. Maybe it's not perfect, but I never said it was. It's just that, well, do you remember all those years ago when I said or did something that made you fall in love with me. Can't you imagine that I could do it again? Can't you imagine that if we talked enough, I'd say the right thing, I'd just stumble across the exact right thing, something that would touch you? Can't you imagine that I could reach into your mouth and down your throat and touch your heart again?"

"That's a disgusting picture, reaching down my mouth."

"Well, I could've approached it from the other direction, but that seemed even less pleasant. What I'm saying, Jane, is that I know what you've been through."

"You know what I've been through?"

"Yes, Jane, I do. I feel terrible for all I've done now that I know how you feel. That's why I want to try to patch things up."

"Why on earth would I want to patch things up? You'd be back for two minutes, then you'd be off to some bar or some restaurant."

Shoogey listened to this prognosis, and smiled a smile just this side of wistful.

"See?" she said. "See? It's pathetic. You're pathetic. Pathetic, pathetic, pathetic. There, another world's record."

"There were some splendid moments, Jane. Don't forget. There were some splendid moments."

"I know there were some splendid moments"—she said "splendid" bitterly, mocking the way he'd pronounced it—"but there were probably some splendid moments in the Spanish Inquisition, too."

"Are you comparing our marriage to the Spanish Inquisition? Is that what you're doing?"

"I thought it was pretty obvious that was what I was doing."

"Comparing our marriage to the Spanish Inquisition?"

"Yes."

"So if our marriage was the Spanish Inquisition, then who am I? Am I Torquemada? Is that who I am? Torquemada?"[141]

"If the shoe fits."

"So you're saying I'm Torquemada?"

"Yes, goddammit, I'm saying you're Torquemada. That's exactly what I'm saying, though I probably should apologize to the entire Torquemada family, wherever they might be."

"That's a terrible thing to say to someone, especially your husband."

"You won't be my husband for much longer."

Shoogey was on the verge of tears and, as people are wont to do under such circumstances, he lost his temper.

"You're a cooking gaslight," he shouted. And here is the strange part: while he didn't say "gaslight," he did say "cooking."

Jane and McClellan each lowered their eyebrows in precisely the same manner, their eyes turning to slits and their heads tipping to the side just slightly.

"He doesn't like to curse," Jane explained to her lawyer. "Lying and cheating is fine. Cursing is a no-no."

"You're a stupid, cooking gaslight with a cooking disease," he continued, "and any man would have to be out of his cooking mind to want to cook you. You're a diseased woman! And don't think I don't know how you acquired your disease. I know. I know. My attorney's provided me with information."

I looked out the window to avoid Jane's eyes. The sky was gray, unsurprisingly.

"Well, if you know," she said, "why would you want me back?"

"I don't want you back. I just said I don't want you back. Are you cooking deaf? Is that a side effect of your disease?"

Jane stuffed her magazine into her handbag, rose from her seat and marched toward the door. She stopped behind me.

"Don't think it hasn't been a slice of heaven, Mr. Ass," she said. She opened the door, but didn't leave. Instead, she turned and walked back toward Shoogey. She picked up the box of pastry and flung it across the table.

"Pastry," she huffed. "That's right, pastry and a stupid poem will make up for everything."

Shoogey's face softened. "Jane, listen, I'm sorry about what I just said. But there were things that…." His voice trailed off, and he gazed out the window as if hoping to find the rest of the sentence written out for him on the Baltimore skyline.

His head fell to his chest, and Jane put a hand on his chin to force it back up. She moved her hand to the back of his neck, pulled him toward her mouth and kissed him deeply, forcing his Adam's apple to bob and his eyes to close.

"That," she said, "was the last time you will ever kiss me, you monster. You poor monster."

Shoogey seemed to be hurled back by the very force of her breath, but, of course, it was more than her breath alone that made him sink to his haunches. He opened his eyes in time to see her leave the room. That moment will never disappear. Shoogey will always be crouched and staring at the empty doorway, his mouth agape. Always, like a character frozen on a Grecian urn.

When McClellan left, I helped Shoogey to a seat. He rubbed his eyes with his knuckles like a small boy.

"That was a bad idea," he said. "The whole thing was a bad idea. I'm really not much of an idea man."

I couldn't think of anything to say to him.

"It was a good poem, wasn't it?" he said.

"It was a great poem, Shoogey."

"Here," he said, and he reached into his pocket and handed me the poem. "I've only written two poems in my life. The first I wrote in the fourth grade. The second one is now in your possession."[142]

Hadn't he once said that he'd written many poems for Jane? *Plain Jane Chicken Lo Mein*? I didn't remind him of that, though. Instead, I fingered the poem he'd handed me, and we sat in silence, looking at the pastries strewn across the dark tabletop like stars on a moonlit night.

Chapter Ten: Mercy

Lawyers do not believe in mercy; lawyers leave mercy to heaven.

I learned that lesson one afternoon the following week, the day Carl DeWitt's secretary summoned me to his office: "Mr. Ashe, Mr. DeWitt would like to see you presently." She didn't give me a hint about why DeWitt wanted to see me, though her use of the word "presently" rather than "now" suggested that the matter, whatever it was, was both serious and urgent.

I walked down to DeWitt's office as quickly as I could, but his door was closed. As I prepared to knock, his secretary grabbed my wrist and twisted it slightly. She was a massive woman, but not unattractive, with massive legs, massive, rubbery arms and the massive breasts of an operatic contralto. But she had a tiny line of a mouth, her lips pinched closed, giving her a distant look.

"Please don't knock. He's on the phone. Please have a seat until he's ready to see you."

I sat in a slim chair by his office, opposite DeWitt's secretary. She had the imperviousness of a hand puppet. A little gold placard above her typewriter read: *HELEN RENKO*.[143]

She typed and popped red-and-white peppermint candies into her mouth.

With nothing to else to occupy me, I listened to bursts of laughter and occasional snippets of DeWitt's conversation that leaked through his door:

"You old dog, Jack. You old *dog*."

"No, we'll just ask for an extension of time."

"Who? No, I've never heard of him."

It was not especially compelling conversation, and my mind wandered.

Finally, DeWitt said goodbye and noisily hung up the phone, and I rose, only to hear him start a new conversation: "Jim, it's Carl DeWitt here."

I took several steps toward my office, but his secretary's eyes compelled me back into my seat as surely as if she'd put her hand on my shoulders and pressed.

"That's certainly one approach to the problem."

"A bird's got to lay eggs, doesn't he?"

"You've got to be an individual, just like the rest of us."

"Six o'clock? No, six o'clock's no good. Six-thirty. No. Yes."

DeWitt conducted at least three more conversations while I sat outside his door as forgotten as a half-finished cup of coffee. Only I knew I hadn't been forgotten. There was something about DeWitt's voice—maybe it was louder than it needed to be, maybe more insistent, like a stage whisper—that suggested that he knew very well that I could hear him. When several moments of pure silence finally seeped through his door, Helen Renko informed me that I could enter. She nodded her enormous head once and said, "Mr. DeWitt will see you now," and when she said the word "see," her upper lip extended to reveal a black gap between her two front teeth, as wide as a tooth itself. It sat like a bug in the middle of her pretty, old face.

"Good afternoon, Ashe," DeWitt said. His voice was considerably quieter than it had been with the door closed. He didn't rise; he didn't even look at me as he stuffed tobacco into the bowl of his pipe. "Sit, sit."

There were two chairs opposite his desk, each upholstered in a dark floral pattern, and I chose the wrong one: the midday sun fell directly upon my face, and I squinted and twisted in my chair to avoid it.

DeWitt lit his pipe, sucking in air to help the fire catch. He made noises like an asthmatic. A tiny bit of smoke escaped, and he drummed his fingers on his desktop. His office looked different than I remembered. The only other time I'd been in, the morning I'd left my note about Shoogey, it had seemed freshly scrubbed and well-ordered. Now, it was an intimidating, hypnotic mess; it looked as if great winds had whipped through the room, and he'd let everything remain where it'd settled. There were papers everywhere, turned at every angle. Pink message slips on his desk and credenza, and on the floor. A stack of books by the door, each with pages paper-clipped or folded down. *Civil Procedure: Fourth Edition. American Criminal Procedure. Litigation Practices and Techniques. Cases and Comments on Evidence. Maryland Rules. Federal Judicial Procedure.* There were wrappers from candy bars and the remains of fast food lunches. I couldn't help but think that he smoked that pipe of his for no reason other than to overwhelm the other odors in the room.

"What's your first name again," he began.

I told him.

"That's an unusual name. Is it a family name?"

I told him it wasn't.

"Are you from Baltimore?"

"Yes, sir. I live in Mount Washington," I said, and I turned in my seat—and directly into the full force of the sun—and made a gesture with my thumb, indicating where that was, as if he were new to town. "I've been here most of my life."

"Is that so? Where'd you go to high school?"

"Magruder."

"Ah, Magruder, a good school. I went to Gilman." Magruder is a public school, Gilman private, and Gilman boys rarely let Magruder boys forget that, even when they're no longer boys. "That's where my boys went, too—Gilman. But Magruder's not a bad school, not bad at all. They had some good sports teams there, if I remember. You play any sports there?"

"Yes, sir. I played a little basketball."

He blew smoke. That and his continued lighting of his pipe served as punctuation to his speech.

"Is that right? I played a little basketball myself when I was at Gilman. In fact, my senior year, we won the state championship."

Four decades after the fact, I congratulated him.

Despite the disorder, DeWitt's office offered a magnificent view of the harbor. The air was clear, and a trick of the light made the murky, tea-colored water appear gas blue. Sailboats weaved deliberately, and on the high ground in the distance, a carousel made slow circles, sending the painted horses bouncing.

"What I wanted to meet with you about, Ashe, has to do with a friend of mine who's running for the state Senate. He's a wonderful fellow—I went to law school with him—and he'll do a tremendous job. Very charismatic, very civic-minded. In any event, we're having a little shindig in a couple weeks to kick off his campaign, and I thought I might invite you and your wife. It'd be a wonderful opportunity for you to meet some people. But, as a Baltimore boy, you may already know everyone. It's two weeks from Saturday, at eight o'clock. Do you think you and your wife might be able to make it?"

I was more than a bit excited about the prospect of spending an evening with the bluebloods of Baltimore, and I told him we'd attend.

"Terrific, that's just terrific."

DeWitt pushed some of the papers on his desk, swirling them in circles, then produced two, white pieces of cardboard that were slightly larger than index cards. There were brown thumbprints on each.

"The tickets are two hundred dollars apiece," he said. "You can just give my secretary a check if you don't have cash with you."

Two hundred dollars apiece!

Four hundred dollars total!

Angie and I couldn't afford to spend four hundred dollars on a dinner, but there was nothing I could do. I slumped some in my chair, thinking about how I would tell Angie about the dinner, about the money, as DeWitt started to speak again.

"Now, let me ask you this: how are things going with our friend Shoogey's divorce?"

"Fine."

"Details. Give me the details."

I gave DeWitt a short synopsis of what had happened, including the most recent development—Jane Shoogey's unmentionable social disease. Only to DeWitt, it was exceedingly mentionable.

"Herpes! The woman has herpes!" he whooped, and, afterward, a sense of danger lingered. There was something wicked in his smile, something predatory. Outside, a boat with sails the color of ginger snaps turned a complete circle.

"Yes, she does."

"Wonderful. That's absolutely wonderful. We couldn't ask for better news."

"Pardon me?"

"We couldn't ask for better news. If the good Lord looked down from heaven and said, 'What can I do for you boys,' this is precisely what we would've asked for. Not for peace on earth, not for good will to all men, not for an end to hunger. No, we would have asked for this."

"Herpes?"

"Yes. We would've asked for herpes. This is something we can exploit. This isn't something that she's going to want the public to know. Her neighbors, her friends, the ladies she plays bridge with. No, this is something she's going to want to keep in the closet, and we can exploit that."

"I'm not sure I want to," I said, trying to be reasonable. "I don't think it's proper. She's a woman, and I don't think it would be very gentlemanly of me to even mention that she has a social disease."

DeWitt pounded his fist against his desktop violently, but, thick with papers, it produced no sound.

"Stop calling it a 'social disease' for Chrissakes. It makes it sound like something clinical. Call it 'herpes.' Disgusting, festering herpes. And as for being a gentleman, I have no idea where you got the notion that a lawyer is supposed to be a gentleman. Where on earth did you ever get that idea? From *To Kill a Mockingbird*?[144] From *Perry Mason*?[145]

I'll tell you, *Perry Mason* was the worst thing to happen to this profession; it made everyone think that this was a profession for gentlemen. Well, it's not. These people who come to us, these people like Shoogey, they trust us. We're a firm of sound reputation, and they know that. They're either so enlightened that they know we know more about the law than they do, so they put their unmitigated trust in us, or they're so *un*enlightened that they put their trust in us because they don't understand a damn thing about a damn thing. But I'll tell you this, there's one thing they all expect from us: they expect us to be ruthless, absolutely ruthless. They expect us to be cruel so they can be kind, heartless so they can be warm-hearted, ruthless so they can sleep at night. And it's in this one regard that we can't fall short. It's for that reason that you're going to take this herpes issue—not this 'social disease' issue or some other nicety, but this 'herpes' issue—and exploit it. Lawyers show no mercy. Lawyers must, *must*, leave mercy to heaven, and that's especially true of M & D's. As long as I'm alive and kicking, M & D's will leave mercy to heaven, or I'll show them the door quicker than you can say, 'Jackie Robinson.'"[146]

DeWitt kept speaking, and my mind returned to how I would explain the purchase of the tickets to Angie. Four hundred dollars. In the distance, the carousel stopped, and I watched the tiny riders step off and a new set of riders climb onto the painted horses. The recurring sight of the sailboats gave me a flash of a sensation I'd known as a child: the tides, the winds, the feathery curls of water, they'd all been created for me.

"Ashe, are you listening to me?"

"Yes, sir, Mr. DeWitt."

"What was I talking about?"

"You were talking about mercy, Mr. DeWitt."

"Yes," he said emphatically. "I was talking about mercy. And how do we feel about mercy?"

"We're opposed to it," I said.

"Yes. Very much opposed."

* * *

That night, I didn't tell Angie about the four hundred dollars. I simply couldn't find a way to do it. In the morning, Angie and I lay still, in silence, like bleached bones in the sand. I considered telling her then, but thought better of it. It would be better to tell her at breakfast with the girls in the room: though she'd still be angry, she wouldn't say anything.

Two men were bantering back and forth on the radio, but I couldn't pay attention.

"Blah blah blah," one of the men said.

"Blah blah blah *blah*," the other said.

I gave them my attention, though, when they read the weather forecast: hot and humid, temperatures in the mid-eighties, a slight chance of rain.

The blah-blah-blah of the voices resumed, and several minutes passed before I heard the soft plops of footsteps in the hallway, then the creaking of the door to the girls' bathroom. The walls were thin, and you could hear everything that went on within the house, especially at night. Talking. The television. The dishwasher. Everything, every little noise, floated like campfire smoke through the house.

I heard the buzz of the girls talking in the bathroom.

"Right, you were here first," I could hear Katie say with a touch of sarcasm in her sweet voice; the sarcasm she learned from me, not Angie.

"You're such a snot."

"No wonder everyone hates you."

"Everyone hates *you*, you snot. Now get out of here or I'm going to get Mom."[147]

"Girls," I called out. I didn't say anything more, just "Girls," and they lowered their voices to a harsh whisper that found its way to the master bedroom just the same. Then the bathroom door closed on their voices.

I turned to look at the clock again. Six-twenty-five.

"Angie?" I said. "Angie, we've got to get up."

"I know," Angie said. Her voice sounded as if she'd just survived a long boozy, nicotine night. She coughed to clear her throat and looked at the empty water glass. "I know," she repeated in her normal voice. Then, removing her covers, she said, "What's it like outside?" and I shrugged my shoulders.

Soon, Angie was in the kitchen, emptying the dishwasher as the girls and I ate breakfast. She wore a pair of my sweatpants and one of my T-shirts, a heavy gray one that read "Property of the Baltimore Orioles" across the front, just above a black-and-orange cartoon bird. That morning, the kitchen seemed oppressive, the air too warm and vaguely malodorous. It may have been the light, too, a bright, unforgiving light meant for peeling cornhusks and scrubbing pots. Whatever it was, it made me feel dull.

I had to tell her about the four hundred dollars soon.

A cup of coffee smoked in front of me, two pieces of toast sat on a plate, and Angie ladled out helpings of Cream of Wheat. When I finished my breakfast, I walked to the bathroom to shower; I'd tell Angie about the four hundred dollars on the way out the door. I dressed, and as I was pulling on my socks I heard a sound like glass shattering and I heard Claire scream.

Wearing one sock, I raced to the kitchen. There was Cream of Wheat smeared on the wall, and Angie was trying to separate the girls. Katie grabbed Claire's upper arm, punching her on the back.

"Girls," Angie said as she pulled them apart, still holding a wooden spoon in one hand. "Oh, my."

"What happened? What happened?" I repeated in a voice that seemed to be marked with fright.

"She called me a bitch," Katie said.

I turned my eyes to Angie.

"Not *me*," Angie said. She cocked her head toward Claire. "Her."

"I did not. I called her a witch. With a 'w.'"

"She did not. She called me a bitch."

"Claire," Angie said, putting her hands on her hips and a stern look on her face.

"I didn't call her a bitch. I called her a stitch."

"Claire," I said, matching Angie's tone and expression.

"I called her a ditch."

Angie gave me a wry smile. "This one's all yours," she said. "This is what I have to deal with twenty-four hours a day."

"I called her a switch," Claire said, laughing.

I ordered the girls to sit, then pulled a straight-back chair away from the table and settled into it. I unbuttoned the jacket of one of my charcoal gray Joe Bank's suits. "Now, you—" I pointed to Claire "—you aren't supposed to call your sister a bitch. You're—"

"I didn't call her a bitch. I called her a flitch."

I had to suppress a laugh. "There's no such word as 'flitch.' And even if there were, you shouldn't call your sister a flitch, or a bitch, or a witch, or a ditch, or a qwitch, or a blitch, or anything like that. She's your sister, and she loves you, and you love her, and you should be good to each other."

I could tell that I hadn't swayed her, so I changed course: "Remember when you were sick with the chicken pox last year? Remember that?"

"Yes."

"Who brought you some coloring books and watched TV with you?"

Claire didn't answer.

"Who brought you your meals to your bedroom?"

"Mom."

"Mom and...," I waited for her to finish my sentence.

"Her," Claire finally answered. Her top front teeth fell across her lower lip like white sheets on a clothesline, and she tucked a stray lock of hair behind her ear, just as Angie was always doing.

"Well," I said, "you have to remember things like that. Especially when you're mad, you have to remember things like that. Now, you, young lady," I said, pointing a finger at Katie, my tone stern again, "throwing dishes. We don't throw dishes around here. Have you ever seen me or your mother throw a dish?"

"No."

"No?"

"I'm sorry. It's just that she makes me so mad sometimes."

"Mad enough to throw—" I stopped and turned to Angie. "What did she throw?"

"A bowl," Angie said plainly, without turning. She took another sip of juice.

"Mad enough to throw a bowl? Geez, you could have killed someone."

"With a *bowl*?" Katie said. Her eyes became huge, and she stroked her ponytail, braided in tight, neat plaits.

"Yes, with a bowl. People have been killed by bowls before."

Katie chuckled. "They have *not*."

"Have so."

"Name one," and she held up an index finger, waving it in front of my face. "*One*."

"Well, I can't think of any offhand," I said, pretending to give the matter some thought before saying, "Abraham Lincoln."

Now, Claire joined in. "Abraham Lincoln was *not* killed by a bowl. He was shot by John Wilkes Booth in the Ford Theatre in Washington, D.C.[148] Any dodo knows that."

"Where did you learn that?" I asked.

"In Mrs. Freedmont's class *last* year.[149]

Mrs. Freedmont said that Abraham Lincoln was watching a play with his wife Martha, and this man, John Wilkes Booth, shot him in the head and they couldn't finish the play because he died."

"Well, you only learned it half-right. First of all, Abraham Lincoln's wife's name was Mary—Mary Todd—not Martha. More importantly, it's not well known, but John Wilkes Booth didn't shoot Abraham Lincoln. No, he threw a bowl of soup, and it hit him right square on the head. Bonk!"—I rapped my knuckles against my skull—"Just like that, he was dead."

"No *way*, Jose," Katie said.

"Yes, way. And Lincoln wasn't the only one," I continued. "Thomas Jefferson—you know who he was—well, poor Mr. Jefferson was killed by a bowl of clam chowder, I believe. Manhattan clam chowder, the red kind. And Cleopatra, the Queen of the Nile, she was killed by a bowl of Texas chili."[150] I bunched my lips together and nodded my head slightly. "So, there," I said, "I think we learned an important lesson today, didn't we?"

Claire rose from her chair. "You are, without a doubt, the weirdest dad in the whole school."

"You say that like it's a *bad* thing, Noodle," I said. "Now, both of you give me a kiss and get out of here."

"We don't have to be at school for another *hour*," Katie said.

"Then shouldn't you both be watching television? Why do you think we bought it?"

The girls headed toward the living room, and I swatted their bottoms with the back of my hand as they left the kitchen. I heard the television set as it popped on, then heard the sounds of dozens of stations as the girls raced through them looking for a show they could agree on.

"You know," Angie said, carrying the trash bin to the table, "it'll just start up again when they get home."

"I know." I took a sip of cold coffee. I picked up a piece of toast, but it had grown cold and hard, so I returned it to the plate.

Moving beside my chair, Angie knelt down and carefully picked up the broken pieces of the bowl with her fingertips, dropping them into the trash bin. Then, with a ragged dish towel, she wiped the Cream of Wheat off the wall. Damp traces of the cereal remained, leaving stains the color of spoiled lemons. Angie scrubbed at the spots, but they wouldn't vanish.

"That was a good bowl," she said. "Now we only have seven complete place settings."

She continued wiping the wall, then, suddenly, she turned to me, and let out a laugh. It rushed out of her.

"What?" I said, my coffee cup poised inches below my mouth. "What?"

"Cleopatra?" she said.

"It's a true story," I said, smiling broadly and opening my eyes wide to arch my eyebrows. "You could look it up."

Somehow, in the confusion, the Cream of Wheat, the name-calling, the broken bowl, I forgot to tell Angie about the four hundred dollars. I forgot that evening, too, but I have an excuse: I was preoccupied in those days. I was preoccupied with mercy.

Chapter Eleven: Mercy, Continued

There's a procedure that is used in litigation that is called a "deposition." It is a procedure I had to study up on because of my inexperience. Skipping some of the legal niceties, essentially a party to a lawsuit will subpoena a witness to appear at a designated place and answer questions under oath, not unlike a trial, save for the absence of a judge or jury.[151]

Depositions usually occur in law offices, and the witness and the parties and the lawyers and the court reporter all gather around a table as if preparing to eat. Rarely are the proceedings pleasant. I've heard stories of lawyers coming to blows during depositions, of witnesses suffering heart attacks or weeping hot tears.

When Jane Shoogey arrived for her deposition, she didn't acknowledge Shoogey or me. She barely acknowledged her own attorney, greeting McClellan only with a glance. She sat with a calm and dignified manner, showing no trace of the ordeal that had come before, which seemed to be a feat of grace and intelligence, or of utter coldness, it was difficult to tell which. She wore a navy blue dress, and her hair was swept back dramatically, pulling her skin taut. She folded her hands on her lap, and as I read my questions from a yellow legal pad, she answered in the calm, distant voice of a telephone operator.

The deposition lasted several hours. As I learned, Jane Shoogey's smart little face concealed a sniper's eye:

Q: Please state your full name for the record.

A: Jane Shoogey.

Q: Have you ever been known by any other names?

A: Yes, I used to be known as Joan of Arc.[152] Before that I was known as Madame Bovary.[153]

Q: Joan of Arc?

A: Yes, you may have read about me. I was burned at the stake. It was in all the papers.

Q: Mr. McClellan, will you please instruct your client that this is no laughing matter, that she should answer my questions honestly and seriously.

MR. McCLELLAN: Jane, this is no laughing matter.

Q: Will the court reporter please read back my question.

(Whereupon the court reporter read the last question.)

A: Yes, my name was Jane Peel before I was married.

Q: Do you understand the importance of the oath you've taken today?

A: Yes, I do, Mr. Ass.

Q: That's Ashe.

A: I guess that's a matter of opinion, now isn't it?

Q: Mrs. Shoogey, please. Do you understand that you can be charged with perjury, a criminal offense, if you don't tell the truth today?

A: Yes, I do.

Q: Do you understand you can be sent to prison for perjury?

A: Is that true? Well, then it's the gas chamber for you, Sam Shoogey.

Q: Mrs. Shoogey, please. Your lawyer will have an opportunity to depose Mr. Shoogey if you wish. But please direct your responses to me.

A: Certainly, Mr. Ass.

Q: It's Ashe.

A: Oh, please, we've gone through this already. You're boring me.

Q: Mrs. Shoogey, have you ever given a deposition before?

A: No, I haven't. I've given a few dinner parties, though. You know, we once had the Emperor of China over for dinner, didn't we, Sam?

Q: Mr. McClellan, will you please advise your client to address her responses to me.

MR. McCLELLAN: Jane.

A: I'm sorry, Mr. Ass. Were you feeling left out?

Q: And please have her address me by my proper name.

MR. McCLELLAN: Jane, please.

A: Oh, if I must. But you boys are taking all the fun out of this for me.

Q: My apologies. Now, Mrs. Shoogey, the way a deposition works is that I'll ask you a question, and you'll answer it. Now, has anyone ever sued you?

A: No.

Q: Other than today, have you ever testified under oath at any proceedings?

A: I don't know. Was I under oath when I said I'd marry that buffoon sitting next to you?

Q: No, Mrs. Shoogey, that wasn't under oath. Other than that, have you ever testified under oath at any proceeding?

A: Yes, I have.

Q: Can you tell me about them?

A: Well, I testified when I was arrested for killing Rasputin.[154]

Q: Mrs. Shoogey, that was almost a hundred years ago.

A: I was very young at the time.

Q: I'm going to ignore your answer and move on. For the record, you're married, are you not?

A: That's just like you lawyers, bringing up unpleasant matters.

Q: But you are married?

A: Yes.

Q: Also for the record, what is you husband's name?

A: My husband's name is Pope Pius III.[155]

Q: Mr. McClellan, please.

MR. McCLELLAN: Jane, please.

A: I thought that was your name, Sam. Isn't that your name?
MR. McCLELLAN: Just tell him his name.

A: Oh, okay, his name isn't Pope Pius III. It's Samuel J. Shoogey.
At least that's what he told me.

Q: Thank you.

A: You're welcome.

Q: And, just for the record, will you state the names of your children?

A: Rudolph and Susannah.

Q: Now, of course, you have filed for divorce from Mr. Shoogey.
For the record, how long have you been married?

A: Eternity.

Q: Could you state that in years?

A: Thirty-something years. But can we have the record reflect that
it felt like eternity?

Q: How long have you known Mr. Shoogey?

A: Too long.

Q: And how long is too long?

A: How deep is the ocean? How high is the sky?

Q: What I mean is, when did you first meet Mr. Shoogey?

A: When was it exactly? When was it that he first began to leech
the life out of me?

Q: Would you say that you were happily married?

A: Would you say you're happily married, Mr. Ashe? There, I pronounced your name right. Would you say you're happily married, Mr. Ashe?[156]

Q: Mrs. Shoogey, I get to ask the questions.

A: What a shame, because I hear things about your marriage, Mr.
Ashe. I hear plenty of things.[157]

Q: Please, Mrs. Shoogey, just answer my questions. Would you say
you were happily married?

A: No.

Q: At any stage were you happily married?

A: If I said, "When he was sleeping," would that suffice?

Q: But you stayed married?

A: Yes, we did.

Q: Why?

A: Because I'm a stupid, stupid woman.

Q: But you did stay together, right? Why?

A: Because we were married, and it was important to try to work things out because we'd made a vow.

Q: But you stayed together for more than thirty years, didn't you?

A: Yes, we did.

Q: But you weren't happily married?

A: No, I wasn't. I stayed with him because of the children.

Q: But you're not staying with him now because of the children?

A: No, I can't.

Q: And why is that?

A: Because he was unfaithful, Mr. Ashe. He was unfaithful a hundred, a hundred fifty times.

Q: And you believe that it's important for spouses to be faithful?

A: Do you?

Q: Yes, I do. But I want to know whether you do?

A: Yes, I do.

Q: And you believe that it's wrong for a spouse to be unfaithful?

A: Yes, I do.

Q: And you believe it's wrong for someone to have an affair with someone who's married?

A: Yes.

Q: Can you tell me who Syd Braverman is?

A: No.

Q: Are you saying you don't know an individual named Syd Braverman?

A: I've never heard of him.

Q: How about Sydney Braverman? Do you know an individual named Sydney Braverman?

A: No, I don't.

Q: Are you familiar with anyone with the surname Braverman?

A: No.

Q: Mrs. Shoogey, I have to remind you that you're under oath.

A: I'm aware of that, Mr. Ass.

Q: You're doing it again.

A: Yes, I know.

Q: Mrs. Shoogey, at any time have you had sexual intercourse with anyone other than your husband?
    MR. McCLELLAN: Clarification, please. Do you mean after they were married?

Q: At any time, before or after they were married. Mrs. Shoogey, at any time, before or after you married my client, did you have sexual intercourse with any other individual?

A: I'm not even sure I had it with him. I mean, it was over so quick, you wouldn't even have had time to boil an egg.

Q: Mrs. Shoogey, have you ever had sexual intercourse with anyone other than my client?

A: Yes.

Q: Who?

A: Let's see. The Baltimore Colts. Most of the Baltimore Orioles, except for the third baseman.[158] The fire department. The guy who hosts *Soul Train*. Most of the Naval Academy.[159] Dwight D. Eisenhower.[160] Menachem Begin.[161] Arnold Palmer.[162]
    The mayor. The governor. Oh, and two girls named Serena.

Q: Mrs. Shoogey, please.

A: Oh, Mr. Ass, you don't have to ask. I'll do it with anyone. Why don't we clear off the table and do it right here. Sam, would you like to watch?

Q: Mrs. Shoogey, please.

A: I told you, Mr. Ass, you don't have to beg. Let's just tear our clothes off and screw right here on top of the table.

Q: Mrs. Shoogey, please be serious.

A: Mr. Ass, how can you be serious when your life is a joke?

Q: Is it your testimony that you never had sexual intercourse with Syd Braverman?

A: Did he play for the Colts?

Q: Mrs. Shoogey.

A: What was your question?

Q: Did you ever have sexual intercourse with Syd Braverman?

A: Is he the one with the fake teeth. No, that's right, *you're* the one with the fake teeth. Braverman's the one with the big ears, right?

Q: Right.

A: No, Mr. Ass, I never had sexual intercourse with Syd Braveman and his All-Ear Band.

Q: How about Mick Cronin? Did you ever have sexual intercourse with him?

A: No.

Q: How about Peter Kaminski?[163]

A: Mr. Ass, are you going to ask me one by one if I slept with everyone in the neighborhood?

Q: As a matter of fact, yes. And then I'm going to subpoena each and every one of them and ask them the same question. Then I'm going to have them each tested for herpes so we can determine who you got herpes from. Now, Mrs. Shoogey, did you have intercourse with Peter Kaminski?

The deposition went on and on like that, for hours and hours until I had asked her about all of our neighbors, and other men, too. The mechanic. The grocer. The gas man. The mailman. I asked her question after question. First she answered them with some amusement, and her answers were funny, too. Then she began to respond matter-of-factly, as if she'd been asked a question about her clothing or what she'd eaten for breakfast. Her indifference became contempt, her contempt hostility, then embarrassment, then sadness, and she was in tears. At last, she stood and said, "May I please have a break?" She left the room, and

McClellan followed her. When McClellan returned several minutes later, he held his hands up in front of him in surrender and offered to settle the case. His offer let Shoogey keep the house, and that, I learned, was all Shoogey had wanted: to stay in the neighborhood. I had Carole type up the settlement documents, and when Shoogey signed them with his sweeping John Hancock of a signature, the case was over, as quickly as the snap of a finger and a thumb.

Shoogey grinned his grin and extended a hand toward me. "Well," he said, "I guess this is goodbye, my friend."

"Goodbye?"

"Sure," he said. "I'm not your client anymore. You're not my lawyer. But you sure have made this whole process a lot more palatable than it could have been. You did a fine job, my friend. Superb. I wish you nothing but the best of luck."

Shoogey's hand was still hanging in the air in front of me. Finally, I said goodbye, and took his hand, the big, soft hand that had brought down ballcarriers at the University of Maryland, the hand that had touched a hundred, a hundred fifty women, the hand that had knocked King Gilmore to the floor and written five novels about a detective named Napoleon Game, the hand that had turned seven men to fertilizer and pure blue air.

Chapter Twelve: Meet Sam Shoogey

Fried chicken with mashed potatoes. That was what we were eating when I finally told Angie about the tickets to the fundraiser, the two hundred dollar tickets. Four hundred dollars that we couldn't afford.

Angie glared at me, letting me know that she understood why I'd chosen to tell her about the tickets over dinner rather than tell her in private, that she would have something to say on the subject when the girls were out of earshot. Still, in a pleasant enough voice, she said, "Ham, you know that's not in the budget."

"I know," I said, "and I don't want to go to this thing any more than you do, but when you're at M & D, sometimes these things are almost obligatory. It's terrible. I hate it, but it's part of the game you have to play when you're an M & D."

"I'm already getting tired of you being an M & D." She'd become more and more frustrated with the hours I was working and the unpleasant mood I was often in when I returned home.

"I know you're tired of it, Angie, but let's try to deal with this situation objectively. For all we know, this may turn out to be fun. Who knows. At the very least, it'll be a good opportunity to meet some of the other M & D's and their spouses. Maybe we'll make some new friends."

Katie interrupted. "Dad?"

"In a second, honey," I said, not looking at her.

"Dad, what are the Empties?"

"What?"

"The Empties? What are the Empties?"

Angie and I exchanged looks of confusion.

"Honey," I said, "I have no idea what you're talking about."

"You said you were going to meet some of the Empties and their spouses."

"M & D's," I corrected her, enunciating the letters carefully. "M is an abbreviation for Morrisey, and D is an abbreviation for DeWitt. So M & D is an abbreviation for Morrisey and DeWitt, see?"

"I don't know," Angie said, "I prefer Empties myself. And I don't want to have to spend a night with them."

"Angie, you're the one who always says we never do anything."

"That doesn't mean I want to spend the night with a bunch of lawyers. And I certainly don't want to have to pay four hundred dollars for the privilege."[164]

"Sweet Potato, they're good people."

"No they're not, Ham, and the fact you'd even say that frightens me."

"What do you mean?"

"I mean, I've met some of the Empties," she said, which was true: we'd been to several small dinner parties and to a holiday party for the entire firm. "Do you know who I liked the most? The secretaries, and the receptionist, and the guys who worked in the file room. They seemed like good, decent, hard-working people. Your secretary, for instance—Carole. I liked her. She seemed very nice. But the lawyers? Ham, they're horrible. A bunch of pretentious, unpleasant men whom I don't care to spend my free time with."

"Sweet Potato," I said. "Please."

"No, Ham, they're horrible. They always try to find some way to steer the conversation around to themselves so they can talk about how smart they are, or so they can talk about their fantastic vacations or their fantastic cars or their fantastic whatevers. They always find some way to get everyone to compliment them on how brilliant they are, like a bunch of high school girls fishing for compliments about how pretty they are. It's sick. Like your friend Shoogey."

"But Shoogey's not a lawyer."

"Maybe not, but he'd be a great one."

I couldn't deny that.

"Angie, he's gone, okay? The case is over. Shoogey's out of our lives. We shook on it."

"What?"

"We shook on it. He's out of our lives."

"I wouldn't be too sure," she said.

When the evening of the fundraiser arrived, Angie was in a surly mood. She wore a periwinkle silk dress and a black felt hat, and she looked lovely and girlish; she looks wonderful in hats. But she couldn't, or wouldn't, smile.

We left the girls in the care of Angie's sister, who brought them pizzas and candy, then we drove downtown, heading toward the Bromo Seltzer tower. The hands were on the *R* and the *Z*.

"What's this guy's name?" Angie asked.

"I don't remember," I admitted.

"We're going to a dinner for a man whose name we don't even know?"

"He's running for the Senate."

"Yes, but what's his *name*? As it is, we couldn't vote for him even if we wanted to since we don't know his name." She opened her black purse, then shut it quickly, retrieving nothing.

I tried to recall DeWitt mentioning the man's name. "It's Bob St. Something," I said. That was all I could remember.

"Bob St. *Some*thing?"

"I don't know. It's something like Bob St. James. Maybe it's Bob St. Louis. Or Bob St. Christopher Medal."

Angie wouldn't smile. She played with her purse, snapping it open and closed.

"Or Bob St. Francis of Assisi. Or Bob St. Thomas Aquinas."

Still, she wouldn't smile. She was determined to have a terrible time, and nothing I could say would change that. She didn't even smile when we saw the banner draped over the entrance to the Belvedere Hotel pronouncing the name of the candidate: it read "Phil Van Marker for a Better Maryland."[165]

"You really need to write things down," Angie said.

"I don't need to write down that I love you," I said. "That's something I'll always remember."

"Nice try," Angie said.

"Did it get me out of the doghouse?"

"Not even close."

We left our car with the valet, then strolled inside. The fundraiser was no small affair. It was held in the hotel ballroom. The room had a lofty, intricately patterned ceiling, high enough for an elephant to pass through, decorated with red-white-and-blue bunting and helium-filled balloons. The floors were parquet and buffed to a high shine like a new pair of shoes fresh out of the box.

At one end of the room was a banquet table covered with a cloth that brilliant shade of purple associated with royalty. At the other end, a long toss away, an orchestra had set up shop. It was not a small one either, no string quartet, but row after row of trumpets and trombones and saxophones and violins and men in tuxedos and women in black dresses. Several times during the cocktail hour I tried to persuade Angie to take to the dance floor with me, but each time I was rebuffed.

Like the musicians, many of the men in attendance wore tuxedos; I wore one of my best Joe Bank's suits and did not look out of place. The women wore cocktail dresses, and some wore thick, gold necklaces and many rings; none looked as beautiful as Angie.[166]

When dinner was served, we sat at a circular table populated by Empties and their spouses, making small talk about their cars. Porsches. BMW's. Volvos. Saabs. Angie frowned at me. We listened to several speeches delivered from the main table, each concerning the many fine qualities of the guest of honor, Phil Van Marker, who smiled throughout as if he'd been frozen the moment after hearing a rich joke. Each of the speakers delivered his address in a halting and formal manner, as if reading excerpts from the Boy Scout Handbook: *when carving, you should always move the blade in strokes away from your body to avoid an accident.* At one point, a gentleman spoke about Phil Van Marker's many contributions to society, then produced a large bronze trophy with a figure of an eagle atop. The guest of honor arose to much applause and took the trophy in his hands, studying it with his fingers as a blind man might.

"As many of you know, in my career I've received a great many awards." He spoke in the voice of a man who has spent a day in England and decided that was sufficient time for him to affect its people's accent. "A great many trophies and plaques and certificates and ribbons and so forth. But I can say without any doubt whatsoever that this trophy, this one that you have honored me with tonight, is the most recent."

When the laughter died, he said, "And now, what we've all been waiting for—let's eat."

His words ushered in a symphony of silverware which, as if some sort of cue itself, struck up the orchestra. They played a piece which I soon recognized as "It Ain't Necessarily So."[167]

The sound they produced was delightful, and I noticed the corners of Angie's mouth curve just a little bit, as if she'd forgotten she was having a terrible time.

The smile disappeared soon after the dinner table conversation resumed. One Empty began to talk about how another Empty outwitted his opponent in a case, and the second Empty waved off the compliment with alarmingly false modesty. Another Empty talked about his days at Harvard: "Here's a funny story that happened while I was attending Harvard . . . ." The story was not funny. Another Empty fingered the pearl necklace he'd given his wife for Valentine's Day while his wife sipped red wine, oblivious to the fingers at her throat. Another Empty complained about the maid his wife had hired. Then I found myself telling everyone about the work we were doing on our house, work I referred to as "renovations." Angie bit her lip, but not in that way I find so appealing. No, I expected blood to flow from the lip.

Dinner arrived in pieces: sorbet, fruit salad, garden salad, chubby dinner rolls with slabs of butter carved into roses, chicken cordon bleu, green beans and mashed potatoes, with some sort of custard for dessert. All in all, it was a good meal as that sort of affair goes, but Angie hardly touched her food, eating only her fruit salad and some of the beans from the side of her plate. The Empties noticed, and repeatedly I leaned over and whispered, "Eat something," to her, but she resisted.

"I've lost my appetite," she said.

Finally, I said, "Eat *some*thing, you're embarrassing me," a little more loudly than I'd intended, which I immediately regretted.

Angie rose and said, "If you'll all excuse me for a moment. My husband's treating me like a child." She took her napkin and wiped her lips, leaving a racing stripe of red on the white linen—was it lipstick, or was it blood?—then placed it on her empty seat and headed toward the restroom. I hesitated, then shrugged to my colleagues and their spouses, that condescending little shrug of the shoulder that men share and understand to mean, *Women!* I excused myself and followed Angie, holding my glass of scotch. I shouldered my way through the crowd on the dance floor and past the orchestra. A woman in a black strapless evening gown left the women's room, and I waited for the door to close before knocking lightly against it.[168]

"Angie?" I called.

There was no response. I took a sip of scotch and thumped my fist against the door again, more heavily this time.

"Angie? Angie Ashe?"

"Get out of here, Ham."

"Angie, you're embarrassing me."

"Then we're even."

Another woman left the restroom, and rather than let the door swing closed, I held it open with one hand. I could see Angie's black shoes beneath one of the stalls.

"Angie, come back to the table and eat something. Or *don't* eat something. Whatever you want to do."

"Go away. I'm taking a pee."

"Angie, people will hear you."

"That's what you get for talking to someone while they're in the bathroom. Now, go away. Go away and tell everyone about the renovations we're doing on the house. Why don't you tell them we're putting in a swimming pool and a tennis court right next to the baby grand piano. That ought to impress everyone."

I knew what she was saying: *You're becoming one of them.*

"Sweetheart," I said, "all I said was that we were doing renovations, which technically is true."

"We painted, Ham. We swept, and we scrubbed, and we painted. We didn't renovate. I've never even heard you use that word before."

"I have."

"We *painted*, Ham. That's all we did. We painted."

The orchestra had stopped playing. The musicians were setting down their instruments and talking among themselves as I walked back into the ballroom. At the far end of the room, a crowd was gathering in the open space before the head table. I snaked my way into the crowd and stood on the tips of my toes to see what was happening, and there I found Carl DeWitt in the center of the group. I hadn't seen him at all that evening, but now he seemed to be preparing to hold court, waving people toward him with open arms like an old man summoning grandchildren. He cleared his throat loudly, then he apologized.

"I'm sorry, but I have a touch of laryngitis," he said, though his voice was booming, hardly a scratch to it.

When all heads had turned in his direction, DeWitt adopted a stiff pose. He ran a hand across his neck, then folded his arms across his chest, and this is what he said: "Friends, thank you for coming this evening to support our good friend's candidacy for the state Senate. We've all heard all about Phil's many, many attributes, so I thought it might be appropriate for me to tell a little story about Phil. Oh, it's a whopper, and, again, you'll have to excuse me for my laryngitis. You see, when Phil was a young man, fresh out of law school, he interviewed for a job with a major law firm, the name of which I will keep secret to protect the innocent. Well, in the midst of the interview, they asked Phil for three words to describe himself. Phil thought for a moment, then said, 'Irreverent.'"

There was a pause, then quite a lot of laughter.

DeWitt should have stopped, but he did not. "Let me tell you another story about Phil," he said. "This happened when Phil was preparing to take his bar examination so he could become a full-fledged attorney and do whatever it is we attorneys do."

DeWitt cleared his throat again, though he didn't need to. He already had our attention, especially the attorneys in the audience, which were more than a few. What was worse, he knew he had our attention, and he grew more and more dramatic, unfolding his arms, then swinging them about like a cheerleader at a compelling basketball game.

"As I was saying, Phil was preparing to take his bar examination. He hadn't had nearly enough sleep, he'd been studying so hard. Some of you will recall what that's like. You recall, Douglas, don't you?"

He gestured toward a tanned, gray-haired man in the crowd who laughed too heartily so that we might all recognize him.

"When the day of the examination finally arrived, he was worn out. He was plumb tuckered *out*. Am I right, Phil? Isn't that true? Well, what could he do? He was so tuckered out that he decided he had to do something to stay awake, all his hard work going down the drain, as it were. He decided to do something he'd never done before. He decided to take some antihistamines—no, no, that's not the word I'm looking for."

DeWitt closed his eyes for a moment.

"Amphetamines!" he said, shaking a hand in the air. "That's what I meant! So Phil decided to take some amphetamines so he could remain awake, little pills the size of lentils that he washed down at the water fountain before the test was distributed. He left the test hours later feeling he'd done well. Fantastic, terrific, wonderful. In fact, he couldn't remember ever writing as much or as gracefully in his life, and that only made it all the more shocking when he learned months later that he hadn't passed the examination. He hadn't come close. It seems that while

Phil had written quite a bit, he'd never turned the page of the test booklet. He'd just written paragraph after paragraph, answer after answer, on *top* of each other, leaving the first page of the booklet a square of navy blue ink. Isn't that funny? Isn't that a funny story about Phil?"[169]

That was DeWitt's story, and when he was through, everyone smiled politely and resumed their own conversations, somewhat disappointed, I suspect. Offended, perhaps. DeWitt stood alone, wearing the look of a man who has something unspeakable on the sole of his shoe. All he could do was rub at his throat, as people often do when suffering from laryngitis.

I pushed my way back through the gathering and returned to our table, which was empty now save for the half-full glasses and the floral centerpiece and a dish of melting butter roses. I waited alone for Angie, running my finger along the rim of my glass. Minutes passed, five then ten, the orchestra started up, playing something bouncy, and when someone took the seat beside me, it was DeWitt, not Angie. He seemed to want to attach himself to someone, welcome or not.

"What did you think of my little story?" he said. He pulled the sleeves of his tuxedo jacket, the fine whitish dust of mothballs adhering to the lapels.

"I thought it was very nice."

"Really? I tried to punch it up a little bit at the funny parts, but it was difficult with my throat bothering me and all."

"Yes," I said, "it was clear that you weren't feeling well. But I think everyone enjoyed the story."

"Really?"

"Oh, yes."

"You don't think it was inappropriate? Some idiot just said he thought it might have been inappropriate."

"Oh, no, not at all."

DeWitt patted my hand. His fingers were tough, as you might expect a longshoreman's to be. He pulled his pipe from his breast pocket and lit it.

"Me, neither. I thought it was perfectly appropriate. It was just my throat bothering me, that's all. Now, how are things going with my friend Shoogey?"

"It's over."

"Over?"

"Yes. We just settled the case the other day. I sent you a copy of the settlement agreement in interoffice mail."

"Hum. Well, if you did I haven't had a chance to read it yet. Did things go well?"

I told him things had gone fine.

"And you took my advice?"

I nodded.

"My advice about mercy?"

I nodded again.

"Splendid. That's absolutely splendid. Shoogey told me you were doing an admirable job. But I wanted your opinion of how things went. Your opinion as a lawyer."

I suppose I could have told him about Shoogey's poem. I could have told him that Shoogey was still in love with his wife, but I didn't think DeWitt had the right to know that. That was personal. Instead, I just said, "Well, it could have turned out better, it could have turned out worse. It wasn't a very pleasant experience for him, but I think Shoogey will do fine in the end."

"Good, good."

DeWitt patted my hand again, then looking around the room he spotted someone he'd prefer to speak with. I have no doubt that that's what happened, nor did I mind. He wished me a good evening, then rose and walked off, leaving Angie's chair smelling of tobacco and mothballs. I craned my neck to look for Angie in the crowd, but couldn't find her.

Just then, one of the gentlemen at the table next to ours leaned toward me. He was a snub-nosed, fair-skinned man—his skin was so white you sensed you could see the movement of blood within him like soda through a straw if only you looked more closely. He had black, beetling eyebrows, so dark that they looked like they'd been touched up with burnt cork, but the hair atop his head was dark yellow and cut close to the scalp like a Marine's.

"Excuse me," he said, "but I couldn't help but overhear your conversation, the tables being so close and all. I heard you and your friend discussing someone by the name of Shoogey. You weren't talking about Sam Shoogey by any chance, were you?"

I told him that we had been, and he slapped his thigh in an exaggerated gesture of delight and with a bright, straight smile said, "Aha, the Baron Munchausen of Baltimore!"

I asked him what he meant, and he said, "You see, Baron Munchausen was a famous storyteller who made up wild stories about his adventures.[170] Stories about monsters he'd slain and knights he'd defeated. Very entertaining, but at the same time very much false. That's Sam Shoogey all over—a lie and a smile. The biggest storyteller in all of Baltimore. If you get him going, he'll tell you about how he shot down thirty fighter planes in the war. Or maybe he'll tell you about how he almost played major league baseball. Oh, he has hundreds of them. All of them meant to convince you he's your best friend so you'll buy insurance from him. The worst part is that he doesn't even have the courtesy to remember the lies he tells you. He'll tell you one day about how he danced with Grace Kelly, and the next day, *the very next day*, you'll say, 'So, was Grace Kelly as pretty as she looks in the movies,' and he'll look at you as if you were talking in gibberish.[171] It's like he writes these little lies with one hand while he's erasing them with the other."

"We must be talking about two different people," I said somewhat defensively. "I'd been talking about Sam Shoogey, the novelist."

"The novelist! The novelist!"

I hadn't seen someone so amused in many years. It was as if someone were tickling his ribs; he laughed so violently that he had to put a hand on the corner of his table to steady himself. The table shook with his convulsions. Coffee splashed over the lip of his coffee cup and into the moat of the saucer, and several of the other guests at his table gave him the disapproving looks normally reserved for bad dogs. I turned my head to see Angie on the dance floor in the arms of a short, bald man in a tuxedo. He was one of the Empties, a partner in the tax department named Will Novak.[172]

Angie's head was tipped back, laughing. He was staring at her throat, or lower.

"Yes," I said, "Sam Shoogey, the novelist."

"Sam Shoogey's a swindler, a con man. This town's just littered with people who rue the day they first heard the words, 'Meet Sam Shoogey.'"

"See," I said, raising an instructive finger, "that's where you're mistaken. The Sam Shoogey we were talking about *is* a novelist."

"You're not talking about those detective novels he writes, are you?"

I told him I was, and then the man dropped his voice several octaves, adopted a stiff pose and became Shoogey for a moment. His hair grew and turned black. His dim teeth turned white. His nose widened at the tip. His suit changed color, then style.

"Some of my novels have sold nicely in Europe," he said, imitating Shoogey. "I don't know why that is, my friend. Perhaps they gain something in the translation. And translation is something I know quite a bit about, my friend. In fact, my friend, I *personally* translated my novel into French, Greek, Arabic, Swahili, Pig Latin and hieroglyphics. Then, I stayed up all night translating it into Braille so the blind might enjoy my work. That's right, my friend, just me with a pin and a ream of paper, translating my work into Braille, my friend."

Finished with his impression, the man shrank back into himself, then released two bursts of laughter through his nostrils and said, "Those books of his, he paid for them himself. They have those publishing houses that will print copies of anything if you pay them. I forget what they call them. There's a name for them." He turned to his companion, a small, similarly complected woman. "Honey, what do they call those places that will print copies of your stuff for you? You know, the ones old ladies use to print up copies of their horrid, little poems about their cats?"

"Vanity presses," his companion replied wearily. She was a pudding-faced woman with black, black hair. She seemed not to have any interest in our little conversation.

"Yes, yes, that's it. Vanity presses. See, Shoogey pays them to print up copies of his books. He writes them, they type them up and slap on a cheap cover, and—wham, bam, thank you, Sam—you've got yourself a book sure to be favorably reviewed by your mother, your sister and your next-door neighbor. He tried to sell me one once, too."

A mortified expression must have come over my face because the man stopped laughing. He wiped his hand across his mouth as if he were erasing his schoolboy grin.

"Listen, pal," he said, "I'm sorry if I offended you. Is he a friend of yours? I probably should have asked that before I opened my big mouth."

"No, he's not a friend."

"An acquaintance?"

"A neighbor," I said, "that's all."

"Well, if you don't mind a little advice, I suggest you approach him with a healthy dose of skepticism. Two hundred milligrams or so, though I'm no doctor. It's just that that Shoogey character—well, let's just say I had my share of problems with him. Sold me some worthless life insurance five or six years ago. It wasn't worth the paper it was written on. I could've shot the guy, but now I figure it's not worth it. It's not as if he's big-time. He's no shark. He's more of a suckerfish, attaching himself to the bigger fish. Besides, I guess it's partly my own fault. I mean, an insurance salesman who writes fiction: what were the odds that *any*thing he said was true?"

I couldn't tell if his question was rhetorical. It wasn't.

"I'll tell you what the odds were: slim and none. You know how he got me to buy those phony policies? Do you know how? He told me some story about some boy from a hick town who was killed during the war, a kid they called Napoleon. You know, like Napoleon Bonaparte. And he kept telling me how much I reminded him of this poor boy—this poor boy who was allergic to chocolate and ended up getting killed in the war—until I was practically crying. I'm a grown man, and I was practically crying, it was so sad. I would've bought the Brooklyn Bridge from him at that point. You've got to be careful about the stories people tell you, I suppose. Everyone has their stories. God knows if they're true."

His companion rolled her eyes. "Well, I wish someone would tell me a story before I fall asleep from sheer boredom," she said.

The man touched my arm and said, "Sorry again," then returned to his own conversation. Angie and her dance partner swayed back and forth to a very slow song, stepping carelessly among the balloons that had lost their purchase on the ceiling and floated drunkenly to the dance floor.

"Oh," the man said suddenly, snapping his fingers. "I thought of the name of the town Shoogey told me that boy was from: Casper."

"Yes," I said, "Casper, Maryland. It's a little fishing town."

The man shook his head side to side. "There is no town in Maryland called Casper. I looked it up. There's no such place."

* * *

Driving home that evening, Angie wouldn't speak to me, but my mind was elsewhere. I turned on the radio. A slow song was playing. I couldn't help but think about Shoogey and the insurance policies, Shoogey and the books.

Though I hadn't planned to, at the last moment I stopped the car in front of his house, sending Angie sprawling forward; she had to brace herself by placing a hand against the dashboard. The engine still running, I put the car in park and told Angie I'd be home in a minute. Wordlessly, she slid over to the driver's seat and drove off, driving faster than she needed, and I walked to Shoogey's porch and rang the doorbell.

"Ham, my friend," he said when he appeared, "you look like you've been out on the town." He was wearing a pair of green pajamas and he rubbed the sleep from his eyes. "Can I—"

"—Don't 'Ham, my friend' me, Shoogey. I want to know if it's true. I want to know if it's true that you sold people phony insurance policies."

Shoogey stepped back, a wounded look came on his face, his astonished mouth an accusation of betrayal.

"Why, I never," he said. "With God as my witness, I've never swindled anyone. Never. How could you think that? You of all people. You're supposed to be my lawyer."

"I'm not your lawyer anymore, remember?"

"Well, you're supposed to be my friend. That makes it worse."

I didn't reply. I stepped inside, and he put his hand on the small of my back, then closed the door.

"It's not against the law to sell insurance, my friend. I told you from the start that was what I did. It's not like I was withholding evidence on that account. If I didn't tell you that I shot President Kennedy, well, I could understand how you'd find that disturbing, how you'd be upset by that oversight. Or if I said I sold secrets to the Nazis during the war. But, the last time I looked, selling insurance was a perfectly legal profession."

"It's perfectly legal if you do it legally."

"I did."

"That's not what I heard." I put my hand behind my ear for effect.

"What it was," he said, "it was the company I was working for at the time. They put some language in the policies. Never told me a damn thing about it. Scout's honor. Had I known about it—had I *known*—I never would've sold the policies. As it was, the second I found out—the very *second*—I demanded that they give everyone their money back. It's documented. I wrote *letters*. In fact, if you come in, I'll get them out of my files."

I took a seat on the couch as he left the room and walked toward the back of the house, his movement as deliberate as a mousing cat.

"Now, as I was saying," he called to me from the bedroom, "I wrote letters the second I found out. I mean, a man is nothing if he doesn't have his integrity. Am I right, my friend? I believe it was J. Paul Getty who said that a man must have three things if he's to succeed. A man needs his integrity.[173] A man needs his dignity. And a man needs to strike oil. Those are the three things every man should have: integrity, dignity and an oil well."

Shoogey went on and on, his distant voice dissolving. On the end table was a picture of him and his wife, their wedding picture. It hadn't been in the room the other times I'd been in the house. It was an odd picture. There was something about the photograph that made Shoogey and his wife appear waxen, entirely unnatural, happy beyond human capacities. Shoogey appeared to have glamorous, pink puffy lips and a cocoa complexion, both of which would have been the envy of any woman. His wife had the same skin tone in the photograph— there was no sign of her freckles—and a romantic pastel circled her mouth like gift wrapping. Her eyes were a deep chocolate, richer still than her skin, a lovely, sparkling, tender, girlish brown that would stir any gentleman of sensibility.

"The thing about it," Shoogey was saying, "was that I didn't even want to sell insurance. It was just something to do to make a living. There are worse ways to make a living. You know, I have a cousin named Deborah—Debbie—and to pass time she makes wedding dresses for pets. I'm quite serious about that. She makes wedding dresses in case people want to have weddings for their pets."

I rose and walked to the mantel, where there was another photograph, a dusty, sun-yellowed photograph of two small children running knee-deep in the surf. The children were no older than my own daughters were at the time. Squint, and they could have been Katie and Claire swinging plastic pails, carrying plastic shovels.

Shoogey was still calling to me as I showed myself out, and I imagine he was still talking as I walked down the street toward our house. Angie had turned the porchlight off, but her sister's car remained in the driveway; they were probably in the kitchen, and Angie was telling her about how horrible I'd been that night. She had every right to say that.

I hadn't confronted Shoogey about his books—there weren't any books, I knew that now—and for that small act I was pleased with myself. A man should have his dignity. His dignity among other things. And as I reached our darkened porch, a thought occurred to me, a terrible, wonderful, hideous, beautiful thought: despite countless opportunities to do so, Jane Shoogey had never exposed her husband as a fraud. She'd never betrayed him. She'd kept his secret like a miser and never said, "The great writer Sam Shoogey has never written anything," but she could have, and who would have blamed her? I felt my heart sink with remorse; Jane Shoogey was a good, fine woman, and I'd shown her no mercy.

Then, as I stepped into the house and saw the light on in the kitchen, I realized something else. I realized that the odor of peaches was with me, clinging to the places Shoogey had touched: my hand, my suit jacket.

Chapter Thirteen: The Silent Treatment
[DELETED]

Chapter Fourteen: Crime and Punishment

Several days passed, and Angie hardly spoke to me. We acted like strangers, and I could think of nothing to do to get her to forgive me. Several times I tried to repair matters with a kiss, but each time she turned her head so I would catch neither her lips nor her cheek, but the flesh beneath an eye instead. In those several days, I actually looked forward to going to work.

It was one of those days that Carl DeWitt came to my office. The intercom beeped, and Carole called out my name.

"Ham?" she said. "Ham, are you there?"

"Mm hmm." I was marking up a contract with a red, felt-tipped pen.

"Ham, Carl DeWitt's on his way to see you. Can you see him now?"

"Of course," I said, and, hurriedly, I set my coffee cup down and took my feet off the desk: it was, after all, his furniture.

The door opened, and the sound of computer keyboards rushed in, a sound like a forest of cicadas. DeWitt stood in the doorway with his cane in one hand and his pipe in the other. He smiled at me, then extended his arm to usher his secretary in. Holding his cane as he did he resembled a carnival barker introducing the next act: *Ladies and gentlemen, for your entertainment pleasure, we are proud and happy to present the man with three arms!*

"Ham," he said instead—he'd never called me by my first name before—"you remember Helen Renko, don't you? Helen's my secretary, and she goes to our church."

Our church? I did not attend the same church as DeWitt. I do not even know what church he attended.

"Sure," I said nonetheless, and, somewhat confused, I rose halfway from my seat and extended a hand to her. Helen Renko clasped it in both of her hands, then sat across from me in one of the wicker chairs, a thin, fragile smile on her face.

"Hello, Mr. Ashe," she said. I was surprised, as I always was, that her large frame housed such a small, girlish voice.

DeWitt was still in the doorway, and he swung the door closed behind him with his fingertips, then positioned himself behind Helen, taking small, careful steps as if his shoes were pinching him. He placed his hands on her shoulders.

"Ham, we've got a situation," he said. "A situation we hope you can help with."

"Well, I hope I can."

"I hope so, too. You see, the problem—and it may not be a problem, it may be a blessing. That's what I've been trying to tell Helen. Some things are blessings in disguise." DeWitt removed his hands from the woman's shoulders and folded them casually across his chest. "You see—how should I say this? I've known Helen through our church for years and years. In fact, I was the one who helped Helen get her job here in the first place. She's been a secretary here for, what's it been?"

"Twelve years," she said. Her words came out slowly, as if they were afraid to leave the comfort of her mouth.

"Twelve years," DeWitt said solemnly. "She's a great secretary, and she's always been just a joy to work with. Just a joy. And you know how we consider M & D to be one big family, don't you? I mean, I've given it my name—DeWitt—just like with my children. You see that, don't you?"

"Of course," I answered. Where was this leading?

"Well, that's how I think of everyone here, like we're part of one big family. Remember that big family that used to have the Christmas specials on TV? All the brothers and sisters and aunts and uncles and nephews and nieces."

DeWitt looked for the name of the family on the ceiling.

"The King Family," Helen said.[174]

"Is that right, the King Family? Well, that's the way I think of M & D. The partners, the associates, the paralegals, the secretaries, everyone. We're the M & D family, so to speak. And when something happens that involves one of the members of our family, well, it's our duty to lend them a hand, whether it be financial support or just a shoulder to cry on."

DeWitt was standing behind the woman once again, and, again, he put his hands on her shoulders. His fingers were thin and bony, and the loose flesh hung from those bones like a dress.

"So," he continued, "maybe you can understand why I was so upset this morning. It was about five o'clock in the morning, and the phone rang, and it was Helen on the other end, and she just sounded terrible. I had to keep saying, 'Calm down, Helen. Just calm down.' And then she finally told me what happened. You see, Helen has a boy named Teddy. Now, I know Teddy from various church functions, and he's a good boy. A bright boy. Very articulate, very intelligent. He might be a little misguided—is that fair to say, Helen?"

"Yes, that's fair. He's had some bad influences." Her eyes were trained on mine.

"Well, he might be a little misguided, but at heart he's a good boy," DeWitt continued. His head down as he spoke, he removed his hands from the woman's shoulders and crossed the room time and again like a man who'd misplaced something on the beach, searching the same plot over and over. "In any event, when Helen called me, she said she was calling from the police station, and that they'd arrested Teddy. Arrested him, can you believe that? Handcuffs, police cars, fingerprints, the whole nine yards. So I said, 'Just sit tight, Helen. Let me get dressed, and I'll get right down there,' which is what I did. So I drove over, and I talked to the police officers, and they showed me the police report, and I can't tell you how shocked I was. You see, they'd arrested Teddy for stealing a car."

"What?" I said, not because I was surprised, but because he'd whispered the last words as if describing some unspeakable disease. Like herpes, for instance.

"A car," he repeated. "An automobile."

"I can't tell you how embarrassed I was," Helen said. "I mean, it's embarrassing to find out that your son's been arrested for stealing a car. I could have—"

DeWitt squeezed her shoulders to quiet her.

"Now, now," DeWitt said to her, "let's not forget that we're part of the same big family." Then, to me, "See, it's just a horrible shame that this has happened, Ham. A horrible, horrible shame. And it would be even more horrible to have this on Teddy's record. It could just ruin his life. Ruin it. If you have something like that on your record, it makes it awful difficult to get into a good college, or to get a good job, for that matter."

"He made a terrible mistake," Helen interrupted, "and I have a good mind to kick him in the rear end. But he really is a good boy, Mr. Ashe. He's never hurt anybody. He just doesn't think sometimes."

"So," DeWitt said, "what I was thinking was, since we're all part of the same family, I thought it would be best if we just dealt with this situation within the family"—he made a pair of quotation marks in the air with the index and middle fingers of his bony hands when he said "family"—"so to speak."

"What do you suggest?" I said. I felt pressure behind my eyes and a burning sensation in my stomach.

"Well, I don't see any reason why Helen should have to go out and hire a lawyer, seeing as she's got a couple dozen right here in the family, don't you agree?"

I nodded and foresaw the rest of the conversation.

"Well, seeing how well you did handling Shoogey's matter, I want you to head over to the courthouse and take care of the bail hearing. See if you can get him released on his own recognizance, no bail. Then see if you can get the owner of the car to drop this whole darned matter. Then, what I figured is that I'll reimburse them for the repairs on the car, and Teddy can reimburse us. Maybe he can work off the debt by working in our mailroom. That way, everybody's back to square one. Everybody's happy."

"Please, Mr. Ashe," Helen said. "I know what he did was wrong—"

"What he *allegedly* did," DeWitt said.

"I know what he allegedly did was wrong, but I'll punish him worse than any prison could."

DeWitt laughed a sardonic *heh-heh-heh*. "He wouldn't go to prison, Helen. It's his first offense, so he'd probably get probation. No, the real concern is that we keep this from showing up on his record. That's the real problem."

I sat with my coffee, wishing they would leave, but they didn't. I was trapped. Again. If it were just DeWitt in my office, I suppose I could have discussed the matter with him, told him that I had no interest in handling criminal matters, but where would that have put me? I couldn't refuse with Helen there, her mouth open slightly. I knew that was why DeWitt had brought her to the meeting.

"Fine," I said reluctantly. "I don't know much about criminal law, but I'll do my best."

Helen thanked me with great feeling. She grabbed my hand. "Thank you so much. You're a very generous man, and God will look out for you for doing this generous thing."

I stood and Helen hugged me to her, and I felt a comfort in the certainty of her skin. It was the hug of a good mother, and, in that moment, I was glad I'd agreed to try to help her.

"Thank you," she said again and again.

"It's okay," I told her. "We're one big family here."

"Well," DeWitt said, "I'm glad we got that resolved." He started to leave.

"Just one thing, Mr. DeWitt," I said. "When's the bail hearing?"

"It'll be sometime today."

"Today?"

"Yes."

"When?"

"God knows. You have to go to the courthouse and wait. It could be this morning, it could be this afternoon."

"But I have a meeting with a client at one o'clock."

DeWitt's expression told me I had no such meeting.

* * *

I waited in the courtroom, holding a textbook I'd pulled from the library shelf. It had a green cover with gold letters that read *CRIME AND PUNISHMENT, VOLUME II*. I studied the section on theft, then sat for hours waiting for Teddy Renko's name to be called. There were at least twenty other lawyers with me, all silent and serious, all doing nothing but sitting and perspiring and waiting. Somewhere, there might be a profession that has more prestige and less dignity than being a lawyer, but none comes to mind readily. As we sat and perspired, the room taking on the aroma of a locker room, it occurred to me that it wasn't the suits that distinguished lawyers. It wasn't the gray Joe Bank's suits; Joe Bank's must sell thousands of suits like that to people in all professions. No, it wasn't the suits lawyers wear; it was their faces, something sitting a fraction of an inch beneath the skin. Only another lawyer can spot it, the way the practice of law erodes the character of those it seduces. There was no sense that they had lives within them. In the younger ones, you could see the fear, the fear that if they practiced long enough it would steal their souls, leaving no corner for the original inhabitant of their flesh. In the older ones, the fear was replaced by—what? Self-loathing, I suspected and never wanted to find out.

The hours passed. I had work to do in the office. Meetings and telephone calls that couldn't wait. I watched as dozens of men pleaded not guilty to dozens of crimes. Burglary. Arson. Armed robbery. Murder. Attempted murder. It was incredible—no one was guilty of anything. I was in a room full of choirboys all being falsely accused of committing crimes. One by one, trial dates were set for each of the choirboys. Finally, the bailiff showed me mercy and called out the name of my choirboy: "Theodore Renko." A small boy, no taller than five-feet-two, shuffled into the courtroom. His chin was tucked into his chest, his wrists shackled. The bailiff removed the boy's handcuffs and suddenly the boy seemed unsure what to do with his arms or legs. Eventually, he crossed his arms across his chest and crossed his feet.

I approached the bench, prepared to make an impassioned little speech about Teddy Renko's many fine qualities. *He's a wonderful student, Your Honor. He works at the church bake sale. He runs the church raffle. Why, I do believe he'll be President of the United States some day.*

Only there was no need to make a speech.

The judge was a handsome, gray-haired man by the name of Charles Hammermill.[175]

He had the thick neck of an athlete, and the demeanor of a grandfather. I introduced myself, and before I could say anything more, he said, "Mr. Ashe, I'm going to release your client on his own recognizance. He'll get killed if we keep him here. They'd eat him alive and spit out the bones. I assume he pleads 'not guilty'?"

"Yes, Your Honor," I said.

"What a surprise."

The judge touched his gavel upon his bench and handed some papers to the bailiff.

A police officer pushed Teddy's shoulders, and Teddy approached me. His eyes were wet. The top of his head came to my chest, no higher. I have no idea how he was able to see over the top of the steering wheel of the car he stole. Of the car he allegedly stole, I should say.

"Thank you, sir," he said.

"You're welcome," I answered. I introduced myself. "I'm Hamilton Ashe. I work at M & D with your mother."

"Oh."

"You've made your mother very upset."

"I know."

He wiped his upper lip with his forearm, and I looked at my wristwatch.

"Teddy, I'm sorry but I really have to run," I said. "I have a meeting

I have to be at. Stay out of trouble." I left him standing alone in the courtroom among the sulking lawyers, one or two of whom would have known enough to give the boy a ride home, or buy him lunch, or have a little talk with him about responsibility.

That evening, I worked late to make up for the time I'd spent at Teddy's hearing, hours I'd lost so I could do no more than stand up and tell the judge that Teddy Renko pleaded not guilty; really, I had done nothing. I listened to the radio while I worked, song after song about love lost and love found, before I completed the projects I'd been assigned. There was no one else in the office when I departed, and Harry Addler seemed surprised to see me when I passed by the guard station.

"Late night, Mr. Ashe?" he said. He was eating a sandwich, drinking from a soda can.

"Yes, it was, Harry." I looked at my watch: eleven-thirty.

"Do you want me to call a cab for you?"

"No, Harry, I'm fine," I said, and I walked the deserted streets to my parking lot, then drove home.

It was nearly midnight when I reached our little house, the porch-light still glowing, the remainder of the house dark. Angie had left a plate for me in the oven. Chicken? Meatloaf? I don't know. I took the plate from the oven and placed it on the shelf in the refrigerator. There were balloons and streamers in the kitchen. Apparently the girls had had a party for one of their friends. I hadn't heard anything about it.

I walked upstairs, changed and climbed into bed. Sleeping, Angie turned her back to me. It was only then that I realized I'd forgotten my own birthday.

* * *

I opened my birthday presents at the breakfast table the next morning, one day after my thirty-fourth birthday. A new basketball from the girls, some new records from Angie. I hadn't played basketball with the girls in weeks; I hadn't danced with my wife since Phil Van

Marker's fundraiser. No, I hadn't danced with her there, had I?

I was apologetic about the prior evening, and I was overly enthusiastic about their gifts to compensate. I even ate a slice of birthday cake at seven-thirty in the morning. It didn't help: I was horrible. When I arrived at work, I found a plate of homemade brownies on my desk. The brownies were wrapped in tin foil, and there was a note attached:

You're wonderful.

Thanks for everything.

Love, Helen Renko.

The note was written in a graceful, rounded backhand that seemed at odds with Helen's bulk. She had the handwriting of a lovely young girl with hair that smelled of strawberry shampoo and teeth that sparkled in the moonlight. I folded the note and put it in my bottom desk drawer, then ate one of the brownies.[176]

Then I ate a second.

Later that morning, I called the owner of the car Teddy had stolen. His name was Weymer, Frank Weymer.[177]

He was a man of about sixty, retired, with no desire to see a young boy's life ruined by an act of bad judgment, especially a boy with tuberculosis, which Teddy acquired in the middle of the conversation; I hadn't planned to say that, but somehow the words came out of my mouth. It was no more than two or three minutes later that Weymer agreed to drop the charges if Teddy would pay him for the repairs. The window he'd broken, the ignition switch, etcetera, etcetera. I called Helen to share the news—I didn't mention that Teddy had contracted tuberculosis—and she began to weep into the phone, thanking me, thanking me, thanking me, thanking me.

The following morning, she left a box of homemade pastries on my desk blotter, walnuts wrapped in dough and covered with cinnamon.

The morning after that, she left a plate of oatmeal cookies.

The next morning, Shoogey called me from New York City to tell me he was in jail. He'd been arrested, he said, for murder.

Chapter Fifteen: A Criminal In My Clothes

"Murder?"

"Yes," he said. There was nothing special about his voice, and it was that quality, that absence of any emotion, that frightened me.

"In New York? What are you doing in New York?"

"I came here to see my agent about my book."

"In New York?"

"Yes. Her office is in New York, so in order to visit her, I have to come to New York. If her office was in Paraguay, I'd be in Paraguay. That's the way it works. Now, my friend, my good friends here at the police station have only given me this one phone call, and I called you. Are you going to help out a friend, or not?"

"Yes," I said, without thinking, "of course. I'll be right up. I don't know how, but I'll be right up."

"Take the train," he said, matter-of-factly.

"Is it faster than taking a plane?"

"No, but it's nicer. It's more relaxing, and you'll get a nice view of the landscape."

"Are you sure?"

"Yes, by all means take the train."

"Okay," I said, and I started pushing pads and pens into my brief-case. My collar was damp with perspiration already. "Let me ask you one thing before I go, Shoogey."

"Anything."

"Did you do it?"

"Ham, Ham, my dear friend" he whispered, "you know the answer to that."

And I did: he'd done it. He'd killed someone. I'd heard the story: he'd killed seven men before, sent them to their graves, turned their bodies to fertilizer and their thoughts to pure blue air. He'd shot the first one in the nose, for godssakes, then smothered him with his bare hands, like he was wringing out a dishrag.

"I don't know New York City, Shoogey. Tell me where I'm supposed to go."

Shoogey gave me the address of the precinct house where he was being held, and I wrote it on a slip of paper and stuffed it in my pants pocket.

"It's not far from the train station," he said. His voice was distant but, still, affectless. "Just grab a cab out front of the train station and give them that address, okay?"

"Okay."

"And hurry."

"I will."

And I did. I hurried out of the office without telling anyone where I was headed. Not Angie, who I knew was at the girls' school for some event I couldn't recall. Not Carole, who was away from her desk. I hurried out without telling anyone the horrible truth, that Shoogey had killed someone. Again.

* * *

I still had the textbook that I'd pulled from the shelf in the firm's library when I'd gone to court to help Teddy Renko: CRIME AND PUNISHMENT, VOLUME II. I studied it as I waited for my train, then on the train as it rattled toward New York City. I read the section on homicide, though I had trouble concentrating. It was hard to think about homicide in the legal sense when a friend had murdered someone in the physical sense. Blood and screaming. The sorts of things you would read about in the newspaper or in mystery novels, the sorts of things you would hear about on the television news, the sorts of things you never wanted to actually impinge upon your own cozy existence.

I kept imagining Shoogey killing someone. A shooting. A strangling. Perhaps he pushed someone from a window. I watched a man fall, his arms fluttering as if he were trying to take flight.

I imagined a knife. A gun. I imagined a fistfight in the street and police cars swarming like bees to a hive. I imagined all that, and I imagined more, and I didn't have trouble imagining it. The murders came easily and swiftly, one after the other, Shoogey killing one man, then killing another, then another.

I saw Shoogey shoot a man in the chest. He shot the man and laughed, haw-haw-haw, as if the man had merely slipped on a banana peel. I saw him choke the breath out of a woman. Her face turned as blue as the sea is in dreams. I watched him push a young couple in front of a fast-moving car, then step back to admire his handiwork. Time after time, I watched him turn strangers into nothing more than flesh and bones and biology that ceased to work.

It was easy to picture him creating fertilizer and pure blue air.

Yes, he was guilty. I knew it, and it was then that I realized that I shouldn't even have been on the train: I couldn't help Shoogey. When he'd called me, I should have found a criminal lawyer for him in New York, someone who specialized in defending murderers, someone who knew what he was doing. That's what I should have done, but I was already on the train and too far along to turn back.

Shoogey had killed someone. I knew it.

The riders on the train were a pale, sullen group, their skin the color of wallpaper paste save for a single black woman at the front of the car. There was no conversation, only the occasional rustling of newspapers and magazines. Across the aisle a young couple sat with an infant. The man, bearded and balding, read *The Washington Post* while the woman bounced the child on her lap. The child had dishwater blond hair cut above the ears. It was impossible to tell if the child was a boy or girl, dressed as it was in red overalls, which reminded me of the baby shower one of Angie's friends planned shortly before Claire was born. Box after box contained blue overalls with a label that read "Oshkosh B'gosh." Angie thanked everyone after opening each, and when we snuck off to the kitchen she said, "We're having a baby, not a farmer!"

I imagined Shoogey killing the bearded man, suffocating him with his newspaper, shoving the words down his throat and plugging his nose.

I imagined Shoogey shooting the man in the nose.

I imagined him pushing open the door to the train, ushering in a great wind, then pushing the black woman out like a pirate forcing a sailor to walk the plank.

I won't say what I imagined him doing to the woman and her child. I won't say, but just imagining it was enough to make me think, *Oh, God,* and nearly speak it out loud.

Then I thought of the last time I'd seen Jane Shoogey only months before, asking her questions that did not merely bare her to the world, but mocked her nakedness:

Mrs. Shoogey, at any time have you ever had sexual intercourse with anyone other than your husband?

Mrs. Shoogey, did you ever have sexual intercourse with the mailman?

Mrs. Shoogey, did you ever have sexual intercourse with Syd Braverman?

Mrs. Shoogey, would you mind telling me how you got a venereal disease known as herpes?

* * *

Someone had left a copy of a magazine in the pocket of the seat in front of mine, and I flipped through it to take my mind off Shoogey, off the murders he was committing one after another after another like a madman on the loose. There was an advertisement that said nothing but *VISIT ARIZONA!*, a photograph of the sun rising behind dark cacti; the curving arms of the plants spelled out something in a long-forgotten language. There were advertisements for shoes and contact lenses. There was another ad that said *A TREAT FROM HAWAII.*[178]

That one had a photograph of a young woman, long black hair framing her brown nut of a face. Her bare midriff was bookended by a pastel blue bikini top and a flowered sarong. The girl held a blue-and-yellow can of pineapple juice in one hand, extending a glass forward with the other as if to offer you a cool drink.

I flipped through the pages. There was a photograph of a beautiful young woman wearing a negligee, her hands stretched over her head, her spaniel eyes staring directly into my own. Above her head was a single word, *MARINA*, in bright red italics.

If Marina Miles could be a food —

the article read

— she'd be a pineapple. "Because a pineapple is all hard and prickly on the outside, but sweet inside," she says with a hearty laugh.

That description sums up her scene-stealing role in the hit movie "Umbrella Steps." As Nicholas Crowder's girlfriend, Marina is a sexy, nutty knockout.

The actress grew up in Manhattan, the daughter of an attorney and a psychologist. She attended New York University for a year before dropping out to pursue acting full-time. Though she made a brief impression in "The Best Years Of Our Short Lives" and as the tomboyish daughter in "Robert Dynamite," "Umbrella Steps" is her first real chance to show her stuff.

"My friends all think I'm moody," says Marina, who's in her mid-20's. "I think that helps my acting. It certainly hasn't helped my dating." Marina holds up her hand. "Joking," she explains, "I'm joking."

The young actress, who still lives in Manhattan, is dating a New York writer. She's now in Florida, "sweating my tuchis off" shooting "Bee King." "I must drink fifty glasses of juice a day just to stay alive."

Pineapple juice, we presume.

I turned the page. My eyes passed over the words, but then I flipped back to look at Marina Miles; she looked nothing like Jane Shoogey, but I imagined she did.[179]

Jane, Jane, Jane.

I ran my tongue over my teeth. *Brack-a-brack-a-brack.*

I reread the article. I flipped several more pages, then returned to the photograph.

In Philadelphia, a thin man in a cardigan took the seat beside me. I allowed my eyes to meet his, then returned to my magazine. The man left the train several stops later, somewhere in New Jersey, though I couldn't tell the name of the town. When the conductor announced the stop through the static, it sounded like he was saying, "Magalumph."

In Magalumph, an enormous man plopped into the seat beside me. He had slick, black hair and folds of skin about his neck. He made gulping noises when he breathed, and he gave me a nasty glance.

Shoogey had killed someone.

I took a legal pad out of my briefcase and, referring to the textbook again, I began to take notes to prepare myself:

HOMICIDE = purposely, knowingly or recklessly causing the death of another under conditions of extreme indifference to the value of human life.

Note: Is Shoogey indifferent to human life?

First degree murder = deliberate and premeditated, or with intent to take life.

Yes, I knew it. He'd done it with the intent to take a life. He'd intended to take a life when he'd pushed a woman off the balcony, when he'd hit her over the head with a club.

Evidence of premeditation = (1) evidence of planning activity, or (2) evidence of motive, or (3) evidence as to manner of killing that shows preconceived design.

Ask Shoogey if he'd planned the murder. Or was it spontaneous? Maybe I can argue that Shoogey's insane. That his mind's left him. That he didn't have the capacity to understand his actions.

THERE IS A VERY HEAVY MAN SITTING NEXT TO ME READING OVER MY SHOULDER.[180]

The man jerked his head away, and I returned to my preparations, drawing up page after page of notes. The railroad tracks fed themselves into tunnels and past huge, ugly mountainscapes of factories and warehouses. It was shortly after three in the afternoon when the train pulled into Pennsylvania Station, lurching.[181]

The man beside me rose and was thrown forward slightly, then back again as the train came to a stop, and his wide posterior swayed before my nose. I gathered my things and slid them into my briefcase, except for the textbook, which I kept tucked under my arm. I waited for the aisle to clear before stepping onto the platform, then followed the crowd into the terminal.

Inside, a man in a windbreaker asked if he could carry my briefcase, and I kept my chin to my chest, ignoring him. A man carried a guitar. There were three boys with identical New York Knicks jackets, the faint smell of buttered popcorn and cigarettes and stale coffee, a teenage girl in a short skirt and wobbly high heels.[182]

I stepped outside, and—whomp! There it was, New York City. It was worse than I'd ever imagined. Cars swerving, food wrappers and newspapers rolling along the sidewalk like tumbleweeds, and the smell of dirty laundry everywhere. And there was Shoogey standing beside the hoardings along the sidewalk. He stood next to a peeling movie poster of a man with a trumpet and a woman with her head resting on his shoulder, the words *Umbrella Steps* hovering over their heads.[183]

"Shoogey, what are you doing here?" I said. I couldn't hide my excitement. "Did they release you?" They'd made a mistake. Shoogey hadn't killed someone after all, and they'd set him free. Shoogey wasn't a murderer.

Shoogey cocked his head slightly and closed one eye, as if confronting a strong odor. "Release me?"

"From jail. Did they release you?"

Shoogey held up a hand and bobbed his head, then smiled his Shoogey smile. "Oh, that's right, my friend. I did say something about being arrested for killing someone, didn't I?"

Everywhere, my muscles grew weak.

Shoogey mussed my hair as one might in greeting a small boy, and I quickly fixed it with my fingers.

"What?"

"I was just kidding around, my friend. I just said that to get you to come up here. New York is a wonderful, passionate city—so much to do, so much to see—but a terrible place to visit alone. You need company if you're going to enjoy it properly."

"You didn't kill anyone?"

"Of course not."

"What about the Eighth Precinct? I thought they were holding you at the Eighth Precinct."

"I don't even know if there is an Eighth Precinct, my friend." He rubbed his nose. "Come to think of it, I'm sure there is one. I've heard of the Tenth Precinct, so there must be at least ten. I sincerely doubt they just skipped over the Eighth. Though they do do that with high-rise buildings sometimes: they skip over the thirteenth floor because it's supposed to be bad luck. The lights on the elevator will say, one, two, three, four, five, six, seven, eight, nine, ten, eleven, twelve, then *four*teen. As if the people on the fourteenth floor aren't bright enough to figure out they're really on the *thir*teenth. Now, what do you say we get something to eat?"

Shoogey raised a hand to hail a cab, then turned to look at me and smiled his smile again. He tipped his head slowly to read the spine of the textbook I carried. "*CRIME AND PUNISHMENT, VOLUME II?* I didn't know Dostoyevsky wrote a sequel.[184] I really have to try to keep up with my reading."

"It's a textbook," I said sternly. "I was reading up about murder because you told me you killed someone. Remember? You called me up and said you'd killed someone."

Shoogey pinched my elbow and steered me toward the curb. "I said no such thing. I said I'd been *accused* of killing someone. And, technically, that's true. I can't tell you how many times Jane's said, 'Dammit, Sam, you're killing me.'"

A little gloating smile touched the corners of his mouth.

"To be honest," he continued, "I thought of killing her more than a few times. Not seriously, just a daydream of sorts, but the sort of daydream all men and women have about their spouses: what if I *did* do it? You want to know how I'd have done it? I'd have done it little by little. A little poison in her meal every night, a little in her drink. 'Oh, here, darling, have another cup of coffee.'"

"Shoogey, you gave me the impression you killed someone. I've been worried sick. I've spent the past two or three hours worried, reading about murder defenses just so I could help you out." I held up by briefcase. "I've been taking notes."

"You can work on trains? That's wonderful. Me, I usually intend to work when I take the train, but I rarely accomplish anything. It's hard not to look out the window and gaze at the moving trees, or just close your eyes and let the hum of the wheels lull you to sleep. With all that, I really don't know how some people are able to work on trains. Or planes, for that matter. It takes a very disciplined mind, I would think. Especially if you know that when the plane or train comes to rest, there you'll be, in New York City of all places."

Suddenly, we were in a cab, speeding along the hectic streets, the driver ignoring the lines painted in the road like a child disregarding the lines in a coloring book.

"Now," Shoogey continued, "I'm more than a bit insulted to think that you'd believe I could actually commit a crime. Me, a criminal? A criminal in *my* clothes?" He was wearing a navy sportscoat with a black turtleneck and gray, pleated slacks. "Not that I haven't thought about committing a crime or two in my day. I remember when I was a boy, we had a neighbor named Mrs. Callahan.[185] A very unfriendly woman who always used to pretend she wasn't home on Halloween so she wouldn't have to give out any candy. In any event, I was shoveling the snow off her driveway one morning and when she came out to pay me she slipped on a patch of ice—boom. She refused to pay me, and when she turned around I thought about whacking her over the head with my shovel, but that would've made a mess, don't you think? Instead I just turned the hose on her driveway until it was like an ice rink."

Shoogey looked at me, waiting for a smile that I wouldn't give him. He tapped the tip of his nose.

"Let's see, let's see. What other crimes did I almost commit? Well, *here*'s one: I almost took a drink into a greeting card store."

Again, he looked for a smile.

"Here's another: matricide. After a really bad night's sleep, I almost took a knife to my Sealy Posturepedic mattress."

Again, I wouldn't smile.

"Another time, I was mowing Mrs. Callahan's yard, and I accidentally ran over some of the flowers in her garden, so she refused to pay me. I started kicking around the idea of running her down with the lawnmower, but something stopped me. I think it was dinner time, or something like that."

I couldn't even look at him anymore.

"Here's another crime I almost committed. This was when I was in high school. I have a cousin by the name of Tommy, and Tommy—"

"Shut up!" When I shouted, something small left my mouth and flew across the cab, landing on his jacket. "Shut the hell up, Shoogey! I'm tired of your lousy stories! Just shut up! Just… shut…up!"

When the cab stopped at a light, I opened the door and stepped out. I pointed a finger at Shoogey, at that nose he was always rubbing, at those teeth he was always flashing.

"You're a liar, Shoogey. You're a lying liar. That's what you are, a lying liar; you even lie about your lies. You could have been anything, Shoogey, but all you are is a liar, and all a liar is is a waste of flesh and bones."

I pulled my briefcase off the seat.

"Where are you going?" he said. "Where are you going to go?"

"Anywhere but here. Anywhere where you're not, you lying liar."

I slammed the door shut then began to walk off. I passed restaurants and newsstands and bumped into people who did not want to hear an apology. Finally, I stopped at a pay telephone and called Angie.

"Sweet Potato," I said, "I'm in New York City."

Before I could explain, she said, "Let me guess. It has to do with Sam Shoogey, doesn't it?"

"Yes."

"What kind of adventure are you two on today?"

"No adventure."

"I don't believe you, Ham. How long have you two had this little trip planned?"

"It's not that at all," I said. "I'll be home as soon as I can."

"That's fine, Ham," she said. "I can't say I was looking forward to your return anyway."

She hung up before I could say anything more.

I began to walk without direction. There was, I must admit, something breathtaking about the city, something that just seemed to grab you by the lapels and drag you on and on. Something that just seemed to say, *Oh, you must see this. And this.*

I passed bars and restaurants and movie theaters. Book stores. Clothing stores. Record shops. Hotels. Liquor stores. That's what the air smelled like. It wasn't dirty laundry, it was liquor a day or two out of the bottle. Bourbon or gin, and it went to my head. I began to wander through the city, buzzing about like a drunken bee, first here, then there. As the afternoon wore on, I felt my anger slip away. I stopped in a record shop and bought two albums to replace ones that I'd previously owned and had inexplicably lost.[186] I bought a book of poems in a book store for Angie, and a new tie and belt in a men's shop.[187]

I'd just passed Radio City Music Hall, still drunk on the bourbon (or gin) in the air, when an old white man approached me, blocking my path. The man's hands were stuffed deep in the pockets of his trench-coat. A black trenchcoat, surprisingly neat. He smiled, and his teeth were the color of cornhusks. He smelled terribly of wet sacking and oily meat. I tried to avoid the man, but he moved nearer, standing closer to me than strangers ought, his breath and my breath meeting, combining, vanishing together like friends into the universe.

I began to excuse myself politely, but before I could say a word, the man pulled a teaspoon from his coat pocket, pressed it firmly against my Adam's apple and demanded my money. We weren't alone, not by any means. Though it was late, dozens of people were still milling about, some passing as close to us as you are to the book you are holding.

"Gimme your money, gimme your money, gimme your money," he said. "Gimme your money, gimme—"

And, without thought, I just pushed the spoon away, and smiled, and said, "Only if you're going to buy pudding."

Only if you're going to buy pudding. As I walked past him, I was pleased with that response. Just then, a cab pulled up to the curb beside me, and the door swung open.

"Ham, get back in the cab." It was Shoogey. His jacket was off, and the sleeves of his turtleneck were pushed to his elbows. "Get back in the cab right now," he said urgently.

"Go to hell, Shoogey."

"Ham, you're going to get killed out here. Now get back in the cab, and we'll go get some dinner, and then I'll put you back on the train if that's what you want. We'll do whatever you want. Just get back in the cab right now."

"I'm not going to get killed. I'm doing just fine, thank you."

"You're doing just fine, my foot. We've been following you around, and you're lucky you're not dead already. That guy could have killed you. In New York, if someone asks for your money, you give it to them, no questions asked. There's no negotiating, my friend."

"He was carrying a spoon," I said, then sarcastically I added, "my friend."

"Ham, did it ever occur to you that anyone carrying a spoon might well be carrying other—*sharper*—kitchen utensils? I mean, who would have just a spoon? You can't even buy a spoon separately. You've got to buy a whole place setting. You have to buy the fork and the knife, too. The guy probably had a whole place setting in his pocket. Now, get back in the cab."

Of course, he was right, and I climbed back in beside him. My textbook was still where I'd left it. I picked it up and held it against my thigh.

"There, there," he said, patting my knee. "You know, I once heard someone say, 'New York is my kind of town—because I have a gun!' That's the way you've got to think up here. Now, let's get some food in you. What are you in the mood for? How about French? No, we want something nice, and the French are so unpleasant. You know, everyone hates the French, but no one ever does anything about it. Let's try Italian instead. Everyone likes Italian."

I ended up spending much of the rest of the evening in the restroom of a little Italian restaurant, expecting to vomit, but not doing so. Shoogey stood beside the door, knocking occasionally to check on my condition: "Ham, are you okay in there? Come out and have something to eat. You need to get something in your system. You have to eat. Eat. Eat. Eat."

I understood then how much I had embarrassed Angie at Phil Van Marker's fundraiser.

"Shoogey, get away from the door."

"Ham?"

"Now!"

My nausea passed after a long while, and I returned to the table. Shoogey and I didn't speak at all; we barely looked at each other, and he turned away quickly whenever he caught my eye. When my appetite returned, I ordered linguini with marinara sauce, which was delivered quickly to our table. The sauce was wonderful; it was sweet and thick and lingered on your tongue, and it is that taste that I try to remember whenever I think of New York City. Unfortunately, try as I might, my mind usually returns to two other thoughts: the thought of Shoogey killing someone, and the image of my teeth left resting in a cup on the train as it pulled away from the station in Baltimore early that next morning, headed toward Washington D.C. and other points south.[188]

Chapter Sixteen: Not Enough Concrete

I watched the train carry my teeth away from me, watched the doors slide closed and the gray steam rise from beneath the carriage. Under other circumstances, I might have raced to the train and pounded my fists against the doors, shouting, "You have my teeth! My teeth! In a cup!" Instead, tired as I was, I stood beside the tracks and peered longingly at the window beside the seat I'd sat in, watching it as the train pulled away the same way you might do if your wife or your girlfriend were departing on a journey across the country; she would gaze out the window, bravely fending off tears, folding her fingers into her palm to wave goodbye, goodbye. My teeth were gone.

I walked through the nearly empty train station, empty save for a small crew of maintenance workers mopping the floors and a single security guard reading yesterday's newspaper. I carried my shopping bags and my briefcase and my textbook through the parking lot, found my car and steered it home through a gray, fuzzy night; it had rained hard, you could tell, the kind of Old Testament rains that seem to find Baltimore too often.

I pulled the car into the driveway at nearly four in the morning. The rain had stopped, and a clearing wind was blowing, scattering the fog. The house and shrubbery in front, still wet from the storm, gleamed in the headlights of my car. I entered the house to find Angie asleep on the couch, in front of the television, a book on the floor at her feet; it was the Henry James novel I'd given her for Christmas. Claire was sleeping, too, her body limp in the posture of a swimmer doing the backstroke. Their mouths were open. That was the way they both slept, with their mouths open in small ovals.

"Like mother, like daughter," Angie had said when I first pointed it out. "It's hereditary, like hair color."

I could hear the two of them breathing over static of the television. It was as if their whole bodies were rattling. I could see Angie's chest, falling and rising inside her blouse, and Claire's shoulders bobbing.

I removed my suit jacket and folded it over the back of the love seat, and I pulled my tie through my collar and laid it on top of the coat. I switched off the television, then bent and squeezed Claire's arm gently with my fingers.

"Noodle?"

She didn't answer.

"Noodle?" and she groaned. "Daddy's going to carry you to your room, okay?"

I slipped my hands under her and scooped her tiny body from the carpet. A sheet of black hair hung behind her, and I rolled her in my arms so I could look at her face. Her eyes were shut, and her body sagged in my hands.

"Fifteen," she whispered in her sleep, her voice different, more guttural than her waking voice. "Sixteen," she said. God knows what she was thinking.

I carried her down the hallway to her room, and, with my elbow, I flicked the light switch up. When the light came on, Katie growled in her bed and rolled onto her stomach.

I shifted Claire on my hip and held her with one arm while I swept her stuffed animals to one side of the bed, then pulled back the sheets. I lowered her to the bed, brushed her hair off her forehead and kissed her lightly there, tugged the sheets up to her chin, then tucked them in between the mattress and the boxspring.

Returning to the living room, I saw that Angie's head was tipped back. One hand was up in her hair, the other flat against the arm of the couch. Her chest was bouncing still, as steady and deliberate as a wave. In her sleep, she was biting her lip.[189]

I sat on the couch beside her, and when I did, it startled her. She jumped. "What!" She looked at the floor, for Claire, not the book. "Where's—"

"I carried her to bed," I told her. She looked at me warily at first, as if she didn't recognize me, and then she closed her eyes and slid closer to me, little by little until our thighs kissed.

"Want me to carry you, too?" I said. Without my teeth, my words were slurred. "I'll just pick you up and carry you like a sack of potatoes."

She put her arms around my neck, then swung her legs onto my lap. Her weight was upon me, and I barely felt it.

"No," she said, "just sit here and don't move an inch."

"Are you still upset with me?"

"Yes, but I'm sure it'll pass someday."

Her head fell to my shoulder.

After a minute or two she said, "Ham, can I ask you a question? Can I ask you a question and you promise to give me an honest answer?"

"Of course."

"Ham," she said. She didn't lift her head from my shoulder, and I could feel her voice echoing off the wall of my chest. "I want to know what it is with that guy Shoogey. I want to know why you're friends with him."

"I'm not," I said. "Besides, he's out of our lives forever."

"Promise?"

"Yes," I said, and I meant it.

"You've made me that promise before, you know."

"I know."

"So how do you know it's true this time?"

"Because. That's all I can say: because."

"Good," she said. "You know, I heard he killed someone. They were talking about it at the ballet barn on Saturday. They said he killed someone."

"Yes," I said. "I've heard."

"Is it true?"

"God knows."

"Your voice sounds funny," she said. Her eyes were still shut.

"I know," I said. "I lost my teeth. They're headed toward Florida."

Angie began to laugh a little, then fell asleep again, a small noise coming from her mouth like air leaking from a balloon. I carried her upstairs. As I did, I stopped to see her face. She was biting her lip.[190]

Then, out of nowhere, she said, "Fifteen. Sixteen."

* * *

My teeth arrived with the office mail several days later. They were in a cardboard box and bound up in a note that read, simply, *Thank you for riding Amtrak.*[191]

I popped the dental plate in my mouth and heard the reassuring *brack-a-brack-a-brack*, then I returned to work.

I left work early that night. I pulled the car into the driveway at half past six, parking it under the basketball hoop. I pulled my briefcase off the passenger seat, said hello to Angie and the girls as I pulled my keys from the lock, then walked to the bedroom and changed into a sweat-shirt, sweatpants, and sneakers.

"Ham?" Angie called to me. "Ham, is everything okay?"

"Everything's fine."

"I mean, why are you home so early? You weren't fired, were you?"

"No," I called back, "I wasn't fired."

"Then why are you home so early?"

"I just wanted to see my family," I said.

"Good," she said. "Good."

"Angie?" I called a few minutes later. "Angie?"

"What?"

"Angie, what's for dinner?"

"Chicken."

"And?"

"Chicken and rice."

At the dinner table, the girls eyed me suspiciously as I ate.

"What are you doing here?" Katie said.

"I live here," I answered.

"You only live here at night," she said, "and it's not night yet."

"Did you lose your job at work?" Claire asked. "I heard Mom say that."

"No, you heard your mother ask me that, and I told her I didn't lose my job. Okay?"

"Okay."

The girls knelt on their chairs, more interested in watching me than in eating themselves. They didn't tell me that they'd done the cooking until I was finished with my slice of Tar Heel pie. I looked at Angie to see if they had in fact cooked the meal, and when she confirmed that they had, I applauded the girls. Both smiled broadly, and I had an odd feeling at that moment. Then I realized what it was: I was very, very happy.

I moved to the living room. The girls pushed their chairs in and began to follow me, but Angie stood in front of them and struck a pose, her hands on her hips. With mock excitement, she said, "Now, let's play a game. I call this game 'Cleaning the Dishes.'"

The girls groaned, and Angie said, "Hey, the rules have gotten easier. When I was a girl, you had to wash them by hand. Now, all you have to do is put them in the dishwasher."

It didn't take long, though, for the girls to begin arguing.

"You had the easy part. I had the hard part," Katie said.

"You did not. Mine was just as hard," Claire said.

"You had the dessert," Katie said, and she rolled her eyes. "Any moron can make dessert. Melt some chocolate chips. Big deal. A baby could melt chocolate chips."

"I'm so sick of you," Claire said. "I'd like to melt you. I'll bet you'd melt like the Wicked Witch in *The Wizard of Oz*.[192] You even look like her."

"You make me want to puke, you little piece of garbage."

With that, Claire tried to slap Katie but missed, hitting the table instead. The girls began to pull at each other, and Angie had to separate them.

I smiled, watching my family.

"Stop acting like children," Angie said, holding each by the forearm.

"We *are* children," Katie said. "What should we act like—judges?"

"Ham," Angie called, "you really have to help me with this."

"What do you want me to do?"

"You take one of them, I'll take the other."

"Fine," I said. "Eeeny, meeny, miny, moe." I was pointing at Claire. "Let's go, Noodle. I'm stuck with you."

"Where are we going?"

"We'll go shoot baskets in the driveway."

I took Claire by the hand. Stopping to pick up the car keys on the bureau, I led her out to the driveway. I moved the car out to the street, then opened the garage door. My new basketball was wedged between the steps of the ladder. I pulled it out, then rolled it to Claire, who was leaning against the basketball pole. She stopped the ball with one foot, then bent to pick it up, and I flicked on the light over the garage door, casting a sickly yellow glow over part of the driveway.

"You okay?" I asked Claire. "You've been acting strange."

"Yes, I'm okay, " she said, then she changed her answer. "No, I'm not."

I pulled the basketball from her fingers, then sat on it so I could look into her face. "Tell your old man about it."

"I don't know," she said. "I mean, I don't even know why you guys even *had* me."

"Well, Noodle, we didn't know it was going to be *you*." Already I could tell that she was suppressing a smile—she turned her head to look at the street—so I continued. "We thought we were going to get a German shepherd. But then, when your mother was in the hospital, the doctor came out to the waiting room and said, 'Mr. Ashe, it's a baby girl.' Well, I figured it was a baby girl German shepherd puppy, so I said, 'Great. Fantastic.' And he took me into your mother's room, and I expected to see her holding a little German shepherd puppy, but to my surprise, she was holding a beautiful, black-haired, blue-eyed baby girl, and I fell in love with her just like that," I said, snapping my fingers. The light over the garage door bounced off Claire's skin.

"It must have been someone else, not me," she said.

"No, it was you."

"You said it was beautiful, and I'm not beautiful. Katie's the beautiful one."

That was it.

"You're both beautiful," I answered softly. "You look just like your mother, Noodle." And, in fact, in the eclipsed light, Claire looked like the tiny specter of her mother.

"You are such a liar. People always say, 'Isn't Katie beautiful' or 'Katie's the beautiful one.'"

I reached into the pocket of my sweatshirt and produced a tissue, which Claire took reluctantly. She wiped her nose, then held the tissue out.

"Ick," I said, "I don't want it *back*."

"It's just little girl snot. It won't kill you."

I pinched a corner of the tissue and slipped it back into my pocket.

"Sweetheart, you *are* beautiful. Trust me, I know."

"I am not," she said. "Look," and she took three, quick bites at the air. "I'm a beaver. Chomp, chomp, chomp."

I leaned in toward her. "You know, I never noticed that before, but you do have a little bit of an overbite, don't you?"

"You never *noticed*? Puh-*lease*."

"Really," I said, folding the thumb and little finger of my right hand into my palm, then holding three fingers beside my face, "Scout's honor. You know what it was, I must have been so overwhelmed by the rest of your beauty that I didn't even notice that one little, tiny thing. That's what it was. I'll tell you what. Would you feel better if we went to see a dentist to see if maybe he could fix it?"

Claire stood up on her toes. "Can they fix it?"

"Of course, they can fix anything these days. Look what they did for my teeth." I bared my false teeth to her. "Would that make you happy if we did that?"

Claire leaned forward and hugged me, and I had to shift my weight to keep from falling off the basketball.

"Want to know how good they are at fixing things these days," I continued, and Claire stepped back. "Promise you won't tell anyone that I told you this?"

Claire nodded.

"You have to say, 'Promise.'"

"Promise."

"Well, when Katie was born, do you know what—she had four noses. She had one here"—I touched the tip of my nose—"and she had one here"—I touched my right cheek—"and she had one here"—I put a finger to my right knee—"and she had a little tiny one down here"—and I twisted my foot and touched the sole of my sneaker.

"She did not."

I nodded. "Yes, she did, she had four noses, but they cut three of them off. Now, you promised not to tell anyone, remember? That's a secret between you and me."

I held up my hand and Claire smacked it with her own.

"Now," I said, "are we going to play some basketball or are we going to sit out here talking like a couple of mother hens?"

I stood and dribbled the ball twice. Claire held her arms out to receive the ball, but I tucked it under my arm.

"Before you play basketball, you have to sing the national anthem, don't you?"

Putting my hand over my heart, I began to sing "The Star Spangled Banner," and, soon, Claire joined in.[193]

Once we finished, I bounced the ball to her.

As she dribbled, I dropped my voice and said, "Good evening ladies and gentleman, and welcome to another Washington Bullets basketball game.[194] As you know, the Bullets were in last place until they signed the magnificent Ashes: Hamilton Ashe, the suave, handsome, young center, and his daughter Claire 'The Big Noodle' Ashe, the beautiful, intelligent, sometimes annoying little point guard."

"I am not annoying," she grunted as she heaved the ball toward the hoop. It clanked off the bottom of the rim. I'd never seen her reach the rim before: it'd been months since we'd last played.

"And Claire 'The Big Noodle' Ashe misses her first shot of the game," I announced, grabbing the rebound after it bounced twice on the driveway, then tossing it off the backboard and through the net. "But Hamilton Ashe gets the rebound and stuffs the ball back in for two points! And the crowd goes wild! Yes, fans, just listen to them." I ran in small circles, my head tipped back, my arms outstretched. "Yes, they love Hamilton Ashe here. Just listen to them chanting his name. They're chanting, 'Ham! Ham! Ham!'"

I stopped running and, looking over my shoulder, whispered to Claire, "They're chanting, 'Ham! Ham! Ham!'" Looking past Claire, I saw Braverman in the distance, standing with his feet apart, regarding the star-filled night.

"Ham! Ham! Ham!" Claire said.

"Louder, I can't hear you."

"Ham! Ham! Ham!" she shouted, and I bowed deeply.

"No, really," I said, waving a hand at her. "Stop. You're embarrassing me. It's really just an honor to play in front of all of you good people."

"You really are the weirdest dad in school," Claire said.

"Smile when you say that," I answered.

Not ten minutes later, Angie and Katie came out and joined us, shooting baskets until it was bedtime. I was very, very happy.

* * *

Angie was reading in bed when I walked into the bedroom. Quickly, I stripped down to my boxer shorts, then carried my shoes to the edge of the bed. I held a shoe on one hand like a puppet, lathered it, then rubbed the polish in with a coarse brush. Vigorously, I ran a rag over the shoe, then worked on the other. When I was done, I set the shoes down and, noticing that Angie had finished reading, I switched off the lamp, then slipped into bed, adjusted the covers, and leaned to kiss Angie on the forehead.

"Ham," she said, "I hope you don't mind me letting the girls cook tonight."

"No, not at all. It wasn't half-bad, to tell you the truth."

"Well, we weren't expecting you home for dinner."

"That's going to change."

"How?"

"I don't know, but I'll figure something out."

We were silent for a moment before I said, "Oh, I found out what's been eating Claire. She thinks Katie's beautiful and she's not."

"She *is* beautiful," Angie interrupted.

"I know, I know. But *she* doesn't think she is. She thinks she looks like a beaver with her front teeth."

"I think it's cute."

"So do I, but, realistically, when she gets older, it won't be cute anymore. So I promised her we'd take her to the dentist and get it fixed."

"Okay." Angie paused, thinking. "The dentist or an orthodontist?"

"What?"

"The dentist or an orthodontist? Which one handles things like that?"

I thought for a second. "You know, I don't have any idea. Would you check it out and take her?"

Angie nodded.

"Can I ask you a question?" Angie said.

"Of course."

Then she asked a question that she asked often: "Do you think I'm a bad mother?"

"Angie, no," I said, and I turned on my side and propped my head up with my hand. "Of course not. Why would you ask a silly question like that?"

"I just think that the girls like you more than they like me."

"Angie, that's not true. Why would you say something like that? They like us both. Just because things aren't always perfect doesn't mean they don't like us. Take Katie, for instance. She's at that age where everything I do embarrasses her."

"Oh, we must be the same age then," Angie said, laughing at her own joke. Then she added, "Seriously, Ham, they like you much more than me. I don't know what's happened, but you always make them laugh now. I don't. I don't think I ever make them laugh."

"Angie, I'm sure you make them laugh all the time. And even if you don't, that doesn't make you a bad mother."

"But you always make them laugh."

"Well, that's because I'm funny."

Angie smiled. "When exactly did that happen, by the way?"

"What do you mean, 'When did it happen?'"

"Don't get me wrong, but I don't remember you being that funny."

"I always was funny. But now I'm the funniest man on the planet Earth."

"You are *not*. Johnny Carson's funnier."[195]

"Johnny Carson couldn't wipe my butt," I said in mock protest.

"Ham! I'm going to smack you if you keep talking like that."

"I'm sorry, I take that back. Johnny Carson *could* wipe my butt. Is that better?"

Angie slapped my chest, and the sting surprised me.

"Ow," I said, "why did you do that?"

"I *told* you I was going to do that. You know I hate language like that." She folded her hands over her chest. "The problem is that I'm just not a funny person. I don't have funny genes. I don't even know any jokes."

"I'll teach you one then," I said, and I moved closer to her.

"What do you mean, you'll teach me one?"

"I'll teach you a joke. Ready?"

"Ready."

"Okay, this is a joke I heard at work. The joke goes like this: what do you have when you have a lawyer up to his neck in concrete?"

Angie thought for a moment before saying, "I give up."

"Not enough concrete," I said, and Angie laughed.[196]

"Okay, now it's your turn."

"What do you mean, it's my turn?"

"It's your turn to tell the joke. Go ahead."

Angie patted her hair and wiped a bead of sweat from her upper lip. "Okay, are you ready? What do you have when you've got a lawyer up to his neck in concrete?"

"Beats me."

"Not enough concrete."

"See," I said. "See, that was good."

"You didn't laugh, though."

"Angie, I knew the punchline, remember?"

"You still should have laughed if it was funny."

"Sweet Potato, I'm laughing on the inside."

Angie ran her hand over my bare chest.

"You know," she said, pushing me onto my back, "if I had a thing of concrete right now, I'd pour it all over you."

"A *thing* of concrete? A *thing* of concrete?" I laughed. "What does that mean?"

"I don't know. I just couldn't think of the right word."

She moved to kneel over me, her knees on either side of my hips, and she pressed her mouth against mine. I squeezed her hips, then inched her nightgown up her legs, and I felt warm when she put her hand where it belonged.

"You know I'm sorry," I said. "You know I'm sorry for everything."

"Of course."

"Good. Just so you know."

Angie pressed her lips against mine again, then ran her tongue over my lips lightly as if she was tracing them.

"Tell me a story," she said.

"What story do you want to hear?"

"Tell me the story about how we met."

"You were beautiful, and you were sweet. You were as sweet as cake batter," I began, and over the next five minutes or so I told her the wonderful story that would lead to us being in that bed together.[197] I did not mention that Angie had been drunk. As I told the story, Angie sat on my pelvis, bending over from time to time to kiss my cheeks, my nose, my ears, my throat.

"Did we live happily ever after?" she asked when I was done.

"Yes," I said, "we were so happy that words could not describe."

I compelled Angie onto her back. She looked young and utterly desirable, and I experienced a sense as heady as complete drunkenness, the sense that I was living a perfect life.

"Turn the radio on," Angie whispered.

I pushed her knees apart.

"Ham, put the radio on," she whispered more insistently. "Put the radio on so the girls won't hear us."

I groped for the clock-radio, knocking a book to the floor. I flicked the knob on, then kissed Angie passionately.

"That was nice," she said when I pulled my head back. I started to lower my head again, but she put her hand on my chest. "Ham, don't forget I need you to watch Katie and Claire tomorrow night. I'm going shopping with my sister."

I smiled. "Oh, Sweet Potato, it turns me on when you talk like that," I joked.

Angie laughed, and she moved her hand to the back of my neck and pulled me toward her, and we made love with the fantastic sloppiness of youth.[198] I closed my eyes, and soon, over the sound of the music, I could make out the sound of Angie's voice as she said, "Oh, my. Oh, my," as faint as the roaring of a shell.

* * *

Sometime in the late hours of the night, I was awakened by my bladder. I'd been in a deep, sweet sleep, the sweetest I'd had in weeks or months or years, and, for several moments, I stood blinking in the cellar-like darkness, then shuffled to the bathroom. I felt a bit sweaty at the armpits. I turned on the lights in the bathroom, then waited for my vision to adjust before putting the toilet seat up. Twice I felt for the waistband of my boxer shorts before remembering that I wasn't wearing any.

In the morning, we awoke among unclean bed sheets. As I tumbled out of bed and headed toward the bathroom, Angie gathered up the sheets, as if destroying evidence. When I entered the kitchen after dressing, Katie was hunched over at the table, scribbling on an index card.

"Mom said we could help her cook breakfast," she said.

Angie and I exchanged glances, and I thought I could see her blushing. She was embarrassed that I should see her now, in the unforgiving kitchen light. She lowered her eyes and pointed to the index card and said, "Toast. Ingredients. Bread. Butter. Preparation. Put bread in toaster. Push button down. Remove toast when it pops up. Butter as desired."

"What do you want for breakfast, Dad?" Claire asked.

"Toast and coffee?"

Claire looked up at her mother.

"I haven't taught them coffee yet," Angie said. Then to Claire she said, "I'll get the coffee. You get the toast. It'll be a team effort."

I ate my breakfast with exaggerated gusto, making noises to demonstrate my pleasure, then rubbing my stomach like a fortune teller running a hand over a crystal ball. I took my dishes to the sink and pecked Angie on the cheek, enjoying the lovely unfreshness of her skin, then kissed the girls on the tops of their heads.

Yes, I was very, very happy.[199]

Chapters Seventeen, Eighteen and Nineteen: Two Years

Two years passed so quickly that you would have thought someone had stolen them in the middle of the night. Two full years.[200]

Imagine the pages of a calendar flipping like they do in the movies. Days and weeks and months passing before your eyes as quickly as a blink.

Imagine Katie and Claire growing out of their clothes, requiring new wardrobes, and imagine them growing out of those new wardrobes, too.

Imagine Claire getting braces, then having them removed, revealing her perfect teeth: she looked even more like her mother now.

Imagine both girls taking their ballet classes on Saturday mornings, leaping and flying, then twirling like the stem of a flower between your fingertips.

Imagine me playing basketball in the driveway with my family. Imagine me helping them dig a hole to China in their backyard.

Imagine me at my little desk at M & D. Imagine my hair thinning, my waistline growing, my eyesight weakening under the dim office lights until I had to purchase eyeglasses. Imagine me driving to work in the early hours of the morning so I could leave in time to have dinner with my family.

Imagine me, author, tired from work, lying on the couch while Angie read to me from magazines and my daughters fed me cookies and cakes and pies they'd baked.

Imagine our family taking a vacation to Florida one summer, and to California the next.[201]

Imagine trips to the beach, the salty night breezes, the unforget-
table smell of wet bathing suits hanging on the door knob.

Imagine two Halloweens.[202]

Imagine two Thanksgivings, and two Christmases, and two New
Years Eves and Days.

Imagine our lives without Shoogey.

Imagine our happy little lives.

Chapter Twenty: The Return of Jane Shoogey
[DELETED]

Chapter Twenty-One: I Am Sam Shoogey
[DELETED]

Chapter Twenty-Two: Cheap Hotels
[DELETED]

Chapter Twenty-Three:
The Return of Henry McClellan, Attorney at Law
[DELETED]

Chapter Twenty-Four: Cheaper Hotels
[DELETED]

Chapter Twenty–Five: My Wife Knows Mercy
[DELETED]

Chapter Twenty-Six: Welcome to Chestertown

Helen Renko stood in my doorway. She was holding a plate of cookies. From her heavy eyes, I knew it was something about Teddy.

Teddy stole another car, she told me. Or, to be more precise, Teddy was accused of stealing another car. This time, it was a black Mustang which he (allegedly) stole from the parking lot outside a grocery store in East Baltimore.[203]

After (allegedly) stealing it, he (allegedly) drove it to the Eastern Shore, where he (allegedly) ran out of gas and (allegedly) pulled the car to the side of the road. A state trooper (actually, not allegedly) spotted Teddy walking back to the car with a can of gasoline and a bag of potato chips. He was being held in a jail in Chestertown, Maryland.

"Can you help him?" Helen asked.

"I'll try," I said. "I'll see what I can do."

"Do you want me to come along?"

"No. It might be better if you stayed here."

"Good. I'm afraid I might kill him if I saw him right now."

"Then you should definitely stay here. If you killed someone in a police station, there's a pretty good chance you'd get caught."

I tried to offer her a smile, but she wasn't looking. Instead, she was inspecting her hands.

"I was only speaking figuratively. I wouldn't kill my own son."

"I know."

"I'll bake you something nice when you get back. These cookies are for your trip."

"Thank you, Helen."

I hadn't been to Chestertown in many years, so many that I could not recall why I'd been there before. It was a small town on the Eastern Shore, a fishing town. Maybe my father had taken me fishing there once. In any event, I had to stop at a bookstore to buy a map just so I could find it. The drive to the courthouse was a long one, made pleasant by the sleepy country backroads and sunny, clement skies. I drove past signs that read *LOCAL CORN 4 SALE* and *GET YOUR CRABS HERE!* There were hills and trees that reminded you of faraway places. Sometimes, the smell of the approaching ocean would make you want to close your eyes, and the sound of the road would be the only thing to remind you that you could not. Fortunately, there was a sign that read, "Welcome to Chestertown, the Heart of Maryland's Eastern Shore." A young girl pointed me in the direction of the courthouse. She was eating an ice cream cone and the ice cream slid over her hand while she spoke, but that did not bother her.

The Chestertown courthouse bore little resemblance to the ones I'd seen in Baltimore. It was smaller and less ornate. No fancy murals, no marble this or that, as if to signal that the fine people of Chestertown were more concerned with justice than the appearance of justice.

A thin sheriff greeted me as I entered. "Morning," he said, touching the brim of his hat. He directed me toward the holding cell where I could find Teddy Renko.

On my way there—a short walk as there were only two courtrooms—everyone I passed said hello. Of course, I knew none of them.

I was allowed to enter a small, green room that held only a table and two chairs. Eventually, Teddy was brought to the same room. The rattle of the sheriff's keys announced his arrival. Fortunately, Teddy said hello first because I might not have recognized him. Like my daughters, he'd grown in the two years since I'd seen him. (Imagine the calendar pages flipping.) He was no longer five-foot-two. Now, he was nearly six feet tall and thick, as if he'd been eating too many of the sweets his mother loved to bake. There was more than a trace of furtiveness in his expression and his ungainly walk. He wore the clothes of a criminal: torn blue jeans, a dirty t-shirt and black boots. His face was wet with perspiration. He seemed to be held together by a series of tattoos that covered his neck and arms, drawings of skeletons and birds afire. Worse, he smelled sweetly of marijuana.[204] Over the years, a gap had developed between his two front teeth.

"Hey, Mr. Ashe," he said. "How's it going?"

"Teddy," I said, nodding solemnly, then took the seat across from him. "You're still high on something, aren't you?"

He laughed and said, "Not as high as I was a few hours ago."

"Did you take the car?"

"What car?"

"The car."

"The Mustang?"

"Yes, Teddy."

"No, I didn't take it."

"Then why were you buying gasoline for it?"

"I was trying to be a Good Samaritan because I saw it there on the shoulder."

"How did you get all the way out to Chestertown if you didn't steal that car?"

"I hitchhiked." He was not a good storyteller. His eyes turned slightly toward the ceiling whenever he needed inspiration. (Shoogey's eyes never left yours.)

"And you were never in the Mustang?"

"Never."

"Then how did they find your fingerprints on the steering wheel?"

He looked toward the ceiling. "Someone must have the same fingerprints."

"That's the best you can come up with?"

"What?"

"Teddy," I said, "I have no idea if they found your fingerprints on the steering wheel. But they will, won't they?"

"They might."

"Stop lying to me, okay?"

"Okay."

"What happened?"

"I saw the car. I liked the car. I took the car."

"See, that was easy. Now, let's see what we can do to get you out of here."

I left Teddy in the holding cell, then walked down to the courtroom, greeted by everyone I passed. I was the only person in the courtroom. Outside, a bell pealed over and over. It was more than an hour before the judge entered and called to have Teddy brought into the courtroom. Teddy took a seat beside me at the defense table. The smell of marijuana lingered.

The judge was a black man named Wagner who seemed to be in his fifties.[205] He had a soft voice like that of a minister or high school counselor, and his gestures were spare, but expressive. He read the list of charges against Teddy, then asked how he pleaded.

"Not guilty, Your Honor," Teddy said.

The judge nodded. "Now, Mr. Ashe," Judge Wagner said. "I have to accept that plea, and I have to conduct a trial. Twelve of Chestertown's finest citizens are going to have to take time off work, maybe a day or two, maybe longer, and I'm going to have to spend just as long. Police officers will have to take time off work. Prosecutors will have to spend hours preparing. Now, before we waste all that time and all that money, can we see if we can work something out?"

"What do you have in mind?" I asked.

"How about this. If your client will enter a 'no contest plea' and agree to spend the next week in juvenile detention, I'll place him on probation for two years. Given his age, if he keeps his nose clean this will all be wiped off his record when he turns eighteen. Do we have a deal?"

I turned to Teddy.

"I don't want to go to juvenile detention for a week," he whispered.

"You have to, Teddy. If we try the case and you lose, they'll sentence you to a couple years."

"I don't know what to do," he said. "What's it like in juvenile detention?"

"I have no idea, Teddy," I said. Then I turned to the judge and said, "Your Honor, he'll plead 'no contest.'"

"Mr. Renko, is that correct?" Judge Wagner said.

"Yes, sir," Teddy said mildly.

"I believe you mean, 'Yes, Your Honor.'"

"Yes, Your Honor," Teddy said.

"Good choice," Judge Wagner said, "very good choice." But then he continued in that way that judges in small towns do, but those in large cities do not. "You've just saved the taxpayers some money," he said. "Now, Mr. Renko, I appreciate that a nice new car is tempting to a boy your age. I was your age once, too, and but for the grace of God I would've been standing in your shoes. I saw some beautiful cars when I was a boy, and it crossed my mind to take one for a ride. Crossed my mind more than a few times. But taking another man's property is wrong. It's just wrong, whether you believe in The Bible or not. But it is forgivable. I'll tell you what I don't find forgivable—dishonesty. You stood in my courtroom today and lied to me. When I asked whether you were guilty of this offense, you lied to me. Knowing full well you were guilty, you looked me at me with those big, sad puppy dog eyes and said you weren't. Well, save the puppy dog eyes for the girls, Mr. Renko. The truth is the most sacred thing we have. It is something to be cherished, not toyed with."

I thought he was finished, but he wasn't. Instead, Judge Wagner turned his attention to me.

"And you, Mr. Ashe," he said, his words rising like steam from soup to fill the little room. "You are not without blame, either. You knew he was guilty, and you let him stand there beside you and say, 'Not guilty.' I watched you. I had my eyes on you. When he said, 'Not guilty,' you didn't even flinch. This used to be a noble profession, Mr. Ashe. It comprised good and honest men and women who cherished the truth the same way you might cherish your family. They may have disagreed, but they held the truth in the highest regard. But today, you lied to me, too, or you might as well have. When the truth is lost, it should leave a hole in you, a hole that's not unlike losing a loved one. I know. I lost my wife last year to cancer. The feeling was similar. So I will ask you both a favor. Mr. Renko, in the next week, you must decide if the truth has value to you. I want you to return to this court and tell me. And tell me honestly. It will in no way affect your sentence. I just want to know for my own curiosity. Will you do that?"

"Yes," Teddy said. He tongued the gap between his teeth.

"And you, Mr. Ashe," the judge continued. "I hope you have not suffered the loss of a loved one. But do me a favor. On your drive back to the big city, think about how it would affect you if you were to lose one of them. Think hard. Imagine it. Because if it leaves you with a hole inside, then there is hope for you yet. When my wife...." He opened his mouth to say something more, but left the thought unfinished.

"I will do that, Your Honor," I said. Then the judge made a small tapping motion with a single finger to direct the bailiff to remove Teddy. I left the courtroom, too, heading in an altogether different direction. On my way down the hall and out of the courthouse, three people I did not know said goodbye to me. The smell of marijuana was attached to my clothes.

* * *

As I left the building, I thought of exactly what the judge had asked me to think of, which is why it's all the more surprising that I even noticed that one of my shoelaces had come undone. As often happens in stories both good and bad, something small like an untied shoelace will lead to some startling discovery.[206]

This is what happened here. I could have stopped on the court-house steps to re-tie it. I could have stopped on the sidewalk or any other of a dozen places, but I didn't. Instead, I set my briefcase down beneath a thick old oak tree and sat down upon it so the seat of my pants wouldn't get soiled. I re-tied my shoelace, then leaned back for a moment against the base of the tree, thinking about loss, thinking of the hole I would feel if I were to lose Angie or one of the girls.

It was only when I put my hand on the ground for leverage as I tried to rise that I felt a piece of metal. It was a small bronze plaque at the base of the tree. I do not know why I chose to read the plaque, but I did. The letters were brown and dull, but readable:

IN MEMORY OF WALTER SHOOGEY[207]
A GIFT FROM THE THEODORE ROOSEVELT HIGH SCHOOL

It was a short run to the library, and I did run. The soles of my shoes made a peculiar sound on the pavement like the keys of a slow typewriter. My tie flapped against my chest. A librarian (female, short, brown-haired, her pants as tight as sausage casings) directed me to the small, dusty microfilm room and showed me how to operate the (turn the handle like you're opening a safe) machine to go backwards through time. She was able to find the microfilm cannisters for *The Chestertown Chronicle* (no longer publishing, she told me.) I sat for hours in the gray light of the microfilm viewer, cranking the handle to skip past the lives of people I never knew and never would, making the weeks and months pass in reverse, December turning into November, November into October, watching people get married then engaged, watching babies be christened then born, watching the dead become ill. I saw stories about homes burning and dance recitals, town fairs, mayoral elections. Then, finally, I found it:

LOCAL TEEN FOUND SAFE, SOUND IN BIG CITY
By Henry T. Booth

Local teen Sammy Shoogey, missing since March after the death of his younger brother, has finally been located by private investigator Stanley Game. The boy was found in New York City, where he had been working as a dishwasher in a Cuban-Chinese restaurant.

"I can't tell you how happy we are to have our son back," said Elizabeth Shoogey of 475 Berkeley Drive.[208] "It was bad enough losing one son. Losing both would have been unbearable." Sammy has returned home and will resume his education at Theodore Roosevelt High School immediately.

I scrolled backwards quickly, from September to March, where I found the following:

LOCAL TEEN MISSING, PRESUMED TO HAVE RUN AWAY FROM HOME
By Henry T. Booth

Local teen Sammy Shoogey has been reported missing by his parents, Samuel J. Shoogey, Jr. and Elizabeth Shoogey of 475 Berkeley Drive. The boy, apparently distraught about the recent death of his younger brother, was last seen at approximately 11:00 p.m. Monday evening. He is presumed to have run away from home.

Local teen Sammy Shoogey, missing since March. Anyone having any information about the whereabouts of this boy (pictured below) should contact the police immediately.

The photograph of Shoogey that accompanied the article was of a young boy playing the accordion. He looked as sad and as graceless as any boy ever photographed while playing the accordion.

I turned the microfilm to the previous week's edition, but there was no mention of any of the Shoogeys, nor was there any mention the week before that. I continued to turn through week after week, and each time I was prepared to end my search, I convinced myself to look at one more edition, then one more after that.

It was not until I'd searched through six months of newspapers that I came across the following article:

HUNTING ACCIDENT CLAIMS LIFE OF LOCAL TEEN
By Henry T. Booth

An unfortunate accident early Saturday morning has claimed the life of local boy Walter Shoogey, age 13 (photograph below.) The boy, a sophomore at Theodore Roosevelt High School, was accidentally shot in the nose while hunting with his brother Sammy, a junior at the same school. The boy, known as Walt to friends and family, was pronounced dead at 9:17 a.m. by physicians at Eastern Christian Hospital. The boy's father, Samuel J. Shoogey, Jr., proprietor of Shoogey Glass Company, witnessed the accident and described the traumatic event to reporters: "The boys were chasing a rabbit. They were running ahead of me, about fifty yards or thereabouts. Sammy tripped over a branch or a twig, and his rifle discharged. It was a horrible accident. I feel as if it's all my fault."

Walter Shoogey will be remembered as a bright, articulate young boy. Victor Gregorson, high school principal, said, "He received some very good grades. He excelled in his English courses and expressed some interest in being a professional writer when he was older. He will be missed."

Services for Walter Shoogey will be held at Whitaker's Funeral Home on Wednesday at 10:00 a.m. Because of the nature of his fatal injuries, there will be a closed casket.

In the accompanying photograph, Walter Shoogey was holding an oversized check made out in the amount of ten dollars. In the lower left-hand corner of the check, someone had written, "First Robin Of Spring!"

The librarian (a different one, male, husky) directed me to a wall of books that included old telephone books and minutes of town hall meetings and yearbooks from Theodore Roosevelt High School. The yearbooks were called *Hullabaloo*. I found the yearbook for Shoogey's high school class. I flipped through the pages looking for pictures of Shoogey.

There were six pages dedicated to the football team, which finished its season with a record of eight wins and four losses, "including a glorious Thanksgiving Day victory over archrival Indian Hills by a score of 42 to 18." Shoogey was nowhere to be found in the team photographs.

The French Club offered "an opportunity to spend a few hours in a French environment. The conversation is strictly en français, et beau-coup des jeux et des chansons are played and sung!" No Shoogey.

There was a page dedicated to Smiles, "an organization which offers students the opportunity to work with young children at the Maryland Home for Children. Here, students gain not only valuable experience, but also a great deal of personal satisfaction." No Shoogey.

There were photographs of the Glee Club and the Student Senate. The basketball squad wore shiny gym shorts with belts. No Shoogey.

The Literary Society had a photograph. No Shoogey. There was a poem that mentioned persons named Dolores, and Rose, and Dody, and Godfrey, and "shy little Madeleine." No Shoogey.

There were photographs of girls and boys dancing at an event called the Winterlude. There were photographs of tug-of-wars. There were pictures everywhere of a couple lovingly referred to as "Our Rosie and Bob." I could find Shoogey nowhere.

Finally, near the back of the book, I came to the section called "Late Senior Portraits," with each graduate who had shown up late for his or her photograph listed and pictured alphabetically. There I found a black-and-white picture of Shoogey. White shirt, solid dark tie, solid dark suit, hair slicked back from his forehead. If you squinted, he looked the same as the man who lived down the street from me, except for the expression. His mouth was turned down at the corners, his eyes seemed focused on something distant and unattainable. He probably was looking at something behind the photographer when the photo-graph was snapped. A dog outside the window, a bird on a telephone wire. Whatever it was, you could tell he could not reach it.

I turned several pages ahead to see if there was a portrait of a student named Jimmy Birnberg. There was none. But, sure enough, there was a boy named Bobby Lombardi, the fat Italian in Shoogey's story; the farting, laughing, fat Italian whose life Shoogey would save. *Comet, it tastes like gasoline....*

I went to one of the telephone booths near the library entrance and found the name Robert Lombardi in the directory.

I telephoned, not knowing what to say. I introduced myself. "I'm Hamilton Ashe," I said, "from Baltimore. I'm a lawyer." I explained why I was calling, as briefly as I could. My words did not sound as foolish as I'd anticipated.

It was the same Bobby Lombardi who'd attended Theodore Roosevelt High School. He still lived and worked in Chestertown. He did not seem surprised to get my call.

"Yes," he said, "I remember Sam Shoogey. Terrible story."

"What was a terrible story?"

"About his brother."

"Yes," I said. "I just read about it."

"You're a little behind on your current events," he joked. "Anyway, I suppose you're calling me to find out whether he saved my life during the war?"

"Yes."

"I never fought in any war, Mr. Ashe. I was too far young to fight in World War II. I didn't fight in Korea. I didn't fight in Vietnam. Does that answer your question?"

"Yes, it does," I said. "You wouldn't happen to know who Jimmy Birnberg is, would you?"

Lombardi laughed. "You mean the man from our platoon? I had Shoogey write a check for five thousand dollars to Jimmy Birnberg, isn't that how the story goes?"

"Yes," I said excitedly.

"Well, I never heard of Jimmy Birnberg, and I never gave him a check for five thousand dollars. Heck, I never gave *anyone* a check for five thousand dollars."

"Jimmy Birnberg wasn't a classmate?"

"No."

We spoke briefly about Shoogey, but Lombardi did not have much to say about him. He went to school. He went home after school. He'd accidentally shot his brother in the nose.

Lombardi ended the conversation by saying, "Please give Shoogey my regards when you see him. It's okay if he tells his little story about me. I don't mind at all. It's nice just to be remembered sometimes, even if the memory isn't true."[209]

I forgave Shoogey for everything, including the death that will end this book. For everything he'd ever done and everything he ever would do. I drove home, and when I arrived I hugged my wife and I hugged our daughters, and I enjoyed the feel of their bones and the smell of their skin.

We ate dinner, we played basketball, we watched television, and when we finally went to bed, I told Angie what I'd discovered: Shoogey really had shot someone in the nose, but it hadn't been during the war; it had been his own brother. I told her about the hunting accident, and about how Shoogey ran away. I showed her the copies I'd made of the newspaper articles. I told her about the Cuban-Chinese restaurant where Shoogey had been found. I told her the last name of the private investigator who had found Shoogey: Game. The rest of the story he'd told us, the story you have read in Chapter One and hopefully have not forgotten, was populated with people he'd met over his life, people like Bobby Lombardi. That is how writers work, I presume. They collect little facts and little stories like trinkets stored in a cigar box. They remove the trinkets when they wish.

"And Jimmy Birnberg?" Angie asked.

"I don't know, probably an old friend."

Eventually, we turned out the lights. I put my hand on Angie's hip and shut my eyes. Of course, I kept picturing Shoogey. After a while, I realized that Angie wasn't sleeping either. She was crying. I don't know which I noticed first: the slight bounce of the mattress or the sounds that came from somewhere in her chest.

"Sweet Potato, are you okay?" I said. I moved to turn on the light, but she put a hand on my chest to stop me.

"Don't turn the light on," she said. "I'm fine."

"What is it?"

"It's Shoogey," she said. "I keep thinking about how horrible I've been to him. I didn't let him in our house: I made him wait on the porch when he came to see you. I pretend I don't see him when I drive past his house. I pretend I don't see him waving. Am I an awful person, Ham?"

"No, Sweet Potato, no."

"Am I terrible for saying I didn't want him in our house?"

"No, Sweet Potato. You didn't know what he'd been through. You had no idea of it."

Still, she kept crying.

"I can't believe how mean I've been to that man after all he went through. I'm ashamed of myself."

"Sweet Potato," I said, "don't say that. You're the best person I know," which was true. She is a good and honest woman. She is kind and thoughtful. She remembers everyone's birthday and bakes cookies for the girls to take to school. She could have done much better than me. And I fell asleep thinking how I would feel if I were to lose her.

* * *

Most of the next day at work I spent on the telephone, making odd calls to try to confirm portions of Shoogey's stories.

Did Shoogey serve in the Army? Did he ever go to war?

I am afraid, dear reader, kindly homicide detectives, that neither the Veterans Administration nor the Army itself has any records of a serviceman named Samuel J. Shoogey III. The only Shoogey who ever served in the United States military was Samuel J. Shoogey, Jr.— Shoogey's father—who, according to records, was in the Reserves and never left the continental United States in that role.

Did Shoogey ever fight King Gilmore? Again, no records. The associate editor of *Ring* magazine informed me that no records are maintained of King Gilmore's sparring partners. They couldn't call King Gilmore to check: he'd died years ago. His body had turned to fertilizer, his thoughts to pure blue air.

Did Shoogey play football at the University of Maryland? Well, dear reader, kindly homicide detectives, let me share my research on that issue. Both *The Sun*, published in Baltimore, and *The Washington Post* contained detailed reports of every football game ever played by the University of Maryland. I reviewed the microfilm of the game accounts for the ten-year period during which Shoogey conceivably played there. There is no mention of a Samuel J. Shoogey. Moreover, I scanned the team photographs for the same ten-year period; the famous number 84 was worn by a procession of young men, none of whom bore his name or likeness. Instead, the young men who wore the number were, in chronological order more or less: Arnie Gelfman, Sean Campbell, Andy Laria, Steve Dupree, Ben Johnson, Scott Johnson, Conor McGee and Sander Lebau.[210]

Did Shoogey even attend the University of Maryland?

I telephoned the alumni office in College Park, Maryland.

"I'm looking for the address of one of your alumni," I told the young lady who answered the telephone.

"Let's see if I can help you," she said pleasantly enough. "What's the name?"

"Shoogey."

Immediately and rather firmly she said, "We don't have any alumnus by that name."

"Don't you need to check? Isn't there a computer listing you need to check?"

"I don't need to check anything, sir. I get a phone call a month from some poor soul asking me to confirm that we had a student here named Shoogey. I've checked a dozen times, maybe more. No such person ever attended the University of Maryland."

"Samuel J. Shoogey, III?"

"Yes," she said, her voice taking on an unpleasant and mocking tone. "Samuel J. Shoogey III. 'Shoo.' 'Old number 84.' Football hero. Etcetera, etcetera, et-cet-er-ah. No such person ever attended the University of Maryland."

"Are you sure?"

"Did he sell you a bad insurance policy?"

"No."

"Are you trying to find out if he was fooling around with your wife?"

"No," I protested, "nothing like that. He's a friend."

"Oh," she said, before apologizing. There was a long silence. "Listen, let me ask you a question."

"What?"

"Do you want me to tell you he went to school here? Is that what you're looking for?"

I thought for a moment before answering. "Yes," I said.

"Okay," she said. Then she rattled some papers near the telephone and said, "Oh, yes, I found it. Here it is. We did have a student here named Samuel J. Shoogey III." She spoke in a slightly different, more girlish voice, the type of voice that would turn a man's head. "I remember him well. Everyone called him 'Shoo.' He played on the football team. 'Old number 84.' He was a star quarterback."

"Linebacker," I said.

"Linebacker," she repeated.

Chapter Twenty-Seven: Every Good Boy Deserves Fudge

The sun began to set, and from my office window I watched it, a perfect painter's sunset, all red and orange and gold, the type of sunset under which cowboys die in their lovers' arms. Then I turned my attention to the work I'd neglected all day in order to make my calls, working until nearly eleven o'clock, long after the cleaning staff had come and gone.

It was then, at that very moment, sitting at my desk as midnight approached, that I came to the sad realization that many men arrive at: I had friends I could number, but none I could count on. Only Sam Shoogey.

Soon, I found myself at his door, pressing my thumb against the doorbell. Although I could see a light on in the kitchen, there was no answer. I rang the bell again. When he finally answered, he was barely recognizable as Shoogey: he was a hundred years older than when I'd last seen him little more than two years before. His hair was long and gray and unruly, chaotic with crazy ringlets spiraling in every direction like springs that had popped through a worn bed. A red-and-black plaid bathrobe covered his pajama top, which was a shade of blue one might associate with anti-freeze. He wore no pajama bottoms, just boxer shorts, and a pair of puffy, light-blue slippers that crept up his ankles like a rain puddle. He'd put on weight, too. He had the beginnings of a second chin, and there was fat around his edges: his face, his neck, his fingers even. In his eyes there were tiny red lines, hundreds of them branching out like tree roots, and there were lines carved like riverbeds into the flesh around his eyes as well.

Shoogey grunted something, I couldn't decipher what, then, leaving the door open, he turned his back to me and walked into the living room, toward the sound of a television. He seemed oppressed by some disease like lassitude, unable to move his limbs freely, as if his bones had been soaked, then rusted. His walk was stiff-legged and unnatural, like a marionette. I entered, closing the door behind me and followed in his wake. Shoogey sat in an armchair in the center of the room, his eyes trained on the television. There were no bare spaces in the room. The floor and furniture were covered with pizza boxes and candy wrappers and newspapers.

I said Shoogey's name aloud in the tone one often uses when speaking to the elderly or the infirm. "Shoogey," I said. "Shoogey, it's me. It's Ham. It's Ham Ashe."

"I know who you are. I know very well who you are," he said in an un-Shoogey-like whisper with an un-Shoogey-like drawl. His elegant, precise tongue was nowhere to be found. Like a layer of shellac stripped away to reveal some cheap wood beneath, it was gone, and in its place was the voice of the Maryland shore, as thick as molasses, but not sweet. No, there was a touch of lemon to that accent.

I walked to the television set and switched it off.

"What's going on?" I said. "Is something wrong? Is something going on?"

"Nothing's wrong. Nothing's going on."

"Something's going on, Shoogey. Look at this place." I held my hands open in front of me, then let them fall apart as if measuring some distance. "Look."

Shoogey kept his eyes on the sleeping television set. His sorrow had grown big and beyond measuring, his features blurry like a postcard left out in the rain. After a while, he coughed, then said, "I just have a little ennui, that's all. A little malaise. That sounds like something you'd order at a French restaurant, doesn't it? 'Oh, garçon, I'll have the ennui, with a side order of malaise. And could I get a salad with that?'" He smiled weakly, a dim copy of his smile.

For want of a better idea, I took Shoogey by the hand and tugged him from his chair.

"What are you doing?"

"We've got to get you ready."

"For what? I've got nothing to get ready for. It's night."

Nevertheless, I pulled at Shoogey, moving him toward the bathroom little by little, then directed him to sit on the lid of the toilet seat, revealing his bald pink knees and varicose veins that zigzagged along his calves.

"What are you doing?" he said as I rooted through his medicine chest looking for a pair of scissors.

"Nothing."

"What are you doing?"

"Shut up, Shoogey," I said quietly.

When I found the scissors, I raked his hair with my fingers then began to snip away at the ends.

"You know, my friend," he said suddenly, "there are things for which we can never be forgiven. Some of us are beyond the realm of God's mercy, it's as simple as that. We're just beyond the realm. Do you know what that means? Are you familiar with the word 'realm'? I've done some terrible things, and for that I'm beyond the realm of God's mercy."

"We've all done terrible things, Shoogey. All of us. There isn't a person alive who hasn't."

"A baby hasn't."

"Other than babies."

"Or people who are mentally retarded."

"Or people who are mentally retarded."

His hair was filthy. It stuck together in clumps as if adhered by gum, and it left my fingers dark and oily.

"Would you like to hear a story?"

"I'd love to," I said sincerely.

"It's a terrible story. It's about when I was a boy. Did I ever tell you about a boy I knew when I was just a boy myself, a boy named Napoleon?"

I told him that he had.

"He was a good kid, I suppose. He wasn't popular, at least not with other children. He'd had the misfortune of being small, and he'd suffered the cruelty that only children can muster. Though he had a small frame, he had a large head which gave him the appearance of a retouched photograph, one person's head attached to another's body. It doesn't take much of an imagination to think of the names the other children called him. Dwarf. Midget. Fathead. Pumpkinhead. Napoleon."

"That's horrible."

"Yes. Anyway, there were other nicknames. Fetus. I think some kids said he looked like a Pez dispenser. Do you remember those, Pez dispensers? They had candy in them, and you tipped back the head, and a candy popped out of the neck.[211] In any event, he grew over the years, and by the time he'd reached high school, he was no longer the smallest boy in the class, but his role had already been defined. Children are like that. Adults, too.

"Well, one day after school I was walking past the boys' locker room. I'd stayed late, though I don't recall why, so there was hardly anyone in the building. As I passed the locker room, I heard shouts and whoops and laughs, and for some reason I decided to find out what had happened. I pushed the door open, and there were a couple of guys from the basketball team in there, kneeling on the ground like they were praying. Did you say you played basketball in high school?"

I told him I had.

"Well, I've never really been fond of basketball. All that running back and forth in shorts in the dead of winter. What's the point? In any event, I'll tell you who the boys were: their names were Bob Schoenfeld, Gary Vinton and Mark Wiper.[212] When I moved closer, I saw they weren't kneeling on the ground at all, and they certainly weren't praying: they were restraining a boy, Schoenfeld holding one arm, Vinton the other, Wiper the legs. Schoenfeld turned his head when I entered and said, 'We caught this little faggot in here spying on us.' Then he said to the boy, 'Did you get a good look at us, you little faggot?

Did you get a little thrill?'

"The boy started to answer, but Schoenfeld slapped him across the face to quiet him. 'Little homo was trying to get a peek at our cocks, Sam.' You'll have to pardon my language, my friend, but the story loses something in the translation if I try to tone it down. Do you mind?"

I shook my head and continued clipping his hair.

"I moved closer, and the boy tried to speak again, but Vinton yelled at him, 'Shut up! Shut the *fuck* up!' The boy lifted his head. As you probably guessed, it was Napoleon. I only saw his eyes, but I knew in that moment that it was him. He looked up at me and said, 'Sam, please.'

"'Sam, please *what*?' Vinton said in a singsong voice. Do you know what I mean by saying he had a singsong voice? I mean it was like a mother speaking to an infant. 'Sam, please let me suck your giant pecker. Is that what you were going to say?' Schoenfeld and Wiper laughed, and their laughter encouraged Vinton. 'Say it,' he demanded, and he put a hand on the boy's throat. 'Say, "Oh, Sam, please let me suck your giant pecker."' The boy shook his head, but Vinton squeezed his throat and said, 'Say it! Say it!' until the boy finally did. 'Not good enough,' Vinton said. 'Say it again, with feeling.' Napoleon repeated it, more loudly this time, and Vinton, Schoenfeld and Wiper all laughed their horrid laughs. I thought that would be it, but it wasn't. Vinton said, 'Come on, Sam,' and gestured with his head for me to join them. When I hesitated, he flicked his head violently and shouted, 'Get the fuck over here and help!' He just looked at me with his desolate pirate stare, and I felt myself walking toward them, as if I had no will of my own. I took the boy's arm, replacing Vinton, who sat on the boy's stomach. With his thumb and middle finger, he flicked the boy's face over and over again leaving red marks like mosquito bites. He said, 'Say, "I'm a big homo."' The boy looked at me, and when he saw I wasn't going to help him, he said, 'I'm a big homo.' 'Say, "I like my father to fuck me up the ass." Say it!' Napoleon inhaled, and a wet sound came from his nose, and he said it. 'Say, "I like to give my teachers blow jobs."' Napoleon said it. Vinton laughed, then said, 'What's your name, faggot?' He wouldn't answer, so Vinton looked at each of us and said, 'What's this kid's name?' Schoenfeld and Wiper didn't know it, and I didn't know his given name, I only knew his nickname, so I told Vinton it was Napoleon. 'Napoleon. Napoleon. Couldn't your parents give you a normal name like Bob or Pete instead of a homo name like Napoleon?' Vinton turned to Schoenfeld with a look on his face like he had a brilliant idea, and he said, 'What was that thing we learned about Napoleon?' Schoenfeld just looked at him blankly, and Vinton looked at me and said, 'What was that sentence they taught us about Napoleon?' 'Able was I ere I saw Elba,' I said.[213] You know, the palindrome: Able was I ere I saw Elba. Vinton repeated it slowly, then he stared down at the boy and said, 'Say it!' The boy did, then Vinton said, 'Good boy. Now say it *backwards*,' and he started to laugh hysterically, then turned violent again and squeezed the boy's throat and said, 'Say it, you little faggot.' The boy said it, 'Able was I ere I saw Elba,' and Vinton said, 'Good boy, very good boy. And a good boy deserves a treat. Every good boy deserves fudge, only that's not what you'll get. We'll give you something you really love.' With that, Vinton stood over the boy and lowered his shorts and athletic supporter, then knelt over the boy's head. Imagine Napoleon, if you will. Imagine him, already cheated by biology, finding himself surrounded by stinking, urgent, raucous boys. You can guess what happened. Imagine the hot tears he cried. For the next several minutes I continued to hold his wrists to the floor."

It was a horrible story. Was it true?

"I'm ashamed of what I did," he said. Indeed, he was a picture of contrition: the grave frown, the lowered eyes, his bathroom as confessional. Perhaps the story was true. We all tell stories where we are victims, to gain sympathy, but who tells stories where he's the aggressor? Who tells stories where he is compelled to hurt his own brother? Who? No one, unless those stories are true.

"We all do terrible things," I said.

"Not babies."

"Not babies."

"And not mentally retarded people."

"And not mentally retarded people."

I'd long since finished snipping Shoogey's hair, and while it wasn't as neat as a barber's cut, it looked fine. There was a semi-circle of flesh over each ear and a ruler-straight part along the left side. I scooped up the clippings from the floor and washed them down the sink, then found a can of shaving cream on the counter.

"You see what I mean," he said. "I did something horrible, and now I'm beyond the realm of God's mercy. It doesn't matter anymore what I do."

I lathered Shoogey's face, rubbing the cream into his stubbly cheeks and jaw and neck, then began to shave it with the cleanest razor I could find in his medicine cabinet. Shoogey stared at my forehead all the while, as if there were a bug there sitting perfectly still, asleep. A trickle of blood appeared above Shoogey's lip. I dabbed at it with a square of toilet paper, then resumed shaving. The blood ran heavier though, and darker, the color of a rose in high spring, but Shoogey remained silent. I pressed another square of toilet paper firmly against his lip to stanch the bleeding, feeling his teeth sliding beneath my fingertips. After several minutes, I removed the paper, which looked like a tiny Japanese flag: white with a circle of red. I wiped the traces of shaving cream from Shoogey's face with a wash cloth, and he leaned forward as if to whisper a secret, but he told me nothing. Instead, he considered me with his old, red eyes. Then he leaned forward again, so close that I could smell his breath. And what did his breath smell of? It smelled of summer peaches.

"There's more," he said hoarsely. "It's very sad what happened to Napoleon," he said hoarsely. "Very sad."

"What happened?" I said.

"Well, in those days, the army used to put people in platoons based on where they were from. One platoon would have a lot of boys from Alabama. Another would have a lot of boys from New York. Napoleon and I ended up in the same platoon, if you can believe it. We didn't talk much. In fact, we didn't talk at all. Not that you can blame him. Anyway, one night he wandered off and got lost. He ended up getting killed. His body turned to fertilizer, his thoughts to pure blue air. He got killed in the most painful way imaginable. Do you know what that is?"

I said, "No."

"He was shot. And do you know where he was shot?"

"No."

And that's when Shoogey said, "He was shot in the nose."

That was as close as Shoogey ever came to telling me about what happened to his brother.

* * *

As Shoogey showered, I called Angie to tell her where I was; it was late, but she was still awake and, I suspect, sitting near the phone. I went through Shoogey's dresser and returned with clean clothes—underwear, pajamas, slippers—which I left in a neat pile outside the bathroom door. I returned to his living room and tried to tidy it up some, putting the magazines and newspapers in knee-high stacks, stuffing the pizza boxes and candy wrappers into the paper grocery bags I found beneath his kitchen sink, wedged against the pipes.

Beneath one of the pizza boxes, I discovered a small notepad lying face-down. Turning it over, I read: *Poor Napoleon*. The cover was worn and curling at the corners like an old photograph. On the cover, along with the title, were doodles, endless triangles inside of triangles and names here and there. The sound of the shower water running continued, and with no small amount of guilt, I opened the notepad. The first page read:

POOR NAPOLEON
Based on a true story
By Samuel J. Shoogey III

On the next page, written with expertise and precision in straight lines:

Oranges
Milk
Ground beef
Cookies
Butter (or margarine)
Ice cream (on sale—coupon!)
Bread
Juice (on sale)
The next page:
Lunch meat
Cheese
Peaches
Peas
Ice cream
Cookies
Lettuce
Tomatoes
Cereal (coupon!)

And so on and so on and so on, page after page. I closed the notepad and covered it with the pizza box, then listened to the sound of the shower as it thumped against my friend's skin.

* * *

That night, after I helped Shoogey into his bed, I slept on his couch, wrapped in an old blanket, using a seat cushion as a pillow. When I awoke in the morning, stiff and sweating, I telephoned home and waited for someone to answer. Two rings, three rings, four, five, six. Finally, I heard the click of the receiver as it was lifted from the hook, then the sound of it bouncing off the kitchen tiles, followed by one of my daughters laughing.

"Sorry," she said, laughing. "Ashe residence."

"Claire, is that you?"

"Mm hmm. Is that you, Dad?"

"Yes. Claire, what just happened?"

"I had butter on my hands from my bread," she explained, "and when I went to get the phone—ka-bam! Where are you?"

"I'm working, honey."

"Pants on fire."

"What?"

"You know—liar, liar, pants on fire," she said, then she swallowed something. "I know you're not at work. Are you and Mom are having a fight?"

"I *am* working," I said, hoping to sound sincere. "I'm working trying to help a friend. Your mother and I aren't having a fight."

"Whatever you say. I just—" The phone bounced off the floor again, cracking in my ear. Angie shouted Claire's name in the distance.

"Sorry," Claire said. "It's the stinking butter."

"Well, be more careful."

"I will. Dad, I have to finish eating so I can get ready for school. Do you want to talk to Katie or Mom?"

"Put Katie on first, Noodle."

"She's right here, doing her *home*work at the *break*fast table."

"You're such a bigmouth," I heard Katie say. "Why don't you just try to get me in trouble." Then, into the receiver, Katie said, "Hi, Dad. I wasn't doing my homework. I was just proofreading it. That's different than doing it."

"That's okay, sweetie. I just wanted to say hi before you went to school."

"Well, hi," Katie said.

"Did you do all of your homework, or just some of it?"

"All."

"Really?"

"Yes."

"*Really?*"

"I swear on my mother's grave."

"Your mother doesn't have a grave."

"Then I swear on some dead person's grave."

"Okay, then."

"Dad, I really have to go."

"Okay. Is your mother there?"

"Yup."

"Can you put her on the phone?"

"'Can I' or 'may I'? There's a difference. When you say 'can you do something', you're asking if the person *can* do it. But if you say 'may', you mean *will* you do it."

"Thank you for clearing that up for me, sweetie. *Will* you put your mother on the phone?"

I heard Katie wrap her hand over the mouthpiece of the telephone.

"Is he okay?" Angie said when she picked up the phone.

"I have no idea. I'm going to stay with him for a couple nights if it's okay with you."

"Of course it is," she said. I heard her as she turned her head to say goodbye to the girls, then I heard the front door close. "Ham, what can I do? Can I come over and clean up or cook or something?"

"I don't think you need to do that."

"Please," she said. "Please let me do something. I need to do something for that man."

Angie sat with Shoogey during the day. She cleaned his house, she washed his clothes, she put fresh linens on his bed, she cooked him soup for lunch.

That night, after work, I moved in with Shoogey; I moved some of my clothes into his daughter's bedroom. After I finished unpacking, I took Shoogey to dinner at a little cafe called Louie's, where we ate hamburgers and salads and drank scotch while a pale, thin-boned woman plunked away at a piano.[214]

We did not talk much, but there was a certain pleasure in just sitting across the table from Shoogey again, in watching him chew and swallow, in listening to the cadence of his voice, even if it was only to order another drink. Afterward, we returned to his home. Shoogey went to bed, and I watched television, I read, I rearranged the furniture to conceal the stains and holes in the carpeting, then I went to bed myself, sleeping on stiff new sheets, fresh out of the package. The room was filled with dolls and stuffed animals, and smelled of powder. That first night, as I lay in his daughter's slender bed, I could smell Jane Shoogey cooking dinner. I could hear their children learning the piano. I could see Shoogey and Jane coupling and quarreling, Jane filling the tub, a party, the television, a baby crying, a dog yelping at the door, someone slipping on wet tile. And this abundance of pasts had an oppressively sad effect.

Sometime in the night, I was awakened from a dream by the sound of a voice. It seemed to be in the same room, as if someone had snuck in to share a secret with me, and my heart beat hysterically for a moment—a burglar?—until I recognized it as Shoogey's voice coming from the room next door, seeping through the wall and curling around my bed.

"It's not too late."

There was a pause.

"It's only two-fifteen. It's only eleven-fifteen in California."

Pause.

"I know you don't live in California. I was trying to be clever."

Pause.

"I know it wasn't clever."

Pause.

"Jane, sweetheart, listen to me."

I tried to block out Shoogey's voice, first with other thoughts, then with my pillow, but I couldn't.

"If I could just kiss you," he pleaded.

Pause.

"Please, Jane."

Pause.

"Of course I know what love is."

Pause.

"Jane."

Pause.

"Jane? Jane?"

It was hours before I was able to fall asleep, and when I did my sleep was a restless one that produced a horrible dream. In the dream, I was driving a car. I pulled the car in front of our house, honked the horn, and waited. I honked again, and, finally, the girls shuffled out the front door then walked mournfully toward the car. Katie crawled into the front seat, Claire the back. They mumbled hellos.

"Cheer up," I said, "we're going to have some fun."

The girls said nothing.

I pulled the car into the street. "Okay, what do you want to do today? Anything you want to do, we'll do."

"I'd like to smack you in the head," Claire said.

"Claire."

"Well, you said we could do whatever we felt like. Didn't he, Katie? Isn't that what he said?"

"That's exactly what you said," Katie said to me.

"Nobody's going to smack anybody," I said. I pulled the car onto a main street. "Have you eaten yet? We could stop and get McDonald's."[215]

"We've already eaten," Katie said.

I tried to make conversation. "Claire, honey, how was school this week?"

"Mind your business."

"Yeah," Katie said, "mind your business."

"But you are my business."

"We're Mom's business. God knows what your business is."

"You're my business, sweetheart. Both of you are. Your mother and I are having problems now, but we both still love you."[216]

"Oh, sing me another song, why don't you."

"What?"

The girls laughed. "Sing me another song," they said in unison, in a way that suggested that was some new expression around school.

"What does that mean?"

"Wouldn't you like to know."

"Honey, that's no way to talk to your father."

"Good," Katie said.

"Besides," Claire said, "how can we even be sure that you *are* our father. Maybe we were adopted."

"Did you have sex with your girlfriend last night?" Katie said.

"Katie. That's no way for a young girl to talk."

"I know you and your girlfriend had sex."

"Katie. Now let's be nice."

"Why don't you be nice?"

"I am being nice. I came to pick you up, didn't I?"

"You're not nice."

"Fine," I said. "What can I do to be nice?"

"Cut your fat head off," Claire said, and Katie laughed and said, "Yeah, cut your head off."

"Honey, don't say something like that to your father."

"You're not our father. You know who you are—you're the devil. You have the devil in your body."

"I'm the devil?"

"You're Hitler."

"Honey, I'm not Hitler. Hitler was a short, evil man with a mustache. Look. Look. See, I don't have a mustache."

"You're Hitler."

"Honey, do you know who Hitler is?"

"He killed a thousand Jews," Claire said.[217]

"That's who you are," Katie said. "You're Hitler, and your friends are the devil and the man who killed John Kennedy and John Wilkes Booth and all the evil men."

I rubbed my nose.

"I hate it when you do that," Claire said. "Picking your nose."

"Sweetheart," I said, "I rubbed my nose. I didn't pick it."

"Liar," Katie said. "Why don't you go have sex with your girlfriend, you liar."

Claire slapped her palm against the window.

"Claire."

"What?"

"Stop that this instant."

She slapped the window three more times: *wap, wap, wap.*

I pulled the car into a parking lot and turned it around.

"Where are we going now?" Katie asked.

"I'm taking you home."

"Good," Katie said. "That's exactly what we wanted you to do."

I returned to the house, and the girls stepped out of the car, slamming their doors closed. They walked up to the porch, and the front door opened for them. Only it wasn't Angie opening the door; it was Jane Shoogey.[218]

Chapter Twenty-Eight: Poor Napoleon

Weeks and weeks passed, and the solstice grew near. Another Saturday came, and I awoke in my own bed, next to Angie; I had stayed with Shoogey for about a month, and he seemed much better for it. It had not been an unpleasant month, not at all. In fact, I will remember it fondly. Shoogey and I had gone to dinner and to the movies, and occasionally Angie and the girls had walked over to cook dinner for us and to listen to Shoogey's stories. He had more stories than I'd ever suspected, and I'd suspected he'd have plenty. He had stories about celebrities, and stories about animals, and stories about people we'd never known but wished we had. They could fill many, many books.

Shoogey had not seemed sad when I left. I imagine he knew I'd seen his notebook—he hid it after my first night there, and I would never see it again—but I believe he appreciated that I held my tongue.[219]

My departure must have come as some amount of relief to him.

The morning sun was clement and pure, and, though the dogs days approached, the air had yet to grow heavy. It remained fresh and fragrant, as if dozens of young women had just wandered past, laughing, their arms bare. Angie and I took the girls to their ballet class. We watched them dance, walking on tiptoe as if barefoot on an August blacktop. We watched them spin and catch and nearly float. My daughters' faces were sweet blank slates, and for a moment I looked at them as if they were someone else's children, only to feel deep within me how much they were my own. I looked at Angie to smile at her. She was biting her lip.[220]

Afterward, we stopped at the library, then returned home. We had lunch, then I took the girls out into the backyard.

I breathed in the clean air as the girls and I worked on our hole to China, digging another three or four inches; we were miles behind schedule. The girls were wearing jeans and sweatshirts and their hair had grown: it hung straight down from the red berets that all the girls were wearing that year.

"We've done enough for one day," I told them, setting down my shovel, then led the way to the garage, where I retrieved the basketball and rolled it toward Claire. Katie went inside to help Angie cook. Claire snaked her arms behind her as if she didn't know what to do with them, then squatted to pull the basketball to her chest. She pushed it back toward me, and I rolled it back. She stopped it with her feet this time and kicked it solidly to me. We continued in this pattern for several minutes, no one talking, the bounce of the ball taking on a pleasant monotony. A small blue car drove past with its windows open, the sound of rock music seeping out. The high sun was captured in its windshield. Though it was proceeding with some speed, the car seemed to move slowly, with that eerie inertia that inhabits events that somehow we know are being transformed into memories in the very moments that they occur.

I held the basketball against my hip and swiveled to watch the car pass one house, then another, the driver twisting his head left, then right, ducking like an old man without his bifocals. In the distance, I saw Shoogey on all fours in his yard. His lawn had just been mowed by one of the boys in the neighborhood, leaving pale and dark ribbons of green, and Shoogey was plucking weeds from the flowerbed with his bare hands and dropping them into a plastic trash bag.

"Dad," Claire called. "The *ball!*"

The car passed two more houses, and Shoogey pulled himself to his feet to look as it stopped in front of his yard. He put a hand to his forehead to peer into the car. The driver's door opened, and a man emerged, dressed in a red-white-and-blue striped polo shirt and faded blue jeans. The car engine was still running and the music still playing.

As the man walked toward Shoogey, I saw that he was holding something in one hand. When I realized what he was holding—a wooden baseball bat—I knew who it was: it was Jimmy Birnberg.

I don't remember dropping the basketball to the ground, but I'm sure that I did as I started running toward Shoogey. I moved as quickly as I could, which I'm afraid was not quickly at all. The man was shouting something, but his words were lost in the distance and what remained was buried by the music. A guitar, a bass, an electric piano, drums, a man singing plaintively about love. Jimmy Birnberg's first swing of the bat struck Shoogey on the left arm, where the bones meet at the elbow. It didn't knock him down, though: Shoogey staggered backward several feet, clutching the spot where he'd been hit. The music grew louder, and I yelled something—"Stop!" or Shoogey's name perhaps or maybe just some long vowel that belonged to no word, but to my heart—but whatever it was I yelled, it had no effect. The next blow caught Shoogey full on the side of the head, right on the ear. He seemed to languish for a moment, then descend, toppling piece by piece like a dynamited building collapsing, then landing on his shoulder in the flowerbed.

Birnberg stood over Shoogey now, straddling him, and with quick flicks of his wrists he rapped the bat solidly against Shoogey's face and neck and chest—boom, boom, boom, boom. Like a beaten prizefighter, Shoogey tried to protect himself with his forearms, but the blows were too quick and everywhere.

"Is this the mouth you kissed her with?" Birnberg yelled, and he brought the bat down against Shoogey's lips.

"Is this what you used to screw her?" he said as he smashed the heel of the bat against Shoogey's groin.

"I don't remember her," Shoogey said. "I don't."

"Like hell you don't."

Just as Birnberg drew the bat back again, I dove on top of Shoogey and tried to cover him. The bat cracked against my wrist, and I heard the bone snap but felt nothing.

A mixture of vomit and blood dripped from Shoogey's lips, and I held his head. The soil beneath us was growing muddier than mud.

"I really don't remember her," he said, and he said this not defensively, but regretfully, as if he'd forgotten a wonderful dream upon waking, recalling only that it had been wonderful.

Birnberg pushed the round, fat end of the bat against my ribs as if he were trying to wake a drunk.

"Get off him," he said. "He was screwing my wife. He deserves this."

He grabbed me by my broken arm and tried to pull me off Shoogey. I felt very heavy, though, and he couldn't move me. I smelled petunias and marigolds and the peach of Shoogey's skin. Somewhere in the background, over the sound of the music, I heard Claire screaming for her mother.

"Stay back, Noodle," I yelled. "Stay back."

"Mom," she yelled as she grew nearer.

"Noodle, stay back!"

"Get the hell off him," Birnberg said. "He was screwing my wife, the son of a bitch."

"You're wrong," I said.

"Don't tell me I'm wrong. My wife told me his name. I've got hotel receipts. Now get off him."

Birnberg raised the bat over his head, the sun behind him. I could see my daughter approaching. She was too close, but there was nothing I could do. But before Birnberg could swing the bat again, I heard a sound like the clapping of hands and watched him fall to the ground beside me. Then I saw Braverman sitting on Jimmy Birnberg, bringing his fists down upon Birnberg's chest so harshly that the blows sounded like drumbeats.

"He was screwing my wife," Birnberg shouted. "You don't understand. He was screwing my wife for *years*."

"I don't give a damn," Braverman said, "you almost hit that little girl." Claire was standing no more than five feet away, safe, scared. She began crying when she saw the mess Birnberg had made of me and

Shoogey. When Braverman saw us, his punches became even more powerful. I would have feared for Birnberg's life if I weren't already busy fearing for Shoogey's. The moisture that soaked my shirt was not water.

* * *

Braverman drove. My arm was in a cast, the cast was in a sling. It was too difficult for me to maneuver the steering wheel in that condition.

Braverman parked his car on the street, and we walked several short blocks toward the hospital. A group of young women stepped off a bus and onto the sidewalk beside us, so close that I could have reached out and touched them, one and all. They wore sleeveless dresses, their hair pulled back off their faces.

Once inside, Braverman began to cough the profane, hacking cough of an old man. We wound our way through the corridors. When we found Shoogey's room, he was dressed in just his boxer shorts. No hospital gown, no robe. He was facing north, looking out the window of his room onto the street below, taking it all in with a seriousness that I could feel. There were bluish bruises over his chest and face. His ear was bandaged, his arms, too. There were exposed stitches along his hairline and under one eye. He nodded a hello to us, and we stood beside his chair at the window. Below, there was a group of boys in jean jackets, sitting on a stoop and on the car parked beside. One of the boys was thumping his fingers against the car's roof. A young couple walked along the sidewalk, then into the liquor store.

Shoogey tried to lower his arms, but he couldn't. There were intravenous hook-ups in each of them: tubes in his forearms, a thick bracelet of white tape about each wrist, holding them in place. He'd let himself forget that they were there, on either side of him so that his arms were fully extended to his sides. When he'd moved his arms to welcome us, the poles tipped.

Outside, the group of boys in jean jackets swelled. There were six at first, now there were thirteen or fourteen. Two of them weren't wearing jean jackets, they were wearing leather instead. The group seemed to have a single life. It moved as one, and slowly.

A woman stepped out of an apartment building. She held out her hands, palms up, looked at the sky, then returned to the building.

Shoogey looked at the sky. It was clear. It was gray.

Another woman was walking a dog. The dog stopped by the group of boys, and some of the boys surrounded it. Shoogey touched the glass of the window, the IV poles clanking when he did, but he saw that the boys were crouching to pet the dog. The woman tipped her head back, laughing.

The phone rang, but Shoogey didn't answer it. It would be too much trouble to move the IV poles.

"Do you want me to get it?"

Shoogey's eyes said no.

Several minutes later, the phone rang again. Fourteen rings, and one of the nurses opened the door and peeked in.

"Mr. Shoogey," she said, "the *phone*."

Six rings.

It was his wife. Or, to be more precise, his ex-wife. That's what Shoogey must have been thinking. It's what I thought, too.

What could she possibly say? "Oh, Sam, I was afraid that I'd lost you forever."

The boys on the stoop left, vanished, and a woman walked along the sidewalk, holding an umbrella over her head. It wasn't raining, and the sky was still clear.

The sound of someone moaning, either in pain or hopelessness, entered the room. Shoogey moved carefully from his spot by the window, using the two IV poles like ski poles to right himself. He found his balance and, with the back of his leg, pushed a chair toward the bed so he had room to slide the IV pole through. He wheeled the poles across to the center of the room, both arms extended still, connected to the poles by strings of clear plastic tubes. He stood there in his navy blue boxer shorts and breathed, nothing else.

Did he want to lie down?

Did he want us to leave?

There was a knock on the door, and Shoogey answered, "Come in." It was the first time he'd opened his mouth since we'd arrived; there was a black hole where his teeth should have been.

The door swung open, and a young woman entered, carrying a brown paper bag. She was a thin woman, but with a round face despite her thinness. Her black hair hung like a canopy over her nose. She was attractive, with the athletic good looks of a tomboy who had outgrown that stage. She wore a silver cross on a silver chain: the cross dangled in her cleavage.

Shoogey didn't say anything. He straightened his back.

"Oh, my God," she said. She brought her hand to her mouth. "I just heard. I didn't know it was this bad."

She approached him and, taking a moment to calculate how to best accomplish her goal, hooked one arm around his neck and the other around his waist and hugged him loosely. She stepped back to see if she'd done any damage. She reached out and touched the stitches under his eye with a single fingertip, then pulled it away as if it were hot.

Shoogey spoke through lips that were only barely parted. "How are you, honey?"

"*Me?* Good God, I'm fine. It's *you* that I'm worried about. I should be the one asking how *you* are?"

"Well," he said, looking at his bare, blue chest, "I've seen better days. I don't know if I've seen worse, but I can certainly say that I've seen better." He looked up at her. "I'm sorry I'm not dressed. I thought you were one of the nurses."

"Don't apologize, Dad. I've seen men before. I used to work in a store."

She set the bag down on the bed by his pillow, then sat on the edge of the bed.

"I hope I'm not interrupting anything," she said, nodding toward me and Braverman. "Hello, Mr. Braverman. Hello—"

I introduced myself.

"Oh," she said, "you're the lawyer. I'm Susannah. It's nice to meet you. I just had to come the second I heard about it. I mean, there I was on the bus this morning, and someone said something about a writer getting mugged—"

"I wasn't mugged, honey."

"Well, someone *said* that, so I asked who. Of course, it was rude to be eavesdropping like that, but it's okay if you're doing it out of concern. But I can't tell you how shocked I was when they said it was *you*. I said to them, 'Sam Shoogey? You must be wrong. He's my father.'"

"It's me all right. But, like I said, I wasn't mugged."

She put her hands flat against the bed, as if steadying herself. "When did it happen?"

"Saturday."

"Are you going to be okay?"

"I think so. They've just run tests so far, so I won't know for a while."

"Good. That's good." She started to rise from the bed. "Listen," she said, "I brought a few things for you. Nothing special. I stopped off in the gift shop and got you some cologne. It's that new Calvin Klein cologne. I hope you like it. The girl let me try some out on my wrist, and I thought it smelled very pleasant. It's in the bag. And there's a picture of me in there. It's the most recent one I have."

Shoogey bobbed his head.

"There's also a note in there from me. Don't read it until I'm gone. It's nothing special really, just a thank you for all you've done for me, but I'd be embarrassed if you read it now. It's just about how I remember you taking me to see *Snow White and the Seven Dwarfs* and *Seven Brides for Seven Brothers*. Silly stuff like that."

"I understand," Shoogey said. "I'll wait until you're out of the building before I read it."

Then the four of us sat in silence for nearly an hour.

"Well, I should go," Shoogey's daughter finally said. "I know you need your rest, and you have company and all. But I'll call later. I promise."

Shoogey nodded again.

"If there's anything I can do for you, just let me know," she said. "Anything at all."

She was almost at the door, and he told her, "No, there's nothing."

She wasn't gone more than five seconds before Braverman said, "Listen, Shoogey, we probably should shove off, too, and let you get your rest."

His mouth shut, Shoogey muttered a thank you, and looked at me blankly. As he stood in front of us, all black and blue and bandaged, I thought, *Let me see your teeth. Let me see your teeth.* I said it over and over in my mind, as if by thinking it I could will him to part his lips and smile. But he didn't.

Braverman and I left the room, and we watched Shoogey's daughter walk down the long, white-tiled corridor and disappear around a corner. I struggled to adjust my sling until Braverman gave it a helpful tug.

I jerked my head toward where Shoogey's daughter had been moments before.

"I'd never met Shoogey's daughter before."

"That was her. She's a good egg."

"I know. It's just that it never really hit me that she actually existed until I saw her in the flesh."

We were still standing outside the door for five minutes, perhaps more, when a man rounded the same corner around which Shoogey's daughter had just disappeared.

"He has a son, too," Braverman said, and he waved to the man. The man waved back, then shook Braverman's hand forcefully when he arrived.

Shoogey's son had the look and demeanor of a man who had done a great deal of work with his hands. His skin was rough and tanned and clung to the bones like chicken meat. His reddish hair was pushed back off his forehead, revealing a small, poorly stitched scar just beneath the hairline. He was, as all this spoke, a man who believed in his own sense of decency. And, like his sister, he wore a silver cross around his neck: Shoogey was a Christian. He wasn't a Jew.

Braverman introduced me to Shoogey's son.

"Yes, yes, I understand you're a friend of my father," Rudolph Shoogey said to me.

"Yes, that's right."

"I understand you know my mother, too." He was not smiling.

"Yes," I said. "That's true."

"Well, let's not talk about that. I understand that you're the one who rode in the ambulance that brought my father here, you and Syd." He tipped his head toward Braverman. "That was awfully nice of you to do that, to look after him."

"It was nothing," Braverman said.

"Don't be so modest. You know, my father's always been the kind of person who's needed someone to look after him. It used to be my mother, but I think she just got tired out. I try to send him a check every month so he'll have some things. And he still has some of the money my grandfather left him when he died, at least I hope so. But as to other matters, well, you've got to let people lead their own lives. Like Doris Day said, *que sera, sera*."[221]

Braverman nodded knowingly, and I heard myself say, "That's very true."

"You know," Shoogey's son continued, "we don't see him very much anymore. We only live a few hours away up in New Jersey, but, well, the time we do share I suppose we should be thankful for." He paused, sniffed, adjusted his stance. "Well, I ought to get in there and see how the old boy's holding up. I wanted to thank you gentlemen again," he said, extending his hand first to Braverman, then to me. When he noticed the cast covering my wrist, he squeezed my arm instead, above the elbow.

"You're good friends," he said. "You've been good friends to my father. God bless."

Braverman and I buttoned our jackets and began to walk away, but not before we heard Rudolph open the door to the hospital room and greet his father. He did not call him "Dad" or "Father" or "Sir" even. He did not call him "Pop" or "Pa" or "Old Man" or any other nicknames sons often have for their fathers, like I had for mine. Instead, I heard him call his father "Napoleon." He said, "How's it going there, Napoleon?"

As Braverman and I walked toward his car, the delicate flap of his ears our only communication, I was struck by the realization that perhaps I now knew Shoogey as well as I ever would, which is to say that I did not know him at all. The lives of anyone and everyone we will ever meet are essentially unknowable. All we can ever know about them are the stories they tell us, and if those stories aren't true, what then? What then?

I couldn't help but smile at this thought, and I was reminded of something Shoogey himself had once said over dinner, or on one of our jaunts to the movies or some bar here or there.

"The world would be funny if it weren't so sad," he'd said.

"Or the world would be sad if it weren't so funny."

I don't recall which, exactly.

But I believe it to be true.

Chapter Twenty-Nine: Guilt

[DELETED]

Chapter Thirty: Agile Monsters

Everyone has a story. Everyone has horrible little stories about cruelties and betrayals and injustices that were suffered. I do. Angie does.[222]

And so do you and you and you and you.

Here's a story.

Harry Addler had a story. Harry Addler, the security guard in the building that housed Morrisey & DeWitt's offices.

The Saturday after I had visited Shoogey in the hospital, I bumped into Harry Addler at the library.

"Mr. Ashe," he said when he saw me, and he extended his hand for me to shake. My wrist in a cast, I had to take his right hand in my left.

"Sorry about that," he said.

"It's okay, Harry," I said. "It's good to see you," and it was. He had always been pleasant to me, and I enjoyed seeing him as much as anyone. "Please don't call me Mr. Ashe though. It's Ham."

"Thank you," he smiled, "but it'd be better if I called you Mr. Ashe. If my supervisor ever heard me calling one of the tenants by his first name, I'd be out of a job faster than you can say 'Jackie Robinson.'"

"That doesn't seem right," I said, "but you do whatever you feel is right."

Harry was dressed in a short-sleeved shirt and blue jeans. It was the first time I'd ever seen him wear anything but his uniform of white shirt, red tie, black slacks. His arms were muscular. You could see the line of his triceps.

"You here by yourself?" he asked.

"No. My wife and our girls are picking out some books. How about you?"

"I'm here with my grandchildren. They're looking for books with Celia."

Celia, I correctly assumed, was his wife.

Harry and I stepped outside and sat on the cement steps outside the library.

"Do you mind if I ask you what happened to your arm?" he said. He touched the cast with a fingertip.

"No, not at all. It was broken when I was trying to help break up a fight."

"You were in a fight?" he asked, astonished.

"Not really. I was trying to break it up. Do you remember a man named Sam Shoogey who used to come by the office?

"Sure."

"Well, he was in a fight with someone, and I tried to break it up. I got off easy. Shoogey's much worse off."

Harry's mouth fell open. "Is he okay?"

"Yes. Or at least I think he will be." I gave him some details about Shoogey's condition, and Harry shook his head side-to-side as I did.

Then, with little introduction, Harry began telling me a story. His sentences ran together like paint bleeding, an effect I will try to approximate here.

"This was a long time ago when they had me in this locker room Mr. Ashe," he said, "and the whole place smelled like horsecrap it was making my stomach sick and I probably would have thrown up if there was something in my stomach but there wasn't since I hadn't had anything to eat since a hamburger and a helping of potatoes at supper the night before. I'd done this once before at a racetrack in New York and I learned that if you've got to spend a day sniffing horsecrap you might as well be doing it on an empty stomach right? And if you've got the brains of a bird you'd put on your oldest rottenest clothes because that horse stink sticks with you like paint it doesn't come off too good in the shower and you usually just have to throw your pants and your shirt and your underpants right into the trash or else your wife and your kids won't come anywhere near you that's how bad the stink is.

"Well they put me in the same changing room that they had all the jockeys and they must have been used to that horsecrap smell because most of them were eating hot dogs and drinking out of paper cups I couldn't tell if it was liquor or soda pop. The very last thing on my mind was putting food in my mouth which I already explained why but just *looking* at other folks doing it was enough to give my stomach a good case of the shakes.

"The jockeys were cackling like a bunch of mother hens they were playing cards and I got undressed. I was thinking about how Celia and Winston Winston was just a baby then I was thinking about how Celia and Winston my baby boy were going to be sitting in the stands and how excited they were going to be when they heard the man say Harry Addler over the loudspeaker and how everyone was going to stand up and applaud for me. I was also thinking trying to figure out how much money would be left over after I paid the rent and bought some food because I saw a pair of those black and white shoes in the window at Loehman's that I was going to buy if I had any money left over.

"There was one of those old electric fans on and I could feel the bumps shooting up on my arms and legs and one of those little pip-squeak jockeys threw an ice cube that hit me right square on the back it must've come out of his drinking cup. He asked me if I was the stupid niggra that was supposed to race against a horse and I said yes sir except I'm not stupid. He laughed right out loud when I said that like I was Charlie Chaplin or someone funny like that and he says don't tell me you ain't a stupid niggra ha ha ha.[223]

"He was laughing at me and I could tell he was making faces behind my back and I wanted to beat the life out of him which wouldn't have been all that hard to do since he was about the size of one of my legs. But I knew that's what he'd like to see me do because they're pretty quick about sending people like me to jail and then who takes care of Celia and Winston my baby boy?

"That's the biggest problem with white folks Ham is that half of them treat you like you're some kind of dumb monster and the other half treat you like you're a regular person when you meet one of them you never know if it's going to be one or the other. Sometimes you think it's one and it ends up being the other you never really know. I'd much rather have the kind that says something to let you know they don't like you than the kind that acts like they do and then goes off and says something terrible about you behind your back and then is as sweet as sweet potato pie the next time they see you. At least with the ones who are rotten to your face you know enough to be rotten back if you know what I mean I bet you do.

"I went back to where my clothes were put on a pair of shorts and a shirt with no sleeves and I sat down on a bench so I could put my socks on. Then I took my track shoes out of the box where I always kept them and put them on my feet and laced them up tight so I didn't have to worry about them coming loose when I was running so I'd trip over them and land smack on my face. I was laughing to myself thinking about how this was an easy way for me to make money easy as pie. I got paid the same amount twenty-five dollars if I lost or if I won which is a hundred times easier than the time I worked in Virginia pouring rubber for twelve hours a day sometimes more or the time I worked digging a tunnel right through a mountain that's backbreaking work.

"Next thing I did was I knelt down on the floor and I said thank you Lord for the gifts you have bestowed upon me your poor servant and thank you for giving me Celia and Winston my baby boy and thank you for taking good care of my family then I got up. One of the jockeys came over with a mustache and he gave me a paper cup with something in it and he told the jockeys to come over by me and they did even the one who was making fun of me. They got in a circle around me it looked like a rainbow because they were all wearing different colors and the one who gave me the cup asked me what's my name. I said Harry Addler and he said we should all drink a toast to our friend

Harry Addler and wish him good luck in his race against a horse I was surprised. I asked him what's in the cup is it liquor because I don't want to be drinking liquor before I run and he said no it sure isn't liquor don't worry we're all your friends. He said cheers and everybody drank their drink right down I drank mine too it stung my throat.

"I said thank you for the drink they went back to their table and I started stretching my leg muscles out so I wouldn't get a cramp which I do sometimes if I don't stretch my leg muscles. I was bending over touching my toes when all of a sudden it was like the devil had a hold of me my stomach was burning up and my face was sweating and everything looked out of whack I couldn't see too good. I went to sit back down on the bench and I almost fell right over and then I started throwing up only there was nothing coming out since there was nothing in my stomach. My mouth wouldn't shut and there was this noise coming out of me like I was choking to death and my stomach was jumping up and down no one was helping me. I was trying to make myself breathe but it wouldn't work and it felt like my stomach would shoot right through the top of my head like a rocket it really did.

"The next thing I knew there was a man standing over me normal size not one of those jockeys. I was laying flat on my back like a dead man on the floor and he asked me if I was okay and I said yes I am. He grabbed my arms and helped me sit down on the bench there was no one else in the changing room anymore and he said he'd go get some ice and be back in a minute. I didn't know what he was talking about but when I rubbed my head because it hurt there was a lump there as hard as a rock the size of my fist I swear. It stung when I touched it so I didn't but then the man came back with the ice and said call me Zac and pressed it against the lump and I wanted to holler. He asked me who I am and I said I'm Harry Addler I'm supposed to run a race against a horse and he said he didn't think I should be running around with a big lump like that I should see a doctor. We needed the money and I told him I had to run and he said it's your life. I took the sack of ice and held it against my head and said thank you Zac for helping me out and he said it was nothing you should really see a doctor and I said maybe later who knows.

"I started to walk down the hallway my head was pounding like a drum my stomach felt like it wasn't even there anymore my legs were all wobbly. I walked along the wall and I wound up in the place where they kept all the horses locked up the stable I think is what you call it. There's hay all over the place and hundreds of horses and the horsecrap smell was awful strong it was getting up in my nostrils and I started to cough some.

"A man with a hat was leading one of those stinking horses around by a rope going right by me. He stopped to ask what I'm doing there buddy and I was about to tell him that I'm supposed to run in a race when all of a sudden the horse went wild I don't know why. It was a giant horse a black one much taller than me probably weighed close to a ton and it started whipping its head around and making noises. It got up on its back legs and I covered my head with my arms so it wouldn't hurt me. The man was laughing at me I took my arms away from my head he said what kind of man's afraid of a horse. I said it wasn't a horse it was a monster and he said you ain't supposed to be here anyway he smacked the horse on the rear like it's a pretty girl. I told him I'm supposed to run a race against a horse and he said oh so you're the boy they got this is Wonderfella the horse that's going to whoop you it's the giant horse that nearly killed me. He told me I should be outside already I'm late and told me how to get out to the track.

"When I walked through the door the sun was so bright it hurt my eyes and I couldn't see a thing. I felt dizzy like I was on a carnival ride you know the one that goes around and around. I fell down and put my hands over my eyes the sunlight felt like a knife going straight into my eyes. Some man came over and grabbed me by the arm and said get up you dumb niggra you've been drinking haven't you that's all you niggras do is drink. I was holding my hands over my eyes so the sun wouldn't hurt too much and my head was pounding and the man was pulling on my arm and said come on you dumb drunken niggra we ain't going to give you a cent if you don't run. I tried to tell him that I hadn't been drinking but he said shut up and showed me where to stand on the track next to the rail.

"My eyes didn't hurt so bad anymore so I looked around and there were thousands of people in the stands I couldn't find Celia and Winston my baby boy there were so many of them and there were signs that said Welcome to Pimlico Race Track Fourth of July in red-white-and-blue. The same man who told me how to get outside brought the giant horse over next to me except now there was one of those jockeys on top I couldn't tell which because they all look the same small. It was hot and I was leaning against the rail I still didn't feel good and I was looking at this giant horse just praying to the Lord that he wouldn't go crazy and crush me like a fly which he could have if he went crazy.

"Down the track a ways there were two men standing holding a stretch of rope between them that was the finish line. It wasn't that far away because if it's too far a horse will beat a man every time. The idea is to get a good start because it takes a horse a while to get going good and you just hope he doesn't catch up with you. Over a short distance a man can win.

"Over the loudspeaker a man said ladies and gentlemen thank you for coming to Pimlico Race Track he had a very good clear voice maybe he was a singer. Then he said as a special treat for the Fourth of July we've got a colored boy who's going to run a hundred yards against Wonderfella one of the fastest horses in the whole world he didn't even say my name and I was hollering say my name say my name but he didn't hear me. Another man pulled me over by the starting line I was yelling say my name he said be quiet you dummy.

"The crowd was making a lot of noise the horse wouldn't stand still he was scaring me half to death and I could tell the jockey was saying something to me his lips were moving except I couldn't hear him the noise was so loud like an earthquake. My head was pounding and somebody said on your mark get set go and shot a gun off. I started running only it didn't feel right my legs weren't working right like they

should and it was like I was running in water and I could feel myself
falling off to the side a bit I wasn't running straight at all. I made myself
go straight again and I felt myself go off to the other side and I could
hear the horse running up behind me and I could hear its feet and I
could hear the sound it made when the jockey smacked it and I could
even hear the breath coming out of its nostrils it sounded like a
vacuum cleaner. I was swerving I couldn't even feel my legs underneath
me anymore and I looked ahead and saw that I was about halfway
there. I didn't know if I could make it to the finish but the horse was
still behind me and I was thinking maybe I could win maybe.

"I was running as fast as I could and my chest started hurting and
I started swerving again but I couldn't make myself go back straight I
didn't know what was happening. My head was dizzy again and I
couldn't stand up I fell down on the track in the dirt and I was thinking
this horse is going to stomp right on my head. There was so much noise
I wanted to scream out loud and I saw the horse coming right toward
me only I couldn't move it was like I was in cement I couldn't even
scream. I was thinking Lord please don't let me die don't let that monster stomp on my brain what'll happen to Celia and Winston my baby
boy when all of a sudden the horse got up on its hind legs just like the
Lone Ranger's horse just before it ran me over and it fell over onto its
back it was a miracle. It rolled over onto its side and got up and just
walked away except the jockey was still lying there he wasn't moving a
muscle.

"A lot of people came running toward him and there was so much
noise I had to cover my ears. I got up off the ground and started
walking I didn't know where I was going. People were pouring out of
the stands jumping over the rails I didn't know if the jockey was dead
or alive where did the horse go? I had my hands over my ears and that
still wasn't good enough because the noise was so loud and I started
yelling stop it because my head felt like it was going to burst.

"People were throwing bottles and cups and rocks and some were
pushing at me and calling me names except I couldn't make out what

they were saying. Who are all these people why are they hitting me I didn't do anything wrong. Out of nowhere a bottle hit me right smack on the head right where that lump was and it split me wide open I could feel it. The blood started running right into my eye I wiped it away but it kept coming and I started running I didn't know where the blood was getting in my mouth and I spat it out. There were people all over the track everywhere and I tried to go between them some kicked me and some hit me with their fists policemen were there too with sticks.

"I was just running trying to stay away from people so they wouldn't hit me sometimes I felt I was going to fall but I didn't I couldn't see too good out of one of my eyes on account of the blood. A woman was hitting me with a book and I could see the horse just standing there by itself it looked small because it was far away and I was thinking to myself if I can just get over there to the horse I'll be okay. I'll get on the horse and we'll take off and no one will catch us. We'll jump over the fence and get out of here and we'll jump over buildings and go down the highway as fast as a race car and just keep running faster and faster until we get out into the country and nobody will say anything to us in the country.

"Then out of nowhere a man came running out of the stands I thought he was going to hit me. Only he didn't hit me instead he stood in front of me and held his hand out to the side and said if you want to kill this man you'll have to kill me to do it. A couple men actually struck him but they were pulled aside by the others and in that moment I saw there was hope for all of us."[224]

The racetrack where Harry Addler's story took place, Pimlico Race Track, was no more than a mile from our home in Mount Washington. A mile from our peaceful little home with the oak trees and the basketball hoop and the hole the girls and I were digging to China.

Finished with his story, Harry leaned back, resting on his elbows.

"Who was the man who helped you?" I asked, and Harry told me his name just as our wives found us on the steps.

"Sam Shoogey," he said, "your friend. Didn't he ever tell you that story? Didn't he ever tell you the story about what he did at Pimlico Race Track?"

"No."

Harry laughed. He introduced me to his wife. I introduced him to mine.

"Celia," he said, "Mr. Ashe is a good friend of Sam Shoogey."

Celia put her hand over her heart. "God bless you," she said, and she clasped her other hand over my cast.

"Mr. Shoogey is in the hospital," he said.

"Oh, my Lord," Celia said, and she moved her hand to her mouth. "Is he okay?"

I gave her some of the details of Shoogey's condition. Although I assured her Shoogey would be fine, her hand never left her mouth.

"Honey," she said to Harry, "can we go see him?"

"Exactly what I was planning," Harry said. He shook my hand and said, "See you at the office, Mr. Ashe."

"Yes," I said, "I'll see you in the office, Mr. Addler."

Our wives shook hands, then we headed off in opposite directions. On the drive home, the girls propped their new books up on their laps, and I told Angie the story I'd just heard. Angie closed her eyes to stave off tears, but she could not hold them off when I revealed the name of the man who had protected Harry Addler.

"Why hadn't Shoogey ever told me *that* story?" I said. "Why?"

And Angie provided the answer I believe to be correct: "He didn't consider it to be his story, Ham. It was Harry Addler's story."

At Shoogey's request, I did not bring criminal charges against Jimmy Birnberg, nor did he. Eventually, my wrist healed and the cast was removed to reveal flaky, mottled skin. Eventually, Shoogey returned from the hospital. It seemed he was there for months; his stay may have been shorter. When he was released, he looked strong and healthy, and his false teeth hopefully were better made than those I continued to wear. Braverman and I drove him home; he did not invite us in. Over the weeks and months that followed, Angie and I invited him to our home for dinner no fewer than two dozen times. We invited him for parties and picnics and trips to the beach. He never accepted, not once. Eventually, we stopped asking him.

I saw Shoogey from time to time, bumping into him here and there, in the grocery store or the hardware store, but there was nothing of substance to our conversations, just the simple, empty "Hello, how are you?" of neighbors compelled to speak by no shared interest, but by the fortune of their residences. Sometimes, we would see each other, our eyes would catch for a moment, just long enough so there'd be no mistake that we'd seen each other, but we'd look away and go about our own business. It happened once in a restaurant. It happened other times as well.

Early one evening, though, walking past his house, I heard him call out my name. He made small circles with his hand, as if cranking a fishing reel, signaling me to join him on the steps of his front porch. Around his shoulders he wore a huge, apathetic black cat like a shawl. As I approached, Shoogey pulled the cat off as you might pluck lint from your clothing and set it down on the porch, then wiped his hands on his pants and hoisted himself up by the railing. He looked enormous, puffy and pink like a woman in the late stages of her pregnancy when she's achy and holding water.

"It's good to see you, my friend," he said, his voice loud and unmusical. He offered me his meaty hand, then popped the gum he was chewing, sending a tiny spark of spearmint into the air. The cat leaped off the porch as if it'd heard a gunshot.

"Yes, it's good to see you, too, Shoogey."

"It's been a while."

"Yes." I couldn't think of anything to add, so I said, "Yes," again.

"Listen, how about I get you a drink. An iced tea? Who can refuse a nice iced tea?" He smiled weakly: his new teeth had been made even more poorly than my own. The gums were more tan than pink, and the teeth themselves were too sharp and made him look like a cannibal.

I shrugged my consent, then followed him into his house, through the post-hurricane living room and into the kitchen. He pulled two tall, green-tinted glasses from the cupboard and filled them with ice, then poured the tea.

"How about something to eat?"

"No, no, I'm not hungry. The tea's enough."

He opened the refrigerator anyway: an entire shelf was weighed down with peaches, some old and bruised blue, some fresh. They were stacked like logs behind a cabin. He pulled one out from the middle, then seemed genuinely surprised when his simple act made the pile shift, and another peach rolled and fell to the floor, then rolled some more before rocking to a rest. Shoogey inspected the first peach like a jeweler, turning it, turning it, and shoved it into his front pants pocket, then picked the second one from the floor and rubbed it against his shirt to clean it, then took a bite.

"Just a little snack," he said, the juice glistening on his lips. "You can get hungry just sitting sometimes, especially if you're thinking. What it is, my friend, is the brain burns up all the calories. Not that these have many calories to begin with, though I should pay more attention to such matters." He smacked his belly with an open hand, producing an extraordinarily plaintive tone.

He waited for me to smile, then extended the peach toward me. "You sure you don't want one?"

I shook my head, no.

"You do really like those, don't you?" I asked.

"Mm hmm."

"Why?"

I wanted him to tell me that he ate them because they were sweet and because he couldn't eat chocolate; I already knew that, but I wanted to hear him say that. Instead, all he said was, "They taste good to me. Isn't that enough?"

I returned to the porch with him. The dusk fell in flakes around us. We sat and looked blankly at the street, at the sky, though occasionally I glanced over at him, at his melting profile. He was bright but not deep, intelligent but not wise, articulate but not eloquent, and I would always remember him more than I would miss him.

"This is a good neighborhood, you know. A darned good neighborhood."

That's all he said.

After a bit, I excused myself and said I had to be leaving. I stood, and he stood with me. He grabbed my hand and shook it firmly, then suddenly tugged me toward him and embraced me, patting me twice between the shoulder blades with his free hand.

"It was good to see you, my friend," he said, then he opened his arms wide to release me, as if he were setting a bird free, though I was no bird. Like him, I'd put on a bit of weight, and then some. My clothes were beginning to pinch me like borrowed shoes.

I felt Shoogey's eyes on me as I walked into the blue night, following me until the trees stood between us. The new leaves, still yellow but hinting at green, waved noiselessly in the breeze. And the smell of peaches stuck to me, to the places he'd touched.

* * *

I didn't know that would be the last time I would see Shoogey, but it was. He was gone within a week, and within another a new family had moved into that house, filling it with different voices and children who were much loved. Angie baked a Tar Heel pie to welcome them to the neighborhood, but I didn't accompany her and the girls when they delivered it. I stayed at home with the television keeping me company.

I only heard from Shoogey twice after he moved. First, there was a jumbo-sized postcard I received in the mail. On the front was a picture of some beach somewhere, sunbathers bunched together like newborn pups in a wicker basket. There was no return address, though the post-mark was from Chicago, Illinois. In tiny, tiny print, his note read:

Dear Ham:

I'll be sending you a package shortly.

I saw a tie in a store window and was struck by two thoughts: 1) Ham would love this, and 2) Ham would hate this. I figure it's a 50-50 proposition, which is a pretty good bet these days. So if you love it, I knew you would. The same goes if you don't.

My new home is wonderful. Roomy with a view of the morning sun. It's a wonder what a change of scenery can do for your spirits. Where before I had a general sense of malaise, I now have a much more pleasant sense of malaise. Malaise Lite! Great tasting! Fewer calories!

POOR NAPOLEON marches on, my friend, a bit more quickly than before. I may enclose a chapter or two when I send the necktie. Don't be cross with me if I don't. I'm not sure it's turning out quite how I expected. Oh, well, thank God for Malaise Lite!

Be well, my friend, and think happy thoughts. You're a terrific lawyer, and I wish you all the best in your budding legal career.

Eat Wheaties!

Your friend and idol,

And then there was his majestic signature—

Samuel J. Shoogey III

The package he wrote of never arrived. No tie, no chapters, and I can't say I was surprised.

The only other time I heard from Shoogey was several years ago. He telephoned me out of the blue one evening, the sound of his voice startling me, not so much because it was unexpected—I had gone through a spell after he'd moved when I'd expected him to be on the other end of the phone whenever it rang—but because his greeting was full of cheer. As we spoke, he seemed to be fine, stable and content, though I may have been mistaken in that assessment: it may just have been the Malaise Lite of which he'd written. He was living in New York City, he said. (I tried to think of marinara sauce, but thought instead of my teeth.) He was working on the final draft of *Poor Napoleon*. He told me he hoped it would be published within a year. Perhaps it would be nominated for an award.

"Imagine that," he said. "Imagine if I won an award for writing a book about Napoleon. Imagine how happy I'd be. You know, my friend, looking back on everything now, I think that everything that I went through, everything I did, good and bad, served a purpose. Maybe there's a moral to my story."

"Maybe so," I told him.

"What do you think it is?"

"The moral?"

"Yes."

"Heck if I know, Shoogey," I said, and we both laughed a little.

"How about this," he said. "How about, You have to sin to get saved."[226]

"That sounds like a good moral."

"Or how about this: Every dog has his day."

"Not as good," I said.

"You're right. Anyway," he said, "will you come to the ceremony if I do win an award?"

"Of course."

"Promise?"

"Promise."

"Say, 'I promise.'"

"I promise, Shoogey."

When the conversation stalled, Shoogey recited his new address and telephone number, which I diligently wrote on the back of an envelope. He asked me to telephone him if I was ever in New York—"We'll have dinner and see a Broadway show!" he promised—and I assured him that I would, though I had no intention of ever returning to that city and, in fact, have not. We said goodbye.

Only then did I recover little pieces of information I wished I'd told Shoogey, but hadn't. Little stories, little observations. I hadn't told him that the Cuban-Chinese restaurant he'd taken me to had closed; in its place was a convenience store that's open twenty-four hours a day, holidays, too. I hadn't told him that I'd resigned my position at Morrisey & DeWitt and had returned to teaching history at Magruder High School. Or that I coached Magruder's boys' basketball team (twelve wins and ten losses in my first season, good enough for third place in the conference.)[227]

I hadn't mentioned that Harry Addler had retired and was my assistant coach; because he could operate a clutch, he drove the team bus, too. I hadn't mentioned that Carl DeWitt had died in his sleep one night and that, presumably, the attorneys at his firm were no longer required to leave mercy to heaven. I hadn't told Shoogey that Angie and I had had a third child, a son (Alexander; nine pounds even; red, wrinkled.)[228]

That was several years ago. Imagine the pages of a calendar flying. I hadn't thought of Shoogey at all for some time, and I certainly wouldn't have thought of writing about him had it not been for a story that appeared on the television news one evening. It was past eleven o'clock that night, and I was camped in one of the overstuffed chairs in the living room, reading a book with the television on and keeping me company.[229]

An attractive young newswoman was talking, though I wasn't

paying her much attention, just glancing up now and again from my book to catch her pushing her butter-yellow hair from her eyes with her fingertips.[230] She spoke about a fire in a warehouse downtown and about the mayor, and, as I read my book, her sentences became words, her words became sounds, and those sounds became a hum as steady and distant as the crackle of a campfire. Through the hum, though, I heard a word now and again leaping like sparks from the fire: "Evening…police officers…funny to hear that…congressman…unexpected delay…it was a sunny day here…"

When the telephone rang, I reached for the remote control on the coffee table, pushing a button to lower the volume on the television before answering the phone.

"Ham?" the caller said.

"Yes," I said. [231]

"Hamilton Ashe?"

"Yes."

There was a raspy, barn-door-hinge quality to the voice that was so familiar that I placed it immediately.

"Ham, is that you?"

"Yes, it's me, Syd."

"Ham, it's Syd Braverman here. Did you see it? On the news, did you see it?"

I leaned forward in my chair, grinning a little. It was a pleasure to hear Braverman's voice. We spoke infrequently after Shoogey moved on. We'd learned, to our mutual disappointment, that without Shoogey we had little to discuss. "Syd, how are you?"

He didn't answer me. Instead, he said, "Did you see it?"

"Did I see what?"

"Hurry. Put on Channel Eight. Hurry, hurry. It's Shoogey. There's been a murder."

I didn't respond for several moments. It was the first time I'd heard Shoogey's name spoken for so long that I'd forgotten how it sounded.

"What?"

"Hurry, hurry."

I switched to Channel Eight and turned up the volume just as the newscaster, a tan, black-haired man, was saying, "The slaying apparently occurred at approximately six o'clock this evening." Over his shoulder was a black-and-white photograph of a man who looked tired or ill or both. The man's mouth was slack. His eyes looked as if he'd just woken from a restless sleep. The photograph disappeared, and the newsman started in on his next story.

"I didn't hear the name," Braverman said, "but I recognized the picture."

"The picture? The picture they had on the screen?"

Braverman huffed as if he'd been running. "Don't you recognize him?"

"No."

"That was Shoogey."

"Syd," I said in a voice that was low and reasonable. "Are we talking about the same person?"

"The man in the photograph. The man in the photograph on the Channel Eight news. It's Shoogey."

"Sam Shoogey? Our Sam Shoogey?"

"Yes, yes."

"Syd, I don't know."

"Did you see him? Did you take a good look? That was Shoogey, I tell you. The eyes, the smile."

The eyes, the smile. I'd only seen them for an instant before the photograph had disappeared. Maybe they had been similar to Shoogey's, but the man in the photograph appeared much younger than Shoogey. Wherever he was, Shoogey was in his late sixties, early seventies. The man in the photograph appeared to be about my age, maybe younger. Also, the man in the photograph had been thin, as if a layer of paint had been brushed on his bones. Last I saw Shoogey, just before he packed up and left Baltimore for good, he was up to 260 pounds, with a barrel of a stomach and the beginnings of a third chin.

His doctor told him to chew Wrigley's gum between meals, which Shoogey did instead of eating sweets.

No, even with the eyes, the smile, the man in the photograph couldn't have been Shoogey. Politely, I told Braverman that he was mistaken.

"I'm not. It was Shoogey. I didn't hear the name, but I recognize the picture."

The sounds of the television filled our silence.

"Okay," I said, "assuming it's him, who did he kill?"

There was a pause.

"No, no, you've got it wrong," Braverman huffed. "Someone killed *him*. Someone killed *Shoogey*."

I heard someone say, "Oh, my God."

It was me.

I switched back to the other television station. The blond woman was flicking her hair out of her eyes with her fingers again. There was no photograph of the thin man, and she did not mention Shoogey. A heavy-set, cheerful man appeared and began talking about sports.

"Did you hear his name, Syd?" I demanded.[232]

I spoke more loudly than I'd intended. "Did you hear them say the name Sam Shoogey?"

"No. I told you before, no."

"Damn it, Syd. Damn it."

"I'm sorry, Ham."

"I'm not mad at you."

"I know."

"Why don't we just clear this up right now?" I suggested. "Why don't we just give Shoogey a call?"

"I don't know where he is."

"You haven't heard from him? I thought for certain you'd have heard from him. You were his best friend."

"That's not true," Braverman said. I could tell he was smiling at the thought. "I thought *you* were his best friend."

I denied it, but I may have been smiling when I did so. If I did, my smile would not have lasted long. It would have stopped as soon as I remembered the way I'd treated Shoogey.

"Well, I haven't heard from Shoogey for at least two years," Braverman said. "Maybe more than that. It might even be three."

"Where was he living then?"

"I don't remember. New York, I think. New York City."

"Well, we could call information up there and get his telephone number."

"No use. I tried once," he explained. "I tried to call him to wish him a happy New Year a couple years back, and they didn't have a listing for him anywhere in New York City."

Neither of us spoke for some time. Braverman hummed into the receiver to let me know he was thinking. I thumped my tongue against my teeth.

"Geez, Ham," Braverman said at last. "What if he is dead?"

"He couldn't be," I said, but I knew he was.

"I don't know," Braverman answered, "the picture. The picture looked like him, which was why I called." Then, wearily, he added, "He was a good egg, you know. I don't give a damn what anybody else says about him. He was a good egg, better than all of them rolled together."

"You're absolutely right," I answered.

"Maybe it'll be in the morning paper. Let's look in the morning paper."

"Good idea," I said, then after a long and embarrassing pause, I wished Braverman a good night. My book still sat open on my lap, but it was unreadable now: the letters floated like bees on the page, darting, swirling. I set the book down on the coffee table, then walked through the living room, shutting off the lights one by one as I did, leaving the porch light for last. It was in that porch light, of course, that I'd first met Sam Shoogey, the cruelest flower, the most elegant wreck.

And it was on that porch that I read the news the following morning: *Longtime Baltimore Resident Found Dead: Foul Play Sus-*

pected. It was Shoogey, after all. He'd been found dead in his home outside Buffalo, New York. The details of his death were not pleasant, not the sort of thing you'd want to read first thing in the morning.[233]

There was blood, and there were deep wounds. Whoever had killed Shoogey had hated him.

Braverman and I drove to Buffalo. Why, I cannot say. There was a police investigation underway, but they told us there were no suspects. There was a funeral in Chestertown, Maryland, the town where Shoogey grew up, and I found myself crying. Braverman put a hand on one of my shoulders, Jane Shoogey on the other, as we stood with Rudolph and Samantha, with aunts and uncles and cousins I had never heard of.

It was shortly thereafter that I learned that my family and I were the beneficiaries of a large insurance policy that Shoogey had taken out on his life, large enough that we will never have to worry about college tuition for Katie and Claire and Alexander.[234]

He had taken out similar policies for Jane, and for his children, and for Braverman. We were, sadly, rich.

It was sometime later, while sitting in the teachers' lounge sipping a cup of coffee, that I realized something terrible. Find Shoogey's insurance policies. Find them, and read them. You will find a clause that Shoogey himself once told me about during one of our lunches, a conversation where he explained the intricacies of the insurance business. Find the policies. Find the suicide clause. If I am correct, it will state that the beneficiaries collect nothing if Shoogey kills himself within two years of purchasing the policy. And you will see that Shoogey died shortly after that clause expired. We had already buried the murderer. He was laid to rest in Chestertown, Maryland, next to his brother's grave.[235]

I've returned to Chestertown only once since the funeral. Our basketball team was driving back from a game in Easton. Alexander was with us, sitting in the front bus seat.[236]

I saw a green sign on the highway that read: *Chestertown 8, Baltimore 57.*

"Boy, what a horrible game *that* must've been," one of the boys yelled, and everyone laughed, myself included. I couldn't help but ask Harry to make a detour. We drove the streets aimlessly, past little shops that bore no resemblance to the stores in Baltimore, past boat yards, and school yards, and tall trees that were only saplings when my friend lived there.

"Coach," one of the boys finally said, "is there a reason we're driving around this town?"

"He's looking for a place to take a leak," one of the other boys said.

"He's looking for a place to drop you off," another boy responded. "What did you have, two points? My grandma could score more than two points."

The boys teased each other for a while before one of them said, "Come on, Coach. Is there a reason we're here?"

"Yes," I said, "a damn good reason." I almost said, "Sam Shoogey killed seven men, sent them to their graves, turned their bodies to fertilizer and their thoughts to pure blue air." But, instead, I said, "We need to find a place for our post-game meal."

We ended up eating dinner at a little luncheonette by the water. Fifteen of us—me, Alexander, Harry and twelve boys in sweatpants—crowded around two tables. We ate hamburgers and french fries, we drank milkshakes and sodas, we relived moments of the victory that had been ours only hours earlier, and we embellished those memories. The boys talked about cars and sports and girls, the very things boys are supposed to talk about at that age; boys that age should not have anything weightier on their minds. While the boys were finishing their meals, I slipped outside with my son. Still sipping a soda, I strolled along the pleats and tucks outside the luncheonette, holding my son's hand in my free hand. I expected to find more there, but the ocean was the ocean, and the boats were boats, and the people people like me and you and you and you.

Since then, I've thought of Shoogey less and less, and eventually I'm afraid I may not think of him at all. I have no photographs of him, and, try as I might, my memory of him is fading and growing yellow and curling at the corners. Someday, I suspect he will just be a name, a name of someone I once knew and liked. Still, whenever I'm in a bookstore or a library, I can't help but comb the shelves in search of his book, knowing with certainty that I won't find it, hoping with the hope of the damned that I'll be dead wrong. I've seen Braverman do the same thing, wandering over to the S shelves, and I've never questioned him.[237]

Somewhere, though, I imagine Shoogey's book sitting open on a tabletop beside an open window. There is a pleasing summer breeze, and it blows through that window and turns the pages one by one by one, whispering his stories to whoever will listen. It tells the truth and the lies in the same voice.

ENDNOTES

1. This is the title selected by Diane Hoffmiller, the editor of this book. It is a rather obvious title, as the reader will no doubt agree upon reaching Chapter Nine. Your author had wanted to name it *This Should Answer Your Questions, My Son*, a title the editor found too cumbersome and "deceptively amusing," whatever that might mean. In paragraph 6(c) of the standard author's contract, signed by your author, your author relinquished all naming rights for the United States publication of this book to the fine publishing house that has printed it, released it, and delivered it to your local bookstore. He has, however, retained all naming rights for any international publication, and will call the book whatever he pleases in whatever foreign lands this book might appear. In France, for instance, it will be called something along the lines of *Something Something Something, Mon Fils*. French is a lovely language.

2. A concession by the editor, for which your author says, "Thank you kindly, Diane."

3. Your author, the son of Richard and Beatrice, who will occasionally refer to himself as "your author," but will more often than not refer to himself more humbly as "I."

4. This epigram is taken from an argument between Hamilton Ashe and his wife Angie that appeared in earlier drafts of this book. The entire chapter where it appeared has been removed, and the reader may

notice several places where it appears that sentences or paragraphs or entire scenes may have been deleted. It may appear that way because it's true. The author has removed all sections of the book that contain any disputes between Hamilton and Angie, and anything that would suggest that their marriage was anything short of ideal or that Angie was anything other than a charming and beautiful woman.

5. Your author, for one, enjoys reading that very kind of novel on airplanes, enjoys the process by which a mystery is ultimately resolved and waits, with neither patience nor impatience but, rather, hopefulness, for the detective novel in which the mystery either is not resolved at all or (even better) only leads to more mysteries, which there simply are not enough pages to resolve: the back cover is approaching far too quickly.

6. "Which war?" you ask. "Vietnam? Korea? *World War II*?" Those are very good questions. Those are *excellent* questions.

7. The Seven Wonders of the World were: Artemisian at Ephesus, the temple of the Greek goddess Artemis; the Colossus of Rhodes; the Hanging Gardens of Babylon; the Mausoleum at Halicarnassus; Olympian Zeus, the statue of the supreme Greek god; the Pyramids of Egypt; and the Lighthouse of Alexandria at Pharos. This was often a final examination question when I taught history at Magruder High School. You would be surprised at how many students were able to name all seven. You would not be surprised at the number who knew I would ask the question; each year, the new senior class would inform the new junior class. I suppose I could have changed the question or removed it altogether, but it was such a joy to see the delight on 30 faces when they saw the question on the examination and just a joy to realize that all 30 in fact had learned the Seven Wonders.

8. This is a reference to *Snow White and the Seven Dwarfs*, one of the Grimm fairy tales. The Walt Disney Company made an excellent animated film of this story, which my daughters loved when they were

about the size of a bag of raked leaves.

9. A reference to the stage and movie musical *Seven Brides for Seven Brothers*. My wife enjoyed the musical; I did not. This endnote, like many others, is intended purely for the benefit of international readers who may not be familiar with such things as *Seven Brides for Seven Brothers*. To readers in Spain, I say, "Hola. Como esta? Soy bien."

10. I do not know whether Shoogey in fact was ever a member of the Boy Scouts of America.

11. I have been unable to find any information about a movie with this title, although a number of people have nodded their heads and closed their eyes and said, "Hmmm," when I mentioned the scene in which a bullet strikes a Bible stored in a man's breast pocket, saving his life.

12. The silver cigarette case also produced a few "Hmms" of recognition.

13. "Breakfast cereal-y" is not a word (or words.) Diane, the young lady who was assigned to edit this book, initially drew a black line through it. However, I prevailed upon her to keep it, which she agreed to do if I agreed to remove a paragraph in Chapter Three and two endnotes in Chapter Eight.

14. This is a fictitious name. I have used the name of a boy I knew in grade school.

15. Lombardi's song is based on a radio advertisement for Comet, an abrasive cleanser.

16. When you set this book down on your night stand, dear reader, you may very well have a different opinion than I about what is true and what is not true. That is the nature of truth, that what is true is merely that which the majority of us believes to be true. If any of you happened across Shoogey and can confirm some portion of this story (or

other stories of his), please send me a note in care of the publisher, whose address can likely be found on the back flap of the book cover, beneath a fancy photograph of your author.

17. I have confirmed with the Maryland State Bar Association that my telling of this story does not breach any ethical obligations I might have as a lawyer since I have not revealed any communications that might be considered attorney-client privileged. To the representatives of the Maryland State Bar Association, I say, "Hello. How are you? I'm fine."

18. Scout's honor.

19. You will not find a listing for "Shoogey" in any Baltimore telephone directory, past or present. For legal reasons the reader can certainly appreciate, I have had to use a fictitious name. Like the name I have given our protagonist for this book, his real first and last names also begin with the same consonant, and his last name also sounded like something secretive and vulgar, like a grotesque and flaking skin condition, like a crooked politician.

20. My profession should explain the endnotes you will find throughout this book: most lawyers cannot even write a "thank you" card without including a footnote or an endnote. Shoogey once explained why he abhorred footnotes (and, presumably, endnotes): "It's like being upstairs making love and having to run downstairs to answer the doorbell." He did not read footnotes, and he did not include any in his books. That is your choice as well. After all, this is *your* book: you paid for it. If you do not want to run downstairs to answer the doorbell, you do not have to. It could just be the paperboy. But it could also be someone with a million dollar sweepstakes check.

21. Although I often found the practice of law to be trivial and unjust, I must admit that it added a sense of order to my life. Then I decided that order is not as attractive as it seems. New York City looks good

from a distance, too. Then you get off the train and—whomp! Shoogey also did not believe in order. Here is what he would say on the subject: "Order schmorder."

22. A fictitious name, for obvious reasons.

23. Shortly after we moved into our first house, my wife baked a loaf of bread and left it out on the counter to cool while we went out for the evening. When we returned, we found that a tunnel had been eaten right through the loaf of bread by a mouse, which lay dead beside it. My first thought was, *My god, the bread was poisoned*! It was not until later that I thought, *My god, we have mice in the house.* We set traps throughout the kitchen and living room each night. We did not catch a single mouse, I'm sorry to say.

24. A pseudonym. My given name appears on the cover of this book, and on the spine. It was the young lady who was put in charge of editing this book who suggested I use "Hamilton," "Ham" for short. It was a good choice, for which I say, "Thank you, Diane." The last name is that of a favorite tennis player and civil rights leader, Arthur Ashe. Mr. Ashe died from acquired immune deficiency syndrome ("AIDS"), the result of a tainted blood transfusion. Rest in peace, Mr. Ashe.

25. "Angie," of course, is also a fictitious name. Those who know us know her name, or should. She's the woman standing next to me in our wedding photos, biting her lip. She's the one in the white dress. She's the one who could have married someone better.

26. This was the first time Shoogey ever mentioned a gun. I had no reason to believe, at this first encounter, that his comment was anything but a joke. I had no reason to believe he would kill two people.

27. John Dillinger was a notorious American bank robber. Pablo

Picasso was a Spanish artist and one of the originators of a style known as "cubism." Mahatma Gandhi led India's drive for independence from Britain.

28. I fell in love with Angie all over again each time she bit her lip. It was a gesture that had to be seen to be appreciated.

29. To protect the privacy of various persons at the law firm, I have chosen not to use the actual name of the law firm. Suffice it to say, it is a large and prestigious firm, often referred to as Baltimore's "silk stocking" law firm in *The Sun* and *The Washington Post* and other publications that might have reason to refer to it.

30. "Stanley McGee" is a fictitious name. Unless there is someone out there named "Stanley McGee" who is unknown to me. I'm sure his name is not fictitious to him.

31. This is true. I did not even learn that my father was Jewish until he asked me to wear a yarmulke at my grandmother's funeral. I was fourteen years of age at the time. For fourteen years, he had explained his refusal to accompany the rest of the family to Sunday mass by claiming to be an Episcopalian. "Episcopalians," he said, "are basically Catholics who don't like to spend time with Italians." My mother, by the way, is Italian, and so, therefore, is your author.

32. I believe Shoogey meant to say "Hindu" as it is Hindus, not Muslims, who consider cows to be sacred.

33. Hershey makes a variety of chocolate products. The company is based in Hershey, Pennsylvania, a short drive from Baltimore. My wife and I took the girls there once for a tour of the factory and to ride the roller coaster at the amusement park. The entire town smelled of chocolate; inhale, and you cannot help but smile. The lampposts throughout the town were shaped like chocolate drops.

34. Budweiser is a brand of beer manufactured by the Anheuser-Busch Company.

35. A reference to a movie entitled, *The Man Who Shot Liberty Valance.* I enjoyed the movie; my wife did not. We saw it well before we'd ever met a man who had actually killed someone.

36. In kissing my wife, I always pressed my lips against that scar longer and more frequently than any other portion of her neck.

37. Jos. A. Bank Clothiers is an excellent store, although I no longer shop there. I purchase most of my clothing these days from Braverman's Menswear.

38. Although "Harry Addler" was not the guard's actual name, it is true that we share the same initials.

39. These cases may all be found in thick gold books knows as the Maryland Reporters. I have omitted the page numbers in the interests of brevity. The last of these cases, *Rigoli versus Rigoli,* involved a woman who asked for a divorce after seeing her wedding photographs. She didn't think her husband looked sincere.

40. A Latin teacher at Magruder High School, has confirmed the accuracy of Shoogey's translation.

41. This was the first time Shoogey would mention murder to me.

42. "Hafets" is a fictitious name. In this case, I have used the surname of a boy who was on my high school basketball team. He had a soft touch and would frequently salt away five or six shots in a row when you needed them the most. He sells computer software these days.

43. Cracker Jacks is the name of a brand of caramel popcorn that is mixed with peanuts. Each box contains a toy surprise. The surprises

used to be of the nature of miniature compasses and decoder rings. Now, they are less interesting prizes, like tattoos or stickers, the result of too many lawsuits filed by lawyers claiming their clients had choked on the prizes, or poked out an eye or suffered some other, horrible fate. "Another example of lawyers ruining a good thing," my wife once said. "That's why no woman of any value would ever marry a lawyer," I said. My wife nodded. It was a few minutes before she said, "Hey, wait a minute!" It was a few more minutes before she said, "Besides, I married a school teacher, not a lawyer."

44. Milton Berle was a comedian who was popular in the 1950's and 1960's. He was Jewish, like my father. For international readers, I must explain that Milton Berle was never the President of the United States. Nor was Babe Ruth, for that matter.

45. A reference to a musical by Lerner and Loewe in which an erudite professor accepts the challenge of turning a poor, uneducated girl named Eliza Doolittle into an elegant young lady. The professor and the girl find themselves very much in love, a not unexpected development under the circumstances. The musical is based on the play *Pygmalion* by George Bernard Shaw. *Pygmalion* also was not an original story. It was based on the Greek myth about a sculptor who fell in love with a statue he had sculpted of a woman. Venus, the goddess of love, made the statue come to life.

46. There is no such street address in Baltimore. I have used the last name of a college friend for the street name. I was an usher at his wedding, which took place in Tom's River, New Jersey. His wife is delightful. Her name is Mary Jo.

47. The first name is accurate. The rest is not.

48. "Wallace Doughty" is a fictitious name.

49. I wonder if he went to my dentist. *Brack-a-brack-a-brack.*

50. This statement was very much at odds with a statement Shoogey would make to me many months later. He was eating a croissant when he said, "I don't normally eat croissants because I always wonder afterward if I have little flakes on my lips. There, that shows you what a terrible writer I am. A good writer would have said, 'I always wonder if I have flakes on my moist, succulent lips.'" Later, when I said I'd call him, he said, "I'll be waiting by the phone. Of course, a good writer would have said, 'I'll be waiting by the moist, succulent phone.'"

51. "Henry McClellan" is a fictitious name. Neither name, "Henry" or "McClellan," has any particular meaning to me. I toyed with other names. As you may know, dear reader, in *Lolita*, Vladimir Nabokov named a pivotal character "Vivian Darkbloom"—an anagram of his own name. While preparing these endnotes, I have given some thought to attempting the same thing: changing this character's name to an anagram of my own. Unfortunately, the best I could do was "Michael Nuk." I'm not a very smart man, and I must admit that I've had a drink or two since I started writing these endnotes.

52. This was how my wife and I obtained the grandfather clock that is in our living room. We bid two hundred dollars more than we'd sworn we would bid. But it is an excellent clock.

53. First names of siblings, cousins, nieces, friends and classmates— though, coincidentally, many are also the names Shoogey actually recited. When dealing with so many women, it was bound to happen.

54. I had a law school classmate named Serena, a lovely blond girl from Cleveland, Ohio. She had a sweet and pleasant sounding voice and was a surprisingly good softball player. But, for all my years on this planet, she remains the only girl I've ever met with that soft and unusual name.

55. Ann-Margret was a very popular, red-haired singer and actress. (Note: in the British edition, she will be referred to as "ginger-haired.") Angie once dressed up like Ann-Margret for a costume party.

56. Oh, my heart. If only you knew.

57. A reference to *The Adventures of Alice in Wonderland*, a book my wife and I read to our daughters no fewer than four times.

58. Not available at Joe Bank's or any other men's clothing store in the area, to my knowledge.

59. Marilyn Monroe was a film star. She had blonde hair, not black, and was famous for her voluptuous figure. Rumors abound that she had an extramarital affair with President John F. Kennedy. As any of my students could tell you, President Kennedy was assassinated on November 22, 1963. As my wife could tell you, November 22 is my birthday. Like many people, I can tell you precisely where I was when I learned that Kennedy had been shot: I was eating cake.

60. Remember that Shoogey said "Walter." And remember how casually he did, as if he was not sure whether that in fact was the boy's given name. Make a note in the margin, if you must.

61. *The Sun* is Baltimore's largest daily newspaper.

62. "Jack Bowman" is a fictitious name. The last name is the name of a childhood friend.

63. The sixteenth President was Abraham Lincoln. Like John F. Kennedy, he was assassinated. He did not, however, have an extramarital affair with the actress Marilyn Monroe. Furthermore, I was not eating cake when Lincoln was shot. I was still many years from being born, as were my parents, and their parents as well.

64. I have *never* had this thought.

65. The actor Gregory Peck won an Academy Award in 1962 for best performance by an actor for his portrayal of the attorney Atticus Finch in the movie *To Kill A Mockingbird*, based on the novel by Harper Lee. That was also the year I was born into this world. Mr. Peck wore a seersucker suit in several scenes in the movie.

66. I have confirmed that this is true through the Foreign Language Department at the University of Maryland in College Park, Maryland.

67. I do not know in which play that line appears. *Henry V*, perhaps. If you know, please be so kind as to send me a note in care of the publisher of this book: perhaps we can clear this up in time for the paperback version of the book, or the international edition. Please be advised, however, that no prizes will be awarded.

68. I have confirmed that this is true: you peel sugar cane. That was how I arrived at Jane Shoogey's maiden name, "Jane Peel."

69. This appears to be true. Although I have been unable to determine the number of Chinese who migrated to Cuba, it appears the number was substantial. When President Chester A. Arthur signed the Chinese Exclusion Act in 1882, barring Chinese laborers from immigrating to the United States for ten years, the number of Chinese who immigrated to Cuba likely increased as a result.

70. The sauce was red, to be more accurate.

71. Abe Lincoln was often referred to as "Honest Abe." Diogenes never met Abraham Lincoln; they missed each other by more than two thousand years.

72. The Cat's Eye Pub is the true name of a bar in Baltimore's Fells Point area. I was there four nights last week alone!

73. The Senator Theater is the true name of one of Baltimore's oldest movie theaters. It is where my wife and I saw *Seven Brides for Seven Brothers.*

74. I have created the name of this movie out of thin air. I simply cannot remember the name of the movie Shoogey and I saw. *Aim High* sounds like the name of a genuine western, in my opinion, something that may have starred John Wayne in his heyday.

75. Also the actual name of a bar in Baltimore, located a block north of the Senator Theater.

76. Briefly, we considered calling this book *Poor Napoleon.* Very briefly.

77. Remember the name "Walter."

78. The number no longer belongs to SMP Construction, either. It now belongs to a young married couple who gave birth to a baby girl shortly before the publication of this book. Please do not call the number to test it: you might wake the baby.

79. This story may well be a myth. In attempting to confirm it, I found no fewer than four persons who acknowledged that they had heard this story but did not know the origins. What leads me to suspect the story is not true is something a tailor said to me: "If he was doing it to keep them from wiping their noses on the sleeves, he would've put the buttons on the *in*side, not the *out*side." There is a certain logic to that, with which you will likely agree if you will bring your wrist to your nose.

80. The last name I have used for the teacher is that of a young lady I dated while in college (before I found my wife again and became happy.) "Hello. How are you? I'm fine," I say, if she should happen across this book.

81. For legal reasons, I again have had to use a fictitious name. In this

case, I have substituted the name of a man with whom I used to play poker on Wednesday nights before our daughters arrived.

82. It is when we were in bed that I was reminded of how *small* my wife was. She wore size 2 in dresses and size 3 in shoes. It was hard for her to find shoes that did not have Mickey Mouse on them.

83. Please note that the editor has removed the word "turpentine-y," which I attempted to use here. She is an *excellent* editor, isn't she? God bless you, Diane. I raise my glass to you!

84. There is, to my knowledge, no such town.

85. Oh, my heart.

86. My wife's parents are no longer with us. Her mother died first, then her father (Parkinson's Disease, cancer.)

87. Once, from my window, I saw my wife and several of her friends performing exercises in her backyard. In one of the exercises they appeared to be crushing oranges in their outstretched arms. As they performed this exercise, they sang together:
We must,
We must,
We must increase our busts.
The bigger, the better,
The tighter the sweater,
The boys depend on us.

A teenaged boy could not ask for much more than that.

88. The note was my father's idea. I told him all that had happened and asked him to return the coat to her: after all, they were neighbors. He told me I needed to do it myself, then said, "If you really want to see her again, I have an idea." You could almost see the light bulb go on above

his head. Were it not for his idea, were it not for the note, I do not believe I would have ever seen her again. And the sun would not have come up. And the world would have stopped turning. So, to my father, I raise a glass and say, "Thank you."

89. There is a wedding photograph on the desk in front of me as I write this sentence. You have never seen a woman look as beautiful as my wife on our wedding day, unless you were there yourself.

90. Every one of these names is, to my knowledge, fictitious.

91. Neither of the two books she mentioned are "junk," not by any means. *The Red Badge of Courage*, by Stephen Crane, is a novel about a young man whose romantic notions about combat are destroyed when he fights in the Civil War. *The Scarlet Letter*, by Nathaniel Hawthorne, is about a young mother in seventeenth-century New England who is forced to wear the scarlet letter "A" on her dress after she is convicted of adultery. She only had one lover. Imagine what they would have done with someone who'd had a hundred, a hundred fifty.

92. "Syd Braverman" is not a fictitious name. I have the owner's express permission to use his name in this book. He believed it would be good advertising for his store, especially his new store at the Owings Mills Mall. Mention this book and receive a 10 percent discount.

93. Reprinted with the permission of Syd Braverman.

94. The young lady who has been put in charge of editing this book wanted to remove the word "pie-hole" and replace it with "mouths" or "traps." She felt "pie-hole" sounded "too 1950's." But it's what Braverman said, and I think it's a fine word.

95. Elvis Presley was an enormously popular singer. He died of a drug overdose in his Memphis, Tennessee home, known as Graceland. Many years later, I met a man from Memphis. He told me that he had driven

the ambulance that had delivered Mr. Presley's corpse to the hospital. He had kept the blanket he had used to cover the body and was in the process of having it authenticated at the time I met him. He referred to the blanket as "The Shroud of Elvis," a reference to "The Shroud of Turin," which supposedly bears the image of Jesus Christ. I do not recall the man's name.

96. The words to the song are as follows:
Shoo, fly, don't bother me,
Shoo, fly, don't bother me,
Shoo, fly, don't bother me,
For I belong to somebody.

I feel, I feel, I feel,
I feel like a morning star.
I feel, I feel, I feel,
I feel like a morning star.

So, shoo fly, don't bother me,
Shoo, fly, don't bother me,
Shoo, fly, don't bother me,
For I belong to somebody.

97. No, Diane, I haven't had too much to drink tonight. Besides, it's not the same as drinking and driving, where someone could get injured or killed. A few drinks doesn't stop me from operating a pen properly. See? See? So, shoo, fly, don't bother me.

98. "But wait," you say, "didn't Shoogey's mother stand up and speak on his behalf when the library wanted to ban his book when he cursed?" No need to flip the pages backward to search for that passage: yes, Shoogey said that.

99. The names are not the names of the students. In each case, I have

chosen the name of an eminent judge to replace the real names used in Shoogey's story.

100. The album was called "You've Got A Date With The Blues." It is available from Polygram Records, catalog number 837-936-2.

101. This was, and still is, the advertisement for a brand of cereal flakes called Wheaties. The boxes feature photographs of well-known athletes set against a bright orange background. It's a fine product, which I wholeheartedly endorse. The legal department of the publishing company that is releasing this book has insisted on including the following disclaimer: "Neither the author of this book nor the publisher has received any compensation of any kind for the preceding statement. The statement was entirely unsolicited. Neither the author nor the publisher assumes any liability for any injury or illness caused by this product, the same being expressly denied." Lawyers take the fun out of everything.

102. On one occasion, while eating lunch at a restaurant called Bohager's, Shoogey noticed we were sitting next to a priest, a rabbi and a minister. "Hey," he said, "I heard a great joke about you guys." The rabbi and the minister laughed.

103. Jonas Salk discovered the cure for polio. He was welcome in our home. He never came.

104. Diane, I thought we agreed to remove this scene. I thought we agreed to remove all of the disputes between Ham and Angie. I thought we agreed to remove anything that would make Angie appear to be anything but an angel. Didn't we? I thought we agreed to remove anything that would even suggest that their marriage was anything but ideal, for obvious and personal reasons that I need not repeat here.

105. Angie's Recipe for Tar Heel Pie
        Ingredients: 3 eggs, slightly beaten

3/4 cup flour
1-1/2 cups sugar
1-1/2 cups chocolate chips
6 tablespoons melted butter
1-3/4 cups chopped pecans
1 unbaked pie shell
1 cup whipped cream

Directions: Preheat oven to 350 degrees. Mix eggs, sugar and butter. Add flour, chocolate chips and pecans. Pour into pie shell. Bake for 1 hour. Serve hot topped with whipped cream.

106. This restaurant closed more than two years ago, before I even contemplated writing this little book.

107. The whining they learned from me, not their mother.

108. An accurate summary, more or less, of the legend.

109. "Lever" was the surname of a boy who played trombone with me in our grammar school band. Once, before a concert, his father said to us, "I'll give you two boys five dollars each to play tonight. I'll give you ten dollars each if you don't play." We were terrible trombonists, I must admit. Imagine cars screeching on wet pavement.

110. George Herman "Babe" Ruth played professional baseball for the Boston Red Sox, New York Yankees and Boston Braves. He is best known for his years as a home run hitting outfielder for the New York Yankees. He held the career home run record of 714, which stood for decades until it was broken by Henry "Hank" Aaron. He also held the single season home run record of 60, which was broken by Roger Maris, whose record has since been broken by Mark McGuire and, later, by Barry Bonds. Babe Ruth was known for his girth and his woman-

izing. His absence from several important ballgames was attributed to eating too many frankfurters; in actuality, he was suffering the effects of a venereal disease. As I've said before, he was never the President of the United States. Although he was paid more than the President. When questioned about that odd fact, Ruth would answer, "I had a better year than the President."

111. Two actors who were equally as popular with male and female moviegoers. Men wanted to be like Robert Redford or Sean Connery. Women wanted to be kissed by them and often wanted more, I suspect.

112. Henry James was my wife's favorite author.

113. A reference to the O. Henry short story, "The Gift of the Magi." In the story, a man sells his pocket watch in order to buy a hairbrush for his wife for Christmas; she cuts off her hair and sells it so she can buy him a watch fob.

114. My grandfather owned a pair. He was a carpenter, and he took as good care of his shoes as he did of his tools. It would not be unusual to watch him polish a single pair of shoes for half-an-hour.

115. No lawyer worth his salt would be caught dead without his business cards. I've seen business cards materialize as if from thin air at the sauna at the YMCA. I don't want to speculate as to where they were being kept.

116. Heavyweight boxing champion who was stripped of his title when he refused to go to war. Apparently, he had no interest in seeing fertilizer and pure blue air being made.

117. The heavyweight boxing champion from 1937 to 1949, Joe Louis was nicknamed "The Brown Bomber."

118. A fictitious name. I have used the name of a collegiate wrestling

champion who was nicknamed "Bruiser."

119. The name I've used is that of a classmate from my days in law school. During our final year, Frank's girlfriend left him in order to marry another man. Heartbroken, despondent, Frank decided to change his life and, somehow, ended up in a beauty parlor, where he was convinced to have his hair dyed blond and permed. The photograph of him that appears in our yearbook (frowning, blond curly-haired) may as well be that of a stranger.

120. It is true that Ernest "King" Gilmore held the heavyweight championship for a short spell in the 1950's. He was born in Mississippi to a family of sharecroppers. He trained in Tronk's Gym in Chicago, Illinois. He defeated James "Bonecrusher" Williams in Chicago to gain the heavyweight title, which he successfully defended half-a-dozen times before relinquishing it to Frank Rodman at Madison Square Garden. (I have been unable to find any nickname for Mr. Rodman.) King Gilmore's lifetime record, as reported by *Ring* magazine, was 42 wins and eight losses, with 21 knockouts.

121. This appears to be true. Apparently, Ernest Hemingway fought in several boxing matches, although his skills were suspect.

122. No offense intended to any Mexican readers. If any offense is taken, I say, "Los siento, mis amigos. Los siento."

123. Canny readers are likely awaiting Braverman's inevitable heart attack, expecting him to topple over. Braverman would not have a heart attack that night. However, he did have one several years later. He had to have a triple bypass operation. My wife, the girls and I visited him in the hospital; my wife baked him a Tar Heel Pie. He recovered and is alive and well as of the date of the printing of this book.

124. "Mick Cronin" is a fictitious name.

125. "Robert Plessy" is a fictitious name too. His name comes from the 1896 Supreme Court decision *Plessy versus Ferguson,* where the Supreme Court upheld segregated facilities for different races so long as the facilities were equal. This "separate but equal" doctrine was overturned by the Supreme Court in the 1954 decision *Brown versus Board of Education.*

126. Diane, why is this still in here? We agreed to remove this section. We *agreed.*

127. You have not forgotten Chapter Three, have you?

128. Franklin Delano Roosevelt held the office of President for four terms. His bold and intricate socioeconomic plan, known as "the New Deal," is credited with helping the nation escape the paralyzing Great Depression. Interestingly, he succeeded in hiding from most of the public the fact that he was confined to a wheelchair, a result of a bout of polio.

129. This theory has survived for years and years. It has never been proved or disproved. A computer program comparing the frequency of the use of certain words in Marlowe's *Faust* and Shakespeare's *Julius Caesar* was inconclusive.

130. Although Baltimoreans might disagree—Brooks Robinson played third base for the Baltimore Orioles, after all—most baseball historians consider Mike Schmidt of the Philadelphia Phillies and Eddie Matthews of the Milwaukee (and, later, Atlanta) Braves to have been superior. An argument could also be made for George Brett of the Kansas City Royals. My wife had a crush on George Brett.

131. These are all characters in Japanese monster movies. To those of you reading the Japanese version of this book, I say, "Konichiwa." I was taught that by a waitress in a Japanese restaurant called Yumi's in

downtown Baltimore. Shoogey took me there on several occasions. The waitress was not Japanese herself, but wore her hair and makeup to suggest otherwise. Her name was Kim, but in the restaurant she was called "Sachiko," which is Japanese for "happy child." Or so she told us.

132. A monster who was not from Japan.

133. Actually, in the novel by Mary Shelley, "Frankenstein" is the name of the doctor who creates a monster from various parts of cadavers; it is not the name of the monster itself.

134. Diane!

135. The scotch was Cutty Sark, blended. Which happens to be what I'm drinking right now! What a coincidence!

136. This is a different venereal disease than that from which Babe Ruth suffered. Reportedly, he had syphilis. He was never the President of the United States.

137. I have confirmed that this is true with Dr. Bruce Lesko of The Johns Hopkins Hospital in Baltimore, Maryland. He was the doctor who took care of my wife and my daughters.

138. Also confirmed by Dr. Bruce Lesko of The Johns Hopkins Hospital.

139. My grandfather had these shoes, too.

140. From time to time throughout the book, Jane Shoogey will refer to me as "Mr. Ass," rather than as "Mr. Ashe." Of course, since my surname in fact is not "Ashe," her purposeful mispronunciation of my surname did not result in her calling me "Mr. Ass." Instead, she mispronounced my actual surname in such a way as to refer to me by a name more crass and vulgar than "Ass." I will not repeat the name by which she referred to me. Instead, I leave it to the reader's imagination.

141. Tomas de Torquemada was the first and most brutal inquisitor-general of the Spanish Inquisition. He was to become infamous for his severity with persons charged with illegally practicing Judaism.

142. I have saved the poem, and it was for that reason that I was able to recite it verbatim earlier in this chapter.

143. This is a fictitious name. The first name, "Helen," I've taken from my grandmother on my father's side of things. She was a good woman who used to make potato pancakes whenever I visited. It was when she died that I learned that I was Jewish (or, to be more precise, half-Jewish.) My father explained that he never told me because he was trying to "pass" in the Baltimore business community; he was afraid that, once everyone learned he was Jewish, he would lose his job. I can accept that. But I still cannot understand why my grandmother never said anything. I can still see her smiling when I wished her a happy Christmas. I can still see her opening Christmas gifts.

144. A reference to the classic American novel by Harper Lee. The novel, published in 1960, confronts racial tension and injustice through the eyes of a child narrator. In recent years, there has been considerable speculation that Ms. Lee's claim to authorship is bogus. Some have speculated that the book in fact was written by Ms. Lee's good friend, the novelist Truman Capote, who wrote *Breakfast at Tiffany's* and *In Cold Blood*, among others. As best my research has revealed, there is no support for the claim that Ms. Lee's book is not her own. Ms. Lee, by the way, is a lawyer.

145. A reference to a long-running television series.

146. Jackie Robinson was the first African-American to play major league baseball. He endured profanities, epithets and threats that few men could have withstood.

147. Diane!

148. She was correct, as any student from one of my history classes can attest.

149. A fictitious name. I have used the name of a local dairy.

150. False, false, false.

151. More detailed information regarding depositions may be found in the *Maryland Rules of Civil Procedure* (for state cases) or the *Federal Rules of Civil Procedure* (federal cases.)

152. Joan of Arc was a French military leader of the fifteenth century. At the age of seventeen, she took up arms to establish the rightful king of the French throne. She was tried for heresy for claiming to have heard God's voice. She was burned at the stake.

153. Madame Bovary is the heroine of the eponymous novel by Gustave Flaubert. Unhappy in marriage, she sought contentment in adultery.

154. Grigori Rasputin was a Russian monk who gained great influence over Czar Nicholas II. He was murdered by jealous noblemen, who tried many methods to take his life before finally succeeding. Poison, swords, etc., etc. I often jokingly called my father Rasputin because of the litany of maladies that struck him one after the other, but could not do him in. Cancer. A stroke. A heart attack. A lung condition (too many cigarettes.) Bell's palsy. Finally, his heart gave out on him while he was sleeping. It was the only cruel thing he ever did to me.

155. I have no idea why Jane Shoogey would refer to Pope Pius III.

156. My answer, for the record, would be, "Yes."

157. This is a lie. This is an outright and despicable lie. Jane Shoogey

didn't hear anything negative about our marriage. There would be nothing negative to hear. I will swear to that. I will put my hand on The Bible.

158. For many years, the third baseman for the Baltimore Orioles was Brooks Robinson—the very same person Shoogey spoke of on our fishing trip.

159. The United States Naval Academy is located in Annapolis, Maryland—the same place where Shoogey took me fishing.

160. An Army general who became President of the United States.

161. Prime Minister of Israel.

162. A famous and skilled golfer.

163. Again, fictitious names. In this case, "Kaminski" was the name of my history teacher when I attended Magruder High School; he had a growth on his elbow that resembled the head of a mushroom. In fact, it was he whom I replaced following his retirement. He died of a sudden heart attack while this book was being edited. Rest in peace, Mr. Kaminski.

164. Diane, we *agreed*. We had an *agreement!*

165. As Marylanders know, Phil Van Marker eventually served a term as governor. He was defeated by Kurt Kiley in his bid for re-election and has returned to the practice of law at, of all places, Morrisey & DeWitt.

166. True.

167. A song from *Porgy and Bess*, an opera by George Gershwin that is set in South Carolina. In the opera, Porgy protects Bess, only to have her leave with another man.

168. Please, Diane, I'm begging you. Please take this scene out. I thought we'd agreed.

169. For legal reasons, I must say that I do not contend this story about Mr. Van Marker is true, nor do I contend that he has ever used unlawful substances. Any suggestion to the contrary is purely unintentional.

170. This is an accurate summary of the legendary Baron Munchausen, as best I can tell.

171. An American film star who became Princess of Monaco.

172. A fictitious name.

173. J. Paul Getty was a billionaire oilman.

174. The King Family was a show business family that used to have Christmas specials on television each year, all the parents and children and aunts and uncles and nephews and nieces singing and dancing their little hearts out.

175. A fictitious name. The surname is the name of a paper company that produces quality computer and photocopy paper. A ream of their product was sitting on the shelf in front of me when I reached this sentence and needed a name to disguise the identity of our judge: "Hammermill." Thus was Judge Charles Hammermill born.

176. Readers of detective novels surely suspect that Helen Renko's note will play some important part in this book. Perhaps Angie would find it, misconstrue the meaning of the note and believe I was having an affair with Helen Renko. That did not happen. The note remained in my desk until the day I left Morrisey & DeWitt, a reminder that Helen Renko was a good and appreciative woman.

177. In this case, I've used the last name of one of my colleagues from

Morrisey & DeWitt. He and his wife provided much help and comfort after the accident. They were the ones who took care of the arrangements at the funeral home. Three funerals in one day. Imagine that. I didn't have to imagine it. Three funerals only a few months before this book was about to be published. Oh, my heart.

178. Hawaii was where my wife and I had wanted to travel for our honeymoon, only we couldn't afford it. We went to San Diego, California, instead, and stayed at a lovely hotel called the Hotel Del Coronado.

179. A note to Hollywood producers: if a film is ever made of this book, I would like to suggest that Marina Miles play Jane Shoogey as a girl. Only "Marina Miles" is a fictitious name "Miles" is the last name of a girl I grew up with. Prettiest girl I'd ever seen. Before my wife.

180. My sincerest apologies to all persons who may be overweight. My actions were brought on by my unusual state of mind at the time and in no way reflect my true feelings. I'm heavy myself now. I eat and I eat and I eat. Sometimes, I drink. I've put on more weight since the accident than you can imagine. Sometimes it seems like I'm wearing someone else's clothes and shoes.

181. Pennsylvania Station is in New York City, oddly enough. There is no New York Station in Pennsylvania, to the best of my knowledge.

182. The New York Knicks are a professional basketball team. My wife was taking the girls to a basketball practice, by the way, when the accident happened. Drunk driver. Rain-soaked streets. Metal hitting metal. You probably expect me to say something about "fertilizer" and "pure blue air" here, but I can't say that about my own wife, my own daughters. And please do not think that I miss the irony of getting drunk in order to try to forget about what a drunk driver did.

183. To my knowledge, there is no such movie.

184. A reference to Fyodor Dostoyevsky's classic 1866 novel, *Crime and Punishment*, in which deluded and handsome Raskolikov murders an old woman and is consumed by his guilt. It is a shame that I must refer to it here, because doing so only emphasizes the tremendous shortcomings of the book you are reading.

185. I've used the name of a law school classmate.

186. John Coltrane's *My Favorite Things* and the Beatles' *A Hard Day's Night*.

187. The poems were by W. H. Auden.

188. That is not true any longer. Now, whenever I think of New York, I think of my last trip there. I think of myself sitting in the doorway of my hotel room, naked except for a towel around my waist, my heart breaking.

189. Oh, my heart.

190. Oh, my heart.

191. My thanks to the fine people at Amtrak, particularly customer service representative Karen Gropper.

192. A children's book and, later, a movie starring Judy Garland.

193. "The Star Spangled Banner" is the national anthem of the United States. It was written by Francis Scott Key, a Marylander, like most of the persons who populate this book. Like me. Like my wife and daughters. Oh, my heart.

194. The Washington Bullets was the name of a professional basketball team. Because of the violent image the name conjured up (all that fertilizer and blue air), civic leaders prevailed upon the owners to change

the name. They did so, and the team is now known as the Washington Wizards. Did I mention that my wife was taking the girls to a basketball practice when the accident happened? Doesn't that sound absurd? Absurd and unfair? Did I mention that I was in New York City when it happened? Did I mention that I was in a hotel room? Did I mention that I am a horrible man, and had I been a good man I would have been home taking the girls to basketball practice myself? I'm not saying that I would have died instead, but that events would have transpired a little differently – perhaps we would have left home a minute earlier or a minute later, perhaps I would have driven a little slower or a little faster – and we would not have been in the intersection at the same moment.

195. Johnny Carson was the host of a late night television show called *The Tonight Show*. He was well-known for the witty monologues with which he began each show, and for a number of characters he portrayed, including one called Carnac the Magnificent who could predict the contents of sealed envelopes. "Absurd and unfair," he would say, pressing the envelope to his forehead. Then he would open the envelope and reveal the question to which he had just provided the answer: "How would you describe a lovely woman and her two daughters being killed by a drunk driver on their way to basketball practice?"

196. There are a great many lawyer jokes, enough to fill several volumes. Other than the one I told my wife on this page, here is my favorite: a doctor, a rabbi, a priest and a lawyer are sailing when suddenly their boat takes on water. Little by little, the boat sinks until the four men are left treading water in the middle of the ocean. A shark appears. First, the shark eats the doctor. He leaves and returns several hours later to eat the rabbi. Again, he leaves and returns. This time, he eats the priest. Again he leaves, but when he returns he doesn't eat the lawyer. So the lawyer asks him, "Why didn't you eat me?" And the shark says, "Professional courtesy."

197. Please refer to Chapter Five.

198. You will find no details here. You are welcome to use your own imagination.

199. Diane, I appreciate your letting me rewrite this scene. I know you would like me to remove the statements that the narrator was happy. But I think it's important to say that. This is how I want it remembered. So, please keep this sentence in. Please end this chapter with the words, "Yes, I was very, very happy." Thank you.

200. Diane, I'm sorry, I'm sorry, I'm sorry. I haven't figured out how to rewrite these chapters. There's too much to change. I'd have to change *everything*. I believe the best thing to do is to just skip over these two years altogether and just say everything was fine. Everything was great. It was a great big slice of heaven.

201. We visited Disney World in Orlando, Florida one year, then Disneyland in Anaheim, California the next. I have great memories of those vacations. They are memories that make you want to laugh and cry at the same time, only your body doesn't know how to do that, so you just end up gasping like you're drowning.

202. One year, all four of us dressed as M&M candies.

"Do you want plain or peanut?" my wife asked us.

"What's the difference?" my youngest daughter asked.

"You need a pillow for peanut."

That's when my older daughter said about me, "I don't think he has a choice. He has to be a peanut," which probably was true. My ribcage came to resemble a barrel.

203. A black Mustang was the first car I ever bought. The man who took my wife and daughters from me was driving a white Honda Accord, in case you were wondering. In the photograph in the paper, it looked like origami.

204. An odor I recognized from my college days.

205. A fictitious name.

206. Think of Desdemona's handkerchief.

207. Walter was my older brother's name. He is no longer on this planet. If he could hear me, I'd say, "Hello. How are you?"

208. A fictitious address. It was actually the street address of my parents' home. This book was dedicated to them until, well, you know. It is now dedicated to my wife.

209. I had a sickening thought just days before the printing presses were being readied to spin and clank and produce copies of this book: what if *Lombardi* were lying? That would change everything, wouldn't it? What if he had gone to war, but was embarrassed about his behavior? What if he had asked Shoogey for five thousand dollars?

210. Again, not their real names. Instead, these are the names of my friends' children. Someday, when they're grown, perhaps they'll each find a copy of this book on their parents' bookshelves. Perhaps they'll read this page and see their names. Perhaps, in that small moment, all that is troubling them will vanish and they will imagine themselves wearing the red-and-white uniforms of the University of Maryland, with number 84 stitched on the front and back of their jerseys. Perhaps they will read this book and stop thinking such terrible things about me. "Children," I say, if you're reading this, "I wasn't a terrible man. I was just sad."

211. I have a Pez dispenser in my top desk drawer. The head is that of a cartoon character named Fred Flintstone. Guess who it used to belong to? Go ahead. Guess.

212. Fictitious names all, for reasons that will become readily apparent.

213. Napoleon Bonaparte was exiled to the Island of Elba.

214. Louie's Bookstore Cafe, which was a nice little place on Charles Street beside Baltimore's version of the Washington Monument. It is gone now. The café, not the monument.

215. McDonald's is a chain of restaurants that sells hamburgers. If you did not know that, you are probably reading the version of this book published in Hungary or Latvia, where I understand there are no McDonald's restaurants at this time. To the fine people of Hungary and Latvia, I say, "You're missing some excellent french fries. You may want to write to your congressman."

216. This was a *dream*. My wife and I weren't having problems. Or, should I say, whatever problems we had were small ones not worth mentioning here.

217. The number is likely closer to eight million, perhaps more.

218. Dammit, Diane. Dammit, dammit, *dammit*. I removed that last sentence. I crossed it out with red ink, and you know it.

219. Until now, of course.

220. Oh, my heart.

221. Doris Day was a pop singer whose most popular tune was called "Que Sera, Sera." It is Spanish for "Whatever Will Be, Will Be." Doris Day didn't know anything about cars, did she? She didn't know anything about cars that speed through intersections, did she? If she's reading this, I say, "Please shut up. Please."

222. Diane! Please. I'm begging you. Please remove this. *Please.*

223. Charlie Chaplin was a well-known comedian.

224. Races pitting men versus horses are not as unusual as one might suspect. The great Olympic champion Jesse Owens raced horses on several occasions in the 1940's and 1950's; he often won. Professional football player Cris Collinsworth raced a horse in the early 1980's; he did not win.

225. Astute readers have no doubt noticed that this is the final chapter of this book, that only several pages remain before you will bump into the back end of this book, and yet Shoogey has only killed one person so far. Your author told you Shoogey killed *two* people, didn't he? Please be patient. There is plenty of room left. There is exactly enough room left. And I'm nearly finished with my last drink. Just a sip or two remain, along with the ice cubes.

226. Several years ago, I stumbled across an excellent album by a singer named Maria McKee. The album was called *You Gotta Sin To Get Saved*. I would have purchased a copy for Shoogey had I known where to send it. I wonder whether the singer ever met Shoogey. Perhaps she did.

227. One of the boys had received a scholarship to play basketball at the University of Maryland.

228. Alexander was named for my grandfather on my father's side of things. Alexander is his real name. He was with a babysitter the night of the accident. I was in a hotel room in New York City. With my editor. Remember that, Diane? Remember the knock on the door from the concierge when we did not answer his urgent phone calls? Remember hiding in the bathroom while I answered the door? Remember how I fell to the ground with a towel around my waist when the concierge told me what had happened? Was it worth it? Please do not take this the wrong way, Diane, but it was not worth it. I was just having a relapse. A relapse of a disease that was in remission. A relapse of a disease that, if it were ever named, should be called "Shoogey."

229. Diane, thank you for changing "apartment" to "living room" and making the other revisions to this scene. But please insert the following after this sentence: "Angie was asleep. The girls were asleep. Baby Alexander, asleep."

230. Her name is Mary Beth Marsden. She is an anchorwoman at WMAR-TV. I met her at a cocktail party once, and found her to be very short (five feet even?) and charming as can be. But not as charming as my wife was.

231. Diane, please insert the following here: "I could hear baby Alexander crying once. I could imagine him rolling over and getting back to sleep."

232. Diane, please insert the following here: "I heard baby Alexander cry. I heard Angie moving in our bedroom."

233. And not the sort I will recount here, out of respect for his wife and children. To his wife and children, I say, "Goodbye now." I did not get a chance to say goodbye to my wife and daughters. Goodbye, sweethearts. I'm sorry. I'm very, very sorry.

234. Alexander, you did not know Mr. Shoogey, but some of the stories I have told you are stories I've pilfered from him. Like the one about the fish.

235. There is no suicide note, you say? Look at what you hold in your hands. Isn't this close enough?

236. Alexander, do you remember that? Maybe you don't. Maybe I'm remembering it wrong. Maybe it never even happened. By now, you've figured out that most of these endnotes were written for you. You're a smart boy, aren't you? You take after your mother. Only now, it's impossible to tell anymore how much of what I've written is true, or based on

the truth, or how much has been distorted and exaggerated, intention-ally or unintentionally. And it's not just the alcohol, Alexander; it's the way the mind works. I can't even tell you for certain whether there ever was a Sam Shoogey (or someone upon whom he was based.) When you boil away all the fat, I suppose there are only three things you can know for certain now: you have just read a book called *You Poor Monster*; it was written by your father; and your father loved you. And I've just thought of a fourth: the end of the book is coming up fast, very fast, and there's barely enough time to say goodbye to you.

237. Braverman, if something happens, please take care of my son. If you exist. Braverman? Braverman?